here
and
now

All Too Well

Here and Now

Against All Odds

Come What May

Won't You Stay

here and now

CORINNE MICHAELS

Here and now

Cover Design: Sommer Stein, Perfect Pear Creative
Editing: James Gallagher, Evident Ink
Proofreading: Julia Griffis & Michele Ficht

Dear Reader,

It is always my goal to write a beautiful love story that will capture your heart and leave a lasting impression. However, I want all readers to be comfortable. Therefore, if you want to be aware of any possible CW please click the link below to take you to the book page where there is a link that will dropdown. If you do not need this, please go forth and I hope you love this book filled with all the pieces of my heart.

https://corinnemichaels.com/books/here-and-now/

one
Miles

"Y ou're late," Eloise says as she opens the door, hand resting on her swollen stomach.

"And hello to you too, my beautiful twin sister."

She ignores me and lifts her hand. "I'm tired, seventy-six months pregnant, and my husband decided to play hockey with my idiot brother two weeks ago and break his leg. *You're late* is all you're getting."

"I didn't know one could be pregnant for that long," I try to focus on that fact instead of the injury that was totally my fault. I mean, maybe not completely my fault, since I didn't break his leg, but the reason he was playing *is* because of me.

She glares. "You broke my husband."

"Not on purpose. And where is the patient?"

"In the living room—with a bell."

Oh, my sister must love that.

"Who gave him a bell?" I ask.

"Your nephew."

Of course he did, because he's a little shit stirrer, just like his mother was.

"To be fair, it's something you would've done," I remind her.

Eloise is the quintessential little—she's three minutes younger—sister. She was annoying throughout my childhood, but she also had a devious side. My grandmother never knew what to do with her, because she was too smart for her own good. I was able to use my excess energy toward hockey, but since Eloise doesn't have an athletic bone in her body, she used it to cause a lot of trouble.

She huffs. "I know, that's why I can't even hate him. Anything to annoy Gran was my goal; it seems my son has picked up the same thought process."

Our mother died when Eloise and I were only four days old. She had a complication that went unnoticed, and our maternal grandma took us in, since our father didn't want to raise two babies on his own. I blame the doctors and the hospital. Someone should've known, should've seen it. Instead, my sister and I lost a mother we never even got to know.

"Where is our young Ethan?"

"Out back, probably spray-painting the barn or some other awful thing that will make me want to rip out my hair." My sister sits on the kitchen chair and releases a heavy sigh, blowing her bangs up in the air. "I can't do this, Miles. I'm at my absolute limit. Between Ethan and his antics, Doug having major surgery on his leg, and I'm about to pop . . . I'm going to lose it."

When Eloise was pregnant with Ethan, it was not an easy time. She was convinced at one point that she would die like our mother did. Thankfully, she didn't even have a single issue. It was a textbook birth, according to her. Today, though, that stress and worry is prevalent in her gaze.

I step closer and sit beside her, my hand resting on her forearm. "I'm here."

She glares. "Yeah, that's not exactly a comfort."

I do my best to remember she's moody and not take offense to that one. "Well, it should be. I'm the responsible adult in this family."

Eloise laughs and pushes my hand away. "You're the one who made him play, and now I have to handle this *alone*."

"To be fair, no one made your husband do a damn thing, but I'll take the blame if it'll make you feel better."

"It would."

"Then you're right, it's my fault."

"It always is," she says as she rubs her stomach.

Then the bell rings, and I swear I see the steam start to exit her ears. Deciding that Eloise is at that point where she might actually kill Doug, I take pity and step in. "I'll go see what he wants."

The tension in her shoulders releases a bit. "Remove that fucking bell from his hands or I'm going to shove it so far up his—"

"Uncle Miles!" Ethan bounds into the room, practically knocking me off my feet as he barrels into me.

I give him a tight hug and then turn my best authoritative principal look on him. "Were you spray-painting the barn?"

"No."

"Doing anything that might send your mother into labor?"

He glances at her and shrugs. "I don't think so."

"Okay, then. Carry on."

Eloise rolls her eyes. "You're so helpful."

"I do what I can."

"Well, go see what the jackass with the bell wants."

I kiss her cheek and then head in to see what the hell my brother-in-law is trying to accomplish, other than making my sister homicidal.

"Yo, asshole," I say as I walk in.

Doug is lying on the couch, his leg resting on a series of pillows, with a side table full of medication, water, and empty plates.

"I'm the asshole? That's funny coming from you. You have tried to get me killed, forced me to marry a psychopath, and now you broke my leg."

"Glad to see you're dramatic as ever, douchebag." I sit on the couch opposite him. "I didn't force you to marry a psychopath. She's my sister, and I'd like to think I bestowed a great gift upon you."

He snorts. "You've met her, right?"

"You know she'll kill you if she hears this."

"I'll take death at this point."

We both laugh. "Also, when did I try to get you killed?"

"Oh, let's see . . . maybe when we were in Europe, and you had me do shots until I puked for so long I thought I'd lost an organ in the process."

"Ahh, the good ole days."

Doug and I served in the US Marines for four years together in the same unit. I joined right out of high school to get college paid for —Doug wanted to see the world. We became best friends then, he followed me back to Virginia, met my sister, and now he's literally my brother.

"Yes, nothing like that one time I almost got shot."

"Almost," I remind him. "You didn't."

He rolls his eyes and winces. "I would've preferred it to this."

"Is the pain bad?"

Doug groans as he tries to shift. "Horrific. I have physical therapy tomorrow, and I honestly don't know how I'm going to handle any of it."

That says something because Doug is a tough son of a bitch. He's never one to complain and usually takes things on the chin.

"Sorry, dude."

"It's fine. I was the asshat who thought I should go full fucking force on the ice. I'm not twenty anymore."

"No, you're not," I agree.

He flips me off. "You're one to talk."

"Yes, but I didn't break my leg and require surgery. Still, I'm sorry you got hurt. It sucks, especially with the baby coming."

"The baby is part of it. I know how to procrastinate like no one else, so all I've heard is how I said I'd get shit done and didn't do it, so El is pissed. The crib, the painting, fixing the solar panel out back . . . all of it hasn't been touched. Also, she broke down yesterday crying that she's afraid about having a baby again."

"I get that. She's the same age as Mom was, and I think that's probably a mindfuck."

It's why having kids isn't high up on my list. I'm happy being the fun uncle and a school principal. I get my fill with other people's kids.

Doug sighs. "I keep trying to comfort her about it, but it's just something we have to endure, you know?"

"Yeah."

"But one of the things I feel the worst about is that I promised her I'd keep Ethan busy this summer. As you can imagine, he's a little . . . bored and reckless during the summer."

"What were you planning to do with him?" I ask.

Last summer, I actually got a call from my sister asking if I could get the school to go year-round because she wasn't sure she was going to make it. That was a fun one, explaining that while I may be the school principal, I don't exactly set the school calendar, the board of education does, and she's welcome to run to be a member of it anytime she likes.

I don't think I got the sentence out before she hung up on me.

Doug shifts. "Well, this is actually why I wanted you to stop by."

Oh fuck my life.

"No," I say immediately.

"No what?"

"No to whatever you're going to ask me to do. No."

School ended two weeks ago. I have one month where I actually get a little downtime before I have to start preparing the school before the next year starts, and I have a feeling my brother-in-law is about to ruin that. I look forward to this every year. It's the only time I have a chance to reset, breathe, and prepare for the chaos that happens when we get ready for back-to-school.

I need this time.

It has been the one thing I do for myself, no matter what, because it makes me a better principal and human.

"I need you to coach his hockey clinic."

I laugh once. "Absolutely not."

Doug tries to sit up but grabs his leg, grunting and gasping as he does. I get up and walk over as though I can help, but he waves me away. "Sit down, you'll make it worse."

I go back to my seat and wait for him to get control. "You all right?"

He lets out a long breath. "I'm fine. My point is, I can't do it."

"What about one of the other fantastic fathers in the town?"

"We can't even get them to fill out the forms properly, let alone step in to coach the kids. They're just a bunch of six-year-olds; it won't be that hard."

Right, because the young ones are easier with sports? No, they aren't. They don't pay attention, they don't know the basics, and they ask a million questions. Not much downtime there.

"Well, as bad as I feel for you, I'm not doing it."

"You owe me," Doug says with a brow raised.

I shake my head. "I don't. I have plans."

"Cancel them."

I scoff. "The hell I will. I rented a cabin in Michigan. I'm going to fish and boat and enjoy the absolute silence and complete lack of children."

Don't get me wrong, I like kids. I work with them all day. However, my job as a high school principal requires me to be around teenagers. Teenagers are not children. They're not adults either. They're pretty much not even humans most days of the week. They're little shells of people who have a never-ending supply of assholeness that's just itching to get out. Some are better at containing it than others. However, it almost always seeps out, and I need to spend the next month without any kids.

None.

Zero.

Zilch.

No traces of little humans who make me question my life choices.

Each July is my happy place. For eleven months out of the year, I'm not allowed vacations or time off. This is truly the only time I can decompress.

"Okay, then *you* can tell Ethan why he can't do it this year because you begged me to play a game."

"Low blow, Doug. Low blow."

He knows I'm not going to tell Ethan that.

He shrugs. "I can't do it. I can't put skates on, let alone coach kids while my leg is like this."

"Just put one skate on, and the other you can put on the crutches," I say, half joking.

It would at least be semi-entertaining—for me.

"Fuck right off."

Apparently Doug doesn't find that funny.

"Anyway, you and Eloise decided to procreate, this is your issue."

Doug nods once. "All right then. Fair enough."

There are those moments when I know that what's being said isn't what is meant, and this is one of those. Before I can go back at

Doug, he bellows for my nephew. Since I'm visiting, it means Ethan is relatively close, because he's always hoping I'll help him cause my sister a few more gray hairs.

He enters faster than I can get up and get the hell away from these absolute pains in my ass.

"Yes, Dad?"

"I have to tell you that since I broke my leg, I can't do the hockey clinic. I know you were looking forward to it, and that I promised I would coach because none of the other dads could, but I just can't. I asked Uncle Miles, since he was almost a famous hockey player, and thought that maybe he'd be able to fill in, but he's going to sit in a cabin on a lake and pray for fish."

I roll my eyes. "Not exactly what I said, but . . ."

"He's just too busy and can't manage it."

"Laying it on a little thick there, Doug," I say under my breath.

Ethan rushes over. "Uncle Miles, you'd be the best coach ever! Please, you're so much better than Dad. Please can you coach? Please? I don't want to be stuck at home all summer with the *baby*."

I glare at my once best friend and then look at Ethan. The idyllic views, fresh air, and days sitting with my lure in the water start to disappear as my nephew stares at me with pleading eyes.

I let out a heavy sigh, knowing that no matter how much my child-free summer was needed, I won't say no to him.

Because I'm a good uncle.

Damn it, I should've stayed home and not come to check on the big asshole.

"How long is the clinic?" I ask with resignation. Already knowing I'll do it anyway.

"Just the whole month of July," Doug says as though he didn't just ruin my entire summer.

"Just?"

He nods. "It's four weeks and only three days a week."

"Oh, only. And let me guess, it's some random day in the middle of the week I'm off?"

Doug grins. "Tuesdays and Thursdays."

Of course. Why make it so that I could go up to the lake house for a long weekend at least? Let's just ruin it all.

"I'll call the rink and fix that," I say.

"You'll do it?" Ethan asks, nearly vibrating like a tuning fork.

"I'll help out since your dad is unable to do anything without getting hurt."

Ethan whoops. "I have to go tell my friends!" Then he runs out of the room, and Eloise enters.

"What is he so happy about?"

Doug looks at his wife with a shit-eating grin. "Your brother is going to do the hockey clinic and keep Ethan out of your hair."

Eloise's eyes fill with moisture, and as much as I hate that this is going to be my one month off, seeing her overcome with joy makes it all worth it. "You're truly the best, Miles Anderson. The best. I'm so lucky to have you as a brother."

I wave her off. "Yeah, yeah, you can pay me back by hiding your husband's painkillers."

She grins. "Deal."

———

"Hazel! I need tea! And maybe a scone. Or a cupcake. Hell, give me all of them," I yell as I enter the doors to Prose & Perk. While I don't normally bellow, it's week one of my should-be-at-the-lake-but-I'm-here-instead vacation.

And I have to head to the rink in an hour.

To deal with kids.

Lots of kids.

"I know you're not yelling at me." She pops out from behind the counter, hands on her hips and a scowl mean enough to make my balls shrink up.

"I'm not."

"Because I'm your only source of caffeine in this town, and I know you wouldn't want to piss me off."

I raise both hands. "I wouldn't dare. I'm eternally sorry."

She smirks. "Damn right you are."

Hazel is a constant in my life. She grew up in Ember Falls, like I did, and even though she's three years younger than me, she was a good friend of mine when we were kids.

"Can I please have some tea with honey, a cupcake, and maybe a name change?" I ask.

"Isn't today the first day of the hockey clinic?"

"How did you know?"

She shrugs. "I heard around town."

"Yeah, I'm sure everyone is just going on and on about it."

Hazel dips back under the counter, heading to the coffee machine. "Let's not forget, a barista is like a therapist. People tell me the most random shit."

"Do tell me all the secrets . . . especially if it's about my sister."

"Not on your life, buddy. Actually, I heard about the clinic from Penelope."

"Your new barista?"

Hazel brings over the cup of tea and leans against the counter. "The same one. Her son, who you met, he's really into hockey and is apparently on your team."

"His name is Kai, right?"

"Yup."

He seemed like a sweet kid. A little shy and definitely nervous when I met him at the elementary school on a day I was helping there. He was incredibly polite, which is a nice change.

Of course I had an incredibly hard time focusing on him when I couldn't take my eyes off his mother. Penelope is stunning. She's short with reddish-brown hair and the bluest eyes I've ever seen. A man could easily get lost in that gaze.

I've been so busy with the end of school that I haven't been able to come in for a drink and breakfast, which is probably for the best since I'd just ogle the gorgeous woman as she made me tea and a muffin.

Sometimes being a bumbling idiot around pretty girls is a curse.

"Good, what's their story anyway?" I ask, trying to seem nonchalant.

However, by the look on Hazel's face—I failed.

"Honestly, I don't know. She hasn't told me how she ended up in Ember Falls, but she's a great employee who shows up on time, works hard, and doesn't complain. To me, she's been a godsend and doesn't cause any issues at all."

Don't I wish I had more people like that around me. I love my job. Being a principal of the high school has brought me a lot of happiness. Kids, while being some of the most frustrating humans known to man, are also amazing. They're funny, and each day I learn something new.

However, my staff is challenging. Teachers are underpaid and overworked. It's a shame, and as much as I wish I could do something to change it—I can't. I have to spend half my days trying to keep them all from walking out.

Not that I'd blame them.

"I'm glad it's working out," I tell her with a smile.

"Me too. I'm surprised you haven't seen her since she lives close to you."

I shake my head. "Haven't seen her around at all."

I live in the north section of Ember Falls. My house is situated at the base of the mountain, whereas the majority of the town is more to the west, where the falls are. The town was really built around them, but I bought a lot of land away from everyone and built my house. I like that I come into town when I need to but have a sanctuary that's away from it all.

There are only two other people who live close to me, Mr. Kipland, who has been there since the dawn of time, and some guy from California who just bought the one property a little up the road from me, which is the house Penelope is renting.

"Well, I know I feel better that she's got you as a semi-neighbor."

I smile. "Yes, I'm known for being social and kind."

Hazel laughs. "Yeah, you're definitely one of the good ones. So how's Eloise doing?"

"She's good. The baby is due soon, and I'm not sure if she's killed Doug yet."

"Would you blame her?" Hazel asks as she hands me a cupcake.

"Not in the least. I'd help her bury the body at this point."

"Considering he's one of your best friends, I'm kind of surprised you'd turn on him so easily."

I shrug. "I should be at the lake. It's his fault I'm not."

Hazel chuckles. "All right then. Well, you better get to the rink."

"Yes, I wouldn't want to be late."

"Listen, Kai is really excited about this. Maybe if you could intro-duce him to some kids and . . ."

I lift my hand. "I got it."

"All the other kids have their dads or could-be-famous uncle coaching. He doesn't have that."

"I'm a good fill-in," I say with a smile. "I'm pretty good at seeing the kids who need something."

"I know."

"Careful, Hazel, you'll warm the cockles of my heart with your kindness."

She rolls her eyes. "Go away and enjoy your new summer fun!"

Yeah, I *can't* wait. Coaching kids hockey instead of fishing—so much fun.

two

Penelope

"Mom! Stop!" Kai pushes my hands away as I try to fix the zipper on his jacket.

"If you wore the other one, it wouldn't be giving me so much trouble." This one always sticks. I swear the kid can't fasten this one without getting it screwed up.

He huffs and I go back to fighting with the zipper. I pull hard on the stupid zipper, which blessedly releases the fabric behind it, and then I zip Kai up.

Now it's time to get his skates on.

Great.

I crouch and look at them.

Umm, so, I have no idea how to put these on.

Do I take the rubber thing off the bottom? Do they lace up in a certain order?

These are the times I really wish I had a man in my life. Not that Kai's father knew a damn thing about sports, but still.

"Need some help?" a deep voice asks from behind me. For a split second fear causes my body to lock up, but I force out a breath.

It's fine. I'm fine. We're all fine. It's not him.

Breathe.

I clear my throat and continue trying to tie the skates. "We've got it, thank you, though."

"Are you sure? He's going to break an ankle if you lace them like that."

I turn to see who the stranger is and my stomach drops. It's Miles Anderson, the incredibly good-looking high school principal we met when I registered Kai for school. He has a hoodie on with the sleeves pulled up to his forearms, a backward baseball hat, and a smile that could melt anyone.

However, it's his eyes that do me in.

Why does he have to have the most arresting emerald eyes?

The first time we met I thought he was cute, but when he came into the coffee shop, I saw he was really attractive. I was a little worried I'd see him again and find him even better looking, but we haven't run into each other—until now.

And yes, he is now past attractive and straight into being hot.

I remember he said something about laces, and I shake my head with a smile. "I planned to fix them. I was just trying to . . . remember how."

His deep, throaty laugh goes straight to my chest.

In the last six years, I haven't found anyone attractive. I thought something broke inside me. My ex loved to accuse me of looking at other guys and raging at me for it. Since him, I've spent my life on the run, trying to escape my past and not looking for a man to fill my broken heart.

Which is exactly how it should stay.

Miles winks at me and turns to Kai. "Do you skate often?"

Kai shakes his head. "I've never skated before!"

"Never?"

He looks to me, a cheeky grin on his handsome face as he caught me in a lie.

"We skated once," I say, trying to salvage this horrible encounter.

Miles squats beside me. "Do you mind if I help you, Kai?"

Kai shakes his head. "My mom really doesn't know what to do. She had to watch videos at home to see what we needed."

Great, outed by a six-year-old.

"Just *two* videos."

Miles chuckles. "Well, there are a lot of good ones."

"Clearly not about skates," I admit.

Miles walks me through step by step, fixing Kai's laces and

showing where to make sure it's tight before moving to the next foot. I pay close attention to the lesson and do everything I can not to watch *him*.

He doesn't look like any school principal I've ever known. He's tall, with brown hair just poking out the back of his hat. What is it about a man and hats? Some can really pull them off, and he definitely does.

Staring at him, cataloging his features, is a really bad idea. I do *not* need to find things that are attractive on him.

All that does is lead to stupid decisions.

So, yeah, I have not found men attractive since my ex.

Until now.

I wish I could explain what makes him different, but there's this ease around him, as though he will protect anyone around him.

"Do the skates feel tight?" Miles asks my son.

"Yup!"

"Good."

Another boy runs over and stands beside Miles. "I didn't get to say it before, but I'm Coach Miles, and this guy here is my nephew, Ethan."

"Hi, Ethan, I'm Kai," my son says excitedly.

"Hey! Uncle Miles, are you ready now?" Ethan asks Miles.

"Not yet."

"Aren't you a teacher?" Kai asks Miles.

"I'm the principal of the high school, but I often go to the elementary school to check on this twerp"—Miles ruffles his nephew's hair—"and help out there since the principal just had a baby."

I smile when I see the obvious love he has for his nephew. "I'm not a twerp," Ethan says.

"You're worse, but I have to be nice, or your mother will never let me hear the end of it."

Ethan grins. "I'll tell her everything you say."

"And I'll go to the lake house and you'll be without a coach," he warns.

Ethan sighs heavily. "Fine. Hey, Kai, do you want to go meet the other kids?"

Kai looks up at me. "Can I?"

I nod. "Go ahead."

"Be on the ice in two minutes!" Miles yells after them before turning to me. "The things we do for the people we love. Do you have siblings?"

Not wanting to be rude, I force a smile and keep my demeanor friendly. "I have a brother."

His eyes narrow just a tinge. "Older or younger?"

"He's older."

"Tell your brother we have a club and he's welcome to join."

I pull up a little straighter. "A club for what?"

"Older brothers with sisters who, no doubt, drive us bonkers," Miles teases and then winks.

I laugh, shaking my head. "I'm pretty sure it's the younger sisters who need the club. Let's not pretend older brothers are easy to handle."

He offers a wolfish smile and lifts both hands. "Me? I'm an angel. Ask anyone."

I laugh. "Quinn would say the same."

"Sounds like your brother is a smart man."

"He's *something*."

My brother is a smart man, a former Navy SEAL, and my biggest protector. He's who found Ember Falls and moved us here. He's been the one keeping me and Kai safe since I left Chicago. As much as he loves me, he would also say I drive him crazy, but the feeling is mutual.

Quinn loved to get me into trouble when we were little.

Miles extends his hand. "We've met, but not officially. I'm Miles Anderson."

I take his offered hand and shake it. "Penelope . . . Walker." I almost forgot and said Miller.

A few weeks ago we moved here to outrun my past, and when we assume new identities, it always takes time to remember the new last name. The one thing I've asked my brother is to always keep our first names the same. It's way too hard to explain to Kai why his name would change.

"It's nice to formally meet you."

His warm hand engulfs mine for a few seconds longer than normal, and I feel sparks in my belly. A warm sensation fills me and I pull my hand back, tucking my hair behind my ear as I try to hide the heat in my cheeks. "It is. And you're coaching the team?" I ask, my voice shaking, and I hope he misses it.

He speaks and we start to walk toward the rink. "I'm filling in. This isn't my normal gig. Ethan's father, Doug, broke his leg and apparently was unwilling to try to coach ice hockey on crutches."

I grin. "I can see why that would be an issue."

"Right, you see it as a dereliction of duty too? A father should at least *try* for his son."

"Well, I mean, sure."

He smiles and my stomach clenches. Oh, I need to get a grip, and I definitely can't be flirting.

I look down before meeting his gaze again.

"Are you settling into Ember Falls all right?" Miles asks.

"I think so. It's only been a few weeks, but everyone has been really nice."

Each person who comes into the coffee shop always makes a point to welcome me, tell me a little about them, and I swear everyone mentions a kid they know or have that would just love to meet Kai.

The last town we were in didn't have that kind of feel. Everyone was nice enough, but no one talked to us unless they had to. In all honesty, I sort of liked it. When we had to pack up, I didn't feel all that bad about it since I didn't have any real connections.

"The town *is* filled with really kind people. We don't have a lot of people moving in, so when we get some new blood, the sharks tend to circle. I promise, they'll move onto annoying someone else soon."

I smile. "Good to know."

"So where are you from?" he asks as we walk toward the rink.

"North Carolina. What about you?"

It's not a lie, it's where I spent a lot of my childhood. My family owned a beach house in Corolla, and it has always felt like home. It's actually the first place that I went to after leaving my ex. However, it wasn't hard for the people after me to find me, since the house was in my name.

"I'm a born and bred Ember Fallsian. The only times I didn't live here were when I left for college, and when I was a marine, but then I came back, and I have no intentions of leaving."

I wish I could say the same. I really do like it here. The place is beautiful, with the mountains flanking the main area of town.

There's one thing he said in there that piqued my interest. "You were a marine?"

Miles nods. "Once a marine—always a marine."

I laugh because it's something my brother would say. Before I can say anything, Ethan yells from the other side, impatience written all over his face.

"Uncle Miles! Come on! It's time to skate!"

"You better go, six-year-old boys are very demanding."

"Yes, and nothing says a fun summer day more than giving them a stick and telling them to skate around."

I let out a soft laugh. "Good luck to you."

He gives me a two-finger salute. "I'm going to need it."

Yeah, he really is.

"Mom, did you see how good I did?" Kai asks, buzzing with excitement.

"I did. You were amazing."

"I was! I hit the puck four times and got it in twice! I can skate good too."

I won't mention that there wasn't a goalie. "I saw."

He throws his gear down on the ground beside me. "I'm such a good hockey player, and Ethan wants to be on my team with me next practice. I love hockey, Mom."

I love that he loves it, and that Quinn found us a town where there's a league. It also works out that Hazel was able to give me time off during his practices. I was so worried I wouldn't be able to find something flexible, but she's truly wonderful and feels family should always come first.

"I'm glad, sweetheart."

"Can we stay here for a long time?" Kai asks, and the hope in his voice makes my stomach ache.

Lying to him would be the easier thing. I'd give him the comfort of knowing he could have what he wanted, but I won't do it. Living our life isn't easy, and I have to be the one thing in his world that will always be honest, since almost nothing else is.

"We'll stay for as long as we can," I promise.

His face falls a little, but he nods. "I understand."

I hate that I've disappointed him. Kai deserves to have people in his life for more than just a fleeting moment. He needs friends that he can play with, know, and grow with, and I worry that all I've done is what causes his anxiety, because each time he gets comfortable, we have to leave. I don't want to keep him in a perpetual state of fear because that's my job as his parent, but I also have to keep him, us, safe.

"Hey, what if we go get ice cream?" I try for a diversion tactic. Ice cream is always a win.

"Can I invite Ethan?"

My first instinct is to say no. The more we stay guarded, the easier it is to leave when we have to, but . . . it could be days, months, or we could get to stay in Ember Falls forever. I just don't know.

But for now, I'll give him everything I want him to have in the hopes that this can be a place for him to stay longer.

I groan internally and nod. "Sure, honey."

He's running the other way before I can say another word. "Ethan! Do you want to come get ice cream?"

The two kids talk animatedly, and I see Ethan pleading with his uncle. He must agree, because the two boys jump up and down and then rush toward me, with Miles behind, carrying all the gear.

"Sorry, I said he could ask him and he took off," I explain when Miles gets closer.

"No problem, I'm sure my sister will be absolutely overjoyed I'm returning him sugar filled."

I smile. "Oh, I bet. Every mother just loves that."

He winks. "It's payback for my canceled trip."

"You canceled a trip?"

"I did. I should be up in Michigan, enjoying the cooler weather with a pole in the water and a beer in my hand."

"Instead, you're coaching hockey. At least there is a cooler climate involved, and you also have a stick, just not in water," I say with a smirk.

"Yes, Eloise noted that as well."

"Is that your sister?" I ask.

"It is. She's my twin, and according to her, she's two thousand or something months pregnant, and I broke her husband's leg, therefore I'm required to fill in as a coach so Ethan still gets three days a week where he's out of the house."

"Wait, you broke your brother-in-law's leg?"

He shakes his head. "Not like that. I had him play a game with me and he got hurt. She blames me since it's easier. It's fine, I'll take her wrath if it means Doug will owe me later."

We start to walk toward the car where the boys are standing. "I know you feel coerced to coach, but it's really nice you're doing this. Kai . . . has had a hard time meeting kids, and this clinic was really important to him."

"Then it's worth it."

"Not for your nephew's sake?" I ask with a grin.

"That too, but . . . I see a lot being a principal, and kids have a hard time settling into a town that's pretty much been inhabited by its founders. I'm glad Kai can transition and that he hit it off with Ethan right away. My nephew knows everyone and he'll show him the ropes," Miles explains.

"Can I ride with Ethan?" Kai asks as I get to the car.

"No, honey. We'll meet them there."

There are certain things I just can't do, and this is one. I need to know where he is and be able to get to him at a moment's notice if Quinn calls and we have to leave quickly.

His face is crestfallen. "Okay."

Miles steps in. "Hey, trust me, you don't want to drive with me. Ask Ethan. It ruins your cool-kid status hanging out with the principal."

"But Ethan said you were in the NHL!"

I turn to look at him, my eyes wide. "You were?"

Miles shakes his head. "No, I almost was, but I joined the marines instead."

"Really? My uncle Quinn was a Navy SEAL, and I'm going to be just like him."

There goes not telling him about my brother's job.

Miles's eyes move to me and a brow lifts. "He was, huh?"

I shrug. "We don't like to put that out there."

"Of course, the SEALs are known for their humility." I snort a laugh and look away. Yeah, humble is definitely not my brother and his friends. Miles returns his attention to Kai. "We'll be right behind you guys, all right?"

Kai nods. "Okay."

On the car ride to the ice-cream store, Kai goes on and on about Miles and Ethan and another boy named Sam. He tells me about how nice they are and how he can't wait for practice this week.

The absolute joy emanating from him has my smile growing with each word. I pray that this time we can stay here. I know Quinn and his team are doing absolutely everything they can to erase any traces of us, but with the men hunting me, it's a game of chicken on who is going to be better at hide-and-seek.

It's exhausting and frustrating because I just want to live my damn life.

As soon as the car is in park in front of Sugar High, the little ice-cream shop, Kai is out the door and running to the entrance of the store, then waiting for Ethan.

Both Miles and I smile at each other as we meet up where the boys already went inside. "After you," he says as he opens the door.

"Thank you."

A teenager in her 1950s soda shoppe uniform smiles warmly at Miles. "Hi, Mr. Anderson!"

"Hello, Matilda," he replies.

"Hi, Mr. A!" another kid calls out from the seating area.

"Grant."

As we're standing at the counter, an older woman I haven't met before walks over to him and smiles. "Miles, how are Doug and Eloise? I was thinking about them the other day. Oh, and who is this?"

"Mrs. Hawkins, this is Penelope. She works over at Hazel's store."

Her eyes widen slightly. "Oh! Hello! I've heard so much about you. Well, not *so* much. It's just that us old ladies are a bunch of clucking hens that like to gossip. They said that you moved here and you have a son?" She looks over to where Ethan and Kai are standing.

"Yes, we came to town about three weeks ago."

"Well, welcome to Ember Falls. I've lived here my whole life, and my daughter Andrea is a teacher at the elementary school. She's usually a second-grade teacher, but she might be teaching first. Maybe she'll have your son," Mrs. Hawkins suggests.

"Maybe. Kai is entering first grade this year."

"Oh, I hope he has her. She's a gifted teacher. I know she's my daughter and there's a bit of bias there, but she genuinely loves these kids."

"I hope so too, then."

Kai's kindergarten teacher was not the best last year. She got angry at his nervous tics and found constant things to criticize him on, which then made those things worse. The school resources were worn thin, and of my many talents, tutoring is not one.

Miles smiles warmly and tilts his head. "We better get the kids their ice cream before Ethan starts a revolution."

She grins. "He's so much of his mother."

"That's what I keep saying," Miles says in agreement.

Miles places his hand on my lower back and leads me forward. "She'll talk for days and always about Andrea. It's best to have an escape plan at all times," he whispers against my ear.

I fight back the shiver that runs down my spine at his closeness. God, he smells good. It's woodsy with sandalwood and hints of amber and sage. It's intoxicating.

I can't be intoxicated.

No, I need to be sober.

What is wrong with me?

I clear my throat and step out of the bubble he created. "I'll definitely keep that in mind."

There's a flash of something in his gaze, but it's gone before I can name it. "I'll try to warn you about the others."

I smile. "I appreciate it."

I've already gotten a ton of advice from Hazel. She's been so helpful in letting us know the area and who is who.

"You've already met the guys from the Disc Jocks, right?" Miles asks after we place the orders.

"I have." Apparently Ultimate Frisbee is quite the sport in this town. There are four guys that play together: Miles, Everett, Lachlan, and Killian. Everett is Hazel's best friend and comes in a lot to Prose & Perk to either have lunch with her or drink a ridiculous amount of coffee. "Lachlan and Everett the most."

"Killian lives in Boston most of the time. You'll see him a lot less."

"Hazel mentioned that he has a big dating app business?" I ask, curious which one.

"He does."

"That's pretty cool."

He laughs. "Yeah, except when he tries to make his friends sign up."

We take the cones from a kid working behind the counter and head to the open booth at the front of the store.

"Can we sit outside?" Ethan asks.

"No way, it's like a hundred degrees today," Miles notes with a shake of his head.

"But we don't want to sit with you," Ethan says matter-of-factly.

I fight back a laugh, but Miles replies without missing a beat. "Good. You two sit over there, and I'll hang out with Miss Penelope."

Ethan nods, and he and Kai head to the other table. "And here I thought kids were only awful to their parents."

Miles laughs once. "If only. I'm around Ethan a lot. My sister and I are pretty close, plus she's married to my best friend. So, if I'm not at work or the field, I'm usually over at their house."

"Do you have other siblings?"

"Nope, just Eloise. What about you?"

"Just my brother."

"Ahh, yes, your *Navy SEAL* brother. You didn't mention that before."

I grin. "Former. He's retired now."

My cone starts to drip a little, and I quickly bring it to my mouth, taking a bit of ice cream away so it doesn't make a mess. I hear a quick intake of air and look up to see Miles's eyes wide as he watches me. I pull the cone away, realizing what exactly it looks like as I'm licking the cone.

Then he reaches out and wipes at my nose. "Sorry, you had some ice cream."

"Oh, right. Thanks." I smile and shake my head.

"So your brother is a former SEAL. Are you guys close?" Miles asks.

"We are. Even though we don't live near each other, I talk to him frequently." Although it's not nearly as much as either of us want. Our conversations are always based on pertinent information or warnings. This is the first time that Quinn has placed us this close to him. Hopefully that means we'll get to see each other more.

"That's good. I called Eloise every week when I was deployed and stationed in Colorado. We've always been close. Our mother died when we were just four days old, so we lived with our gran after my father took off. Gran still lives in town. You'll meet her, God help you."

"Why God help me?"

"That woman is the reason meddling exists. She probably knows your entire life story already. You tell one person one thing, Donna knows within minutes. She's like the mayor."

I highly doubt she knows anything about my life story, since nothing is true, but Donna sounds like an amazing woman if she raised her grandkids.

"I'm sorry to hear about your mom and I can't wait to meet Donna."

Miles chuckles. "You'll regret that last one, but thank you. Eloise and I were lucky to have my gran. She's really the best. What about your parents?"

My parents cut me off when I got pregnant and they've never met Kai. No matter how much Quinn has tried to defend me to them, in their eyes, I'm a sinner who is unrepentant.

Never mind that my brother got his wife pregnant before they were married. That's Quinn—he's perfect to them.

But I don't tell Miles any of that. Instead, I settle for a portion of the truth.

"My parents aren't around since I had Kai, so . . ."

"Oh, I'm sorry, Penelope."

I shrug. "It's fine. At least I have my brother and please, call me Penny."

He smiles and I feel a flutter in my belly. "You mentioned you grew up in North Carolina, but Kai was talking about how you guys moved from Tennessee."

Thankfully, that's probably the only place that Kai can remember we've lived. When I first left Chicago, we went to North Carolina, then to California for about three months before there was something that alerted my brother he needed to move us again.

After, Quinn moved us to a small town in Oregon called Rose Canyon. I had about two years there, loved it, and then made the mistake of sending a photo to an old friend. She sent me a text two days later, telling me that my ex's business partner offered her $250,000 for any information on me. She was broke and needed the money. So she sold us out, but she let me know once she had the money, so I could get out.

Jackson, my brother's boss, was at the house in six hours, and we were gone. That's when we went to Texas, which I hated, so Quinn moved me to Tennessee. I stayed there for a year. It was fine, but . . . somehow they found us again.

Now we're here and I have no idea how long we'll have before it's time to run again.

"Yeah, we were there for about a year."

"What did you do there?"

I know he's only being polite and making conversation since we're stuck at a table together, but a part of me can't help but wonder . . .

What if he knows who I am?

What if he's not who he says he is?

Rationally, I know this sounds ridiculous. I mean, he's from Ember Falls. He grew up here. His family is here. He's a freaking high school principal and isn't in the same business Edward was.

I know this.

However, I trust nothing.

"Worked, mainly."

"Ahh, so you're a traveling barista?" he jokes before taking a bite of his ice cream.

I laugh and do the same. I opt to lean back into our cover story and the things Quinn has laid out for me. Stick to the script.

"No, I gave up the rat race to come to a small town where I could focus on what matters—Kai."

"There's a rat race for baristas in Tennessee?"

"You'd be surprised," I say, looking away and hoping this will end the inquiry.

"I'm sure I would."

"Mom! Mom! Can Ethan come over to our house?" Kai asks with a hope I wish I didn't have to squash.

"Not today, buddy. We have boxes everywhere, and I have to go to work soon."

His face falls. "But . . ."

"Maybe in a few days, once we're settled more and the house is more put together," I say, trying for a consolation.

"Fine," he says, clearly dejected.

Miles speaks up quickly. "Listen, Ethan isn't going anywhere, and he's going to stay with me whenever his mother goes into labor. Maybe we can have some meetups at the rink and other things I'm going to be doing to keep him from being super bored with his old uncle."

I chuckle, but that seems to mollify Kai. "Really?"

Miles nods. "Absolutely. I think it'll be fun . . ."

But the way he looks at me at the end of it makes me wonder if he's saying fun for Kai and Ethan or fun for him.

three
Miles

I finish my eight-mile run in record time. I have sweat pouring off me, but I don't care. I feel great. I could do another eight miles if I had to.

Running makes me feel alive. I shut everything, and everyone, off. All I focus on is myself and my breathing.

There's a rhythm, a cadence, that forms and allows me to escape my thoughts and worries, focusing only on the pavement.

I'm stretching, reaching to the sky, opening my lungs, when I hear a loud whistle. "Hey, hot stuff, you single?"

I laugh and turn to see Everett hanging out of his truck window. "Only for you."

He chuckles. "Are you coming to practice tonight?"

"I'm always at practice."

"Yeah, yeah, that's because you have no life."

"That's rich coming from you," I toss back.

Everett's life is his business and taking care of his mom. She suffered an injury years ago that flipped his entire life around, but Everett didn't blink and stepped up.

"I'll have you know, I played six games of Scrabble yesterday with my mother and won them all," he informs me.

"Yes, a life that every man dreams of. When was the last time you got laid?"

He shrugs. "Real men don't kiss and tell."

"Funny, I don't see any other real men around but myself."

"Dickhead. Hey, listen, Lachlan changed the time of practice because Rose has cheer. They sent a text."

"I didn't see it. I left my phone in the car."

"You could at least get one of those watches that tells you when someone is looking for you."

I shrug. "I could, but then I'd know when you were trying to reach me."

Everett flips me off. "All right, princess, I'm going out to check on a pregnant cow. Want to meet me after?"

"Sure, let's meet at Prose & Perk," I suggest, knowing exactly why I want to go there.

"What?" Everett asks with confusion. "Why there?"

"We can get a drink before," I say as though it should be fairly obvious. I don't know when Everett doesn't have a cup of coffee in his hand.

"Yes, well, I know why I would get that, but you don't even drink coffee!"

No, but . . . I like the barista.

"I'm aware of that, thank you, jackass. I need to carb up and Hazel has . . ." I search for something I've seen that will make me not look like it's because I just want to see Penelope. Then I remember she just got new snacks in. ". . . protein bars and granola."

He scoffs. "Right, that's what you're looking for?"

Fuck. He knows something isn't right, but I refuse to admit defeat. "Obviously."

They know that I fucking hate coffee and only go to Prose & Perk in the morning for tea and breakfast.

He shakes his head. "Whatever. Meet me there at four."

"Sounds good."

Everett is the town vet, and I swear, no one works harder than him. We're mainly a horse farm area, but we have a few farms in the area that have a variety of animals. He usually spends two days a week going to the surrounding area, and the others he's at his office in town.

I make the ten-minute drive back home, toss my keys in the bowl by the front door, and hop in the shower.

Once I'm done and dressed, I check my phone and notice I have seven missed calls, all work related, and a shit ton of text messages. I'm sure it's the freaking group chat.

LACHLAN

I need to move the practice tonight back two hours.

EVERETT

And we all live to accommodate you.

LACHLAN

Thank you. I appreciate that you do. It's for Rose's cheer team so don't be a dick or I'll tell her Uncle Everett made her miss.

EVERETT

She'd never believe you. I'm her favorite.

KILLIAN

That's a lie.

LACHLAN

If it is true, it's because he acts her age.

KILLIAN

Sorry, guys, I won't be there since I'm in Boston and can't leave.

EVERETT

Slacker.

KILLIAN

You're in rare form.

LACHLAN

Really? This seems like his only form—dickhead.

KILLIAN

That's true, he's always a punkass.

EVERETT

You both really know how to insult others. I'm over here, saving a calf's life and you're just being mean . . . tears . . . please stop hurting my delicate feelings.

I laugh at that one. He doesn't have feelings, let alone delicate ones.

LACHLAN

Anyone know if that's going to work for Miles?

EVERETT

I just passed him after he was running, he's fine. Not like he's good at Frisbee anyway. Missing him might actually be an improvement.

LACHLAN

This is true.

I jump in, grateful this didn't go even longer.

I fucking hate you all. Let's be real for a second, the weakest link is definitely Everett.

LACHLAN

Oh, look, you're alive. Is the new time okay?

Of course I'm fine with it, I would never deny your daughter a chance to cheer. Talk to you idiots later, I have to put out fires at work.

LACHLAN

Leave that to the professionals.

EVERETT

If you know of any of those, please share their names.

. . .

Oh, Lachlan is going to love that one. I put my phone on the charger, knowing that this conversation is going to take a turn for the worse, and grab my laptop.

I'm supposed to be on the lake, not caring about any of these emails, but there are four marked URGENT. Which . . . well, as much as I'd like to pretend I don't care—I do.

Mr. Anderson,
   I'm writing to let you know that I will not be returning next year. I know I previously committed, however, things have changed and this is my official resignation.
   Sincerely,
   Megan Hunt

Of course the head of the fucking English department just quit.
   I open the next email.

Mr. Anderson,
   Please find attached my request for my son's schedule. As you know, Sloane is very gifted, but requires a certain order to his subjects to be successful. I look forward to your care and attention to this requirement.
   Best,
   Jennifer Sanders

Oh, yeah, like that's going to happen. I keep going. Some are from parents, a few teachers asking for specific room assignments or other ridiculous things. When I was pretty much forced to take this position, I had no clue what I was in for. I'd taught for six years and the superintendent came to me, asking me to apply for his position since I was already certified. I laughed, thought it was ridiculous, but agreed because he was a friend.

I never in a million years thought I'd actually get it.

However, with my military background and the fact that I know this town like I know myself, it hasn't been that bad.

Until I get stupid emails like these.

I reply to the few that don't require much thought and then close my laptop. While I'm not in Michigan, I do have access to fishing, and that's what my plan is for the day.

I grab my pole, ready to be out on the water, even if it's just the river, when there's a knock at my door.

That's fucking weird.

I walk over, yanking the door open to find Ethan and Kai.

"What the . . . ?" I stop myself before I finish that one.

"Hey, Uncle Miles."

"Ethan . . ."

"I'm playing with Kai today, and I told him that you live real close, so I had to prove it."

I raise one brow. "Had to, huh?" I look to the non-troublemaker in this duo, pretty sure my nephew is going to corrupt this one. "Does your mother know you both came here?"

Kai shakes his head.

Great. Fishing ruined again.

"Let's walk you both there before she realizes you took off." I step outside, and we make our way toward their house. The boys chat about what they were doing and how they were on an adventure walk, which led them to me.

If I had Penelope's number, I'd call and let her know they are safe, but I don't, and Kai said he doesn't have it.

"Kai! Ethan!" I hear screaming, but it's coming from another area than where we're heading. "Kai! Please, God, Kai! Ethan! Boys!"

There is absolute terror in her voice. "I have the boys here!" I yell back.

"Kai!" She screams again and her voice cracks.

"Penny! I have Kai!" I yell louder, moving toward where she sounded like she was. "Come on," I say to them and we jog that way.

When I get closer, Penny is on her knees, tears streaming down her face, and I get to her first. I quickly crouch and keep my voice soft. "They're safe. They were just being kids who walked off and they came to my house. They're safe."

Her gaze lifts, and her red-rimmed eyes break my heart. She shakes her head. "H-he d-doesn't run of-f."

I nod. "They were doing an adventure walk," I try to explain, even though it sounds stupid. "They're okay."

Her chest is heaving and then Kai comes close. "I'm sorry, Mommy. We were looking for bugs."

She looks to him, and tears continue down her face. "You. You c-can't do th-that to me a-again."

Kai nods. "I won't. I'm sorry."

"It's o-okay." She wipes her face, but I can see that she's still not okay.

"How about we walk back to your house together? It's hot and we could all use some shade and water." I stand, extending my hand to Penny. She takes it, rises, and her lips tremble.

Even Ethan, who normally isn't rattled by much, looks frightened.

The four of us quietly make our way back, the two boys walking a few steps ahead. I slow my pace to match Penny's.

After a minute passes, I speak. "Are you all right?"

She turns her head, almost as though she forgot I was here. "Not fully."

"Scared the shit out of you, huh?"

"They were playing out back one second and then they were gone. I don't know that my heart has restarted yet."

While I don't have kids, I know that moment of panic when you think you're missing a child. "When I was a fourth-grade teacher, we went on a field trip out into the mountains. I taught earth science, so we had the cool trips. Anyway, we were in groups of four, but one of the groups had five. We'd do a one, two, three, four head count every fifteen minutes. It was sort of a sound off. We did this a bunch of times, always getting to five, but to be funny, one of the kids pretended to be another number so they sorted into the wrong group. It was . . . the most fucking terrifying twenty minutes of my life, looking for that kid. I was screaming his name, running up and down the creek. I swear, every horrific scenario anyone could come up with, I'd played out."

Her long lashes flutter. "Yeah, my imagination wasn't kind."

"Ember Falls is pretty safe," I try to reassure her. "Our last murder was in, like, 1907 or something. The worst crime we had was when Everett shoplifted, to which his mother dragged him to the town meeting and made him recite an apology letter . . . where every other parent, mine included, made us come to see what happens to sticky-fingered little kids."

She smiles for just a moment. "That's good to know. Although I'm not sure crime sprees typically come with notice."

"True, but we all look out for one another here. Just so you know, the boys and I were on our way to you. As soon as they showed up at my door, we were heading back."

Penny's eyes lift, and the shimmering tears still linger, but she looks as though she can breathe a little easier. "Thank you. And for walking us back. I really appreciate it."

"Of course."

We reach the entrance to her driveway and she clears her throat. "Thanks again, Miles. I'm sorry I freaked out so much before."

"I would've done the same if it was my kid."

Although maybe not to that extent. Penny was beyond anxious, it was beyond terror even. I've never seen someone so distraught, as though she was sure he was dead or worse. Thankfully, she seems a little calmer now.

She turns to Ethan and Kai. "I think you boys should play inside until it's time to go back."

"Is my sister coming to get him?" I ask.

She shouldn't be driving with her being so close to giving birth, but trying to tell Eloise what to do is like trying to stop the rain.

Penny shakes her head. "No, I'm going to drive him home before my shift."

"I can take him if you need," I offer. I'm not sure why I offer, because it seems there's a perfectly good plan already in place, but something has me wanting to stay, or at least make this day a little easier for her.

"It's fine, I'll do it." She takes a step back and wraps her arms around her middle.

"Are you sure you're okay?" I ask.

While we've been talking the last few minutes, it's clear she's still rattled.

"Yeah, I'm good."

"I can hang around if you want . . . I'm pretty good at keeping Ethan out of trouble."

She smiles but shakes her head. "I promise, I'm fine."

"All right. If you need anything, I'm right down the road."

"Thanks again, Miles. I'll see you around."

I flash my most charming smile, if I even have one, and dip my head. "I'm sure we will."

I can't stop thinking about Penny.

On my walk home, I kept wanting to turn around and make sure she really was okay. However, that would've been a little intrusive, so I went back, worked on the asinine emails I had, trying to respond with professionalism instead of—*are you fucking kidding me with this shit?*—and made sure my nephew didn't appear again.

Not that I think he'd be that stupid to try it again after he saw Penelope's face and how terrified she was.

Now I'm at practice and still thinking of her.

I need a hobby.

"Dude!" Everett yells. "Catch the fucking disc!"

I look over and it's lying on the ground to the right of me. "Didn't see it."

He throws his hands up. "Clearly! We have our first tournament in a few weeks. You might want to at least *try* to give a shit."

I shrug. "I could try, but there would be no fun in that. Hey, after this, I was thinking we could get coffee."

"Coffee?" Lachlan asks.

"Yeah, you know that stuff that your fiancée is so hard up on. She basically keeps Hazel in business."

He rolls his eyes. "Yes, I know what it is, Ainsley clearly does, but you don't drink it."

"No, but I could start."

Everett stands there, jaw slack. "Okay, now I'm sure something is wrong with you. You *hate* coffee."

I roll my eyes. "Maybe I just haven't had the right kind."

Maybe I just want it made by a beautiful woman with auburn hair and blue eyes.

Or maybe I'm an absolute idiot.

That last one is highly plausible.

Still, I want to see her and this gives me the perfect excuse.

"So let me get this straight, you want to try to like coffee for some odd reason?" Everett asks before tossing the Frisbee at me.

"Yes."

"Did we hit you in the head with the Frisbee?" Lachlan asks.

"No."

"Okay, then maybe you're having a medical episode. This is really not like you to *want* coffee."

He's not wrong, I hate coffee. The shit is nasty. It tastes like dirt. However, I don't hate being around the woman who serves it.

"I didn't realize my drinking habits were studied. I want to give it a try."

Everett snorts. "It's not the coffee he wants to try, it's the woman who works there and owns it?"

For a second I think they've caught on that I want to see Penny, but then I actually register what Everett said. "Wait, what?"

"Hazel."

"I know who owns it, putz, but why would you think I like Hazel?"

Everett rubs his forehead. "Well you've been making excuses to go in there and while you don't have a shot in *hell* of dating Hazel, you're giving it a go. Is that it?"

I ignore the jab about dating Hazel because he's a prick, but the fact he's noticed has me a little concerned. Hopefully Penny doesn't notice that I've been in almost twice a day.

"Nope, I just don't feel like cooking and the pastries are great. Hazel has been bringing in new snacks lately."

"You're so fucking weird," Everett says with a laugh. "And a liar."

"Projecting much?" Lachlan asks. None of us are able to resist a good jab at one or the other.

Everett scoffs. "Yeah, and you're just the walking poster for normal?"

"Normal is a relative term," I say quite philosophically, if I do say so myself.

The two of them chuckle. "Yeah, we're not even going to talk about Lachlan," Everett replies before flicking his wrist to send the Frisbee flying—the wrong way.

"One would think by now we'd be good at this," Lachlan mutters under his breath.

"Hey, we're good when we want to be," I say, defending our terribly ridiculous team.

"Not since entering the professional league," he reminds me.

This is a pretty sad fact. Prior to this year, we played as a college team. The four of us enrolled in community college, which allowed us to enter the collegiate league after recruiting a few other players. We were good.

We were gods.

Maybe not gods, but seriously, we fucking kicked ass.

Then we got kicked out.

After our last tournament win, a bunch of the other schools filed complaints because we . . . won all the damn time.

The official collegiate league met with us and told us we either had to be full-time students in a four-year school, or we needed to join a different league.

Which means we needed to join the adults' professional league or disband the team.

Well, no one puts the Disc Jocks in the corner.

We rallied and found a new league to dominate. Only to find out that—we suck.

"News flash, boys. You were never good!" Ainsley, Lachlan's girlfriend, yells from the sideline.

"Fuck off, sweetheart," Lach yells at her.

"Love you too, sugarpie."

I roll my eyes. "You two are couple goals."

"Whatever." Lachlan grins.

He's such a moron and so completely in love with that girl it's almost uncomfortable to watch.

Everett clears his throat. "If we can get back to the topic at hand."

"Yes, how do we improve?" I remind them.

"I was talking about your stupid-ass request to go drink coffee."

For fuck's sake. "Can we just drop this?" I ask.

"Not a chance, douchebag," Everett says, arms crossed over his chest.

"Who cares if I don't like coffee? I want to go, so what?"

Everett smirks. "You're right. Let's all go get coffee and see what really is on the menu that you want to sample."

The three of them grin at each other, and I'm pretty sure I'm going to regret every second of this.

We pack up and head to the cars, which means I get to see Penelope again, and really it's only because I want to make sure she's okay.

four
Penelope

"Mom, do you think I can have a dad again ever?" Kai asks as we're on the way to Prose & Perk.

Thankfully, my reflexes keep me from veering off the road.

"A dad?"

He nods. "I was thinking it would be good to have one."

"You were?"

Apparently I'm unable to do anything but ask questions to each statement.

"But my dad died," Kai says with a mix of sadness and longing.

Oh, how much I wish I could take it away for him.

At first my brother and I argued about how much to tell Kai. He's a kid and I really didn't want to burden him with the truth about his father. While I may not speak to my parents anymore, I had a great childhood where I felt safe and loved, at least when I was living the way they expected me to.

Kai never would have that. He will never know the love of a two-parent home. Regardless of the fact that Edward VanderGroef was a monster and I didn't want him anywhere near us. I do hate it for Kai, though.

Quinn felt I was doing more harm by keeping him completely in the dark. After about thirty minutes of back-and-forth and more tears than I care to admit, I agreed. Kai needed to know his father was gone, because if he was approached by anyone asking questions, he had to be prepared.

"Where is this coming from?" I ask.

"A dad would know how to lace my skates and teach me how to hit the puck. You're cool, Mom, but you don't know that stuff."

No, I don't. "Not all dads know that, though."

"Coach Miles does. He's super cool. He even played hockey in college, and he knows how to do all that stuff."

Oh, this is going to go great. "Then it's a really good thing he's your coach, because he can help you with all that stuff, without being your dad."

"Ethan said that he's the coolest uncle ever. That he always comes to his house and he plays games and sneaks him things that he's not supposed to have."

I smile. "Like all good uncles and aunts do. Uncle Quinn does that for you too."

He sighs. "Yeah, but I don't get to see Uncle Quinn all the time."

I reach my hand back and take his. "I know, but it would be really hard if I met someone who I could actually like and then we had to leave. I think, for right now, it's best if it's just the two of us. Am I cool enough to maybe try to learn about hockey skates and hitting the puck?"

Kai sighs heavily, as though I've just asked him to do math homework. "I guess. Maybe one day I can have another dad, though?"

"Maybe one day, baby."

Maybe one day we won't have to worry about the fact that I'm worth more dead than alive. Maybe one day we will be able to have a home, a life, a family that I want just as much as it seems Kai does.

I can hope.

But for now I need to be realistic, and that means working and letting my brother and the team he has do what they can to protect us and keep searching for answers that will allow us to be free from the people hunting us.

"Ethan says it's great having a dad."

A tear forms and I do my best to stop it from falling. "I'm sorry, Kai. I really am. I know it's hard for you."

He shrugs and looks out the window. "I hate the rules."

"I hate them too."

The rules are the worst part of our life even though there are only four that must be kept. I've drilled them into Kai.

Do not talk to strangers. Ever.

Never post anything on the internet.

Don't tell anyone our real names or where we live.

If someone ever says he knew his dad, he should scream and find help.

"Do you think the bad people will find us?" he asks, almost absently.

Every single day I worry about it, but my only concern is staying alive and away from the men who killed Edward.

We pull into the back parking lot of Prose & Perk, and I turn to face him with a smile and do my best to reassure him.

"No, honey, I think Uncle Quinn and his friends are doing everything to keep us safe, and it's why we got to come to Ember Falls, because it was the best place he could find. It's why we follow the rules, because we don't want to move again, right?"

"Yeah, I guess."

———

My phone rings in my back pocket, and I see my brother's name on the screen. I turn to Hazel. "Do you mind if I step out and take this call?"

She shakes her head. "Of course not, you're due for a break."

"Thank you!"

Seriously, she's the best employer I've ever had.

I walk into the back area, where I can see Kai but he can't hear me. "Hey, is everything okay?" I ask, my heart already beating faster.

"Yes, everything is fine. This is a check-in." He chuckles. "Hello, my darling sister, Penelope."

"Hello, Quinn."

My brother is literally my knight in shining armor, or maybe my knight in camouflage with a gun. Either one works.

"How are things?"

"Well, today your nephew gave me the scare of a lifetime."

"Oh?"

I fill him in on the adventure walk he took and how it shaved about ten years off my life. I've never, ever, felt that kind of terror before. I was sure someone took them. I screamed and screamed, tears running down my face. The worst part was, I didn't do any of the things my brother told me to do if this ever happened.

"Why didn't you call me?" Quinn's voice is hard, and I know he's reining back his anger.

"Because, in that moment, I froze."

He sighs heavily and then my sister-in-law, Ashton, is suddenly on the phone. "Hey, Pen."

"Hey, Ash."

"Your brother is starting to turn red, so I figured it was best I take the phone before I had to rip it out of his hand and lecture him for an hour about not yelling at you. Anyway, I miss you tons. How are you?"

"I'm okay. I'm at work now."

"Oh! The coffee place! How do you like it?" Ashton asks.

I tell her about Hazel and how much I like working here. She lets me bring Kai to work and he hangs out in the back area, which is set up like a living room. Hazel was raised by a single mom and understands how hard things were.

"That's amazing. I really hope you guys stay there for a bit. Is Kai liking it?"

"He loves it here. I know it's only been a few weeks, but he's honestly the happiest I've seen him. He met a friend, Ethan, and some other boys from the hockey clinic. His anxiety is already better. I just . . . I hate the idea that this . . ."

Ashton cuts me off. "Hey, don't think that way. We have no idea what the future holds. Your brother and the guys at Cole Security are working really hard. Trust in that."

"I do."

There's no one in the world I trust more than Quinn and his friends. Jackson, Mark, Quinn, and Liam have all come to my aid more than once. They've done it without question or compensation. I will never take the fact that I have any of them for granted. Not every woman in my situation has the same privilege.

"Good. We're going to come visit next week as long as everything checks out."

I really hope they can. Being alone is something I've learned to accept, but I hate it. More than just for myself, I hate it for Kai. I want him to have the experiences I did. Where we went on vacations with our aunts and uncles, cousins multiplied each year, and you never felt alone.

Instead, he has a life where we are constantly moving and changing our names.

Some days I feel like I've failed as a mother to give my son the life he deserves.

"I'll keep my fingers crossed." I look down at my watch. "My break is just about up. Tell Quinn I love him and kiss my handsome nephew for me."

Ashton laughs. "I'll do both. Be safe, and hopefully we'll be in town next week."

"Sounds good."

I hang up and go to where Kai is watching a video of some guy playing a game online. "Hey, bud, are you doing okay?"

He smiles up at me. "Yup."

"Good. I'm going back out there. Just pop your head in if you need me."

Kai turns, going back to his video. I seriously question what in the world is fun about that, but he loves it. He has three gamers he watches religiously and says they're far superior to the others. Whatever that means.

When I get out into the store, Miles, Lachlan, Ainsley, and Everett are pushing through the door.

My heart pounds just a little faster at the sight of Miles. He's wearing a tight shirt with basketball shorts, and his skin looks slightly bronzed from the sun. The way his dark-brown hair is pushed back is so freaking sexy and makes me want to run my fingers through it.

Which is dumb.

There will be no finger running in any man's hair. Much less Miles's.

I force a smile and walk toward them. "Hey, guys."

"Penny!" Everett calls my name boisterously. "How is my favorite barista?"

Hazel snorts. "You are a fickle man, Everett Finnegan. You do realize that I make your coffee most days?"

He leans against the counter. "Yes, but Penny is much nicer."

"She hasn't realized what a jackass you are—yet."

I laugh softly. "The *yet* on the end tells me it's coming."

He winks. "Don't let her scare you, love. I'm the favorite."

"Oh, please," Miles says, shaking his head. "You're not even close."

Everett stands up, jutting his chin at his friend. "And you are?"

Miles's gaze meets mine and I feel warmth down to my toes. "I think Penny knows I'm a good guy. I'm coaching hockey, I return missing things, and I'm much better looking."

I fight back my laugh, but Everett is unable to let that go without jumping in. "Well, we both know that last part is a lie. Penny, which one of us is hotter?"

I lift both hands. "I'm not entering this fight."

"Come on, we need to know," Miles says with a smirk. "You can tell him the truth."

This is never going to end well. "Fine, I think that Lachlan is the best looking," I say, grinning at Ainsley.

"I second it. Motion passed," Ainsley jumps in, saving me from this fight.

"Now, what can I get you guys?"

Ainsley, Lachlan, and Everett get their normal coffee orders, and then it's Miles's turn.

All eyes turn to him and I feel like I'm missing something. "Miles?"

He sighs heavily. "What do you recommend?"

I blink a few times. "I'm not sure how to answer that. Everything is good, and we can adjust the flavors however you'd like."

"Okay, how about the most un-coffee-tasting coffee."

"Umm, is there such a thing?" I ask.

"He hates coffee," Hazel notes as she's leaning against the counter beside me.

My eyes widen a bit. "You hate coffee?"

Miles shrugs. "It's not my favorite."

That's weird because he comes here all the time. Yeah, he gets tea and a snack, but he could definitely get those at home or at the bakery down the street since that's where we get the baked goods from.

"Have you tried all the different kinds?" I ask.

Miles clears his throat. "I have not."

"Then maybe you just haven't had the right kind."

Hazel practically squeals beside me. "Yes! A tasting. Penelope, let's get creative."

five
Miles

There is way too much excitement in Hazel's voice about getting to make me drink this. Although this trip here was my idea because I wanted to see Penny.

"Trying a bunch of coffee wasn't what I was going for, but if you think you can fix me"—I say to Penelope—"I think we should try."

Penelope smiles broadly. "I hopefully will find you the good stuff."

She already has, it's just not in a mug.

Lachlan snorts and puts his hand on my shoulder. "I see what you were looking for now, buddy." He taps my chest. "Let's go before you start drooling on the new girl."

Penelope and Hazel come around a minute later, and the good stuff has already arrived, but it's not in the form of coffee.

I don't know what it is about this girl, but I like her. She's sweet, and after hanging out with her at the ice-cream store and then our walk, I just . . . I don't know, I like her.

"Are you sure you want to do this?" Penelope asks.

I shake my head. "Not especially."

"This should be fun then."

"Maybe you and Hazel can turn me into a new man."

Hazel scoffs. "Please, I've been trying to fix all you men in this town for years, it's going to take a lot more than coffee."

Everett shakes his head. "Please, I'm not broken."

Hazel's eyes narrow. "You're the worst of the lot. At least Lachlan got his head out of his ass and went after Ainsley."

"There's no head up my ass, sweetheart. I'm perfectly happy being single," he explains.

She rolls her eyes. "You're perfectly happy being a pain in everyone's ass."

"That too," he agrees.

Penelope looks to me and I shrug. This is just their friendship. They're worse than me and Eloise bickering, and that's saying a lot. For a long time, I thought there was some kind of underlying sexual tension brewing between them.

As the years have gone by, I've realized that is absolutely not the case. In fact, there's not an ounce of attraction between them.

They really are just like brother and sister.

Hazel focuses on me. "What about coffee don't you like?"

What the fuck kind of question is that? "How the hell would I know?"

"Well, is it the aftertaste? Is it too weak? Do you like something that'll put hair on your balls?"

I glare at her, and Penelope laughs softly. Great, she's making me look like a fucking dweeb in front of her. "I hate how it tastes."

She rolls her eyes. "You're hopeless. Okay, we'll start with the strongest and work our way back. Be ready for so much coffee you're going to swim in it." She turns, pulling Penelope with her. "Also, today's tasting will be sixty bucks!"

"Oh, great, I get to pay to drink sludge."

Lachlan slaps my shoulder. "As much as I'd love to sit around and watch this show, I have to pick Rose up from cheerleading, and I'd rather be anywhere than with you."

Rose is his six-year-old daughter, whom I adore. She's big into competition cheerleading, and there's nothing more entertaining than watching Lachlan be a girl-dad. He loves every second of it and has zero shame.

"I'd rather be with Rose than you too."

He grins. "See you later, Romeo."

Everett sits opposite of me. "I'm here for the long haul."

"Goodie."

He grins. "Listen, what about that barista?"

"What about her?" I ask, keeping my voice neutral.

If Everett suspects I have a thing for her, then he'll be relentless in his teasing. Lachlan is much more mature when it comes to this. It's best I keep this to myself for now.

He glances back where she is, keeping his voice low. "What do you think? She's beautiful."

Yes, she is. "Okay."

Everett huffs a heavy breath. "It's a wonder why I'm friends with you."

"I wonder why too."

"Anyway, I'm thinking I should ask her out."

Absolutely fucking not. Not only because I'm attracted to her, but because Everett just got back on Hazel's good side after sleeping with her last barista. "Did you learn nothing after sleeping with Cherish?"

"Ehh, Hazel will get over it."

"Or not."

He leans back in his seat, stretching his arms up. "Probably not. You're right. Hazel really likes Penny. She said she's smart, hardworking, and has some great ideas on ways to improve."

"Like what?" I ask.

"I didn't say I paid attention after that," he jokes.

Before I can, once again, tell him what an asshat he is, Hazel and Penelope come with trays.

Multiple trays of coffee.

This was such a bad idea.

Penelope places down the tray and hands me a cup with very little in it. Well, I can at least chug that much if she's watching.

"All right, this is going to be the strongest coffee possible. It's an espresso, but a very bold one," Hazel says as she sits beside me.

"For sixty bucks I better get desserts too," I say, taking the offered cup.

"Sure, honey, we'll get you a cookie."

I laugh with a shake of my head. "Bottoms up."

I take the first sip and want to spit it back out. God, that is so freaking gross. "No."

"No what?"

"No, I'm not drinking this."

She sighs. "It's strong, but it's meant to show you the varying bean possibilities."

"There is no possibility that I will like or want to consume this—ever," I tell her, putting it down.

We go down a few more cups, and I'm about to give up when Penny walks over with a cup. "I've been listening to you talk about the things you like and don't like. I made this version and . . . I don't know, if you want to try it . . ."

I look up into her deep-blue eyes, and no matter how terrible it is, I know I'll drink it. Because I'm clearly a stupid idiot.

"I'll try it," I say immediately. "Under one condition."

"What's that?"

"You go on a date with me?"

Penny's eyes widen. "You'll drink the coffee for a date?"

"With you."

Hazel laughs, but then turns it into a cough. "Smooth."

I ignore that. "What do you say?"

"I'm sorry, I . . . just moved here, and I'm not really ready to date right now. Plus, I have these rules and, well, I just wouldn't want to give you the wrong impression."

The only impression I have is that she's adorable and I want to spend more time with her. It's why I'm here, looking at the coffee in her hand.

"I understand. How about I drink this coffee and you think about it?"

"Seriously, you're embarrassing yourself," Everett says under his breath, but loud enough the people next door could hear.

"Shut up, asshole. I'm talking to Penny."

She smiles and I swear I could fucking start singing show tunes.

Yeah, I know, I'm definitely ridiculous.

"Just think about it?" she says, taking pity on me.

"Yup. You just think about how great dating me would be."

Penny looks down at her feet. "I can do that."

And that's progress. "Perfect," I say, extending my hand. "Pass it over. It can't be worse than the shit Hazel has been making me drink. What's this on top?"

"Just try it and I promise I'll explain what it is," Penny offers, and then she chews on her thumbnail.

I take a sip and it's the oddest experience. The top is a thick foam that has a sweet vanilla flavor, and then you get a taste of the coffee. It's smoother than the last cup I drank, not acidic and harsh.

My eyes meet hers. "What is this?"

"Do you like it?"

"I hate it the least," I say, but I take another sip to see if I actually do like it.

"So you kept talking about the bitterness, which is from the acid in coffee. When you cold brew it, you remove a lot of that, and then the foam on top sweetens it so that you're getting the coffee, but not all at once, giving your tongue a chance to take them in separately."

I take another sip, this time focusing on what Penelope said. She's right. It's like getting two different drinks, and neither stays for too long. "This isn't bad."

Hazel laughs. "Well, that's the highest praise we've gotten so far!"

"I don't love it, but I don't hate it."

"Well, that's something," Penelope says, looking away and tucking her hair behind her ear.

"It's something all right," Hazel jumps in. "I've been trying to get this man to drink coffee for years! I'm like the coffee whisperer and he's had me stumped." She looks to Penny. "If he comes back more than five times, you're getting a raise."

Everyone laughs, and I know that I'll be back tomorrow, if for no other reason than to make Penelope smile and ask her out again.

———

I didn't make it into the coffee shop yesterday, but there was nothing that was keeping me away today.

The bell chimes as I walk in and Hazel is at the front. Immediately I feel deflated.

"Happy to see you too," Hazel reads my mood.

"I'm always happy to see you," I lie.

Hazel snorts. "Penelope! Can you come out and help a customer? I need to run to the bakery for more scones."

Penelope comes rushing out. "Of course!" Then she turns to me. "Oh, hi."

I look to Hazel and smile. Okay, maybe I am going to be eternally happy to see her from now on. She winks and then heads into the back.

"Hey."

"You're back?" Penelope asks, tucking her hair behind her ear. "What can I get you?"

I lean against the counter. "I was hoping for a scone."

She laughs softly. "Seems we're out of those."

"Damn. I hate it when that happens."

Penelope pulls her lower lip between her teeth. "Sorry, you can wait if you want, I'm sure Hazel will be right back with them."

I shrug. "I can wait."

I'd wait for an hour if it means I can talk to her.

"Do you want another cold brew with foam while you're waiting?" Penelope asks.

As much as the coffee she made me wasn't absolutely the worst thing I ever drank, I didn't exactly acquire a taste for it. Still, I'm going to drink it.

"I'd love that," I say and nearly whoop when she smiles.

Fuck, I'll be drinking ten of these a day if I can make her happy like that. I'll surely be getting a date at this rate.

Maybe I'm not such an idiot around women.

"Great! I'll make it now."

She turns around, grabbing the cup and doing whatever the hell the drink requires, and then faces me, handing me the coffee.

Her eyes don't leave mine as she waits for me to take a sip.

I school my features, trying to summon up the acting class I had to take in college for an easy A, and drink.

God, it tastes like shit still, however, on my face, you'd never know.

"This is great. Thank you," I say and Penelope smiles warmly.

Yeah, totally worth drinking the garbage.

"So, how is Kai?"

"Good, he's in the back, just hanging out while I work."

I nod. "He's doing really great with skating. Not every kid can pick it up the way he is. Honestly, he's a natural."

Kai is already improving with skating and stick drills, far faster than I would've expected. Ethan and I have always played hockey, since the time my sister would allow it at least. Doug and I both grew up playing and I like being with my nephew, so it was kind of our thing. Ethan skates rings around the other kids, which I've had to try to tamp down a little.

However, Kai is getting really good at the basics.

"That makes me happy," she confesses. "I always worry with him. You know, it's hard moving to a new town, but a customer mentioned the hockey clinic and I hoped maybe he'd like it. He hated soccer."

"Hockey is much better," I say with a lot of bias.

She laughs softly. "Well, you are a town legend."

"I am, huh? You've been asking around about me?" I lean closer, going for a cute flirty type of encounter.

"Not even a little."

I stand up, clutching my chest. "I'm wounded."

"Should I call Everett?"

"To finish me off?"

Penelope laughs and shakes her head. "He's a doctor."

"He works on cows and horses. Are you comparing me?"

She shakes her head again. "No, not even a little."

I smile. "Good, that wouldn't bode well for me." I bring the coffee back to my lips and force down another sip. "Especially since we could be here, planning our date."

Penelope raises her brows. "We could be?"

"Yeah, I mean, you're supposed to be thinking about it."

"I am."

"Thinking about it or planning it?" I ask.

"Thinking," she says slowly.

Before I can ask another question, Hazel pops back around from the back. "Scones."

I'd like to shove that scone—

"Great!" Penelope says with a little too much enthusiasm for me. "Miles has been waiting for one."

Penelope takes a scone off the tray and places it in a bag. "Total for the scone and coffee is twelve dollars."

"How much is the coffee?" I ask. Usually I get a pastry and a tea and it's five bucks.

"The coffee is five dollars."

"Five dollars for the coffee?" I ask, now turning my attention to Hazel who shrugs. Right. Well, even if it was eleven dollars, it would be worth the encounter I just had with Penelope. I got to spend a few minutes with her and honestly, that's the only reason I came here anyway.

I could've made my own breakfast and tea at home.

I pay and give Penelope a tip. Since my lifelong friend is clearly trying to cockblock me, I grab the coffee and scone, lifting the bag up. "Thanks for everything. I'm sure I'll see you tomorrow."

Penny nods. "See you tomorrow."

———

While I had all intentions of going to get coffee from Penny again, my sister needed me as soon as I left the coffee shop that morning, causing me to miss it for the last four days.

Only she's forgiven because I'm holding the tiniest, most beautiful little girl I've ever seen. She's a day old and already owns my heart.

"Now, no matter what they tell you, Cora, I'm your favorite uncle, and I didn't put the hole in the wall. Your mother did."

Eloise rolls her eyes. "You're already lying to your niece. Nice example you are. You totally put the hole in the wall and blamed me."

One day, when we were kids, there was a mystery hole that appeared in the living room wall of our grandmother's house. At least it was a mystery as far as Gran was concerned. Of course, Eloise and I know exactly how it appeared there. However, my diabolical sister always thought if we just stuck together a little, Gran wouldn't punish us as harshly.

That time I went along with it. We told Gran neither of us knew how it got there. Surely it wasn't the fact that Eloise and I were playing baseball in the house. We'd never do such a thing.

Gran was never able to prove anything, and she's a stickler on fairness and evidence. Therefore, we got away with it, and each time someone wanted to blackmail the other, the hole became the chip we used.

Even to this day.

I grin. "It was you who did it, El. We both know it."

My sister sighs, her head turning to look out the window. "Yeah, yeah, but Gran doesn't know. Hey, thanks for keeping Ethan a few extra days. I hoped I wouldn't end up having a C-section, but this one was clearly not willing to make things easy on me."

"You don't have to thank me—he's my nephew."

"I know, but . . . still. I know you wanted to be on the lake this summer."

I rock Cora in my arms, as her brother is running around out back. "I'm where I need to be."

She reaches her hand out, resting it on my arm. "She's really perfect."

"She is."

"Do you ever wonder what Mom would've been like?" Eloise asks.

That question takes me back a little. "I guess. I wonder more what our lives would've looked like if we had parents."

"Gran definitely would have less gray hair."

"And probably not scowl as much."

She laughs. "Careful or I'll tell her as much."

Like the saying goes about calling the Devil, she enters the living room. "My hearing hasn't gone yet, Miles. Watch yourself."

"It's hard to steal the hearing from an angel," I say, trying to win her back.

She scoffs. "I know all your charms, Miles Anderson, which means I know you ain't got none."

"Please, I'm the most charming person you know, Gran."

At least that's what I believe. I'm the grandson for the ages.

She sits in the rocking chair, shaking her head. "I think Ethan is leagues above you."

"I taught him everything I know."

Gran smiles and reaches her arms out. "Give me my great-grand-daughter, please."

I get up, placing Cora in her arms, and all that piss and vinegar dissolves as she holds the baby.

"She looks like Eloise," I say, remembering all the photos of us as babies.

Gran leans in, kissing Cora's forehead. "She does, only cuter."

"Hey!" Eloise protests. "I was adorable."

Gran scoffs. "Until you could talk. Then all that cuteness went out the window."

I chuckle. "You know, Gran, it's a wonder with all your praise and adoration that you dole out that Eloise and I are so humble."

"I prefer honesty over flattery," Gran says while stretching her neck.

"Except when we're talking about her," Eloise says with raised eyes as she stares at Gran.

Which is true. Gran denies any story that doesn't paint her in the light she feels is accurate. Not that Eloise and I have much to complain about. Gran was loving, firm, and always willing to do anything for us. She had raised her kids and didn't hesitate to do it again, even though life wasn't going to be easy.

"Miles, why didn't you go see your sister in the hospital?" Gran asks, already knowing the answer to that.

"Because I don't do hospitals."

"Until you need one, and then you're not going to be able to be so smug about it."

"I'm not smug," I tell her.

Eloise sighs heavily. "He's always been this way, Gran, he's not going to change now. He's convinced that people only go to the hospital to die. Clearly we've proven that wrong."

"You have issues and I have mine. I'm aware that it's not rational, but I just can't do it."

I believe that grief and fear manifest in different ways for everyone. I'm fully aware that being afraid of the hospital is irrational. It saves more people than it harms. I can literally walk through all the truths and it doesn't matter. I fucking can't do it.

When Doug got hurt, I made it to the front doors and froze.

When Gran had a fall, I was furious with myself for having a full-fledged panic attack as I tried to walk through the hospital doors and couldn't.

I can't do it.

I've tried. I've talked to the school counselor about it, hoping maybe a trained professional could shed some light on why a grown man who has no other issues, and is fully able to rationalize things, can't walk through the damn doors.

Since I can remember, I got nothing other than hospitals are a trigger, and it all ties back to my mother's death.

"If either of you think I want to be this way, you're unhinged," I say, tossing my ankle onto my knee.

"Would you do it for a kid?" Eloise asks. "If Ethan or Cora needed you, what then?"

"Let's hope I'm never faced with it, although I'm pretty sure I'd do what needed to be done. I was perfectly happy waiting for Cora to come home and keeping Ethan from terrorizing the nursing staff."

Gran chuckles. "That boy is all his mother."

"Yes, he is." I push that topic, knowing it'll be much more enjoyable than my fears. "He's just like her. I feel like we should examine why that is? Is it a genetic trait? Nature versus nurture, maybe? I guess we'll know once little Cora grows up and we can see if she's like Doug more."

Eloise rolls her eyes. "I'm going to enjoy every moment when you become a dad."

"Since I plan for that moment to happen—never—it's a dream you'll have to let die."

And people die, which is why becoming a parent isn't on my list of things I want. I'd rather not take the risk.

six
Penelope

"This place is so cute!" Ashton says as she looks around the house. "You did such a great job, Penny."

It's come together nicely. Much better than the last place we lived. "I really like it."

"And Kai seems to be happy?"

I nod. "He likes the house, but meeting the other boys on the hockey team has made all the difference."

Ashton plops on the couch, sighing heavily. "And you?"

I sit beside her. "I'm fine."

"Do you like the town?"

"I do."

"Good. I like that we're only a few hours away too. It gives me more of a chance to see you guys. You know the offer still stands that you can stay with us."

I smile softly. As much as I appreciate her saying that, I couldn't do it. First of all, I'd kill my brother after the first time he told me what to do. Second, I need my space. Not to mention being a single mom is my responsibility. More than anything, I wouldn't want to do that to Quinn and Ashton.

The two of them have dealt with some pretty horrible situations, and while I get that it's what my brother is trained for, it doesn't mean I want to be the one to walk it back into his life.

"I love you for saying it, but this works for now."

She takes my hand in hers. "I get it. I just miss you and wish we had more time together."

"Me too."

"So tell me about the town. Have you made any friends? Kai couldn't stop telling Gabriel about his coach . . ."

Of course he'd tell my nephew, but I have a feeling my brother was there as well, which could be a really bad thing.

"Oh?" I try to sound nonchalant.

Her eyes narrow slightly. "He said he was a big hockey player, was going pro but didn't? Said he's super nice, a marine, and you guys see him a lot?"

I'm going to have to put a stop to this. "That's the rumor I heard about hockey. And, yes, he is very nice, was in the marines out of college, and, no, I don't have a thing for him, which is what I think you're insinuating."

She leans forward. "Is he hot?"

"Are you hearing yourself? I am not dating anyone or allowing any attraction to form. I'm a damn mess and no one needs to walk into this shitstorm."

Ashton doesn't give up. "Penny, you're young, beautiful, smart, and have a nice rack. What more do you think a guy wants?"

"Financial and emotional stability?"

"Ha!" she shouts. "It's the rack they want. Anyway, Kai mentioned that he lives close . . ."

"You're like a dog with a bone."

"No, I just want you to get boned . . . get it?"

I roll my eyes. "You need help."

"Probably, but after all this time with your brother, it's only natural that I've got a few screws loose."

"That is true. He has that effect on people."

We both laugh and Ashton squeezes my hand. "In all seriousness, is he . . . attractive at least?"

I could lie, maybe that would get her off my back, but then I think about the fact that I miss having a friend or girl talk. I miss having someone to even just giggle with, and Ashton is the least judgmental person ever. If there's anyone I can tell—it's her.

"He is."

Her smile is so wide it could split her face. "I knew it! Tell me everything."

I don't have much to say about it, since I really don't know Miles. However, I give her the very brief rundown. Touching on how sweet he was when he brought the boys to me and didn't make me feel like an idiot for being such a wreck after. She laughs about the coffee story and him asking me to think about going on a date and the fact he's come in to get more almost every day. I haven't seen him in a few days, but he's keeping Ethan busy since Eloise had the baby.

"So you're not even thinking about it?" she probes.

It's all I think about, but I'm never going to admit that.

"No, I'm not thinking about it. How the hell do you even approach the story of my life? Hi, super-hot guy who seems to like me, I'm currently in hiding from my horrific ex's business partner, who sort of tried to kill me. Oh, and they're hunting me now, because that's what one does when they have unlimited resources. Yeah, I'm a total catch. Every man's dream of a drama-free girl."

Ashton scrunches her face. "Well, I wouldn't lead with all that, but maybe the super-hot part would be a keeper."

I lean back, pulling my legs under me. "Honestly, I started my rules years ago, and they're for the best. No dating. No sleeping with random people. No friendships because the only people that get hurt in the end are them when they realize I lied about everything. It's just . . . for the best."

"For you or for them?"

"Both."

"I don't know about that part. I think we make rules like that to protect ourselves more than others," she says, giving me a soft smile.

"And what if that's true? Is it so bad to want to protect myself a little?"

"No, it's not."

I wish this wasn't my life. I wish I could just see a cute guy, go on a date, do the whole getting-to-know-you thing, but that's not my reality. I can't tell him about my past, where I'm from, what I did, a last name—nothing. I have to do whatever is necessary for Kai's safety and my own.

"Then it's what I have to do."

Ashton takes a sip of her wine and shrugs. "If you say so, but I vote for the dirty sex with the hot ex-hockey player turned marine."

"You would."

"Hey, what can I say? I have a thing for a man in uniform."

I snort. "I know."

"You know, if you really want to piss your brother off, tell him how much better the marines are than the SEALs."

I laugh and drain the rest of my glass. "I think I'll keep Quinn on my good side for now."

"You do that, I'll keep pushing for you to live a little while you're here."

"I *am* living."

"Okay, live like a twenty-seven-year-old woman and get some then," Ashton says as she refills my glass.

"And where does that get me?"

"Orgasmville if there's such a place."

I laugh, loving my sister-in-law for giving me some girl time, which is clearly something I needed. "If there is, it's been a while since I've visited."

"I'm going to hold back my commentary since I'm married to your brother."

"I appreciate that."

"Just know it's a lovely village and worth the trip. If this hockey coach wants to take you for a quick trip, I wouldn't say no," she suggests.

"I'll keep that in mind."

"You do that. So what's his name?"

I drop my head back. "Ugh, you're killing me."

"You know, if you weren't being so weird about it, I wouldn't keep hounding you."

I'm not being weird about it. I'm being pragmatic. There can be nothing between Miles and myself. We're not even really friends. He's just a nice guy who lives in town.

"You know you're making this up in your head," I tell her.

"I see it on your face, Penny, you like him and I would bet my paycheck that the next time we talk, you're going to admit it."

I shake my head, refusing to even consider it, because all that will happen in the end is that I leave this town, and I can't afford another broken heart.

No, this is for the best. Keep to the rules and stay away from the sexy former marine and all his charm.

———

"Do you want an update?" Quinn asks from the kitchen table. We finished dinner and the boys are out back playing.

"I don't know, do I?"

My brother shrugs. "I'm not sure if it's much of an update, really."

Ashton sighs. "You're really bad at this, babe."

"What? Last time you told me I updated her too much and gave her anxiety, like she didn't already have that. Now I'm asking, like you *instructed* in the car—"

"Instructed?" Ashton's voice turns lethal. Oh, he's in for it now. "I do not *instruct* you, Quinn. I merely educate you on how dumb you are."

"Tell him, Ash," I encourage. "I'm sure it's an ongoing education process."

She turns to me. "It is. It's also *exhausting*, and the pay isn't that great."

"I bet, you should demand a raise and compensation for mental health."

Her smile triggers my own. "I will." She faces him again. "I think you need to tell her what she needs to know, but not make it like this doom-and-gloom thing. Here, I'll show you." Her eyes meet mine. "Someone filed a missing person report on you and Kai. Stated they were family, and we're pretty sure it's going to be listed in the national database. Now, the last photo they have is the one you sent your friend, and Kai has changed a bit since then. Which is good, but . . . you know, you're the same. Do you remember my best friend, Gretchen?"

"Not really," I admit, trying to control my rising anxiety.

Ashton gives me a soft smile. "Okay, well, she's a lawyer and an amazing one. I talked to her, and she thinks she can get it removed from the database since it was a false claim. There's no reason to be nervous at this point, okay? Gretchen is doing what she can on our end."

I nod. "Does she know where I am?"

"No. No one other than the people who have to know are aware of where you live. You have nothing to worry about."

What an easy thing to say. Nothing to worry about. I have everything to worry about. My life will never be normal.

"I don't know about that, Ash."

"No, I guess it's a pretty flippant thing to say, and I'm sorry. Of course you'll worry, just the same as Quinn and I do about you."

I look to my brother. "Do I have anything to be worried about?"

As much as Ashton is a no-nonsense person and doesn't hold back, I know my brother will never lie to me. He won't sugarcoat it or give me false hope.

"No, I worry for you so you can just focus on Kai. We're still going through the book, trying to find the connections, because Edward talked in riddles. There are names, dates, but nothing aligns. Each time we look into something, we have no evidence that those people were there at that time." Ashton runs her hand down his arm and takes his hand. Quinn's eyes meet hers and he smiles.

God, I want that.

I want to be loved so much that someone else just knows what I need and gives it. In all my life, I've never gotten to know what that feels like. Edward played the part for a little while in the beginning. He would buy me flowers, show up at my work with my favorite lunch. There were lavish gifts and fancy dinners, but the minute I moved in, it all ended. It was as though a switch was flipped and there was nothing I could do to get back the man I thought I had.

Whatever he got mixed up in killed him and destroyed me.

"There has to be something. Some tie to make them all a part of whatever he was in. I think it was drugs, but I can't be sure. Look, I like it here, Quinn," I tell him. "Kai likes it here. He's making friends, and I really don't want to move again."

"I know."

I push my fingers through my hair. "Then please, we need to find something that we can use to stop them from hunting me. I don't want to do this anymore."

"There is nothing leading to Ember Falls. Every trace, every lead, everything has been wiped clean. I've gone over everything I possibly could. Just stay off the internet, which I know you do, but the less of a digital footprint you leave, the better."

I was taught that the day he showed up to help me disappear. I have no social media under my name. It's all fictitious, and the only thing I do is scroll. Penelope Miller doesn't exist anywhere, or at least those accounts have gone dead.

Now I get to watch my old friends have families, lives, and do all the amazing things through social media. At least, the ones who have their accounts public. Quinn does reach out to two of them to let them know we're safe, but that's it.

Sometimes, if I'm feeling maudlin, I think about how this is what it must be like to be dead. People move on with their lives, forget about you, maybe randomly will see or hear something, and you pop into their brain for a minute before they go back to life.

"I'm careful. I don't like or comment or do anything. Everything on the new account is literally just scrolling. I don't even follow anyone just in case they're watching that."

"Good. One more update. About three hours after we moved you from Tennessee, a private investigator and someone else did show up at your last house. It was good we moved you when we did."

I lean against the counter, looking out the back window, where Kai and my nephew are playing. I used to wonder when this would ever stop, but I quickly realized that it never will.

That's the sad part. I saw the only proof of why Edward was killed.

All they want is for me to be silent forever, and the only way they can accomplish that is to kill me.

"Penny?" Ashton calls my name.

"Yeah?"

"You should visit that town I was talking about."

I burst out laughing, ever grateful my brother married this woman.

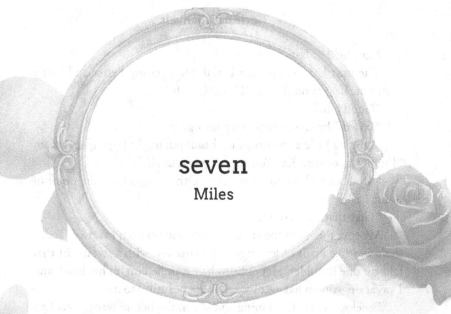

seven

Miles

"All right, kids, skate from goal to goal three times. Go!"

That should tire them out a little.

Who am I kidding? It's not even going to deplete their ever-refilling reserves of energy.

It's been a long time since I've been around young kids this much, and after just an hour, I'm beat. I'm going to propose a raise for our K through five teachers. They're the freaking heroes of the teaching world.

Although middle schoolers are pretty tough.

The ones in high school are mostly little assholes.

So, all in all, there are various ranges of suckage.

"We're done!" Ethan says as he skates up to me, struggling to catch his breath.

Next in the line is Joe, who cracks me up because he's a total natural with skating. However, he has zero hand-eye coordination when it comes to the puck. The kid can do figure eights around the ice, but put that stick in his hand and forget it. I'm not sure how to tell his parents that maybe figure skating would be more his speed.

"You're done, huh? What about your teammates?" I ask the boys as they're starting to approach.

"They're slow," Ethan notes. "No one can catch me."

"And that earned you another lap. Teamwork is everything, and you never leave your team behind. Go." I point to the other side.

Now he'll be last.

The next kid to approach is Kai. He's getting better and better each time he gets on the ice. "Done, Coach."

"Good job."

"I tried," he says in between panting.

I laugh a little as he drops his head, pulling in huge gasps of air. "I'm proud of you, Kai. You're giving it your all."

"Mom says I have to try my best. Otherwise, what's the point of doing it?"

"I like that. She's right."

My gaze moves to the stands, where she sits each practice. Today she's wearing a pair of leggings and a tank top with a sweatshirt that falls off one shoulder. Her auburn hair is pulled up on her head, and I swear no woman has ever looked more beautiful to me.

Penelope's gaze finds mine and she smiles before waving. As I go to lift my hand, I see Kai waving frantically at his mother and thankfully don't make a freaking fool of myself because I thought she was waving at me.

When I glance back down at him, his gaze meets mine. "Do I need to do another lap too, Coach Miles?"

"No, buddy, you're good."

He grins. "Can we hit the puck at you again?"

There is zero doubt what their favorite part of the clinic is. Try to hit the coach as goalie.

"We can. Let me get my gear."

I head to the side area, and Penny is standing there, having moved from the stands. "Hey."

"Hey." She smiles and my chest tightens.

Fucking hell. I really need to get it together or I'm going to look like an idiot. Well, more of an idiot than I do at the end of each practice.

"Everything okay?"

She nods. "Yeah, just wanted to see if practice was almost over? I have to get to work."

I glance down at my watch. We're already five minutes over. "Shit. Sorry I ran a little late. We're almost done. I was just about to start their favorite part of the day."

She grins. "Ahh, it's when you stand in the goal and they just continue to hit you with pucks?"

"That's it." I start pulling my gear on, not that it helps, because the fuckers always manage to find an open spot.

I wasn't a goalie, but Doug was, and I'm using his stuff—only he's a good four inches shorter than me, so I have some exposed areas.

"Well, I'll let you get to it. I'll just need to grab Kai as soon as I can. I would take him now, but I'm pretty sure he'll never forgive me."

"If you need to go, I can bring him to you."

Her eyes widen. "Oh, no, that's okay. I can call Hazel."

"Penny, it's really no big deal. I'll get the boys done and bring Kai to you. I'll even share my location with you so you can watch us drive to you."

She pulls her lower lip between her teeth. "I don't know . . ."

"I've had about six thousand background checks between the marines and the schools. I have been left in command of thousands of kids, and I'm just an overall good guy. I promise, he's safe with me. Eloise would never leave Ethan with me if I wasn't capable."

I normally don't have to beg to let me help them. In Ember Falls, it's usually the other way. I have to say no, because otherwise I'd be a damn nanny all summer. Which is what I think Eloise has basically decided I am.

There's a flash of panic in her eyes; then she closes them, inhales, and blows out a long breath. Glances down at her phone and then to me. "All right. I really can't be late. I know Hazel is great, but I can't push it. You're sure?"

"I promise. What's your phone number?"

Her brow lifts. "Is this a ploy?"

"Completely," I confess. Only half joking. "No, it's so I can share my location, remember, that was part of the deal?"

"Right, part of the deal."

I flash my signature smile, but before she can agree, which I'm pretty sure she's going to, one of the impatient children decides to ruin my game.

"Coach Miles! We're ready!" Joe yells. No doubt Ethan put him up to it.

"Relax, I'll let you have an extra three hits if you don't ask again."

"Each?" Ethan does speak up this time.

I swear, that kid is going to be the death of me. "If you behave!"

I go back to Penelope, who is trying to suppress her grin. "Now where were we?"

The laugh she was holding back comes out. "Sorry, I just . . . now I don't know that I want to leave and miss this."

"I won't go out there until you're gone."

"Oh?"

"Nope. It's contingent upon me having to drive Kai to you."

She purses her lips. "Hmm, well, in that case, I wouldn't want to deprive the children of their fun."

"Yeah, it's all about their needs," I agree, but the sarcasm is dripping from each syllable.

"All right, I'll text you so you have my number." She grabs her phone out of her purse and I give her my number. "I just texted you. I should go. Thank you for doing this and don't forget to share your location or I'll be a nervous wreck."

I laugh. "Not a problem."

Penelope waves at Kai, who waves back, and then dashes out, almost as though she wouldn't really go if she didn't run.

I skate out to the kids with my ill-fitting goalie gear and sigh. "All right, you little ankle biters, it's time for the make-a-goal game." They all yell with an extreme amount of enthusiasm. "Settle down. Today instead of five chances, you each get an extra three. Now, the rules today are like normal, except you can't hit someone else's puck if you think they have a better shot at hitting me, okay? We'll line up and have two rows."

The boys probably didn't listen to a word I said past the extra shots, but last practice, one of the kids gave his turn to Ethan because he's got deadly aim. It's why I have a cup on this time.

I get in my spot and they let me have it. I block quite a few, which makes me feel pretty proud, but both kids go at the same time, so there's really no chance to focus. It's all instinct and reflexes.

After, all the kids yell and skate around. It's fun, and this is what I wish I remembered about playing hockey.

The friendship and the way the sport just made me laugh. By the end of my time, it was all about numbers and injuries and the never-ending bullshit about what I was actually worth. I just realized that *winning* was all the coaches put worth in—not me.

But these kids, they don't know a damn thing about that, and I hope they always love days like this.

"All right, I'll see you in a few days. Go home, shower, drink some water, and be ready for our next skill lesson," I say as I herd them off the ice. "Kai, I'm going to take you to Prose & Perk. Your mom didn't want to be late."

"Cool! Thanks, Coach!"

I nod once and then start to remove all the pads.

"What I wouldn't give to be able to shoot some pucks at your head," Eloise chimes in as I'm pulling my skates off.

I stand and scoff. "Please, you have zero athletic ability."

"I have enough rage, though."

That part is true. "I still feel pretty safe."

She shrugs and then yells for her son. "Ethan! Get your shoes on, we aren't hanging around. I need to get home before Cora wakes up!"

"You left the baby with Doug?" I ask, questioning my sister's decision-making skills.

"Gran is there, and even if she wasn't, Doug is just fine watching the baby. He's a great dad, just not a great hockey player."

I toss my shit in my bag and throw it over my shoulder. My sister falls in step beside me as we head to where all the kids are.

"No, he's really not, but I give him an A for effort."

"How magnanimous of you. God knows you were always stingy with the As."

I grin. I really was. I loved that about myself. "Anyway, why did you want to pick up Ethan and not have me drive him as part of my penance?"

"I needed to leave the freaking house."

"So it wasn't because I'm finally forgiven for breaking your husband's leg and you just wanted to see me?" I ask.

"Not a chance in hell."

I laugh and pull her against me, kissing the top of her head. "No matter how old we get, Weezy, you'll always be my favorite person to annoy."

She pushes away from me and shudders. "You're gross."

"You love me."

"Because I have no choice. We shared a womb."

"You're welcome for not ingesting you and allowing you to be the mole on my ass."

Eloise makes a gagging noise. "I swear, you need a priest or a therapist. Maybe both."

Ethan and Kai come running over. "Can I go with Uncle Miles?" Ethan asks my sister.

"Not this time."

We say goodbye and I get Kai in the car. "Ready?"

"Ready."

We head from the Ember Falls Recreation Area up and over to Main Street, where Prose & Perk is located. It's no more than a ten-minute drive.

"So how are you liking Ember Falls?"

"I love it here! I hope we get to stay. Ethan is my new friend and I like Joe too. Kyle is kind of weird, but today he was nice."

I let out a short laugh. "He's got six older brothers who like to give him crap. He's usually the lowest man on the list and is trying to see if he can outrank someone. Don't take it to heart."

"I won't."

"Good. Did you play hockey where you lived before?"

Kai shakes his head. "Nope. I skated with Uncle Quinn once, but I didn't play. I like to watch it, though. Mom will make popcorn and let me stay up when her favorite team is on."

"Yeah? Who is her favorite team?"

"The Red Wings."

I can get with that. "I like them too."

"Who is your favorite?"

"I loved the Devils. My gran is from New Jersey, and she made sure we loved all her teams. Do you like football?"

He shakes his head. "We only like hockey."

"I see, well, it is the best sport. Other than Ultimate Frisbee. That's one that everyone would love if they ever got to see it."

Kai looks slightly confused but doesn't say anything. Which I'm grateful for, since my sister and Doug have no shortage of commentary regarding my new sport.

We pull up in front of Prose & Perk, and Kai and I head in. He's telling me about his new room and how he really wants to put a gaming system in there, but his mom said no.

"You're here." Penelope lets out a long sigh of relief as she comes around the counter. "I wasn't worried or anything."

"Of course you weren't," I say with a grin.

She smiles back at me and then pulls Kai to her chest. "Why don't you go in the back room, put the TV on, and I'll get some food for you."

He looks crestfallen and I feel bad. It can't be a fun way to spend your summer, cooped up in the back room of a coffee shop. "Do I have to?" he asks.

"You know the rules. I'm only here for a few more hours, and then tomorrow I'm off."

Kai looks up at me. "Thanks for today, Coach."

"Sure thing."

Without any complaints, he heads into the back, leaving me with Penny.

"Thank you for bringing him. Hazel had to run an errand and I said I'd cover, but practice and . . . well, you know."

"I'm sorry it ran over."

She shakes her head. "No, no, it's not a big deal. I just appreciate you helping."

"That's what we do here. It's all part of the small-town charm."

Penny smiles and tucks her hair behind her ear. "Well, thank you again."

I lean in against the counter, doing my best to look suave. "Can you make me one of those foam cold brews I love so much?" I ask.

"Of course and it's on me," Penelope says quickly.

Not a chance in hell I'm going to let her pay, but she turns around quickly, grabbing the supplies to make the coffee I'll toss as soon as I get home.

I drink about three sips to make it look like I love it, but . . . ugh. It's still nasty.

As she has her back turned, I go in for the real question that keeps me up at night. "So have you thought about it?"

"About what?"

"Going on a date with me?" I flash her a smile.

Penny laughs. "I have, but I don't think you'll like the answer."

"Then don't give it to me."

"Why is that?" She hands me the coffee.

"It just means you haven't thought hard enough if the answer is no. See, I have a lot of really great reasons why the answer should be yes." I force a sip down, letting the time pass so I can be around her longer.

"And what are those?" she asks, and suddenly my playful idea seems dumb. I have no idea if my reasons are great, but I know I like this girl and I want to at least see if there's something between us.

I tick them off on my fingers. "I have a great job, financially secure, which is a very good indicator of responsibility."

She snorts a laugh through her nose. "That is one good thing, sure."

"I'm good with kids, again, a sign of a good man."

"You work with kids, doesn't mean you're good with them," Penny tosses back.

"I'd like to disagree based on the fact that your son thinks I'm a great coach. If I wasn't good with the kids, they wouldn't want to be around me."

Penelope lifts one shoulder. "Okay, I'll give you that one. Kai and Ethan both seem to adore you, but you know, six-year-olds are pretty easy to win over."

"Well, you see a lot of my high schoolers, poll them on whether they think I'm a cool principal or not."

If those kids ruin my game, they'll be in detention. Not really, but I'll threaten it, at least. Or just remove their ice-cream machine and watch anarchy descend in the lunchroom. Although that might bite me in the ass more than them. I'll find something to punish them. I'm pretty confident that won't be the case, though, because my students actually do like me, for the most part.

"I'll do that."

"So, like I said, think some more until you come up with the right decision."

Penelope leans in, and her smile brightens her beautiful eyes. "And what if the answer is still not what you're hoping for?"

I grin. "Then I'll have to come up with more of my glowing attributes to sway you. Besides, we're practically dating as it is."

She leans back. "We are?"

"Yup. We've had coffee almost daily, we spend three days a week together with Kai, went for ice cream, and I walked you home that one time. So I'm counting at least six dates."

"Umm, this is my place of employment. That doesn't mean we're dating because you come in here to get coffee." Her smile is just starting to form at the end.

"Semantics."

She shakes her head. "Okay, as for your other times, you're the coach of Kai's team, so yes, I see you those days, and ice cream was with the kids . . . those weren't dates."

I stand straight and smile. "If you say so. I see them as dates, and so far, you've been pretty happy each time that we've spent time together."

Penny laughs and crosses her arms over her chest. "You're ridiculous."

I tilt my head. "The word you were looking for was *relentless*, and I'll see you in a few days with Kai."

"For practice."

"It's a date." I wink and then walk out, hopefully leaving her at least smiling.

eight
Penelope

"Hey, Penny!" Eloise calls to me as I'm sitting off to the side, watching their clinic. "Come over here, sit with us."

I've done my best to stay back from the other moms. Not because they're not kind or anything, but because I need to maintain my distance. I know Ashton thinks it's stupid, but if we have to run tomorrow, I don't want to feel worse about it as I'm leaving friends without any explanation. I don't need any more reasons to feel like shit about myself.

Still, saying no to them after being invited isn't really an option. So I smile, gather my bags, and shift over.

"Hey," I say as I sit down.

"Penelope, this is Maryanne. She's Joe's mom. This is Amari. Her son is Briggs, by far the best skater here, and then the blonde down there banging on the glass because her son is chipping the ice with his skates is Darlene."

"It's nice to meet you all officially. I've met Amari a few times in the coffee shop. It's great to see you again."

Amari smiles warmly. "You too. I'll be heading there after practice because there is not enough coffee to keep me running today. School can't start soon enough."

Eloise laughs. "Tell me about it. The summer feels longer this year."

"Probably because you have a newborn," Maryanne notes.

In my perfect life plan, I would've been Eloise right now. I wanted two kids, a few years apart, but not more than seven. My brother and I are far apart, and I always wished we were closer. While I love having only Kai, sometimes I wish I could at least have options for more, but again, no one wants to be with a woman who is running from her past.

"That would be why, still, Miles has been amazing with helping. He's kept Ethan busy so much for me, but it's still exhausting. Between Doug still not being mobile and Cora waking all the time, I just wish I had a few hours during the day where I could . . . sleep," Eloise says, and you can almost feel the exhaustion.

"Your brother has aged like a fine wine," Maryanne says as she bites her lip.

Eloise makes a gagging noise. "Stop it."

"What? I'm single, he's single. I'm just saying that Miles is still hot."

I glance over where he's waiting at the end, watching the kids trying to learn how to stop while on the ice. I say *try* because most of the time he ends up catching them as they're flying by, unable to get their feet in the right position to stop the way he's trying to teach them.

He's wearing a baseball hat backward, and the way he's squatting right now gives a really good view of his ass.

Not that I'm looking.

Because I'm totally not.

I mean, maybe a little, but just because Maryanne mentioned it, not because I do think he's incredibly good looking and I might be developing a stupid crush on the guy who is kind, thoughtful, and makes me smile.

However, I'm not going to ever admit that out loud, and as a sister to a brother, Eloise definitely doesn't want to hear it. Growing up, I always had to listen to my friends go on and on about Quinn. It was nauseating. First of all, he was my brother. And second, just ewww.

"He's also absolutely not your type," Eloise says, shuddering a little.

Oh, this is interesting. I listen a little closer and stop looking at Miles's butt.

"What, he doesn't like girls who are single?" Maryanne asks, raising a brow.

"I think you mean he likes girls who are stable."

Maryanne laughs. "Touché."

Eloise turns to me. "Maryanne has been relentlessly flirting with Miles for so long it's become a joke."

I grin. "I'm sure he loves it—deep down."

"See! I'm starting to think it's the male population instead of my terrible taste," Maryanne notes.

I'd tend to agree with her since my experience would support that theory. I didn't actively look for a terrible guy. In fact, he never showed any red flags until they all went flying at the same time.

"Miles is nothing like the guys you date," Eloise informs her.

"I know, that's why I just admire him from afar. I'm pretty sure I'd get bored of his goody-two-shoes attitude and being nice and all that."

Eloise sighs heavily. "Well, there are not many men like Miles, and I'll just say that whatever woman he ends up with is going to be extremely lucky. He's a good one."

"And he's hot," Maryanne reminds us.

"Anyway, I'm not even sure what I'm saying at this point. I'm pretty sure I just complimented my brother, so that should tell you how fucking exhausted I am."

"Is Cora sleeping in longer increments yet?" I ask.

She shakes her head. "No, that girl is up every two hours. During the day, she'll push it to three, or she tried for four yesterday, but I've been forcing her to nurse on schedule during the day with the hopes at night she'll sleep, but . . . it's not working."

I remember how absolutely miserable I was right after Kai was born. I never knew what tired was until he came. It made matters worse that I was pretty much alone until Ashton came. She was a godsend and helped me through the first week and a half before she had to go back home. I remember being so exhausted I would just cry, because I had no energy to do anything else.

"She'll get there," Amari encourages. "The first few weeks are the worst."

Eloise yawns. "I know, but . . . I'm older this time, and it just feels so much worse. Ethan literally is nonstop with wanting to do things. I don't know how that kid functions on that level of energy. I sit down, he needs something. I cook, he hates it. I clean up, he destroys it. I close my eyes while Cora is finally napping, and he's screaming and begging me to do something. No matter what I try, he's just always in my hair, and I know it feels worse because I'm so tired, but . . . I just need *sleep*."

I can't imagine what she's feeling. Doing it with just Kai was hard, but at least I could sleep when he did.

"If you want, I can keep Ethan overnight after work," I offer. "He can have a sleepover, which I know Kai would love, and since I'm off the next day, he can just hang at the house. You can sleep or whatever you need to if that helps."

Eloise's eyes fill with unshed tears. "Are you serious?"

"Absolutely. The boys can play, which will keep Kai busy. I wasn't planning on doing anything but clean a bit. I can take them to the bike park if you want too?"

"You are an angel, Penelope. An absolute angel. That would be . . . amazing. Gran is coming on Friday to help a little, and I could sleep . . . oh, I don't even know what to say. Thank you."

I smile. "It's nothing. It helps me too. Kai will love having his friend over, and the two of them can keep each other busy."

"When do you work again?"

"I work tonight."

"Then you have to let me keep Kai for the rest of today. The same logic applies. He'll keep Ethan out of my hair, and Doug can supervise the boys. That way you don't have to take Kai into the coffee shop and he can just hang by me."

The panic that's always a small ball in my stomach grows, making me feel like I can't breathe. I force a smile. "That's too much. You have the baby and adding another six-year-old into the mix will be a lot."

"No, I promise, it won't. At this point my house is a zoo and what you said is right: it'll keep Ethan occupied and Doug can hobble his ass outside while they play. Doug and I were going to take the boys to watch Miles's Ultimate Frisbee match, and when we're there, Ethan is always trying to run onto the field. Maybe with your son, who actually behaves, we won't have to threaten to tie him to his chair." We both laugh. "Please, it'll be a help to both of us."

It's as though my mind is being torn down the middle. On one side, I have the rational part of me that says I should let Kai do this. It's normal for kids to have sleepovers and playdates. What is not fun is sitting in the coffee shop for hours each day, and it's not fair to him.

This will give him something to do, and if Eloise is offering, I shouldn't turn it down.

But the side of me that's ruled by the fear I've lived through says not a chance in fucking hell. No way should I let my son go to someone's house. I don't know Eloise and Doug well enough. I've met her only a few times, and I can't let Kai be away from me.

What if I have to grab Kai?

What if he's far away and I can't get to him?

And then I think, What if that never happens? What if my brother has hidden us well again and we have years where we get to live in this town? Heck, we could have forever.

I force myself to take a deep breath and think. Fear is never going to make sense. It's a liar and a thief. I can make it to Kai in just fifteen minutes, and my brother always gives us more of a notice than that.

I can do this. I can let him go for just a little while. I need a middle ground that will appease both sides of my brain.

"All right. If you can keep Kai while I'm at work, I'll pick both boys up after, and they can sleep at my house. Then we have the whole next day?"

She smiles. "Deal."

I can do this. I did it the other day with Miles driving him, and I can handle it this time.

At least, I hope.

————

I check my watch for the hundredth time, no texts or calls from anyone. This is a good thing. It means that Kai isn't in trouble and no one is close to finding me. All is good.

Everything is fine.

Maybe if I tell myself that enough, I'll believe it.

The door chimes, alerting me that I have customers. When I look up, it's Miles, Everett, and Lachlan.

"Hey, guys," I say, forcing myself to be calm and collected.

"Penny! My angel of caffeine. Load me up with a double espresso, please, and put it on Hazel's best-friends-drink-free pass," Everett says with his arms wide.

I laugh and shake my head. "She revoked that."

"She wouldn't."

I shrug. "She specifically told me that you pay for your coffee from now on."

"That woman is more temperamental than a vintage car. I swear, she gets mad and takes it out on my coffee addiction."

Lachlan shakes his head. "Maybe stop pissing her off."

"It's what I do best."

"So coffee that is *not* on the house?" I ask.

Everett sighs heavily. "Fine. I'll take it up with Hazel tonight."

"She's coming to the game?" Miles questions, leaning against the counter.

"She is. Apparently now that we suck, we're drawing a crowd. The only thing this town loves more than a winner are terrible losers. I'm sure we're going to be featured in some ridiculous article that Ainsley will no doubt be behind," Everett notes.

I'm glad my back is turned to them so they can't see my smile. Ainsley was in earlier, working on an article for her paper that was about elder men who still like to play sports as though they're in their twenties.

I laughed. A lot.

It was very clear that Lachlan was on her shit list and this is some sort of retribution.

"I wouldn't doubt it. She loves to find ways to make me look stupid," Lachlan says with a laugh.

"There are so many options. How does she choose?"

"Fuck off, Everett."

"No, boys, let's not fight. We have a game in an hour, we need to be prepared," Miles says, stepping in with all the pragmatism of a principal.

There's a short silence, and I use this as my chance to hand the coffee over. "Here you go."

"Thank you, sweet Penny. You're my favorite woman in this town," Everett says with a wink.

"I appreciate that."

"Miles here feels the same," Everett says, leaning his elbow on the counter. "He was telling us today in a group chat how he asked you out and you shot him down."

There's a low grumbling noise from where Miles is standing.

"I didn't shoot him down."

"Did you say yes?" Everett sips his espresso and raises one brow.

"I didn't, but I didn't say no either."

"So it's a maybe?"

"That's enough." Miles steps in, pushing Everett to the side. "Ignore him. He's mad about the lack of free coffee."

"Dude! I was helping. You have no game. I was letting you borrow some of mine!" Everett comes back closer. "One date with Miles, Penny. If it sucks, I'll take you out and show you a good time."

I laugh and feel the heat flaming my cheeks.

"I'll kill him," Miles warns.

"Come on before he actually does it," Lachlan says as he's pulling Everett from the coffeehouse.

"I'm sorry about that," Miles apologizes.

"Don't be. Remember, I have a brother, and he would do the same for his best friend." Honestly, I'm pretty sure Quinn has done far worse to Liam. Any chance he has to mortify him, he takes it and vice versa.

Miles gives me a half smile. "Yeah, friends are great like that. Where's Kai? I'd love to say hi. Is he in the back?"

"Actually, he's with Eloise. He's going to your game tonight."

"Really?"

I nod. "Yeah, I'm going to take the boys from there back home, and Ethan is spending the night. It'll give Eloise some time to just sleep."

"I tried to offer to keep him the other night, but she wouldn't let me."

"Postpartum is a really hard time. Most days you think you want something you don't, or you do want it and tell yourself you don't. I'm sure she regretted not taking you up on it."

I felt like I was a yo-yo after Kai. One minute I was up, then down, then back and forth. I just couldn't get a grip.

"I can only imagine. So are *you* coming to watch me play?" His grin is adorable, and I'd like to kiss it off his perfect face.

Which is a bad idea.

Instead of doing that, I lean back a little. "Not exactly. I'm coming to pick up the boys."

"And that, *coincidentally*, means you're coming to the game."

"Sure," I say with a laugh.

"So it's kind of a date."

"No, it's a coincidental meeting location."

"Also known as a date." Miles tilts his head. "I'm just saying, we're having a lot of these lately. I'd like to plan something a little more formal."

I chuckle. "I bet you would."

"With all the thinking you've been doing, I've been doing some as well."

"Have you?"

He nods. "Yeah, so, how about this? We coincidentally meet on . . . say, Thursday night? I'll just happen to have some kind of coffee emergency that you have to come to my house to fix. The neighborly thing to do is help someone in need."

"I see."

Miles continues on, letting out a long sigh first. "It's just . . . the way it goes. I've helped you, you help me. When you get there, I'll just be finishing up cooking, so you can just—stay."

"It's a very orchestrated coincidence to have a coffee emergency, which I didn't even know was a thing—while cooking," I say, crossing my arms over my chest and fighting back a grin.

God, he's cute.

He's cute and he's funny and he's sweet and I don't want to like him, but I do.

Damn it.

"It is, but fate has a way of making things happen." Miles shrugs and stands up. "I have to go, but I'll see you at the field."

"I'll see you then."

"What a way these coincidental dates keep happening, Penny. You're going to have to accept that maybe some things are out of our control and we're just fighting the inevitable."

I snort a laugh. "I guess we'll have to see what happens . . ."

"I guess we will."

nine
Miles

"If you fuckers don't start playing well, I'm quitting," I warn everyone.

Lachlan huffs. "Yeah, because we're trying to look like fools, just to piss you off."

I wouldn't doubt it. "Let's remember how you were when Ainsley came to watch. You weren't exactly easy on anyone since you looked like a tool."

Everett pipes up. "He still does. Now he's just in love with her, and for some reason, she sees past his ever-mounting flaws."

"Yes, and yours are piling up, too, which means catch the fucking disc!"

I swear, Everett has dropped more passes than ever before.

"Maybe we should change up who is where," Killian suggests.

Nothing seems to be helping since we started playing in this league. Maybe Ainsley is right and we're just terrible. I sigh and look over just in time to see Penelope walking toward the families who are lined up with their camping chairs.

My sister sees her and waves her over.

Great.

Now she's going to see that we do not, in fact, have big-disc energy. We're more like floppy discs.

I groan. "Look, I don't ask you guys for much, but maybe for the next half hour we could step it up?"

Lachlan looks over and smiles. "Penny's here."

"Yes, I'm aware."

He slaps me on the back. "I'm going to enjoy all of this."

I bet he is. "You realize your girlfriend is also with her?"

"Yup, but I already got the girl. You're still trying."

I'm getting closer. At least, I think I am. She's resisting, but my hope is to just keep proving it's at least worth one damn date.

I glance back again to see her with Eloise. The two of them are laughing, and then Eloise points to where we're standing. I smile a little, and Penny lifts her hand in a small wave. I nod once, because waving would make me look ridiculous and I don't need to give the guys any more ammo to ruin my chances.

"So you want us to be better so you can get a date?" Everett asks. "What do we get out of it?"

I huff. "Dignity."

"Nah, I lost that a long time ago when I lost the bet and had to get Brutus to be the official school mascot."

That was a fun one. "He loves every second of it."

"Yeah, and I just love spending every Friday night schlepping him up to the football games, where I have to watch and then walk him out for the halftime show."

Honestly, it was the best bet I ever won. Everett is one of those guys who can't turn down a dare or a bet. The school's trusty bull-dog, Samsonite, passed away two years ago, and I went to Everett since he's the town vet, asking if we could borrow his new puppy going forward. The best thing about our home games was Samsonite coming out during halftime. The kids loved it, and he was our lucky charm.

Everett grumbled, said no way, that he had better things to do on his Friday nights, and so I proposed a bet. If he could beat me at a race, I would let it go, adopt my own dog, and call it a day, but if I won . . . it was his job.

Spoiler alert—he lost.

"It gives you a purpose," I say pragmatically.

"A purpose? I'm the fucking town vet. I think I have a pretty big job already. What do you do? Sit in your office and pretend you're molding the youth? Look around, these kids are all a damn mess, so you're doing a pretty shitty job."

"That was fucked up, man," Killian says, shaking his head. "Anyway, are you two about done? We have a game to finish."

"I think the game is finishing us. Maybe there's a mercy rule in this league," Lachlan says.

"We just need to score once. I can't have a complete blowout with Penny watching," I say, willing it into the universe.

"What are you willing to do for it?" Everett asks.

"What?"

"Well, you want it bad, we're all assuming it's because Penelope is watching. If you want us to kill ourselves so you can get a date, then we need to be incentivized."

I really hate my friends. "I'll pay for your coffee for a month."

"Two months," Everett counters.

Killian rolls his eyes. "Let's not pretend you don't want to win too."

Everett huffs. "Fine, one month." He puts his hand in and we all follow. "All right, let's give it all we have. I need free coffee."

We break and try for the one play that seemed to work before. Lachlan takes the disc and flicks it to Killian, who is about ten yards downfield. Instead of going for big gains like we've been doing—and failing—we're going incremental.

Killian catches it and then throws to Everett, who finally catches a fucking pass. Now we need to keep leapfrogging. I line up to take the next one, but the defender is pretty much attached to me. I move right, then left, but he stays with me. Lachlan is catching up and moving, and Everett tosses it to him.

Thankfully he's able to get it and move forward.

Now I need to do something other than get shown up by some twenty-five-year-old who clearly is in better shape than me.

"Come on, Uncle Miles!" I hear Ethan yell.

I'm trying, little dude.

I move around again, kind of giving this guy a stiff-arm, and am able to break away. I call out to Lachlan, who makes a pretty ridiculous move and tosses it around his defender. It's a little high and, honestly, I'm not sure I'm going to catch this, but I leap into the air and somehow grab it.

What I don't do is land.

Instead, I kind of half fall, but on my way down, I flick the disc toward Killian and pray it gets there. I slam into the ground, my breath leaving me for a second, and hear a loud cheering.

I really hope the other team didn't catch it.

I lift my head up and see Killian with the Frisbee over his head.

Thank God.

Now I can lie here and die.

I drop back to the ground, really fucking hurting for air, and see my three friends' heads in my vision.

"You dead?" Everett asks.

"I'm not sure."

"He looks dead," Lachlan notes.

"Well, he thinks he's still young, and today is going to remind him he's not." Everett again. Always the asshole.

Lachlan looks over at them. "Should we tell him that Penny didn't even see it?"

"Fuck off."

They laugh. "Not dead."

"Did she see it?" All three turn to find her in the crowd, and I groan. "Smooth, assholes. Really fucking smooth."

Killian, the most mature of this group, chuckles and speaks up. "She saw. She's watching for a sign of life."

"I'm going to get up and need you to make sure it looks effortless."

If I'm going to come out of this heroic event, I at least need to look cool doing it.

"Do you need help?" Lachlan questions. "Because if you do, that's not exactly going to look effortless. It's going to make you look like an old guy who can't get up."

Everett nods. "I'm thinking you need to kind of spring up. You know, launch yourself like a real athlete."

I roll my eyes. "I am a real athlete."

"Really? I don't see it," he supplies—unhelpfully.

I can't stand my friends some days.

"Just back up and let me stand," I warn.

Wanting to pop up, a little the way Everett suggested, I push myself to a sitting position and then sort of jump up from there. Not the best, but definitely not the worst.

There's some clapping and I raise my hand, purposely not looking toward where Penny is.

We head to the sideline to get some water, and Ethan and Kai rush over.

"You did so good, Coach. So good," Kai says with a smile.

"Thanks, bud."

"We all saw you fall, though," my nephew informs me. "Mom got video."

"I bet she did."

I'm so going to get that footage from my sister before she posts it.

"She posted it online to show everyone how cool you are," says Ethan, ruining my damn night.

"Did she show the end where I threw it and Killian caught it?"

He shrugs. "I don't know."

Which is probably a no, because Eloise lives to make my life hell.

I turn to find my sister and make a motion of slitting her neck, and she smiles and waves with just her fingers.

Yeah, totally doesn't have that ending on it. I'd bet my left nutsack.

And I really like the left one. Honestly, I like them both.

"I saw it!" Kai says.

"I'm glad one of you guys did." I rub the top of his head. Everett calls my name as he's jogging back onto the field. "I gotta go. I'll see you guys after the game. Don't leave until we're done. I need to tell you something."

I just lied to my nephew and I don't even feel bad about it. I want them to stay, and I plan to use the rest of the game to come up with a way to spend a little more time with Penny.

————

We lose in the most ridiculous fashion. The second half of the game was actually not half bad. The Disc Jocks managed to score another six points, and considering we were in a complete blowout, we were feeling pretty good.

Until they had a substitution player.

I don't know what freaking supplements this man is taking, but I feel like I've been kicked around for a solid half hour. This dude ran circles around us and made us look like the old men we've been accused of being.

Absolute bloodbath.

"Uncle Miles! We stayed," Ethan says as he rushes over, and I groan.

I forgot about how I needed to come up with something to tell him.

My brilliant idea to have people stay to watch the massacre. Way to go me.

"You sure did."

"That was brutal," Ethan says with a smirk. "It was like when I played that war video game with Dad, which I'm not supposed to talk about, and all you saw was blood and guts because the other side was better than him. That's what it reminded me of. They just kept killing you guys. Over and over and—"

I lift my hand to stop him from letting me know just how bad it is as my sister and Penelope get close. "I get it."

Ethan, the unhelpful one, continues, "I'm just saying you guys suck. Really bad. I thought you were good? When did you stop being so good?"

"Just today, which is ironically when I decided you're not my favorite nephew anymore," I mutter.

He chuckles. "I'm everyone's favorite and I'm your only nephew."

"You're also a pain in the butt, you know that?"

Ethan smirks. "Mom says it every day."

"Hey there, big brother," Eloise says with a little too much pep in her voice. "Interesting game there."

"It was," I agree.

Giving Eloise the least reaction is going to get me out of this quickly—I hope.

"I'm glad I came," my sister says with a smile.

"I bet you are."

She laughs and then Penny comes up beside her. "I've never seen an Ultimate Frisbee game before. I had no idea it was so competitive."

"Some more than others. This wasn't a normal game," I try to explain.

"No?"

"Normally, it's not such a blowout."

Eloise snorts. "What he means is that when they played against the college kids, they were great. Now that they had to enter a professional league . . . not so much."

I glare at my sister. "Thanks for the clarification."

"You're welcome."

God save brothers from sisters.

"Anyway," I say tersely, hoping Eloise catches on. I'm sure she will, but won't care regardless. "You're taking the boys tonight?"

"I am," answers Penny.

"Great, well, if you need anything, I'll be home."

"Thanks."

"I hope you need something." And I wonder why this woman isn't falling at my feet? I'm a clown and embarrassing even for myself.

"Good to know," Penny says as she tucks her hair behind her ear. "All right, boys, let's get going."

"Thank you again, Penny. I can't tell you how much I need this," Eloise says, sincerity ringing in every word. "I'll come get him or I'll have Miles bring him home if that's okay?"

I guess she just assumes I have no plans for tomorrow.

"Sure, El, I'd be happy to interrupt my day to do you another favor." I let the sarcasm flow.

"Good, I knew you would."

Penelope fails at trying to hide her smile. "Perfect. Just text me and let me know."

Both boys give me a hug, and then Ethan squeezes his mother. Eloise takes his face in her hands and gives him a reminder of what she expects as a report back on his behavior. She reminds me so much of Gran when she does that. She was the queen of threats before we got in trouble.

Which Eloise always did, and then Gran was great at follow-through.

"Bye, everyone," Penny says as she takes the boys.

"Bye."

When she's about halfway to her car, my sister laughs and slaps my chest. "You like her."

"What?"

"Oh, don't play dumb. You really like her."

"I think she's beautiful, kind, and that's about it," I say, moving to grab my bag.

"Give me a break, Miles. I know you, and I also think we still have that weird twin thing, because I could feel how uncomfortable you were just then. You like her and you're not sure how to proceed with her."

"I have a plan," I defend myself.

"You really don't, but that's okay, I think it's just a male thing. Doug had no plan to woo me, and if it weren't for me basically letting him know we were going to start dating, I'm pretty sure that wouldn't have happened. So I'll intervene for you."

I laugh once and scoff. "You will do absolutely *nothing*."

"Look, consider it a . . . charitable offering. You're single, no kids, a bit of a loser because you don't even date . . . it's okay. I'm here. I'll help."

"Eloise, the absolute last thing I want is your help with this. If Penelope and I start anything, it'll be between us and not with your meddling."

Her lips part and she gasps. "Meddle? Me? Never. It'll be helpful guidance."

"It's unwanted."

"Too bad." She takes my face between her thumb and other fingers, pinching my chin like Gran did. "I just want to see my big brother happy." She releases me. "And I'm going to do just that."

"Eloise, you just had a baby. You're married to an unstable human and have a six-year-old who is either a genius or in need of an intervention. Do you really think my love life is another thing you need to add to your plate?"

"I do." She kisses my cheek. "Now go home and shower. You smell like ass."

I once again ponder why I decided to live close to family after the marines.

ten
Penelope

"**M**om!" Kai screams as the lightning flashes, lighting up the sky after the power just went out.

"Stay there, I'll come with a flashlight!" I call to them.

Using my phone's flashlight, I rush into the kitchen, grab the actual flashlight from under the sink, and head to the boys.

Both are on his bed.

This storm came out of nowhere and arrived with a vengeance. The wind is howling, and the sound of the rain pounding against the roof has me hoping the house is strong enough to withstand it.

A loud crack comes from outside and then a crash.

They both yell and I rush to them, pulling them into my arms. "It's okay, it's okay," I say over and over.

There's a groaning noise, and I'm terrified to see what the hell came down outside, but either way, I don't have a great feeling about staying here.

"Come on, let's go to the back of the house."

There are fewer trees there, and if that was a branch that came down out there, I don't want us to be near it.

I get them settled in the bathtub and give them the lantern. I remember something about storms and that being the safest place. "Can you boys stay here? I want to go look outside and see if there's any damage."

"We'll stay," Kai promises.

"Okay, just sit tight."

Once I close the door, I look down at my shaking hands. I hate storms. I've always hated them, and having Kai and Ethan here is making this one especially bad. I close my eyes for a second, take a few deep breaths, and focus on going to check on things.

When I open the front door, my worst fear is real. Either the wind or lightning hit the tree at the end of the walkway, and a large branch is dangling. One gust of wind and it could fall on the house or my car.

I rush back inside and grab my phone to call Hazel. I need to get out of here, but I'm not sure where to go.

As I'm scrolling to her contact, Miles's name pops up on my screen.

"Hello?"

"Penny, it's Miles. Listen, I just got a notification that lightning struck right behind you. Are you guys okay?"

"No, I mean, we're okay, but it hit here, too, and we have no power. I need to get the boys out of here. There's a huge tree limb hanging over the front of the house."

"I'm coming."

"No! You can't come here. This storm is absolutely horrific," I say quickly.

"Get the boys, get in the car, start driving to that clearing at the end of your street. I'm on my way there now," he commands.

"I can't. I'm not even sure it's safe to get to the car."

Right where the tree branch dangles over the vehicle.

"Then I'll get to you." The sound of his engine igniting is in the background. "I'll be there in four minutes. Get whatever you need and then go to a safe place in the house. I'll be there as soon as I can."

I nod, even though he can't see it, relief filling me. "Okay, but please be careful."

"I'm fine."

I head into Kai's room, tossing some stuff in a bag and grabbing Ethan's. Then I do the same for myself, grabbing some essentials and my burner phone. I send a quick text to Quinn, letting him know what's happening and where we're going. We communicate about locations on that phone.

. . .

> There's a horrible storm and we had some issues.
> I'm going to stay with a neighbor with Kai and his
> friend until it's done. Ethan is Kai's friend, and the
> neighbor is his uncle.

QUINN

You're okay, though?

> Yes. We need to leave, the lightning hit a tree out
> front and it's been really scary.

QUINN

Be safe, Penelope.

> Always. Do I take this phone?

QUINN

Yes. Especially because you'll be gone overnight.

I really hate bringing the burner anywhere. When I'm home, Quinn says it doesn't matter, because he can find me easily. It's for when I'm not and the internet is not secure.

> Okay. I'll text you tomorrow and let you know
> what's going on. Love you.

QUINN

Love you too.

A few seconds later a new text comes through.

QUINN

Ashton wants to know if the uncle is who she
thinks it is . . . now I'd like to know what that
means as well.

. . .

If I could, I would kill Ashton for this.

> Tell her thanks a lot and yes it is.

QUINN
> I'm going to assume I don't want to know what
> this is because she just squealed.

> You probably don't.

I unlock the front door and head into the bathroom, where the boys are. "We're going to Miles's house to ride out the storm. There's a big tree out front, so we're going to be super careful, okay?"

"Okay, Mom," Kai says as they both nod.

"All right, we're going to stay in the bathroom until he gets here and tells us it's safe."

There's a banging on the door, and then I hear Miles. "Penny?"

"We're in the back bathroom!"

"Are you guys okay?" he asks loudly.

"Yes, we're coming out." I look to the boys. "Grab your bags and stay behind me."

The three of us file out and find Miles in the hallway. "Uncle Miles!" Ethan yells, and Miles moves toward us.

He scoops him up and then grabs the bag from Kai. "Hey, little man."

"Hi, Coach."

"Do you have everything?" Miles asks me.

"Yes, this is it."

"Okay, the branch is definitely weak, so we're going to stay to the left of the tree and go to my car. Penny, where are your keys?"

I dig in my purse and grab my car keys. "Here."

"I want you to get the boys in my truck, and I'm going to move yours."

A part of me wants to argue with him, but by the look in his eyes,

I can see that's a losing battle.

I pull the two boys in front of me, and we follow Miles out. He leads us to the left and has to yell over the wind. "Run to the truck!"

The three of us do just that, the wind whipping my hair in my face and the rain soaking through my shirt. This is like hurricane-force gusts. We get to the door and I pull it open, holding it so the boys can climb in the back.

As I'm getting around to the passenger side, my car backs up quickly, and just as he gets close, the sound is unlike anything I've heard—loud cracking as the tree branch gives and crashes right where my car was parked.

Miles keeps coming to where I am, the window down, and he yells, "Drive my truck, and follow me!"

Giving me no room to argue, he keeps moving so he's now positioned in front of me in my very old, very not cute, but very paid off, car.

I hop in his incredibly luxurious pickup truck and have to move the seat forward so I can touch the pedals.

The lightning dances across the sky again, illuminating just how much debris has fallen.

I follow him down the road, moving around the fallen branches and leaves painting the dangerously slick street.

We pull up to his house and I park behind him. Immediately he's out of my car and walking to my door.

"All you guys get inside. I'll grab the bags," Miles informs us.

I want to argue, but my nerves are shot. He helps me out and I grab both boys' hands. When we get inside, Ethan flips the light on.

How the hell does he have power?

A few seconds later, a dripping-wet Miles comes through the door, putting our bags down.

"You have a generator?" I ask.

"I have a whole-home one that keeps the house as though we have normal power."

That's pretty nice. "Thank you for coming to get us. I was worried, especially because I have Ethan too."

He smiles warmly. "Of course, I would've come regardless if you had him or not. I would never let you both stay like that."

My gaze drops to my feet, and I fight back the warmth flooding my cheeks. "Well, that's incredibly sweet."

"I told you, I'm a great catch."

I laugh and meet his eyes. "You did tell me that."

"Uncle Miles, can we go in the big guest room?"

"No. You and Kai can take the room next to mine, and Miss Penelope can have the big one."

"It's okay," I say quickly.

"No, that room is much more comfortable. The boys are able to rough it for a night, right? I bet they can build a fort in there."

Kai nods quickly. "Sure thing! Come on, Ethan, let's go build one!"

The two of them rush off. "Here, I'll show you to the room so you can change."

Miles grabs my bag and I follow behind him, my clothes making a swooshing noise from being soaked through.

His house is definitely not what I pictured. It's simple, masculine, but also really mature at the same time. The whole place is a warm taupe color and looks like it was newly renovated. The floors are a light oak, and he has a lot of blacks and grays that give such a nice contrast.

He opens a door, moving so I can step through. "This is the big room, as Ethan calls it."

The room is spacious, more of what I would expect for a main bedroom with a cathedral ceiling and exposed wood beams.

"This is gorgeous," I say, taking it all in.

In the center of the room is a king-size bed with rattan furniture accent pieces.

"Thanks, Eloise is an interior designer. She loves to spend my money."

"Is she really?"

That's what I went to school for. My dream was to work for a firm and design average people's homes. I wanted to find a way to make a space feel elegant on a budget. I would've been great at it, at least I think so. I just never got to try.

"Yup. She sold her company when she got pregnant with Ethan, but still helps anyone who she can bully into it." He leans against the wall, arms crossed over his broad chest. "When I bought this place, I knew it was a total gut job. We took everything down to the studs and rebuilt. Eloise was all too happy to redesign this place into a masculine retreat in the woods, as she calls it."

"She did a great job," I say, walking around.

"I agree, as much as I hate to say that."

I laugh once. "It really sucks when your sibling is good at something and you have to admit it."

"Absolutely, she's gotten used to having to do it with me, though."

"Has she?" I ask with a grin.

"Yeah, I mean, there's very little I'm not good at. It's almost like she was surrounded by my perfection so she just . . . accepts that I'm good at most things."

I laugh. "Your humility is really in check."

He winks. "I agree. You take as much time as you need. I'm going to change and get the boys set. Whenever you're done, I'll be in the living room."

I pull my lower lip between my teeth and bob my head. "Okay."

Miles closes the door, his eyes staying on mine until the last moment. When it's finally shut, I exhale and cover my mouth with my hand. What am I doing? I'm staying the night here? I mean, my alternative was at the house with falling trees, but still, this is . . . not a great idea because it's Miles.

The guy I like or . . . maybe like.

Definitely the guy I'm attracted to.

Gah.

Okay, think, breathe, focus. I can do this.

First thing, I need to get out of these wet clothes and then call Eloise to let her know we're safe and at her brother's house.

I pull out the sweatsuit I grabbed and head into the bathroom. This room is double what I have at the house. It's a beautiful beige slate, almost feels like the slate has been here since the dawn of time. Between the double sinks there's a large window that looks toward the woods, everything is pitch black except when the lightning illuminates the sky.

I tug my sopping-wet shirt off and hang it in the shower, then my pants, and put my dry clothes on. Once I find my phone in my purse, I dial Eloise's number.

"Hey, are you guys okay?" she asks as soon as she answers.

"Yes, we're fine. I just wanted to let you know we came to Miles's house."

"Oh, good! I was hoping you might, because he has that generator. We have the same one, and I was going to offer if you could make it here."

Eloise lives on the other side of the valley, and I'm honestly not sure I would've. "It's really bad out, so I'm grateful we're here now. He came up to get us because of the tree outside my house. It was . . . well, terrifying."

She lets out a weary sigh. "I'm so sorry, Penny. I didn't know we were going to get a storm like this or I never would've sent Ethan. You're okay, though?"

"I'm good now."

"Okay. If you need me to get Ethan, just tell me."

"No! He's fine. We're with Miles, and honestly, no one should be driving in this storm."

To further punctuate that point, the thunder booms so loud I swear the house shakes.

"Yeah, I would agree there." Cora lets out a huge wail, and I hear Eloise trying to shush her. "I should go. Cora isn't enjoying the storm. Call me if you need anything and stay safe."

"You too."

We hang up, and I head out to the guest room, where the boys are. They've transformed the room into sheets and blankets hanging off things. "You boys okay?"

Kai's head pops out from the bottom between two sheets. "We built a fort."

"I see that."

"Coach Miles helped!"

I smile. "That's nice. Do you need anything?"

"No, but I'm sorry to say this to you, Mom. No girls allowed in the fort."

I back up, raising my hands. "I see, well, have fun in the fort."

"We will!" he says before disappearing under whatever they've created in there. I walk back down the hallway toward the center of the house. The house seemed to split like a Y. When we entered, we went to the left part where the bedrooms are. I'm assuming the other branch is where the kitchen and living room are.

Sure enough, it is.

Miles is sitting on the couch. He changed out of his wet clothes into a white T-shirt and blue joggers. He looks relaxed, sexy, and like a freaking ad for a men's underwear collection. His legs are propped up on the coffee table, and he has his phone in his hand with his black-rimmed glasses on, television on mute.

Seriously, I just wish he wasn't so freaking appealing. Why is he so hot with those glasses on?

He's sexy without trying and my stomach clenches.

No, no stomach clenching allowed. Keep it together, Penny. He's a friend. He's not delicious and completely fuckable. He's . . . off-limits.

"Hey," I say softly, entering the room.

He puts his phone down and looks up with a smile. "Hey, did you see the boys?"

"I did. They are very happy in their fort where no girls are allowed."

He chuckles. "Last time Ethan built one, it was adults, so this is no doubt thanks to Kai. Make yourself comfortable."

I don't know that that's going to happen, but I come around and sit in the corner of the sectional. "Thank you again."

"Penelope, you don't have to thank me. I would never let you sit in that house like that."

"You didn't know the tree was going to fall," I say, tilting my head.

"No, but I knew there was a chance something could be wrong. I know the area pretty well and could see the bolts striking all around."

"It felt like the ground was cracking," I say, shuddering a little.

Miles pulls his glasses off, tossing them on the table as he sits up fully on the couch. "I'm not really a fan of storms, but this one is pretty wild. So much so that I was slightly afraid at one point."

"Only slightly?" I ask, pulling my legs underneath me.

"Do you want me to admit that I almost shit my pants?"

I shrug. "Maybe."

"I didn't."

I laugh. "Okay then. I'm pretty sure I would've if that branch fell while we were in the house."

"You don't have to worry now. You're here."

I am, and I'm not sure I don't have to worry.

"Right."

There's a moment of awkward silence, and then he reaches for the remote. "The cable is out, but I can pull up some stuff I downloaded."

"Whatever you want." I'm not a big television person. Mostly because it's fake, stupid, and I can't afford it. So we tend to read or do outdoor activities as much as we can.

"They're mostly superhero movies," he warns.

"You would love my brother," I say with a laugh. "It's all he watches and usually the same ones on repeat."

He chuckles and then pushes play on one. "Do you want popcorn or anything?"

"No, I'm good."

"Okay. I'm grabbing chips because we have to have something to do with our hands."

My eyes widen. "We do?"

"Well, I do. Otherwise I might reach over and think this is a date, where I could hold your hand." He laughs, indicating it's a joke, but . . . is it?

And why does the idea of that make my stomach drop?

I don't want this to be a date because it can't be. It's not. It's a storm.

Dear Lord, I need to stop this thinking.

While he's in the kitchen, I mentally prepare myself to watch a movie, at his house, while the boys are playing. That's all this is.

It's a nice guy who came to my rescue because of the storm, not another coincidence date thing.

Since that's not even a thing.

When he comes back in and sits on the couch, I need to dissuade him of this whole date thing, since it's not one. "If this was a date, it would be going pretty terrible, don't you think?"

Miles shifts, his joggers tight against his thighs, and I can see the thick muscles there. "Or . . . it could be going pretty freaking amazing. I mean, you're here, it's late, and you're staying the night."

He waggles his brows and I burst out laughing. "Because of the storm."

"Again, happy coincidence."

I lean back into the couch, not even capable of hiding my smile. "You're relentless."

"I am."

I let out a long sigh, hating that the reality of my life means I can't date him, no matter how charming, attractive, and kind he is. Miles can never really know the truth of my past. He stands to get killed, and I couldn't live with that.

Also, I don't even know that we'd work, and then what? If things end badly, I'd have to leave Ember Falls, which I know is a possibility anyway, but I don't want a breakup to be the reason.

Kai and I like it here. It's not perfect, but the last few weeks have been easy and felt more like a home than Tennessee ever did.

"Miles, look, I . . ." I scoot forward onto the edge of the couch. How do I even say this? I just have to be as honest as I can. "I don't have the greatest track record with men, and I've been hurt really badly. It's just . . . not a good idea for me to get involved in a relationship right now."

"I'm not asking for anything. I'd just like to be your friend, and if that leads to more, then . . . so be it."

I stare into his green eyes, wanting so badly to be someone else. A girl who doesn't look at a man and wonder whether he has a jealous streak. Or whether he's a man who seems perfect in the beginning, only to reveal flaws that you explain away, making you complicit in them.

I did that with Edward.

When he would yell, it was always something I did to provoke it.

When he first touched me in anger, it was because I asked too many questions and should've let him be.

It was my fault he would scream and have me cowering in a corner. It was something that was wrong with me.

It wasn't until I found out I was having Kai that I realized the only thing I did wrong was stay and allow him any excuse.

Miles moves closer, leaning in slowly, and my heart begins to race. His eyes are like liquid smoke, and I could get lost in them.

"Just friends," I remind him.

"Just friends."

He keeps coming. The heat of his body starts to warm other parts of me, and . . . oh, God. He just said he wanted to be friends and understands, but now he's definitely looking like he's going to kiss me.

I'm still for a moment, not wanting to misread this and look stupid. He stops when he's close enough that I can smell the scent of clean soap, and his cologne of sandalwood, amber, and sage fills me.

I can't breathe.

I can't move.

I can't let him kiss me.

Miles watches me, not moving or speaking, and I know I have to stop this.

"You just said you wanted to be friends and understood . . ." I barely croak out, my throat tight. "Now you look like you're going to kiss me."

He smiles. "What, you don't kiss all your friends?"

I shake my head. "No, I don't."

He leans back instantly, chuckling a little. "That's too bad. I think it should be something you consider for our friendship at least."

I grin and the nerves subside as he goes back to his spot on the couch, trying to decipher if I'm relieved he didn't kiss me or disappointed. I'm not sure which one is winning out.

eleven
Penelope

I roll over, glancing at the clock, waiting to see it tell me it's been fifteen minutes since I last checked. I nearly leap out of bed when I see it's actually ten in the morning.

How the hell did I sleep until ten?

Well, I didn't fall asleep until after six in the morning.

Why, you ask?

Because all I did was replay that moment on the couch about Miles almost kissing me. I replayed it a hundred ways, me telling him off, me kissing him, the way his lips would feel, the way he'd taste, if he would be soft and sensual or rough and dominating.

All of it was like a stupid movie that wouldn't shut off.

I'm surprised there's not a bald spot in the carpet from me walking to the door and back as I talked myself out of just going to his room and kissing him so I could stop imagining it.

However, I held back, used some self-restraint I didn't know I possessed, and stayed in my room. Counting down the minutes until it would be eight and I could get the boys and go see if my house was still standing.

I seem to have screwed that up.

Quickly, I brush my teeth and then head out to see if the boys are awake. I stop mid-step when I see the scene before me. Miles is at the stove, and the boys are sitting at the table. Miles is in a pair of basketball shorts and an Ember Falls Bulldogs shirt.

His smile is easy as he chats with the boys, and all the reminders, rules, and restrictions I put on myself disappear at the sight of him cooking breakfast for my son.

"You have to eat bacon with pancakes, it's a law," Ethan tells Kai.

"It's not a law."

"It should be."

Kai sighs dramatically. "I don't like bacon."

Miles drops the spatula. "You don't like bacon?"

My son shrugs. "Mom says I'm weird."

"It is weird. Everyone likes bacon!" Ethan protests.

Kai looks over, seeing me. "Mom! Tell them I'm not weird."

I chuckle and enter the kitchen fully, keeping my eyes off the very sexy man at the stove. If I don't look at him, I can't ogle his perfect body.

So I turn to Kai. "You're totally weird, dude. Bacon is the best."

"Thank God, I thought I was going to have to stage an intervention," Miles says with relief.

"No need for that."

"There's bacon and pancakes on the counter. Help yourself to whatever you want."

Now I really want to kiss him. "You should've woken me. I'm sorry."

"I went in your room, but you were snoring," Kai informs everyone. "Coach said to let you sleep and the men could handle breakfast."

I smile. "He did?"

"I do know how to make the essentials," Miles says, flipping a pancake and then pointing to the food on the counter with his spatula.

I take my cue and grab a plate, loading it up with two pancakes and some bacon.

"This looks great," I say.

"I made you coffee as well."

My eyes find his. "You made coffee?"

"You do like coffee, right?"

"Yes, but no one has ever made me coffee, that's my job."

He smiles warmly, and I feel it through my veins. "I think you deserve to have someone make you coffee for a change."

Yeah, that warms me in other places.

Miles goes back to cooking, and I pull my lip between my teeth while heading to the coffeepot. I thought by now I'd be sick of coffee, but that's not the case. I still have my very strong addiction to it.

With my cup of caffeine and breakfast plate, I sit at the table beside Kai. After I slather my pancakes with syrup, I take a bite and moan. Oh my God, these are incredible. They're lemon blueberry with something else that gives it this creamy center. I swear, I might just fall off my chair.

"Good?" Miles asks with a chuckle.

"Very," I say between bites. "What is this?"

"Lemon blueberry with ricotta. It's Gran's famous recipe that she demanded Eloise and I learn when we were kids."

"Well, it's heavenly."

"I'm glad you like it. Once everyone is done eating, we can head back up to your house while it's daylight and assess any damage and what we need to tackle, if that works for you?"

"That would be great, but you really don't have to do that," I tell him quickly.

"It's what friends do."

That word again. "Yes, I guess that is something friends do."

He smiles boyishly, and I'm pretty sure we're both thinking about what friends wanted to do last night.

I drop my head to avoid his eyes and keep my cheeks from view. If the color matches the heat, I'm definitely giving away my inner thoughts.

"Can we go back in the fort?" Ethan asks.

"Go ahead, and then you're going to need to break it down before you head home, Ethan."

"Awww!" they both complain.

"Kai, you need to clean up your mess. Coach Miles was very kind coming to help us in the storm, and it would be rude to leave his room a mess," I say so that Miles doesn't have to be the bad guy. "Do you understand?"

"Yes, ma'am. Come on, Ethan!"

They take their paper plates, putting them in the trash, and the silverware in the sink, before they disappear.

Miles shuts everything off and makes himself a plate, sitting beside me. "Did you sleep okay?"

"I did," I lie.

"I didn't," he admits.

"Why? Was it the storm?"

It howled almost all night. The thunder seemed to come in waves one after another, and it definitely is the excuse I'm using to tell myself it was not the almost kiss.

"It was not." He pops a piece of bacon in his mouth. "Since we're friends and all, can I tell you about my issue? You know the one that kept me up at night?"

Oh boy.

"As your friend, I guess so," I say hesitantly.

"It's this girl," Miles says, leaning back. "I like her. I'm pretty sure she likes me, too, but . . . she isn't ready for dating."

I can play along with this. "I see, that's gotta be hard for you."

"Tremendously."

"Do you see her often?"

Miles nods. "Almost daily."

"And does she know how you feel?"

He leans in, his hand a breath away from mine. "I'm pretty sure she does."

There's this incredible tightness in my chest from his nearness. He smells so good. He's so close. I could just kiss him once, see if the dreams were even close.

I debate it for another second, lingering over his features, studying the way his eyes show no hesitation.

If I do this. If I moved closer, just a bit, he'd kiss me, and I know, in the pit of my stomach—it would be good.

But I don't know that I can do it.

This is a really bad idea when I remember all my reasons. Edward's killer hunting me, running, them finding me, threatening Kai . . . each one tallies up in the con column, but then . . . my heart wants something else.

It wants *him*.

"Mom!" Kai yells, rushing into the room, and two things happen almost at once.

I pull away so fast my momentum causes me to knock the chair back, my legs flying up in the air as I tip over.

"Oof!" I yell as I hit the floor, thankfully smart enough to lean forward and not hit my head.

The other is Miles leaping out of his seat and calling my name. "Penelope!"

I want to just die of mortification. Truly. I've never been more embarrassed in my life. I just went ass over head in a freaking chair.

Maybe if I keep my eyes closed, for a second, this will prove to be another variation of the dream.

However, it's real. My dreams wouldn't be that bad, and I don't have that kind of luck for this not to have happened in reality.

I lift my hands when he reaches for me. "I'm fine. It's fine. I meant to do that."

Yeah, I definitely didn't.

"You're okay?"

"I'm . . . great."

At least Miles has the decency to turn when he tries to stop from laughing. All I see is his shoulders shaking, but there's no sound.

I get up, put the chair to rights, and then sigh.

"Did you hurt yourself?" Kai asks.

"No, honey, just . . . what did you need?"

"I just wanted to know when we're leaving."

Immediately, so I don't have to look at Miles. "In a few minutes. Start cleaning up."

He rushes back out and Miles turns to face me. As soon as he goes to open his mouth, I stop him. "Don't speak of it."

He chuckles. "Okay."

"I'm going to help wash dishes and never look you in the eye again, okay?"

"If you say so."

"I do," I tell him and walk to the sink, keeping my eyes down and hoping I can wash away the shame with soapy water.

———

"Why don't we just head to your house from here? I have the chain saw, and my truck will get up the mountain better than your car," Miles suggests as we stand outside Eloise's house.

He used the same logic when it came to bringing Ethan back here. I figured we'd drop him off, and then I could go home with Kai and get to work on cleaning up.

However, that's not the case. At Eloise's insistence, Kai is staying with her. She has a whole-home generator as well, and after the night we had, she wouldn't let it go. I agreed to let him stay, at least until we assess the house and see what's going on. For all I know, a freaking tree fell on it.

What I didn't intend on was Miles deciding to spend the day with me, claiming if there was debris in the road, it made sense for him to come to clear it, and then stating how he would be able to help with any home issues.

Of course, under the guise that friends do this for each other.

So friends we are, and he's making sense, so I tamp down my need to be independent a little and just allow someone to help.

"All right."

We get in his truck and head back toward our side of town. When we get past Miles's road, it's like the entire area seems to have changed. I'd swear we had a tornado touch down. There are branches, leaves, and even more debris than I remembered from last night.

"I'm going to have to cut this one," he explains when we get to a big branch that's blocking the road.

I get out of the car, helping him clear the cut-up branch. "I can't believe how strong the storm was."

"Yeah, it was pretty intense. Just fair warning, you're going to be without power for a bit. We don't get things restored around here quickly, and they focus on the other parts of town before this side."

"Why?" I ask, not even thinking that could be a thing.

"Population. We're like four people up here where the other parts of Ember Falls have more homes. It's why I put the generator in."

"I wish I'd known that."

He smiles. "Mr. Kipland put one in last year after we had a freak storm that left him without power for weeks."

"Weeks?" I scream. "I can rough it for a few days, but weeks. I can't handle that."

"I'm sure it'll be fine. Parts of the town are already back online," Miles tries to reassure me.

Of course my brother put me in this remote side of town where I'd lose power for weeks. That is, if the house even survived.

"I hope so."

"As a friend, I'm just saying if you need somewhere to stay, you and Kai can always stay with me. No strings, just so you don't have to suffer in the heat."

"You're a good friend," I say, grateful that he even offered.

Not that I could ever take him up on it. I need sleep and not to be dreaming of the man across the hall.

We get the downed tree off to the side and pass through. As we approach my house, I pray it's still standing. I let out a huge sigh when I see that it at least looks intact.

There are leaves and debris thrown all over the yard, but that can be cleaned.

We cut down the huge branch that almost took out my car and push aside twigs and leaves so we can get inside. The power is still off, but nothing looks damaged.

"Let's check the back," he suggests.

We exit the kitchen door and I gasp.

"Holy shit," Miles says from behind me.

The tree we have in our backyard is split almost down the middle. "That was really close to the house," I say, just looking at it, wondering how the tree is still standing.

"Yeah, it was. We need to call a company to get that taken care of. We're not due for another round of storms, but I don't know how long that'll hold."

I nod. "Okay, do you know anyone?"

"Of course. I'll call now."

He takes me around to the front of the house, pulling his phone out and making a call. Whoever is on the other end of the line causes him to laugh. Miles then explains the situation and replies with *yes* and *of course* a number of times. After he disconnects, he gives me a smile.

"Can they help?" I ask, hoping for a good answer.

"Yes, but not until tomorrow at the earliest. Look, *friend*, I'm just saying that staying here tonight isn't a good idea. Do you want to call Hazel? See if you can stay there if you're not comfortable staying with me until it's fixed?"

Great. I really don't want to stay at the coffee shop. The back room is good for maybe a few hours, but the couch is lumpy, and there's no way I'll be comfortable.

However, I absolutely think staying with Miles is a huge freaking mistake. I like him.

I like him a lot and that's stupid.

I don't trust myself.

I don't trust my judgment, or the fact that I've sung this song before, and the lyrics aren't going to change. There might be a new melody, but it will morph into something else and I'll be broken by the bridge.

No, I have to stay strong.

I need to say no and that I'll just spend the night in the spare room at the coffee shop.

"We'll stay with you," I say instead.

Because I'm an idiot.

Because I clearly have no self-control and I'm just . . . dumb.

He grins. "Good. Too bad we had the boys break the fort down. I bet Kai would've liked to have another night in there. It's fine, I'll rebuild with him."

And I'd like a night in his fort.

Oh dear God. Where the hell did that come from? Because he said he'd rebuild a fort?

I need to put a stop to this.

Hazel's it is. I can't stay with him because he's scrambled my brain.

Once again, I open my mouth to tell him my change of heart, but I think about Kai and how much safer it is to stay there. "He'll like that."

"Come on, I'll start cleaning up the front, and you can grab whatever you guys need."

"You said tomorrow, right?"

Miles's eyes meet mine. "At the earliest. I'll call tomorrow and push him, I promise."

"I don't know about that," I say in disbelief. "I'm starting to think you're planning this."

He laughs. "You know, if I can control the lightning, then I'm bordering on Godlike. If that's the case, you're totally going to fall in love with me."

I shake my head. "I was talking about the fact that the guy can't come until tomorrow—at the earliest."

"You heard the call."

"I heard half."

He hands me his phone. "Okay, oh-distrusting-one . . . call him. He's the last number dialed. His name is Justin."

Now I feel bad. "I trust you."

He pulls the phone back. "Good. Now I'll get to work."

I watch him walk away, trying—and failing—to not stare at his ass. Why does he have to be so damn cute?

After mentally slapping myself, I head into Kai's bedroom and quickly grab some clothes for him.

Then I go across the hall to my room to pack a bag. I don't need a lot if it's just one night, but I grab way more than I need in case the tree does fully fall and my house is destroyed with all my belongings.

I need to let Jackson know since he owns the house. I'm not sure which phone to use, but I grab the burner, because at least I know that one is totally untraceable.

"Penelope?" Jackson's deep voice comes through the line after the second ring.

"Hey, I didn't know if I should call, but we had a massive storm. It's bad, and there are trees and limbs and . . ." I relay the facts about the tree and Miles.

"Wow. Are you guys okay?"

"We are, but there's some damage, and I need to get a tree removed."

He cuts in quickly. "I'll pay for everything. Just do whatever you need for the house to be habitable."

"No, that's not why I'm calling." I've taken so much from him, there's no way I'm asking him to pay for this. "I just wanted to tell you and get permission to handle whatever. You are my landlord."

He chuckles. "I guess I am. Of course, send all the bills to Quinn. This will all be covered. You need to worry about you and Kai, not this shit. The company will pay for everything, and we have ways of hiding things."

"Okay, that really isn't necessary."

"I know you feel like you're taking advantage or whatever, but you're family, Penelope. We take care of our families in this company. Not only that, but we need to keep any paper trail clean, and if you were renting from anyone, you'd do it this way. Keep with the script."

"Thanks, J."

"Of course."

"Tell Catherine and the girls I said hi."

"I will. Be safe, Penny."

He hangs up and I sit on the edge of my bed, letting out a long sigh. Sometimes my life is just exhausting.

Nothing is normal or feels like it's real. It's part of why I'm fighting so hard against this . . . thing . . . with Miles.

He lives in a world where everything is as it seems. Bringing him into a web of lies feels like the most unkind thing I could do.

I just don't know that I'm going to be able to hold out, because the desire just keeps growing, no matter how much I tell myself it's a bad idea.

twelve
Miles

We spent about six hours working on cleaning up her property. It was hit hard, and then she suggested we stop and check on Mr. Kipland. It was a good thing we did. While he has power thanks to his generator, there were a lot of downed branches and trees we were able to clear for him.

Both of us were sweaty, tired, and in need of clean clothes and a hot shower.

Penny comes out into the living room, hair still damp from her shower, of which I spent the entire time she was in there imagining the water floating down her body while she was soapy and . . . wet.

Which led to me needing to take a cold shower myself and then jacking off because not even the cool water could stop my thoughts.

She sighs as she sits on the couch. "Eloise said the boys are fine with her tonight."

I really love my sister right now.

"Ethan and Kai get along so well. I'm sure it helps her."

Penelope smiles. "It means a lot to me that he has a friend like him. I got a text from Hazel saying the power is still out in the center of town."

"Yeah, I think the amount of trees down is the issue. Which is why I'm hoping Justin can make it tomorrow for you."

Most of that statement is true, except that I hope he fixes it. I wouldn't mind this little bit of forced proximity happening. It gives me time to win her over.

"Yeah, fingers crossed."

"Although you still won't have power . . ." I remind her.

"That is true, but thankfully Eloise mentioned that she has a portable generator that we could borrow."

I forgot about that. More like I was hoping Penelope would.

"Whenever you want to grab it, just let me know."

"Thanks, Miles."

"No thanks needed. Is pasta okay for dinner?" I ask.

"Pasta is great."

"Do you like Italian food?"

She nods. "I do. I used to get great food when I lived in Chicago. I think that's the one thing I miss more than anything. Pizza, pasta, amazing food options that most small towns don't offer."

I recline, my arm resting on the back of the couch. "I didn't know you lived in Chicago."

The sound that comes from her throat is a mix of a cough and almost choking. "Yeah, when I was . . . in college. I lived there."

"Really? Where did you go?" I ask.

"University of Chicago."

"Awesome, I went to Loyola."

She smiles and scooches forward a little. "That's so funny that we were probably there around the same time. Do you miss the city?"

I shrug a little. "Not much. I usually go back each summer. The only time off I really get is the month of July. Already my email is starting to fill back up with teacher issues, student scheduling conflicts, and coaches who want to know if I submitted things since the teams come back next week."

"I don't know how you do it. I hated school. Truly hated it. I'm not . . . academic, I guess. I tried and did the college route because that's what I was told I needed to do. I made it through somehow."

"What did you study?"

Penelope pauses as though she has to remember. "Advertising. Which gets you nowhere these days since anyone with a camera and the internet can do it." She claps her hands and gets to her feet.

"However, to answer your original question, yes, I love Italian food. Did you need help cooking?"

I feel as though I just got whiplash. I'm a pretty intuitive guy. I can sense evasion like a hawk; it's why I was good at my job in the military and why I'm a great principal. Sniffing out when someone doesn't want to tell me something is a superpower, and my senses are tingling.

If this was a student, I would push or at least try to get them to tell me, but the way that Penelope is looking at me, almost pleadingly, has me pulling back.

Instead of badgering anything out of her, I want her to choose to tell me. To trust me because she knows I won't hurt her.

So I let this drop and don't push any more about Chicago.

"Help would be great," I say, getting to my feet.

We head into the kitchen, and I start getting things out to make my gran's famous baked ziti.

To be honest, I'm not a great cook.

I can hold my own, but it's not gourmet in my house. I cook what I know I can make and time my visits to Gran and Eloise's for dinners at least three times a week. Regardless of what they say, I think they like my stopping by.

"How did you learn to cook?" Penny asks.

"Gran is one of those who thought kids learn best by doing, so Eloise and I were always hands-on in the kitchen."

She grins. "I love that. I taught myself off the internet. My mother was the opposite and wouldn't let us in the kitchen if she was working."

"After being in the education system for as long as I have, I think Gran had the right idea."

"I'd agree. It's why I have Kai in the kitchen with me a lot."

"Kai and Ethan both loved helping with breakfast," I say, after setting the pot on the stove to boil the water for the pasta.

"Kai just likes to help with anything. He really likes you."

"He's a great kid," I tell her. "He's kind and polite. I'm glad he and Ethan formed a friendship. I know Eloise thinks Ethan is a handful, and he can be, but he's a good kid. I know that my life is infinitely better since he came around."

Penelope pulls her lower lip between her teeth. "You really like kids."

It's partially a question and yet it feels like a statement. "This is going to make me sound stupid, but . . . I do. I think that kids are the most important humans on this planet. We have a responsibility to them in so many ways. They'll be the ones to take care of us and this earth as we grow older. They're going to be the ones who will come up with cures to diseases and fix problems we haven't even thought of. They're smart, and their naivety feeds curiosity that adults often tamp down. I think that kids are underrated, and while some days I'd like to walk out of my job and never see another kid again, most days I just want to be around them because they make me a better adult."

"I—I don't even"—she stutters—"wow. That was probably the most amazing thing I've ever heard."

I shrug because it's all true. "Kids are pretty amazing."

"Well, not everyone agrees with you."

"It's their loss."

Penelope comes around the island closer to where I am. "I guess it is. What can I help with?"

I have something I need help with, but I'm pretty sure she's not talking about the desire to lay her on the counter and kiss every inch of her.

So I go with the appropriate answer. "Can you grate the cheese?"

"Of course."

The two of us fall into a comfortable working environment. We talk about my job and what it's like to be a younger principal. The challenges I face with being both cool and also being respected. I tell her some stories about former kids, and she laughs at the one about the kid who tried to convince me that the drugs we found weren't really drugs, they were herbs.

She's sitting on top of the counter, long legs swaying as we eat the rest of the cheese we didn't use. "Did he think that was some new tactic?" she asks through her laughter.

"Apparently. When I said that I didn't believe it was oregano, he said I clearly didn't know my weed from a weed."

Penelope snorts, and I swear it's the cutest sound I've heard. "Pathetic."

"Agreed. I honestly didn't want to suspend him because I worried missing school would be more of a crime."

"Clearly he needs to be taught better."

"And what about you?" I ask, reaching around her for a slice of cheese, not minding that I brush her bare legs.

She clears her throat. "What about me?"

"Tell me some story about you in high school."

"Hmm." Penelope looks around before grinning. "Okay, so this one time, my best friend, Teresa, convinced me that there was this group of cannibals who lived on this road in our town. The legend had it that if we went there before midnight, we'd see them sacrifice their next person. Of course, the smart people didn't go because if this was true, you didn't want to *be* the sacrifice, right?"

"I'm guessing you were not the smart people."

She laughs once. "We were not."

"Of course, proceed."

"So we go at eleven thirty and park on a different street, because why would you want your escape vehicle close? Much better to have to traipse through the woods when running from the cannibals who kill people."

"Yes, much better," I say with a chuckle.

"So, Teresa and I are out there, on this dark-ass road where I'm pretty sure we had a better chance of being killed by a driver than these people, and we wait there, standing in someone's yard, hoping to see—I don't even know what, because if we actually saw what we were there for, I'm pretty sure we would've shit our pants. However, we waited, and the only thing we saw was the police car when he rolled up because the person's lawn we were on called them."

I laugh, shaking my head. "Kids."

"We were all stupid."

"Agreed."

Penelope hops off the counter and stands next to me, bumping me with her hip. "Okay, now you go."

"Go where?"

She rolls her eyes. "I heard your students' dumb stories, but now I want one of yours."

I raise my brows. "Me? I don't have any."

"Yeah, right."

"I was a saintly teenager."

"Saintly?" the disbelief is clear in her voice. "If I called Eloise right now, what would she say?"

"You can't believe a word that comes out of her mouth. She was the second twin, and we think she had a lack of oxygen. Messes with the memories."

Penelope bursts out laughing. "I think you did some really dumb shit."

"I'm pretty sure you would think that."

She turns, moving so quickly she almost falls, but I catch her arms and steady her. There's an instant shift in the atmosphere. A charge that fills the room as I have her in my hands.

Her lips part and she stares at me for a beat.

The urge to kiss her is stronger than ever. Being around her, just talking like this as we made dinner, is everything I've wanted.

I know I don't really know her.

I know this is just chemistry at this point.

But I'm really fucking good at science.

Penelope lifts her hands, resting them on my chest. "Sorry," she says softly.

"For what?"

Her big blue eyes are locked on mine, and then, as if she realizes what's about to happen, she steps back, tucking her hair behind her ear. "For falling . . ."

When she starts to turn, I gently grab her wrist and she faces me again. "I'll catch you. Anytime I'm near." She glances down at her wrist and then back up to me. I can feel her pulse racing, and then she steps to me. Her hands go back to my chest, and I take her face in mine. "I want to kiss you," I tell her.

"Good, I want that, too, but . . . we can't be more than friends."

I brush my thumb against her cheek. "I think we already are."

Her lids lower slowly and then lift again. "We can't."

"Whatever you say."

I incline my head to hers, moving slowly, tasting the moment and savoring it. She's clearly hell-bent on keeping me at a distance, and that's fine. I have plenty of patience.

Penelope lifts up on her toes as I move in to kiss her. I take a breath, resting our foreheads together, allowing her the time to back away if she wants to, but hoping she doesn't. "Did you know that what we're doing right now would be kissing if we were turtles?"

She lets out a soft laugh. "I didn't."

"If we were otters, we'd hold hands, and that would be their way of kissing," I tell her, wanting her to be at ease.

Thankfully Penelope doesn't move away. Again I move my thumb softly against her cheek. "I like the way humans do it best, though."

She lifts her head, eyes meeting mine. "You do?"

I nod. "Do you want me to kiss you?"

Her head moves just the slightest amount. Penelope lifts up again, her eyes closed, hands on my chest, and she digs her fingers in just a touch, gripping my shirt. I pull her tight against me and press my lips to hers.

I stay still, absorbing the feel of her, drinking in the soft inhale she makes, and then her fingers loosen and she wraps her arms around my neck, molding her body against mine. I move deeper, kissing her just a little harder.

Her lips part and I take the cue, kissing her and sliding my tongue into her mouth. The wet heat is intoxicating. There's a hint of tomato from when she licked her finger after tasting the sauce.

Each swipe of our tongues makes the kiss more intense. Penelope's fingers move to my hair and she wraps them around the strands.

Moving us both, I anchor her against the island, and my hands move down to her back, pressing her tight against me.

I could kiss her forever. Do nothing for the rest of my life than this, and while I want nothing more than to strip her down right here and take her, I can't.

I also need to stop before I do exactly that and fuck up any progress I've made.

Slowly, I temper the kiss, bringing it back down in intensity. Not wanting to break away from her completely, I go back to resting my forehead against hers. Her breathing is labored, and once she's a little calmer, I lift my head to gaze at her.

She's fucking gorgeous. Her eyes are lust filled and her lips a little swollen. I brush my thumb against them, wiping away some of the moisture. There's a storm starting to brew in her gaze. I can see the regret or fear hovering over the desire.

I need to break the tension and make her laugh again. "I'm glad we're not otters."

Penelope giggles softly. "Me too."

"But as a friend, I'm happy to hold your hand too." I step back, releasing her, and wink. "Or any kind of kissing that you'd like to test."

She shakes her head, laughing, and then lets out a long sigh. "I'll keep that in mind."

I hope she does.

thirteen
Penelope

At Eloise's insistence, Kai is spending the night at her house. I guess they are playing some game and then going to help with the horses. I was really uneasy about agreeing to it, but Kai pleaded so I . . . let him have his first sleepover.

However, this now leads me to spending the night—alone—with Miles.

This is *so* bad.

All I can do is replay that kiss. I have never gotten so lost in someone before. All the thoughts and worries disappeared the second his lips were on mine. It was only him.

And I was really stupid to let it happen.

Staying in my room, though, feels like the coward's way, so I'm going to go out there, not kiss him again, and stay focused on my rules . . . no dating.

He's in the living room watching television, and I take my spot on the couch.

"All right, now is when we really test our friendship," Miles says, and dread pools in my stomach.

"Why is that?"

"Are you coming with me to the field or staying here?"

"The field?"

"I have practice tonight."

"Oh! For your little Frisbee thing?"

Miles pulls his head back. "Little Frisbee? Little? Woman, I am a member of the Disc Jocks and we are a championship-winning team." He scoffs and throws his hands up. "Little Frisbee . . . I'll have you know we were kicked out of our league for being so good."

Since I saw them play the other day, I had no idea they were good. I mean, they didn't do all that great.

"That's not at all hard to believe," I tease.

"You're thinking about the game you saw? Don't take that as an indicator of our talent. We're much better; we just had an off day."

I fight back a smile. "I see. Eloise and Ainsley were saying that you guys are usually worse than that."

"They lied. They wanted to make me look bad," he explains and then gets to his feet. "I have to leave in about five. If you want to come, Ainsley and Rose will be there. Also I think Hazel is going as well, since her power is still out."

Staying alone in his house seems a little weird for me. Plus, it would be nice to hang out with the girls. It's not like I've had any of that in six years.

"I'd love to go."

"All right, grab whatever you need and I'll get you a camping chair."

I'm not sure what I need, so I grab a sweatshirt, not that it's remotely cool out, but you never know, and I meet Miles out front. He's loading his truck and opens the door for me as I walk toward him. "Your chariot awaits."

I hop up and smile. "Thank you."

He winks and then closes the door, leaving me feeling like a sixteen-year-old girl who has her first crush.

I'm a mess.

I focus on my fingernails so I don't stare as he walks around the truck. He gets in, he turns the music on, and we head to the field.

"It's so strange because while the town is super small and not exactly a metropolis with lights everywhere, this feels so . . . eerie," I say after a minute or two of silence.

"I feel like Main Street is really where it's different. The entire town feels desolate."

I nod in agreement. "But the park lights are on?"

"The park lights run off a generator, so we didn't have to worry about that."

"I see."

"Listen, I need to tell you something. It's very serious."

"Oh?" I ask. "Of course you can tell me."

He sounds so concerned I kind of am now.

"My friends, the guys on the team, are all suffering from a disease that the medical community is still trying to get under control."

Well, now I'm not concerned. I cross my arms over my chest and shift to look at him as he drives. "Really? What disease is that?"

"Stupidity. I mean, we know some things about it, but there's a lot the doctors are still trying to unearth."

"I see, and do you also suffer with this affliction?" I ask, fighting back the urge to laugh.

"No, I was cured of this a long time ago."

"Oh, but you had it once?"

Miles grins. "Depends on who you ask."

"But you're not sure?"

"I'm pretty sure I had a mild case, but it was easily treated."

"With?" I ask.

"A kick in the ass from my gran."

"I really want to meet her," I say, not thinking about how that sounds.

Why would I want to meet her? We're not dating. We're definitely *not* going to date. We kissed once, it's over, I'm just staying at the house one more night so that I can get the tree in the back taken down and not die in my sleep.

All things that don't require the meeting of any family member.

Now, if Eloise wants to introduce me, that's one thing. She's . . . not going around kissing me.

"I'm sure Gran will love you," Miles says with a little swagger in his tone.

Great. He thinks it means something too.

"Does Eloise think your case of stupidity was cured?" I ask, bringing it back to the easy teasing we had going.

"Definitely not."

We pull up to the field, and Miles grabs the chair and his bag from the back. When we get down from the parking area, the lights illuminate the field. All the guys are on the sideline stretching, and Everett is taping Killian's ankle.

"Hey, hey, if it isn't Miles and Penny. Let me guess, Romeo came and rescued you in the storm?" Everett asks.

"He did, actually."

Lachlan walks toward us. "I heard about the tree in your yard, you're staying somewhere safe, right?"

"I am."

"Like I was going to leave her and Kai in that house," Miles says with a hint of irritation.

"No, but I also know that if it was between a tree falling on me or having to spend time in a house with you, I'd take my chances with the tree." Lachlan elbows him, and then the two of them start to do that weird guy tackle thing. After a few seconds, Miles releases him and Lachlan comes back toward me. "I just wanted to make sure. I know Justin can't get out there today; he's been helping us clear branches that fell on power lines."

"Hopefully he can get to the tree before it falls. Otherwise, it looks like I'll be moving."

"We'll get it taken care of," Miles promises.

"Are we planning to practice or what?" Everett yells.

Lachlan flips him off, and then a water bottle hits him in the back. "I'm going to kill him," Lachlan warns.

Oh, this is going to escalate. Sure enough, Lachlan runs after Everett, and Miles sighs. "Go hang with the girls. I need to handle the children."

Laughing at their antics, I head over to where Ainsley and Hazel are hanging out. "Hey, guys."

"Fancy seeing you here," Ainsley says with a grin. "Do you have power yet?"

"No, you guys?" I ask them both.

"Not yet," Hazel says.

"Ours came on literally as we were walking out the door to come here. Hopefully more people will be online soon."

Hazel drops her head back, fanning herself with her hand. "It's so damn hot. I can't do another night in that apartment."

"Come stay with us," Ainsley offers.

"I might take you up on that," Hazel says.

"Good." Ainsley turns to me. "You're also always welcome to stay with us. Rose loves Kai, and I'm sure they'd have a great time hanging out."

Sometimes it feels like a bizarre world I've stepped into here. People are just so *nice*. They offer to help anyone in need, and it's really amazing. It's just not the normal I'm used to, which is a sad thing in and of itself.

We should strive to be more like the people in this town. I think the world would be a better place, that's for sure.

"Thank you. It means a lot to me."

Hazel smiles. "She's staying with Miles."

"I figured as much," Ainsley says and then waggles her brows.

"It's not like that," I say.

I mean, it's not. We're not sleeping together. Sure, we kissed and it was the most extraordinary and fantastic kiss of my life, but that's just because it's been so long for me.

Years since I've felt like this for a guy at all. Years since I've even considered letting a man touch me.

That's the only reason.

The only reason, my ass, my brain chimes in.

"Why?" Ainsley asks.

"Why what?"

"Why isn't it like that? Miles is a great guy. We all love him. He's got a great job, loves his family. I mean, look, he canceled a trip to Michigan that he paid a lot of money for just to coach his nephew's team. He's a former marine and has a good head on his shoulders. I don't know, it seems like green flags everywhere I look." Ainsley sits back in her lawn chair after making my head spin.

I know all of this about him. I tell myself his list of attributes on a daily basis and then have to remind myself that it's not really about *him*.

It's about me and Kai.

I am protecting not only myself against being hurt, but him too.

They always find me and it's not an *if* . . . it's a *when*.

When it happens, I'll have to go.

I can't.

My heart is racing and I feel sick just thinking about it.

"Penny?" Hazel calls my attention.

I turn to her, forcing a smile and pushing the panic that was rising back down. "No, I know he's great. Truly I do. I think, for now, I just want to settle in more. Getting into a relationship isn't really a good idea."

Hazel nods once. "That makes sense."

I'm glad it does to someone.

There's a knot in my stomach, sinking lower with each breath I take, though. I know that men like Miles don't come around often. There are far more assholes than good guys—at least it feels that way. I'm sad because I want Kai to have a father and for me to have someone to love and grow old with.

That fantasy has never faded.

I know that real love and happiness are possible. I've seen it with my brother, my friends who are in wonderful marriages, and Ainsley and Lachlan love each other beyond reason.

It's just not in the cards for me.

I stare out at the field when the guys start yelling. Miles catches the Frisbee and then grins as our eyes meet.

If only my dreams never became nightmares, because I could've lived this one.

———

To my relief, not only was the power back on when we got back to Miles's house, but Justin called letting me know he was in the area and went and cut down the tree for me before it was dark.

It doesn't seem that Miles is too happy about this, but it's honestly for the best.

"Let me drive you back at least," he says, standing in the doorway of the room I put all my stuff in.

"I have my car."

"Okay, then let me follow you back. What if Justin cut down the wrong tree?" I grab the heavy bag, tossing it over my shoulder. Before

I can even take a step, Miles is there, taking it from me. "I'll carry that for you."

"You are making it really hard to resist you."

He turns to me, his eyes feel like a caress. "That's my goal. I'm an irresistible guy. However, that's not why I'm going back to your house with you. I'm going because I want to make sure you're safe."

I sigh, my heart aching from the pull I feel towards him. "If it will really make you feel better, then you can follow me up to my house and make sure that your very capable friend—who you promised was great—didn't cut down a different tree than the one that was struck by lightning that's hanging over my bedroom roof."

Then I realize I just invited him to my bedroom.

Miles takes a step to me, nodding slowly. "Good. That's settled."

Most of the debris has been cleared off the road, and my little crappy car makes it up without any issues. I look at the tree in the front and want to weep. The branch that offered me so much privacy is gone. It looks like he trimmed some of the other branches that were really close to the house.

Miles comes up behind me. "Good man for doing a little extra. I'm going to have to make sure his son gets an A in his math class."

I snort a laugh. "You can do that?"

"No, but . . . I can at least tell him I did. His son is a straight-A student, so it bodes well that'll be the case anyway."

"You're ridiculous."

"And charming."

"And that," I agree.

"Look at that, you admitted it. Next thing you know *you'll* be asking me out."

"I wouldn't count on that," I joke and then we make our way to the front door. The lights in the foyer turn on, and he follows me through the little space out to the back. "Look at that, the right tree was removed."

"I guess you'll be safe here then."

I smile, my hip resting on the countertop. "I guess I will."

"You know, I might have other reasons why I wanted you to stay another night."

I bet he did, and those reasons keep me up at night, dreaming about what it could be like if I gave in to it. Keeping up our playfulness, though, I raise one brow and grin. "Oh?"

"Not like that!" he says quickly. "There is a little of that, but it's not what I meant."

I chuckle. "Please explain then."

"I need coffee."

"Coffee?"

"Yes, you've created a monster, and I think it's only fair you continue to feed that monster now with ground coffee beans that are cold brewed only."

Playing along, I nod once. "I see, and you can't get that at your house why?"

"Because I can't make it like you do."

"That's sweet, but . . . it's not hard."

"Yes, but you're an expert."

I sigh heavily. "What if I bring you coffee on my way to get Kai in the morning?"

"Not the same."

"What?" I ask, laughing at the same time. "How is it different?"

"We're not on the same well. Your water might be more acidic or have more lead in it. That's something you should test."

"Lead in the well water?" I ask to clarify.

"I'm just saying, it's happened somewhere."

"You'll get some cold brew tomorrow, but for now, I need to do laundry, clean up, and enjoy having a house to myself for the first time in well—ever."

Miles lets out a long breath and pushes off the wall. "All right. You have your night of freedom and I'll go back home—alone—and think of coffee I won't be getting."

"You'll survive," I tell him.

"Remember that the next time a tree almost falls on your house and car."

"You'd let that happen?" I challenge. Partially because while I'm pretty sure he's joking, I don't always trust myself.

"No, God no. I would never. Did you think I would?"

I shake my head quickly. "No. Of course not."

Just for a second and I knew it was stupid.

He moves to me, his hands cupping my cheeks. "Anytime you need something, call me. Anytime. I'll always show up for you."

As though he can sense the storm that's raging in my chest, he gives me a moment to let it sink in.

I thought I was a mess before, but it's nothing compared to now. I've never had someone, other than Quinn, make me a promise like that, and I believe it.

He was so honest, so sincere, that I'm questioning everything.

Then, with the tenderness of how you'd handle a breakable doll, he slowly brings his lips to the tip of my nose before releasing me. "Always."

Miles walks out the door, and I stand here, wishing I'd said something, but not sure what it would've been.

fourteen
Miles

"Okay, Miles, here's a doughnut and that cold brew coffee you asked for," Mrs. Hendrix, my secretary, says as she places down a plate and cup from Prose & Perk on my desk in my office. "Don't know when you started drinking coffee, but I'm not asking questions."

"No, you're just making an observation."

She grins. "Five years of dealing with you and I've never seen you drink coffee. In fact, I've listened to you gripe about the amount of money the school spends on coffee beans."

"Consider those days behind us, Mrs. Hendrix. From now on, it's good coffee for everyone."

"Pfft, you just like that pretty young barista; that's what the change is."

She's not wrong. "Did Penny make me this?"

"Yes, she did. I told her that I had strict instructions that she was the only one allowed to make it, which earned me a strange look."

"You get strange looks all the time from students and staff," I remind her.

"This is true. Usually it's because I'm giving one of your dictates."

Lois Hendrix is one of the best secretaries that has ever lived. She's kind, firm, thoughtful, and remembers everything that I don't. I truly don't think I could make it through a school year without her.

Since my head of the English department quit, we've been in scramble mode to get a replacement. Being that it's nearing the end of summer, all the candidates I probably would've hired are already taken, leaving us with slim pickings. However, sometimes you find a pearl among the clams, and that's what I'm hoping for here.

I grin and then drop the coffee cup in the garbage.

"Wait, you're not even going to drink that?" she asks incredulously.

"No, I hate coffee."

Her eyes are wide. "You just bought it."

"Yes, I paid for it, Penelope had to think of me as she was making it, and now I'm done with it. This is my daily routine."

"You are a mess. Do you know that?"

"I do. Now, how many interviews today?"

"Twelve."

I glance up at her, hoping I misheard that number. "What?"

"Twe-elve," she says slowly as though I'm a three-year-old who doesn't understand.

"I heard that, but what the hell made you think I wanted to do twelve of these with Belinda on vacation?"

My assistant principal actually got to take her vacation. I'm stuck here thanks to Doug being unathletic. I originally was going to wait for her before doing these interviews, but that scares me even more. I need to hire a teacher before it's too late.

"I know you don't want to, but it's your job." She pats my arm. "Eat your doughnut. I have a dozen at my desk."

"Oh, no, you're in here with me."

She crosses her arms over her chest. "I have work to do."

"Yes, and you have to do this."

"Would you rather I work on the student schedules or be in here taking notes?" Lois asks.

"Both."

The look on her face tells me she thinks I'm a total dumbass. Which is fine because I am not doing these today—alone. I need her to see the things I miss.

"Fine." She takes the plate with the doughnut. "But you don't get this anymore."

I would pout, but she's got more at her desk, and surely I'll need to use the bathroom.

———

The first interview went well. And when I say *well*, I mean it wasn't a total train wreck. The teacher at least had a certification and was well spoken. There was just something about her that didn't sit right.

"She wasn't bad," Lois says.

"I didn't like that she kept talking about her former district."

She nods. "Yes, that was a little uncomfortable. However, she seems like she wants the job."

"And that scares me that she doesn't already have a job."

Lois shrugs and hands me the next résumé. "This one seems promising."

I look it over and, yes, on paper it definitely does. She taught at another district that I'm familiar with. She has all the right certifications and even was the cochair on a curriculum board. That could be helpful.

"Let's bring her in."

Lois gets the applicant, bringing her into my office.

We sit and go over the normal questions about her education and what she's looking for in a new school.

Stephanie crosses and uncrosses her legs. "Honestly? I'm looking for a place that values what I bring to the table."

Not an unreasonable request. Most people want to work where they're appreciated. "And how did you feel your last school wasn't doing that?"

"They didn't allow me to bring my dog."

I blink and then meet Lois's eyes. "Your dog?"

"Yes, all day long I'm gone and Gianna is home alone. I think it's fair that once I prove myself to be a capable and respected teacher, certain allowances should be made. Dogs are allowed in certain places."

Oh boy. "They are. Is Gianna a working dog?"

"She is."

I swear, if I could breathe an audible sigh of relief I would. "Well, if she's a service dog, then that has to be allowed by law."

"She's not my service dog. She works for food, love, attention. All dogs are working dogs, Mr. Anderson."

Just when I thought we weren't going off the rails. Lois fights back a grin, and I wish I could flip her off—lovingly. "As you can understand, we wouldn't be able to accommodate that request. Dogs, whether working or just regular house dogs, aren't allowed in classrooms."

"You're the Bulldogs, are you not?"

"Yes."

"Then how can you support an animal and not allow them to be a part of your learning environment?" Stephanie asks.

"Because . . . that's our mascot, not our educational focus. If we were a dog training facility, then, yes, we could make concessions for that. I'm going to be up front now and let you decide if this is going to be an issue, unless your dog is a service dog for a specific need that you have, we won't be allowing you to bring Gianna in here either."

Stephanie nods once before gathering her bag off the floor and getting to her feet. "I wish you much luck, Mr. Anderson."

I rise and extend my hand. "You as well."

Lois escorts her out and then stands in front of me, fighting back a laugh. "That was . . ."

"Please tell me they get better."

"Probably not." She hands me the next résumé.

We get through four more. I don't know how because I'm pretty sure these were a joke. One guy apparently had a typo on his résumé when he put his graduation year, because he was older than Gran. That wasn't happening.

Then we had another who told us about her ten-year plan, which included moving by year three—yeah, hard no.

"We have a break, what do you need? You've eaten all the dough-nuts," she informs me.

"I had no choice after that last interview."

She bobs her head. "Yeah, that was a shit show, but I wanted that last doughnut and would've fought you for it."

"I would've won."

"And I would've found a way to win later."

If there's anyone whose threats I worry about—it's her.

"I need you to go get another coffee."

"Let me guess, it has to be cold brew and only from Penelope which you'll toss when you get it?"

"Yes, can you please do that for me?"

Lois sighs deeply. "Fine, but you're buying me lunch tomorrow."

"Deal."

I grab my notepad that Eloise gave me—it says *World's Okayest Principal*—and write a note to her.

Go out with me tomorrow night. Coincidentally at least.

I grin, knowing she'll probably roll her eyes and laugh, which makes the rest of my day slightly bearable.

I walk out as Lois is grabbing her purse. "Here, give that to her for me, please."

"Now I'm passing notes? You know you run the high school, Miles, not attend it."

"I'm aware, it's cute."

She chuckles softly. "Oh, you men, you're all the same. I'll hand your note to the girl you like."

"I appreciate it."

Without another word, she heads out, and I go back to review the notes we took on the candidates. I really have no idea what I'm going to do. We promoted another teacher to the head position, but that leaves her classroom open. I have kids returning in a few weeks without a teacher in place. When schedules go out, I have to have a name in that slot or I'll have a whole other issue with parents.

It's like a merry-go-round in my head, spinning between them, hoping something lands and I pick the right horse.

Before I know it, Lois is back. "You look deep in thought."

"I was hoping I'd see an option out of the ones we've spoken with."

She places the coffee down with a note on it: *No date, but coincidentally, I might see you at practice tomorrow.*

The stupid smile that forms should be embarrassing, but I don't care. It's been a few days since I've seen her, other than when she waves as she picks up Kai after clinic.

"Miles?"

I look up. "Yes?"

"Get it under control, we have our next interview," Lois says and then walks out.

This interview is actually going great. I like this girl. She's smart and worked out of state, moving back to this area of Virginia to be closer to her family. There are no real red flags and from what I can see, the reason she's not already taken is she just moved a month ago.

I might actually have someone.

"Can you tell us a bit about your last school?" I ask Trinette.

"I loved it. New Jersey is where I grew up, and I planned to stay there, but then my aunt got sick and I just thought it was better to come stay here and help. I taught ninth and tenth grade, which was really wonderful. I can handle any English time period, but my two favorites are British literature and Shakespeare. However, I'm open to anything."

"All of that sounds great. Do you have anything to ask us?"

Trinette shifts. "I do. Can you tell me about the school's goals? Meaning, do you teach more to testing or do you work toward other goals?"

I smile at Lois, feeling confident that we might have found our teacher. "We're a mix of both. Most schools are scrutinized over the test scores, as you probably know. We do want the kids to keep achieving the goals the state has required, but we are a little unique in that our students don't say they feel that pressure. We do a lot of things, and I encourage my staff to find ways to just make learning fun."

Trinette's lip starts to tremble, and then her hand covers her mouth. I start to move, and then she just bursts into tears. I'm talking a sob that sounds like a wail.

What the . . . ?

I get out of my seat, as does Lois. "Are you okay?" I ask quickly.

She raises her hand. "I'm sorry. Yes."

Lois and I look to each other and she shrugs. Great, she doesn't know either. "Can I get you something? Are you sick? In pain?"

Trinette shakes her head. "No, no, I'm sorry. I just . . . I need a minute."

"Of course."

I step back and replay that last conversation, trying to figure out what the fuck I said to trigger her into a full-fledged meltdown. A few minutes go by, and then she sniffs and seems to have control again.

"I apologize."

"It's all right. Can you explain what upset you?" I ask.

"It's just . . . Mercury is in retrograde, and I felt the tug against my heart. The planets are telling me this isn't the right fit."

And just like that . . . I'm still teacherless.

"Beer," I say, holding up a six-pack at Lachlan's front door. "Beer."

"Yes, that's beer. I'm assuming we're going to drink it."

"Beer."

He chuckles. "That kind of day, huh?"

"Lots of beer."

The day ended with having to do another round of interviews, because we did not find anyone worth even a second interview. So, yeah, beer. That's all I got.

"Ainsley!" Lachlan calls. "We have company."

She pops around the corner and smiles. "Miles! Hey! What are you doing here?"

I grab the six-pack and lift it. "Beer."

"All right then. You're going to drink beer."

Lachlan steps in. "Yes, apparently that's all he can say. Are you cool if we head out to the falls?" he asks her.

"Have fun. I've got Rose and Kai."

"Kai is here?" I ask.

"Oh, now he has words," Lachlan says with a snort.

Ainsley smirks. "He is. Penny will be here in about fifteen minutes. Maybe don't drink *all* the beer before then."

"How about we hang here?" I suggest.

Lachlan's stupid grin tells me he knows exactly why. "Yeah, I saw that coming."

We head into the living room, and Rose and Kai come running in. "Coach!" Kai yells and then launches himself at me.

I catch him and chuckle. "Hey, little man."

"I didn't know you were going to be here."

"I didn't either," I tell him.

"Hi, Uncle Miles," Rose says with her hands behind her back.

"No hug?" I ask.

She rushes over and I get the best hug. "Kai is my friend, and Daddy said I can tell him the town secret."

"Good call, he does live here."

She giggles and the two of them head out. Lachlan sits in the recliner, and Ainsley plops on his lap. "So why all the beer?" Lachlan asks.

I fill him in on my day, having to go back and explain the sudden departure of Megan Hunt and how if she'd told us this months ago, we could've planned.

"It's part of my job, I get it, but the people today were just absolutely a mess. I mean, crying? Because of Mercury being in retrograde? What the hell does that even mean?"

Ainsley grins. "I, for one, am enjoying the story."

"Clearly."

"I'm sure you'll find someone, Miles. You just need to get through the unqualified candidates."

I hope she's right. I'm getting much too close for comfort to not having someone in that spot. If another teacher decides to leave, I'm going to be fucked—and not in the good way.

"If I don't, I'm going into hiding."

Lachlan snorts. "I'm sure Killian will allow you to stay in one of his barns."

"Oh, yes, that's my dream."

"You could always stay with Everett."

"I'll take the barn," I reply without a moment of hesitation. "Also, thanks, asshole, you have a house, land, part of the damn Ember Falls, and you haven't offered me lodging? Dickface."

His laugh makes me want to punch him in the face. "Ainsley and I like to explore those falls without anyone watching."

"Lachlan!" She slaps his chest and turns to me. "What he's saying is—"

"You like to bang in the woods, I get it."

Her cheeks paint a new shade of pink. "I hate you guys."

"You love me," Lachlan tells her.

"I do, for some stupid reason." She stares at the man she loves with absolute adoration.

Watching the two of them makes me both happy and sad at the same time. I'm happy because they really do love each other. They are each other's other half, like Eloise and Doug. Just being around them, though, makes it very clear I don't have that.

Before I go down the road that I really don't need to travel down, there's a knock at the door.

Ainsley hops up and grins at me before going to see who it is. "Hello, Penny."

"Hi, thank you so much for taking him for the afternoon," Penelope says, her soft voice filling my ears and my heart.

God, I sound like a dumbass. Fills my heart?

"Of course, come in."

Penelope enters, and I swear it's like the fucking sun rising. The sky brightens, the day feels as though anything is possible, and there's an air of hope that fills me. All that by just seeing her face.

Who cares if I sound like a dumbass? It's just the truth.

"Miles," she says my name softly, eyes wide as it's clear she didn't expect me here. "Hi."

"Hello." I grin, feeling like my bad day just got a little less crappy.

She smiles warmly and Ainsley comes up beside her. "Don't mind him if he doesn't say much. He's had a shitty day and came here to drink beer."

"Oh? Is everything okay?" she asks. Her big blue eyes are filled with concern and I can't look away.

"It's looking up," I admit.

Lachlan clears his throat. "Hey, Penny, have you ever seen the falls?"

Her eyes shift to him. "Falls?"

"Ahh, so Miles didn't tell you the secret either?" he tsks. "Well, since Kai is here and he and Rose are out playing, why don't you two go for a walk and he can let you in on Ember Falls' greatest secret."

"You have secrets?" she asks.

Lachlan chuckles. "Doesn't everyone?"

She shifts and nods. "I guess they do. I just didn't know the town had one."

"Miles knows the story."

Yeah, today is definitely looking up, and I'm starting to think Lachlan isn't so bad after all.

fifteen
Penelope

I t's been a few days since I've seen him, and the way my heart began to race the moment my eyes met his is seriously an issue.

However, it's nothing compared to how it is right now. The two of us walking down this dirt path, away from the world.

"So you had a bad day?" I ask, wanting to talk instead of letting my mind wander around.

"I'm in the middle of trying to hire a teacher, and let's just say the end of July, the worse the chances are of finding the right fit."

"I can imagine that would suck."

He chuckles. "It definitely does." Miles stops, and his hand grips mine. "Now, before we go further down the path, I have to ask you a few questions."

I work hard to control my breathing and not focus on the way his hand feels in mine. "Okay."

"First, do you swear to hold the secrets of Ember Falls with your life and never repeat them?"

I blink at that. "What?"

"The secrets that are about to be told must remain—a secret. You have to swear it."

"Wow, this must be some great secret."

"It is." He drops my hand and I already miss the warmth of him.

I nod. "Then I swear to keep the secret."

"Okay, you passed the first one," Miles explains. "Now to see if you're worthy of being told the secret is a little harder."

"Why do I feel like this is going to be a huge letdown?"

"It could be."

I laugh softly. "All right, that's encouraging."

"First part of the question. Do you have a pure heart?"

I'm not really sure how to answer that one. "Umm, maybe?"

"Maybe? What kind of answer is that?" Miles asks.

"Okay, fine. Yes, I do. If I didn't, I would've just lied off the top."

"Are you lying now?"

I shrug. "You'll have to figure that out."

He steps closer with a grin and my skin tingles. "What I'm hearing is that you want to go out and let me get to know you."

"You need a hearing exam." However, he's not wrong. I want that very much.

"That's not a no."

"It's not a yes."

"I'll take it." He steps closer into my space. "Do you want to know a secret, Penny?"

I'm not sure if he means about him or this mythical town thing, but I nod anyway.

"Come with me."

Miles extends his hand again, and I let my fingers entwine with his, doing exactly as he asked, following him like a moth to a flame, hoping I don't end up burning my very fragile wings.

We walk down the path, and then he pushes a few branches aside, allowing me to walk through.

When I do, my jaw drops. "This is . . . incredible."

There is a beautiful waterfall that has a pool at the bottom before going to a few smaller falls. There are trees around both sides, and the way the moonlight glints off the water is . . . so pretty.

Miles's voice is soft as he says, "Welcome to the Ember Falls."

"They're amazing."

Miles chuckles. "Now, they have actual magical powers, or at least that's what the legend says."

"There's a legend?"

"All small towns have them," he says with a grin.

"Please, do tell then."

He shakes his head. "I'm afraid I can't do that."

I purse my lips. "Umm, why is that?"

"You have to be dating someone in the town to know the legend. People with permanent addresses can know of them. I think I'm breaking some town laws by actually showing you, but I plan to just blame Lachlan, so I'm not worried about it."

I laugh, crossing my arms across my chest. "Do you all have meetings about this?"

"Monthly."

I turn back to the falls, wondering if they're warm or cold. "Can I touch this magical water?" I ask.

"Again, that's only once you at least agree to date someone who lives here."

He's relentless, and a part of me loves it. "I see. So all the single people in the town can't touch the water?"

Miles grins. "Well, those of us who were raised here get a free pass."

"I wonder if Everett would be willing to go out with me," I tease.

Miles doesn't seem to like that. Fire flashes in his warm green eyes, and he steps to me. "I don't think he would."

"No?"

"No."

"Why is that?"

"Because you know how I feel about you." He steps closer. "You can go out with any man you want, but know that I won't give up on you. I'm going to show you that I'm the only man worth your time, sweetheart."

My stomach clenches and then my breath quickens. I want so badly to be someone else. A girl who could step to him, ask him how he feels. To give myself over to these damn feelings. To know that I could have a life, love, friendship, or even just a damn good time.

Then I think about what is in my past, the men who want to kill me and my son.

But what life am I living anyway?

I live in fear and if I tell him what this can be, and he accepts it, it could be enough.

"Miles," I say his name softly. "There are . . . things in my life . . .

and I can't . . ." This is so fucking hard. Part of what Quinn has said is that I can't tell anyone. The entire point of me staying hidden is that no one can know. I huff, suck in a breath, and say what I feel safe saying. "I like you. I like you, even knowing it isn't a good idea, and that scares me."

He takes another step forward, his hand moving to my face, and I flinch. "Penny, I'm not going to hurt you."

My jaw trembles. "In my past, I made bad choices, and those decisions had consequences. One of them is that I don't trust easily. I also will always put Kai first. Always."

"I would never ask you to put your son anywhere but in the front."

This is why it's so easy to like him. He's . . . amazing.

And he can never be mine. Not when I know I wouldn't be strong enough to leave him. If I let him in, he'd take hold of my heart and I'd never get it back.

For Kai, I have to be strong and be ready to protect him.

"I can't date you."

"You can."

I laugh once. "I can't, Miles. I can't do it."

"Why? Tell me one good reason and I promise I'll stop."

I don't want him to stop.

Which makes me want to cry, because he's literally offering exactly what I'm asking for. Yet it's not what I actually want.

I hate my life some days.

"Because I'm not ready to date anyone, and even though I care about you, it doesn't change things. I . . . ." I move closer, my hand resting over his beating heart. "I can't give you more than this. We can do these coincidental dates and the flirting, but I can't be in a serious relationship. Right now, I need to focus on getting my life together and making sure Kai is safe and happy."

His finger moves under my chin and tilts it up. "And who is going to make sure you're safe and happy?"

"Me."

He shakes his head. "No, sweetheart, you have me to do that for you too. I hear what you're saying and I understand it. You have a past? I do too. I'm sorry anyone ever hurt you, but I never want to be the cause of any pain in your life. So we'll coincidentally keep running into each other. Maybe we can happen to see each other for dinner tomorrow?"

I can't say anything because I'm pretty sure I'm about to break down in tears, so I nod. "Maybe around six?"

"I could maybe bring something to the house and we could eat?"

My head and my heart are at war. I want everything with him, but then I can't find a way to convince myself that it's okay.

But then I think about what my sister-in-law said. What Ainsley and Hazel say about Miles and who he is. All the things he's shown me over and over and . . . we've already shared moments and I'm still standing.

What if I . . . took a small part of it?

What if I give in to just something?

Before I lose my nerve, I speak. "Miles?"

"What, sweetheart?"

I breathe in, giving myself a sliver of permission. "Could you maybe kiss me?" I ask.

"I can definitely kiss you. If that's what you want."

He leans down, his mouth just a breath away from mine. It feels like a choice. That he's allowing me the option whether or not to let it go further. He has no idea how much that little pause means to me.

My hands move up his chest, cupping his face, and I bring our lips together and melt into his touch.

———

All day I've been a bundle of nerves. Each time the door chimed that there was a customer, I kept hoping it was him. Then, as I was leaving for work, I thought maybe Miles would be there at my car. Why? I have no idea. I just wanted to see him.

Instead of him showing up, Justin, the tree man, as I've now dubbed him, is here on my front step with a shovel and a *tree*.

"Hi, Justin."

"Ma'am. It's good to see you."

"You as well. Are you doing okay?"

"I am."

That's good. "Did my landlord not pay you, or is there another tree with an issue?"

He shakes his head. "No, ma'am. I'm here with a note and directions to stay until you've made a decision."

"Okay . . ."

I take the note from him and smile.

Penny,

Trees have roots and roots grow deep. I think you should put some roots down here in Ember Falls. Make Justin plant this anywhere you want where you can watch it grow.

Miles

"Why does he have to be so sweet?" I ask aloud.

"I think his gran has a lot to do with it," Justin replies.

I look up, forgetting he was there. "Right. Sorry. So you have to plant this?"

"Miles gave me strict instructions you could decide where it went, and I'm not allowed to leave until it's in the dirt."

"I see. What if I don't know where to put it yet?"

Justin looks a little afraid and shifts his weight. "Umm, well, then I guess we can put it in a pot and just tell him it was planted."

I burst out laughing. "I think that defeats his purpose, but I sort of love the idea."

"Do you want to do that then?"

"Yes, let's do that. I think I saw a big enough pot out in the shed."

"All right."

I head to where the previous owner had a lot of gardening supplies. Back in the corner is a huge ceramic pot that will be perfect. It'll also be funny, since I know for sure that this isn't what Miles had in mind.

I heft the thing out of the corner and roll it. After ten minutes and sweat trickling down my forehead, I call for Justin.

He comes back, and together we move it close to where the tree that almost took out my house is.

"Do you think you can put it here?" I ask.

"Not a problem. I'll get some soil and be back to get it done."

"Thank you."

I head back out front to unload the few groceries I picked up for dinner tonight while Kai is at practice. Since Miles is going to just happen to stop by tonight, I needed to make something really good.

Not that I'm that great of a cook, but I can google like the best of them.

I'm going with something that I've done a few times and was good: pork chops, stuffing, and my grandma's homemade macaroni and cheese.

I check my watch and hurry out the door. "Justin, I have to run to get my son. Are you okay to head out the side yard?"

"Yes, ma'am. I'll let Miles know it's in dirt."

I chuckle. "Good play on words. Thank you again!"

"Of course."

The entire drive I can't wipe the smile off my face. He's so sweet to give me a tree and the note and to have Justin actually plant it. Just . . . so freaking adorable.

I find a parking spot, and Eloise is outside the rink. "Hey!"

"Hey, Eloise. How are you?"

"I'm good. Cora is finally sleeping more, which means I'm sleeping more. Doug goes to the doctor tomorrow, where hopefully he's cleared to start weight bearing, and then . . . I might fly to Mexico and leave him with the kids."

"Take me with you," I joke.

"Don't tempt me with a good time." She sighs. "Anyway, how are you? I heard that you have learned of our magical secret of the town?"

"That news traveled fast."

She shrugs. "I got coffee with Ainsley this morning and it came up. Lachlan's land owns half of the falls, and the other half is Gran's. I was mentioning that we were going tonight and would probably take the kids down to swim."

I didn't know that. No one mentioned that Lachlan owned the falls. "I didn't know anyone owned them."

This town is just full of surprises. I will say, the falls were pretty cool, and I can't wait to hear more of the history of them.

"Did Miles tell you the stories behind it?"

"He said I needed to be dating someone."

She bursts out laughing. "Did he?"

"I'm going to guess that's not true."

Eloise shakes her head. "No, but then again, it might be. We learned about them when we were kids, since it was our backyard growing up. You know what? He might be right. There is all kinds of weird shit in the town oath. Anyway, I'm glad you know now and you're an official Ember Fallsian."

My heart swells at those stupid words. She thinks I belong here, and I have never felt more at home since moving here. I want to always stay here, but wants aren't truths, and I'll have to face that at some point.

I force a smile, not letting the sadness take over. "Thank you for the welcome."

We head inside just as practice is finishing up. It's the part of their day they love the most. They get to hit pucks at Miles. I laugh as he gets pelted over and over again and that there seems to be a frying pan-looking thing hanging from his belt.

"Oh dear lord," Eloise says when there's a loud gong sound as the puck hits his makeshift cup. "That would've hurt."

I would agree with her there. Another puck hits the same spot, and Miles points his finger at Ethan, who laughs and then lines up for another swack at the puck and once again hits the pan.

"Ethan has great aim," I say.

"He really does. That kid is outside all the time hitting pucks into the net. He loves it, and he loves figuring out how to make them go where he wants. I'm pretty sure my brother is going to stop this drill now that Ethan is aiming for his balls."

Practice stops and the boys filter off the ice.

"Mom! Did you see us?" Kai yells as he rushes to me.

"I did. You boys did so good."

"Ethan is amazing. He was able to hit Coach Miles four times!"

Miles is heading toward us, his dark-brown hair is pushed back, and he has his gloves slung over his shoulder. There's something incredibly sexy about a man a little sweaty and rugged after playing a sport.

"Eloise," he says as he walks over. "Your son is trying to ensure I don't have children."

"Miles, you're the one who taught him hockey. You only have yourself to blame."

He turns to me. "Are you like this with your brother?"

I shrug. "Sometimes."

Eloise links her arm in mine. "Us sisters have to make sure you boys know your place. Are you coming for dinner tonight?"

He looks to me. "Coincidentally, I have plans tonight. I'll come by tomorrow, though, hang out with Doug, and watch the game."

She jerks her head back. "Plans? With who?"

"None of your business." Then Miles smiles. "It's a nondate date."

I can feel the heat flaming from my cheeks when Eloise's gaze moves to mine. Her smile widens, and the knots in my stomach tighten. She totally looks as if she would break out into song and dance.

"A date?"

I shake my head. "No. Not a date."

"She doesn't date. Not on purpose at least."

I huff and roll my eyes. Now he's making me sound ridiculous. "That's not what I said."

Eloise looks intrigued. "How does one date accidentally?"

"It's more of . . . if we're in the same place at the same time thing."

"So you're just going to stop by Penny's house when she's making dinner?"

Miles raises his brows with a smirk on his perfect lips. "It'll be a happy coincidence if it happens."

"If I'm making dinner."

"Maybe I'll find out in an hour."

"Maybe you will."

sixteen
Penelope

Miles should be here any minute and I'm back in my bedroom, changing my shirt for the sixth time.

I'm not sure what I should wear. I want to look cute, but not like I'm trying to look cute. So I have on a crop sweatshirt from college with the neck off, a pair of leggings, and my hair up in a topknot.

Cute, but casual.

"Mom! Someone is at the door!" Kai yells.

I take a deep breath, blow it out, and head toward the door. When I open it, it's not Miles there, it's my brother.

"Quinn?"

He smiles broadly. "Hello, sister."

I blink and my pulse races. "Is everything okay?"

"Yes, completely fine. I'm just here to see you and Kai. I wanted to call but thought it would be more fun to surprise you."

"Fun. Right."

As much as I absolutely love my brother and always want to see him, *fun* isn't the word I would use for any time he just shows up. The minute I saw him, all I could think was—this is it. We have to leave again.

"Are you angry?" he asks.

"No, not at all, just . . . you know, when you show up without a call, it's not usually because you missed us."

"I'm sorry, Pen. Can I come in?" he asks sheepishly.

"Of course." I step back and allow my brother to enter.

Kai pokes his head out and yells as soon as he sees his uncle. "Uncle Quinn!"

"What's up, bud?"

He scoops him in his arms and then ruffles his hair. "I had an awesome day at hockey today! I got a goal two times."

My brother smiles, pride showing on his face. "I knew you'd be great at sports, just like I was."

I fight back a laugh. "You weren't great."

"I was better than you," Quinn tosses back.

He's not wrong. I swam, but more because my mother said I had to play one sport or join band. Since I have zero musical ability, I went with swimming since I was fairly decent at it. Quinn was a three-season player and was marginally good at each one.

"*Anyway*, neither of us were great."

He chuckles. "You're ruining my street cred."

I place my hand over my chest. "I'm so sorry." My eyes meet Kai's. "Your uncle was the best there ever was."

"Better than Coach Miles?"

"Probably not, but for your uncle's sake, let's pretend."

Quinn huffs. "I heard that."

I smile. "I wasn't whispering."

Quinn places his hand on Kai's shoulder. "Did you finish the Lego set?" Kai shakes his head. "Why don't we work on that in a little bit. I'm just going to hang with your mom for a little, okay?"

Kai looks at him like he hung the moon. "Okay! Can I go play my game, Mom?"

"Go ahead."

He rushes out and Quinn looks to me. "He reminds me so much of you."

"Me?"

"Yeah, you loved games and I freaking hated them. Gabriel is the same. All he wants is to play that one building-a-world game online or watch people on the internet do it. Which is a whole other level of confusion for me."

I laugh softly. "Yeah, I don't know how that became a thing. Kai likes to watch them play, almost more than I think he likes to play."

It honestly confuses me. What is fun about watching someone build a world when you could do it yourself? What's even more confounding is some of these people are making a fortune. While I'm just making coffee.

"Kids are weird."

"I'm glad we weren't like that."

Quinn scoffs. "Dad would've kicked our asses right outside."

"He didn't need to. We wanted to be outside from the minute we woke up."

It was a different time. I know this, but truly we longed to be outside playing with our friends. Quinn and I would scarf down our breakfast and be out the front door before we finished chewing.

Now it's like pulling teeth to get Kai to play out back.

To be fair, there's not much to do as an only child. I had the luxury of a brother who had no shortage of ways to find trouble.

"Well, I'm glad you came to say hi."

He pulls me against his side. "Me too."

We head into the open kitchen area, and my brother looks around. "Were you expecting someone?"

"Huh?" I ask, surprise in my voice.

He tilts his head toward the table. "You have three place settings."

"Yeah," I say quickly. "He's a neighbor and . . . umm . . . Kai's hockey coach. He was going to come by."

Quinn, who doesn't miss a damn thing, crosses his arms over his chest. "He?"

"It's not what you think."

"What do I think?"

That this is a date, which it's not. It's just a coincidence.

I'm such a liar. It's totally a date.

"I'm not dating anyone. I'm not going to make the same mistakes," I explain.

My brother steps forward, his arms dropping. "Whoa, whoa, Penelope, slow down there. Way to jump to conclusions."

"I'm not. I'm just saying that I don't want to relive history. I'm not going to put myself or Kai in that situation again."

"That's not what I was thinking. I don't think you're stupid or going to be in a worse-off situation. I think you're brave and strong to have called me and let us get you out of the position you were in. I think you're an incredible mother who has literally sacrificed everything just to keep Kai safe. If you want to date, you should."

I shake my head. "And what? Where does it go? How do I explain any of it?"

He sighs. "I don't know, but we put you in Ember Falls because it's safe. I've gone over every lead, trail, anything that could lead anyone here, and it doesn't exist. Our communications and cyber guys do constant checks and leave bad intel just in case his people were to find anything. You're safe here, Penelope."

I wish so badly that I could believe that. "Did you put me in an unsafe situation in Tennessee?"

"No."

"Then why am I in Ember Falls? Because nothing is safe for too long. They found me then, they'll find me again."

Quinn comes closer. "No, they won't."

"You can't promise that."

"You're right. I can't."

The admission causes me to jerk back. "What?"

"I can't promise it. I can't promise that a tree wouldn't almost fall on your house either. I can't promise that things won't go wrong. I shouldn't have said that to you."

I hear his words and a part of me hates them. "Okay."

"I also can't promise that Edward's men won't meet their untimely demise. That you'll spend the next ten years in Ember Falls without a single issue. I can't promise you anything, Penelope, other than you're safe right now and I'll do everything to keep you safe."

He doesn't get it. "And that means that dating someone isn't a good idea."

"Why?"

"Why?" I repeat him, my anger growing. "Because I could . . . I could fall for Miles."

"And?"

I swear, I love my brother, but I might have to kill him.

"That would be terrible."

"You know, you'd think after being married for years, I'd finally understand women, but I don't. So what if you fall in love? You can't predict the future, Penelope. Miles is a great guy from what I can tell."

Now I'm stunned. "What can you tell?"

"Did you think I wasn't going to run background checks on everyone you're around? Miles has an exceptional military service record. Not as good as mine, but, you know, I'm a grade-A badass."

"I had another adjective in mind," I say, cutting him off.

"He's loved by his staff as well as all the students he's taught and been around. The town loves him. I couldn't find any red flags, and trust me, I looked. I know this might sound stupid, but if you were going to fall for someone in the town, I'm glad it's him." Quinn takes a step forward. "He'd protect you, Penny. Honestly, I feel better just knowing there is someone like him in this town."

Little does he know, he already has when he thought I was in danger. I think about Miles's face when he got to me. How he drove up this road, during the worst of the storm to make sure Kai and I were okay.

I can't imagine he'd ever let anything happen to us.

That said, I never want to test it, and I will always choose Kai's safety, even if it means I have to hurt myself or anyone else.

"I don't want to hurt him or Kai."

"I think you're worried about another person hurting too, Penny." My brother calls me out, just like Ashton did earlier.

"I'm worried about everyone getting hurt."

My brother takes two steps forward. "I'm doing everything I can. We keep searching, and I promise I'm trying to make sense of the information."

"I know, and I'm stuck because I can't go to the police about it. I can't explain these half theories to anyone. They'd laugh and they're also involved, if I understand the part of the book I read."

Quinn, who has been trained to hunt, kill, protect, and always do what's right, steps closer. "I will find the answers. I know it's been years. I know we've been working on it for what feels like forever, but when you have a crime ring this big, this . . . established, it's not easy."

Both he and his team have explained it, and I'm fully aware. This involves people with a lot of money and even more power. When we are able to do something about it, we will, but until then, this is my life.

"And that's why I can't let myself get sucked into this pretend life."

Quinn reaches his hand out, resting it on my shoulder. "That's where you're wrong, Penny. This is the life you have. We only get one. We don't get to go back and make different choices based on the knowledge we get afterward. You aren't living anything pretend, this is what it is, so take hold of it and live it, Penelope."

"Just to lose it?" I ask as my tears come unbidden.

"I would've rather ripped the heart from my chest, stomped on it, felt every ounce of pain possible, than to never have loved Ashton. Take the hurt, because without it, you will never know what real happiness feels like."

That might be the most beautiful thing I've ever heard. I think about his words and what it all means for me. Is it better to protect my heart? Is staying away from Miles even possible? I like him a lot. I want to be with him, but the fear of what could happen keeps me from taking that jump.

I think about Kai. How much it would hurt him to get closer to Miles and then to have to leave.

"And what happens if I get close to him, I have to build a relationship on a bed of lies."

Quinn's face falls slightly. "I know, and I would bet he knows how hard keeping secrets is. There were so many times I couldn't tell you the truth about where I was, what I was doing, and lying is never fun, but you don't have to lie, just omit parts of your past. Once we have this missing person file under control, which Gretchen is working on, I'll let you know it's safe to tell him more."

"I'm scared," I admit, wringing my hands.

"I think you have every right to be, but you have a lot of people who are doing what we can to protect you. Trust us. Trust me, Penny, I wouldn't let anything hurt you." A tear falls down my cheek and my brother, unable to handle any type of emotion, shakes his head and steps back. "All right, enough of that shit, now I'm going to build Legos with my nephew and crash your date."

———

I go to grab my phone to send a text to Miles, warning him that our date is *really* not going to be a date, since my brother is here, but before I can fire off a text, there's a knock on the door.

"Penny, your date is here!" Quinn yells, and I groan.

"Please behave," I implore my brother.

He chuckles and I can imagine the shit-eating grin that's probably on his face.

I send off a silent prayer that I can get through tonight without my brother making me want to scream and open the door. "Hey."

Miles has a wide smile and then moves his hand from behind his back, and I wait to see flowers, but . . . it's a garden hand shovel. "Hi."

"Oh. Umm. Thanks?"

"It's so that you can plant around the tree." He chuckles nervously when he sees the expression on my face. "You know . . . I should've just gotten you flowers."

"No! No, it's perfect. It's really thoughtful and cute. Thank you."

His eyes narrow slightly. "Liar."

"I'm not. I love it." I extend my hand, taking the shovel from his grasp. "However . . . I have to warn you."

Apprehension fills his eyes. "Warn me?"

And then my door opens a little from behind me and I gasp. "That her brother dropped in unexpectedly," Quinn says, and I realize my prayers are not going to be answered.

seventeen
Miles

Her brother being present on our first nondate date isn't great, but nothing seems to go easy with me and Penelope. However, she's worth it, and as a big brother myself, I get it.

I extend my hand with a smile. "Miles Anderson, nice to meet you."

"Quinn Walker, nice to meet you as well."

"Coach Miles!" Kai runs out and I squat down to give him a hug. "My uncle Quinn who was in the navy is here!"

"I see that." I stand back up. "We loved you navy guys. You were great at giving us a ride."

He chuckles. "I didn't give anyone a ride. I came in to save your asses when you got lost. It's fine, though. I just love having marines indebted to me."

Penelope sighs. "Great, it's going to be like this all night."

"We're just getting it out of the way," Quinn says. "So the more important question is . . . what's your favorite football team?"

"What's yours?" I ask, not wanting to give my hand away too quickly.

Quinn's eyes narrow and then he laughs. "Well played. I think we'll be just fine. As long as it's not someone from the NFC East."

Well, good thing I didn't say my team then. Otherwise, this would've made for an even more uncomfortable night.

We head into the kitchen area, where there's a small table off to the right that's set for three, indicating she wasn't expecting her brother. We all take our seats, and there's a dish with pork chops, mac and cheese, stuffing, and a salad.

"So, Miles, Penny said you're the principal at the high school?" Quinn asks, leaning forward, resting his arms on the table.

"I am. I got promoted about five years ago."

"Do you like it?"

"I love it," I admit. "I didn't think I would, but it's been a really great experience. Unless I'm having teachers quit at the last minute and doing interviews with people who shouldn't be near children." I chuckle.

Penny giggles and that sound, so musical, so sweet, makes me want to hear it more and more. She doesn't laugh like that often, and man . . . I plan to change that.

"Miles had a pretty interesting string of interviews yesterday."

I nod. "It was ridiculous, but it led to a great end of the day." I look to her, hoping she knows I mean I got to be with her.

Penelope's cheeks turn the most beautiful shade of pink, and then she looks away.

Quinn clears his throat. "I'm not sure I could handle being with kids all day. I have a seven-year-old, and I can't imagine having that nonstop. Although some days it feels like I deal with children in my line of work."

"What are you doing now that you're out of the service?" I ask him.

"I work for a start-up company in Virginia Beach."

"Oh? A start-up for what?"

If I weren't who I was, I wouldn't have noticed the little tic in his jaw or the slightest drifting of his gaze to the left, but I was also trained well.

"Internet security."

The way he says that has my senses tingling. He's withholding something.

"Probably something you'll excel in. I wish your company a lot of success," I say, wanting to assure him that I believe the lie. He clearly is doing something secretive, and it's not my business.

"I'd like to think I'm good at everything security based. We're not a group to let anything happen to the people we're working with. We know when to act on something and when not to."

And there he just confirmed it. To Penny or anyone else, they might miss it, but he just told me that he knows I know he lied, and he respects that I didn't push.

"I understand that. I, too, am very protective of my kids and the people I care about."

Penelope looks to me, then to her brother, then back to me. "I feel like this conversation is like a secret message between you two, and I'm okay not being involved. However, dinner is done."

We both smile, and I take the bowl of salad from her. "Thank you for making dinner."

"Thank you for everything. Kai and I would've been miserable if you hadn't come to our rescue during that storm, right, Kai?"

Kai nods. "Your house is so cool. Uncle Quinn, Miles's house has power all the time. No matter if it storms and he has a room we made into a fort!"

Quinn chuckles. "I love a good fort." Then he turns to me. "I appreciate you coming up here. I heard about the tree almost falling on the house. I'm glad my sister and nephew were safe."

"There's no need to thank me." I would've done anything for them.

Penny speaks up. "This side of Ember Falls isn't as inhabited as the other. Miles was just being neighborly."

"I wouldn't say that," I explain. "I didn't check on Mr. Kipland."

She drops her head, but I catch the smile beforehand. "Well, not during the storm, but we did after. So you still care in a neighborly way."

"No, I came because I was worried about both of you."

I meet her brother's gaze, and he doesn't hide his gratitude, nodding once. I return the gesture and pass the bowl.

Dinner is easy, and the conversation flows effortlessly. Quinn and Penny tell childhood stories, and Kai is close to bouncing out of his seat when he talks about how much he loves hockey practice.

I know I went into coaching the team begrudgingly, but it's actually been a lot of fun. The kids are all great, and the fact that Kai has made friends with Ethan makes it better.

Quinn stretches and then places both hands on the table. "Well, I better get going."

"I'm glad you stopped by," Penny says, placing her hand on his. "Next time maybe call first."

He chuckles. "And ruin the fun? Never."

"It was great meeting you," I say as I get to my feet and extend my hand.

"I feel the same. Be good to my sister."

"I will."

Penelope huffs. "Come on, let's get you in the car." She places both hands on Quinn's back and pushes him toward the front door. Kai follows them, laughing.

I start to clean up in the kitchen, giving them all time. As I'm washing the dishes, she comes back in.

"Miles! What are you doing?" she yells.

"The dishes."

"Yes, I know that, but please stop. You're my guest."

I want to be much more than that.

"And you fed me. The least I can do is clean up."

"This night is really not going the way I expected," she says under her breath.

I chuckle. "Where's Kai?"

"Getting in the shower and ready for bed. Please, I beg you. Leave the dishes."

"How about you dry and I'll wash?" I offer.

She shakes her head but grabs the towel and leans against the counter. "Thank you for doing the dishes and being so great with my brother."

I smile warmly. "What, you don't bring your big brother on all your dates?"

Penny laughs. "I don't. It was definitely unexpected. I thought that we were . . . going to be able to . . . you know?"

"No, tell me," I push.

"You just want to hear me say have a date?"

"I really do."

She laughs softly. "Well, too bad. I'm not going to say it. We were having dinner so I could thank you."

"Well, then, I guess we're going to have to have a proper date."

There's something in her eyes. Something that wasn't there before. A little bit of trust mixed with desire. She wants to date me. She just doesn't want to want it.

She pulls her lower lip between her teeth. "You think so?"

I can't explain in words what it is about her, but I'm drawn to her. I want to be her comfort, her safe place, the person she can't wait to tell good or bad news to. I want to be her person, the one who soothes her worries and gives her a reason to smile.

Looking at her, with that soft expression in her eyes, tugs at my heart.

She's afraid, and the need to relieve that is too much to ignore.

I put the dish down, shut the water off, and turn to her. "What has you hesitating?"

Her blue eyes are watery. "I don't want to hurt you. And most of all, I don't want to let Kai or myself get hurt."

"The last thing I want to do is hurt you or Kai."

"I know."

Does she? I wonder if she truly believes that.

"Then trust me." I step closer, placing my hands on her waist. "Let me take you out tomorrow."

"Tomorrow?"

I nod. "Tomorrow. I'll have Eloise watch Kai and we can go out."

She sighs, and her hands move to my chest. "Okay. One date."

I grin. "I'm going to kiss you so it officially seals this deal."

I bring my lips to hers before she has a chance to reply, and she melts into me. I hold her tightly as we share one of the most innocent and intimate kisses I've ever had in my life.

I could spend the rest of my life doing this. Cleaning up after dinner, kissing her in the kitchen, and then carrying her to bed and doing a hell of a lot more than that.

But for now we'll start with a date tomorrow, when I plan to secure many more in the future.

eighteen
Penelope

"I have nothing to wear!" I complain to Hazel as she's sitting on my bed.

I didn't plan to tell her about the date, but Eloise couldn't watch Kai. Hazel was my next choice and she could tell I was being weird and jumpy, so I finally caved and she offered to watch him.

"I honestly think what you had on was great."

I glance at the jeans and lacy top that's on the bed and groan. "It was giving 'trying too hard.'"

Hazel chuckles. "Shirts can do that." She gets up and grabs the blue off-the-shoulder top. "What about this and the jeans? That way the top is a little sexy, but jeans are super casual."

Do I want to be sexy? No, because we're going to have this one date, and then I need to figure out my life. I know my brother thinks I should live, and I want to, but my heart doesn't have the ability to keep a part held back.

If I let myself date him, I'll fall.

I've already fallen way farther than I ever intended to.

The way he looks at me, kisses me, makes my heart flutter—it's a problem.

And here I am now, trying to find the perfect first-date outfit.

"Maybe I'll wear sweats and a stained shirt," I say, feeling like an idiot.

Her brows raise. "Considering he has feelings for you after seeing you at work with coffee grinds all over and during the storm, I think your plan is flawed."

I laugh. "Great."

"Penny, he doesn't care about any of this. He cares about you and wants to give you a fun date."

"I care."

She lifts one shoulder. "Okay, what did the text say?"

I grab my phone and read it again.

MILES

I'll pick you up at six. We're going to dinner and something after. Very casual and wear sneakers.

She purses her lips. "Okay, jeans for sure, and I think the crochet top or the off-the-shoulder will fit both."

Kai comes running in my room. "Where are you going, Mom?"

"I'm going with Coach Miles for a little while. Hazel is going to hang here with you."

"Can I come?" he asks, nearly bouncing up and down.

"No, buddy, it'll just be me this time."

He looks crestfallen. "But I want to go with Coach Miles."

I smile and press my hand to his cheek. "Maybe another time."

Hazel jumps in. "Hey! I'm a hoot. We're going to have way more fun than they will."

Kai doesn't look like he buys it, but he smiles anyway. "If you say so."

I burst out laughing, and so does Hazel. I spend the next twenty minutes getting ready. I curl the bottom of my hair, letting it fall in ribbons down my back, and go for a subtle smoky eye, not that it really looks like a smoky eye, because I'm terrible at makeup, but I try.

I decide to go with the crochet top because it's cute, but also casual. I come out, and Hazel makes a long whistle. "And you are trying to downplay this? Girl, you look hot!"

"Ugh, I can't go."

But before I can turn to go anywhere, there's a knock at the door. "Do you want to tell him or do you want me to?" she asks.

"Yeah, right, you'll just tell him where I am."

She shrugs.

Putting aside my fear, I open the door. Miles is there, this time with a beautiful bouquet of peonies, which happen to be my favorite.

"These are stunning."

He smiles. "Better than the shovel?"

I laugh softly. "Well, prettier at least."

Kai runs over, giving him a big hug, and Miles ruffles his hair. "Hey, little man."

"Can I come out too, Coach?"

I sigh heavily. "Kai, I already said no. Maybe another time, though."

Hazel comes over. "You guys go. I've got Kai, and we're going to have our own fun tonight."

My heart is racing at the idea of tonight. Not just because it's been, like, a million years since I've gone on a date, but also because I'm leaving Kai. I keep hearing Quinn in my head, telling me we're safe and that I should live my life, but my life never feels safe.

It's hard to explain to anyone not living it, but my life feels as though I'm walking on a balance beam, and at any point my footing will falter and I'll fall.

I squat down so I'm eye to eye with Kai. "Be good for Hazel and remember the rules, okay?"

He nods. "I won't break them, Mom."

I kiss his nose. "Have fun and I'll see you soon."

"Now go, you two crazy kids. Have a good time and don't do anything I wouldn't do," Hazel says, shooing us both out.

I grab my purse and Miles places his hand on the small of my back, leading me to the car. He opens the door, and I smile at the gesture. "Thank you."

He winks and then shuts the door.

My nerves continue to grow, but I promised myself I'd get through tonight and do my best not to be a basket case.

I've left Kai a few times since living here, and everything has been okay. It will be fine this time too.

"Ready for our date?" Miles asks.

I nod once. "I am."

"Good."

"Where are we going?" I ask.

Miles backs the truck out of the drive and grins. "Dinner, and then after we will be doing something fun. I promise."

"Oh boy. The fact that you had to promise tells me that it might not be fun."

"Or it's telling you that it's going to be the most fun you've ever had because I'm a pretty fun guy."

I smile. "You are, huh?"

"I am. There's a poll that went around town, and I was definitely the winner."

"Well, if there's an official poll, how can that be disputed?" I tease.

"Exactly."

As we drive, my nerves settle a little. The more I'm around Miles, the safer I feel. However, even as we're driving, he's hyperaware, almost as though he's assessing the risks and possible danger at every corner.

We chat about our days and how he's a little sad that tomorrow is the last hockey practice.

"I've loved working with the kids," he admits. "I'm around miniature adults all day that act like kids, but when I'm at clinic with the boys, it's just the fun. They're funny and willing to learn. I can see why Doug likes to coach Ethan's teams."

"I have no athletic ability, so I just appreciate that there are parents and uncles who will step in," I say, shifting to face him. "I'm glad that you were Kai's coach."

"I am too, Penelope. I am too." The deep timbre in his voice leads me to think it's not only because he likes Kai and the other boys.

I clear my throat. "Right. Well, I know Kai will be sad he won't see you every week."

"He won't, huh?"

"Well, I mean, the clinic is over."

He grins. "That's not where I plan to see him."

Oh.

He means me.

Sometimes I am so awkward it's beyond embarrassing.

"You're anticipating this to go beyond this date?"

"I told you, I'm a catch. You're not going to want our date to end."

I chuckle and then clear my throat. "I see. You're going with the lay-it-on-thick strategy?"

"It's more like the honesty and confidence side of it."

"Isn't the motto usually underpromise and overdeliver?"

"I'm more of a promise what you can deliver on," he says with a smirk.

Could this man be any more adorable? I sure hope not.

Miles finds a spot right in front of the restaurant that's a town over. Ember Falls has some options, but none of the places in town are fine dining. It's more pizza, and there's a bar at the end of Main Street.

"I hope you like whatever they're serving tonight," he says with a laugh.

"What does that mean?"

"Their menu . . . well, it's the best we're going to get unless we want to drive an hour. It changes each day, depending on what side of the bed Marge wakes up on. Some days she feels a bit French, other days she thinks Italian. We just never know until we show up."

"That's . . . one business model."

Not really sure how that works, but then again, we're not the only car here, so clearly the people in the area just go with it.

"It's something. I should also warn you that Marge is my gran's best friend. She is going to do everything in her power to embarrass me. Anything she says is a lie."

"Anything?"

"Literally anything."

I grin. "So if she says you're a great guy . . ."

"I retract my last statement. Anything *bad* she says is a lie. I didn't do it. I was the perfect child growing up. I have many great attributes and zero bad. No matter what she says."

My lips form a tight line as I attempt to withhold my laughter. The look on his face is part fear and part joy. "I'll do my best to keep the good and discard the bad."

"Good. Stay there."

Is this also a drive-through? I'm so confused.

Then Miles is at my door, opening it. "My lady." He extends his hand.

Okay, he *can* be cuter. Damn it.

I place my hand in his, allowing him to help me out of the truck. However, he doesn't let go once I'm safely on the ground, and he tucks my hand into the crook of his arm.

We walk inside, where a woman nearly screams when she sees him. She's short with long gray hair and big-rimmed glasses, and she clearly loves Miles. She rushes around the hostess booth and slaps his chest.

"You little stinker! You didn't tell me you were coming for dinner."

"Marge, this is Penelope, my date. I didn't tell you because I thought the surprise would be more fun."

Her gaze goes to me, and she has one of those smiles that is so much like a parent. Her eyes are full of warmth, and it's clear she's happy Miles is on a date. "Hello, beautiful girl. It's so nice to meet you. I'm Auntie Marge, and I've known Miles since the day they slapped him on the ass when he was born."

"It's great to meet you," I say, stifling a laugh. I have a feeling I'm going to be doing that a lot tonight.

"I'll tell you, he was a handful, but oh"—she clutches her chest —"the way he could melt your heart with that smile. He's the best, but you know that, since you're on a date with him, I suppose."

"He's definitely the best," I agree.

"He does have bad qualities," Marge says quickly. "I don't want you to get the impression that he's perfect. No man is. Trust me on that. They're all a little dense and often stupid too."

"Same meaning," Miles cuts in.

"See what I mean, had to correct me. You know, they never learn either. I've been married to my husband, William, for sixty-one years. Sixty-one. It's like . . . purgatory without an end other than death."

Miles sighs. "Regrets. So many regrets."

She elbows him in the stomach.

This time my laugh does escape. I seriously love this place, and I haven't even stepped past the entrance.

"I bet you'll have regrets when I'm done telling her all the things about you, Miles Anderson."

"How about we don't and you feed us whatever is on the menu? It's our first date, and I'd like to make sure there's the option of a second."

Marge clutches her hands to her chest. "First date? And you brought her here? Oh, I'm just so honored. Come, let's get you the best table."

We follow her in and Miles leans close. "I warned you."

"I love her," I whisper back.

She sits us in the back corner. The restaurant is old, but clearly loved. It has a cabin-like feel with exposed logs and glass chandeliers that have one individual light. All the tables have white tablecloths and a single candle in the middle.

"Here, this is the lovers' nook."

"I'm sure it's not," Miles says with a sigh.

"It could be if you don't mess it up."

I snort and place my napkin on my lap.

Marge looks to me. "Would you like some wine?"

"I'd love some."

"For you?" she asks Miles.

"Whatever you bring will be great. Not like I think you'd bring what I ask for anyway."

She shrugs. "If you made the right choice, I'd bring it."

"Okay, I'll have a beer," he says.

"Wine it is."

Marge walks off, and Miles looks at me with a smile. "Sorry, I should've known better."

"You have nothing to be sorry for, this is amazing and she's amazing."

He stares off in the direction she left. "She really was like a second mother to me. Marge would watch me and Eloise when Gran was working or just needed a break. She and Uncle Will mean the world to me. He's who taught me how to skate, and he put a hockey stick in my hand for the first time when I was ten. Not having a mom or a dad was hard when I got older, but this community of people in our lives softened the blow."

Hearing that makes me ache for him because it's eerily similar to what Kai is experiencing.

"I think being a parent is the hardest job in the world, but add on when you're doing it alone, it sometimes feels impossible."

He reaches his hand out, resting it on top of mine. "You're doing the impossible. Never doubt that. Kai is a great kid, and he's so lucky to have you as his mother."

The guilt that settles in my gut makes it hard to breathe. If he knew . . .

If he was aware of the person I let into my life, who I loved, who I trusted, would he think Kai was lucky?

I think he'd see me as a fool.

Marge appears back at the table and places our wine down, causing us to break apart. "Have you looked at the menu?" she asks.

"Not yet," I admit with a smile.

She takes it from us both. "Don't. I'll make something just fabulous and unique that will be an aphrodisiac. Maybe oysters! Those are supposed to do the trick. Oh! And definitely chocolate with pomegranate for dessert. Yes, we'll just load you two up on them."

Miles covers his face with his hands. "I should've taken you for fast food."

Marge humphs. "Please, I'm just helping here. Lord knows you need all the help you can get." She turns to me. "He's how old and never married? His sister is married, two kids, and this one over here can't get it together." Seeming to realize what she said, her eyes widen. "Not that it's a bad thing. I'm sure he's just looking for the perfect woman, you know." She winks.

Oh my God, she's the best.

"I'm sure he'll find her."

She pulls her head back. "Honey, what if you're her?"

Miles clears his throat. "First date. First date, Aunt Marge. Let's cool it. We don't need oysters, which I don't even think you've ever made."

Her back straightens, and she turns her head slowly to look at him. "I haven't, but I'm a chef and I can make anything. However, by the time your uncle gets his shoes on and finds oysters, it'll be tomorrow, so . . . I'll cook you both our special for the night." Her eyes find mine. "Are you allergic to anything, sweetheart?"

I shake my head. "No, ma'am."

"Good."

And then she's off again.

I glance down at my phone once more, making sure I don't have any missed calls or texts—so far nothing.

"Everything okay?" Miles asks.

"Huh?"

"You keep checking your phone."

"Oh, just making sure Kai hasn't called."

He smiles warmly. "Do you want to check on him?"

I bite the corner of my lower lip. "Do you mind?"

"Of course not. Call him."

Immediately my anxiety settles a little. I get up and head to the front, dialing the phone that Quinn gave him.

"Hi, Mom!"

"Hey, buddy. Everything going okay?"

"Yup! Hazel and I are watching a movie, and then she's going to take me for ice cream."

I release a heavy sigh. "That sounds great. I'm glad you're having fun."

"Are you having a good time?" he asks.

"I am. Miles and I are having dinner, and then we're going somewhere after."

"Cool. Tell him I said hi!"

"I will. Be good. I love you."

"Love you too, Mom!"

He hangs up before I can say anything, and I feel a little foolish for needing to make that call, but also better for having done it.

I head back to the table. "Everything good?" Miles asks.

"It's great. He's having a good time."

"Good. Are you as well?"

I lift one shoulder. "I could be."

"Could be?"

"I mean, I have to ask Marge . . ."

He smiles. "She'd tell you that you're having a great time, because I'm her favorite person."

"Really? It kind of seems like she'd tell me that you're not all that special."

"That's her way of using reverse psychology."

I nod slowly. "I see. It's working then."

"I knew you'd finally realize it."

The first course comes out, and it's a simple salad with some bread and butter. "Here. This is my special salad. I grow the lettuce myself. I had William make one of those hydro gardens, and I only serve this to the customers I really like. That's you, sweetie." She places it in front of me. "I gave you the bagged stuff from the supermarket," she says as she gives the plate to Miles.

The two of us laugh, and she winks before heading back.

"I swear, I regret all of my choices," Miles says as he grabs his fork.

"Did you find a teacher yet?" I ask as I pick up some of the special lettuce.

"I have not."

I hate that this has been so stressful for him. "Are all the candidates just . . . bad?"

"No, we had one that wasn't awful, but that's not the kind of staff I look for, you know? I want someone who is going to thrive at their job and care about the students and their education. There's a big difference between teachers who love to teach and feel like it's their calling and those who have no other options. Part of my job is not only to find those teachers, but foster an environment where teachers can thrive."

"How do you do that?"

"Fuck if I know," he jokes.

"No, I'm serious."

Miles finishes chewing and then puts his fork down. "Well, I hold biweekly meetings with my heads of each department. We discuss what they're seeing, issues, and possible improvements. Then, the other two weeks, I meet with the teachers without the heads of the departments. I feel like I get the most out of those meetings."

"Why?" I ask.

"Because they're honest. Brutally honest. I get a very full picture after those meetings, and it's not any sugarcoating. I've made big changes because of some of the things I've been told during some of them. I'm also every teacher's advocate when it's required. I'll take the heat from parents."

"So you want the right person in the position." It's not a question, it's a statement. I imagine how many people would want to work for him just because he's a great boss.

He nods. "There are good administrators and then there are leaders. My goal is to be good at both. I need to lead while doing my job too. It's why having good people around me is essential. Plus, the kids deserve a good teacher."

What I wouldn't have given to have had someone like him as my teacher. To care so much feels like such a gift.

"You know, you're a good man."

"I try to be."

"Well, I see you as that. You came to my aid without a moment's pause, and you stepped in to coach the hockey clinic—"

"I was coerced. Let's not get that confused."

"Okay, you still did it. Then you gave me a tree and a shovel, not something a lot of men would do."

He laughs. "No, probably not, but I was going for memorable. Did it work?"

"Very much. I mean, we are on a date."

"We've been dating for weeks, Penny."

I roll my eyes at that. "We have not."

"Listen, we've done a lot in our short relationship, and then in two days, you're coming to my Ultimate Frisbee tournament. It's starting to get serious," Miles says with a big grin.

"I didn't know I was doing that."

"You agreed."

"I did?"

Miles nods. "Yup, you said, Miles, I would love to come to that tournament and cheer you on."

"Boy, I was really excited about it," I say, teasing him.

I actually really do want to go. Ainsley came in yesterday and couldn't stop talking about how interesting their full-day tournaments are. She asked me to come with her if I had off, but . . . I'm not going to tell him that.

This is much more fun.

"You were. It's because you're crazy about me, I know."

I laugh, shaking my head. "I guess I'll be there."

My phone buzzes in my lap, and I grab for it so fast I almost knock over the water. "I'm sorry, I just . . ."

It's a text from Ashton.

ASHTON

How's the date going?

> I'm on it. You just scared me with this text and I almost spilled water on myself.

ASHTON

So, it's going well. Have fun. Love you. Get naked with him!

I ignore that last one and look up at Miles. "I'm really sorry. I thought it might be Kai."

"Don't be sorry. It's not easy being away from him, huh?"

That's the understatement of the year. Little does he know just how much more complicated my story is.

"No, not really. I just worry over him all the time. While the kids you teach aren't yours, they are when they're with you."

"They really are. If anything were to happen to them . . . I'd be a mess."

My leg starts to bounce as I fight the urge to check my phone. Talking about kids and things happening is causing my anxiety to spike.

"Penny?" Miles calls my attention.

"Hmm?"

"Are you okay?"

I nod quickly. "Yeah, fine."

His head tilts to the side. "Honestly?"

Not wanting to lie, I decide to give a little of the truth. "I just don't like leaving Kai. It's really stressful for me to not be able to get to him in a few minutes. I know it sounds ridiculous, but there are . . . reasons . . . and I want to be here with you. I'm having a great time, truly. I'm trying to keep myself from calling him again."

He reaches his hand out, and I place mine in his. The warmth that comes from him is felt everywhere. "I'm not going to ask for your reasons. I just hope one day you'll trust me with them." Miles lifts his hand and Marge comes over. "Can you do me a favor?"

"Anything. What do you need?" she asks.

"Can you box our meals, whatever you've decided we are eating without asking?"

She looks to him, her jaw slack. "What?"

I echo her. "What? Why?"

He faces me. "Because I never want to be the reason you're stressed or anxious. We can take this meal, go home, eat, and hang out on the couch, and that will be the perfect date. All I want is to spend time with you. We can even take Kai with us for the rest of the date."

Yeah, I'm so going to fall in love with this man.

nineteen
Miles

Penny looks over at me, her head against the seat rest. We got our cheese tortellini to go and ate them outside her house in the car. Marge put extra bread and dessert in the bag, too, for Kai.

This might be the best date I've ever been on. We laughed, she was a million times more comfortable being closer to Kai, and it was just effortless.

"You're sure about this?" she asks as she looks at me with a smile.

"That I want to take Kai with us? Yes."

She's a single mother, and her son is a part of being with her. I'm not ignorant to that fact. If anything, I want him there too. I'm pretty sure he'll help me out. No, but in all honesty, I just want her to be comfortable.

"You're making resisting you very difficult."

I grin. "I already told you that was the plan. Come on, let's get him and go on the rest of our date."

I get out of the car before she can protest or try to end the date and open her door.

"You're home already?" Hazel asks as we enter the house. "Miles, I thought you had a little more swagger than this."

I roll my eyes. "You sound just like Everett."

She scrunches her face. "Don't say that."

"I speak the truth."

Penelope cuts in. "Miles and I decided to change things up a little. We're going to take Kai on the second part of the date."

Hazel grins. "I take it back. Game you have. Well done, sir."

I shake my head. "No games."

Kai comes running out and sees us there. "Hey, Coach!"

"Hey, bud. Listen, I have a problem and I was really hoping you could help out."

His eyes widen. "A problem?"

"Yeah, see, I have tickets to monster mini golf, but I'm a little afraid of the dark, and your mom didn't think she could be much help. Do you think it would be okay if you came with us? You know, make sure that I'm safe and all."

The way he comes to life at this simple request is fucking adorable. He puffs his chest out and lifts his head. "I can do that."

"Perfect."

"I'll get my sneakers so we can go!" he yells before running toward his room.

Penelope leans against the wall, her eyes warm, and I can almost feel her layers melting away. "Thank you for this."

"Don't thank me yet. You can save that for later," I tease.

———

"You have to hit the ball in the hole!" Kai explains after I missed—again.

I thought I was going to be good at mini golf. Apparently I'm having performance anxiety, because it's a par three and I'm on shot six. So, yeah.

"I'm trying, dude," I say, lining up my shot and then, when I didn't think this golfing could be worse, I'm proved wrong when I hear the heckling behind me.

"Mr. Anderson can't get it in the hole!" Then comes laughter.

I turn to see four of my students standing off to the side. "Hello, Jacob, Tyler, Hawk, and Ryan. Why don't you play ahead," I suggest.

"Not a chance," Hawk says.

Of course not.

I go back to lining up my shot and actually make it this time.

"Nice shot, Mr. A!"

I grab the ball out of the hole and lift it up before walking over to Penny. "Just to be perfectly clear, I have no problems finding or getting anything in the right hole."

Even in the dark I can see Penelope's cheeks redden. "Right," she says quickly. "Good to know."

Well, that worked to my benefit. I place my hand on the small of her back, guiding her to the next starting point where Kai is waiting.

"I apologize in advance."

"For?"

"Those four."

She smiles. "After Aunt Marge, I really didn't think it could get worse, but think of it as a good thing."

"A good thing that everyone is intent on embarrassing me?" I ask.

"Yeah, I'll know all the bad stuff in the beginning. So if I agree to a second date, you know I definitely like you."

I huff a laugh. "I'll hope for the best then."

Penelope is a natural, and whatever magic Kai has with golf I'm going to call beginner's luck.

I apparently have no luck or skill here.

You'd think I'd be excellent. I played hockey for fuck's sake. The entire game is based on getting the puck in the net.

Yet here I am, at monster mini golf, sucking it up like a loser. I'm going to blame it on the fact that it's dark and the only light is from black lights. As if we're in the nineties and in Gran's basement.

They both golf first and then it's my turn.

"Don't miss," one of the boys says from behind me.

I turn my head and glare. "Remember school starts soon, and I'll hold all the power then . . ."

They quiet down as I focus. I imagine this is the ice and that windmill with the glowing smiley faces that spin is a goalie. I can do this. I'm going to get it in the net—or through the windmill.

I time it, take a breath, and . . . fail.

The stupid ball bounces back at me.

"Do you need help, Coach?" Kai asks.

"Apparently I do."

He comes over and taps the ball, which goes through. Penelope laughs and then covers her mouth.

Yeah, I know, I look like a dumbass.

Thank God the Disc Jocks aren't here to see this. I would never live it down.

"Thanks, Kai."

He gives me a big smile. "You're welcome."

Tyler comes up behind me and clasps my shoulder. "Mr. A, I gotta warn you, if this is a date, you're doing a bad job at looking like a stud."

"I'm doing just fine."

I hope.

He sighs heavily. "I don't know, man, it's not looking good from where we stand."

Jacob chimes in. "Maybe you can take her to a movie or something next time."

"Shut up."

They laugh and I walk away toward Penny and Kai.

We play the rest of the course, laughing—mostly at me, even though I wasn't half bad by the end. Kai and Penelope started missing more and more as the course progressed, and I actually improved.

It was a nice change of pace.

We're on the last hole, and I'm determined to go out on a high note. Penelope got hers in five and Kai was nine. My goal is not to lose.

If I can make this shot, I'll be at three.

Penelope walks over, looking at where I'm standing, and tsks. "I wouldn't do that."

I turn my head, still in position to tap the ball. "Why not?"

"Your angle is off."

"My angle is just right."

She grins. "I don't know about that."

I crouch down, looking at the trajectory. I'm totally right. "You're trying to make me miss."

"I would never do anything like that," she says, all innocence with her lies. She and Kai share a look.

"Oh, and you're in on it too? The shame. I thought you were going to help me, not team up with your mom to make me lose."

Kai laughs. "I want you both to win."

I hit the ball. It misses because of course it does, but I look over at Penny. I can see the laughter, the joy, and the desire swimming in her eyes. I put that there. I gave her this and I swear, I feel like I'm a hundred feet tall and could move mountains with that single look.

I move close to her and keep my voice low. "I might have lost this game, but I've already won something much better."

———

I lift out of the car a very exhausted and deeply asleep Kai. After mini golf, we went to get ice cream, and somewhere in the middle, he zonked out.

"I can take him," Penelope says as I heft him into my arms.

Kai doesn't even stir as his head rests on my shoulder. "I got him."

Penelope walks in front of me, opening the door and leading me toward Kai's room. There is very little furniture, just a dresser, the bed, and a folding table next to it. I noticed the same around the rest of the house when I was here for dinner.

The place almost feels like it's someone else's. There are no decorations or pictures up. It's like she's not really living here.

I put Kai down, and Penny takes his shoes off. "I hate that he's going to sleep in his clothes, but it is what it is." She brings the superhero comforter up, tucking him in.

We slip out, closing his door, and stand in the hallway, so close, but not touching.

"I hope you had fun on our date," I say, breaking the silence.

"I did. I had a great time. Thank you for not being upset about leaving dinner and then bringing my kid on our date."

"He's part of who you are. If I can't accept that, I shouldn't be asking you out."

Penelope smiles at that. "Are you asking me out?"

"Do you want me to ask?"

I want to ask her to block out every weekend, but I need to use caution.

I step a little closer. "I asked you first."

She has to tilt her head back to maintain eye contact. "Maybe."

"That's not really an answer." I lift my hand to cup her cheek, and she closes her eyes for a moment. "Do you want me to ask you out?" I repeat my earlier question.

Penelope's eyes find mine, and I can see the storm rage. "Can I answer you when this date is over?"

"You want this date to keep going?" I ask, even though I really want to push her against the wall and kiss her until she can't think of a reason to say no.

"I think we could . . . for a while."

I lean into her slowly, waiting for her to push me away. Not that she has before, but I always want her to feel like she can.

"What do you want to do for the rest of the date?" I ask.

She pulls that lower lip between her teeth and places her hands on my chest. "You."

twenty
Penelope

I can't believe I just said that.

Oh my God.

I told him I wanted to do him.

I mean, I do. I *really* do.

Especially after tonight.

He cares about me, truly cares. He showed up during the storm, took us in without questions. He bought me a freaking tree because he wants me to put down roots. He's made me laugh, smile, and given me a safe place in all the chaos that is my life. When I don't see him for a few days, I miss him. When I am around him, I don't want to leave.

Each day he's made me fall harder and harder and . . . I like him. I trust him, and even if I can't keep him, we can have each other for a little while.

No other man would ever end the dinner early, take it to go, eat in the car outside my house because I was worried. Then, on top of that, bring Kai on the rest of the date.

Tonight was . . . the very last brick I had in defense of caving.

The wall was already crumbling, and I couldn't stop it if I wanted to.

"Say it again," Miles urges, his lips hovering over mine.

"I want you."

Before I can draw breath, he kisses me, a low groan reverberating from his chest. Our lips meld together before the kiss deepens. His hands move to my back, holding me tight against his body, and I hold on to him.

My back is suddenly against the wall, and the contrast to the heat of his body and the coolness of the wall is so striking I can't help but shiver. His tongue slides against mine, and I drink him in. He kisses me as though I'm giving him air, and it feels as though he's robbing all of mine.

I want this so much.

I want him to make me feel again.

To show me another way where it's not a game and I'm just a chess piece.

His hands drift lower, cupping my ass, but he breaks the kiss. "We don't have to do anything more than this if you're not ready," he says, breathless.

One more brick falls.

I don't say anything. I just take his hand in mine, leading him toward my bedroom.

Once we're inside, I step toward the bed, feeling nerves hit me like a freight train.

He looks around a little, taking in the plain space that could be anyone's. I've never found the need for decorations, since I always have to leave them behind.

Like I will have to do with him.

I immediately push away those thoughts, focusing on living in the moment. For once. To have this night with him and however many I can have.

"Miles?" I bring his attention to me.

"Yes?"

"Do *you* want this?" I ask hesitantly, because maybe I'm misreading the situation. Maybe he doesn't want me and I'm imagining things.

He takes four long strides before he's in front of me, his green eyes intensely locked on mine. "I want you more than I've ever wanted anyone. I think about you all the time. I took up drinking coffee just because I needed to be around you. Do I want you and this? I want it all. Everything you'll give me. So never question if I want you, Penelope. I do and always will."

My heart is pounding, and I force myself to breathe. "Why do you say things like this? Why are you so intent on making me fall for you?"

Miles smiles and brushes the hair back from my face, tucking it behind my ear. "I'm just telling you the truth, sweetheart. Don't fly away from me tonight."

I don't think I can take any more of his truth.

Surprise fills me when I register what he said. "What do you mean?"

He smiles. "You like to sit and watch, but when someone gets too close or you feel threatened, you take flight."

God, if he only knew how close to the truth he was. My vision becomes blurry as my eyes fill with tears. "I don't want to fly away. I want to give you all I can."

The slide of his thumb against my cheek is like a feather's caress. I feel it, but it's delicate and won't harm me.

"Then stay here with me. Let me show you that I won't hurt you. Trust me to give you everything you need, but you need to tell me what you want." His voice is rough as he moves his hand down to my neck.

"I want you to touch me."

"Where? You have to be specific, beautiful."

His fingers move across my collarbone.

"I've never been in charge before, and I don't know how to do this." I'm not one of those women who can just . . . say what they want.

My wants and needs were always irrelevant in the past. But with Miles, it's never been the case.

"I'm at your mercy. You will always have control when you're with me. I'll always ask if you're okay with something." The truth in his eyes is so clear.

"And if I need to stop?"

"We stop. I may need a cold shower, but you say the word and it ends."

I brush my thumb across his lips. "I feel . . . embarrassed."

He gently nips the pad of my thumb. "Never be ashamed or embarrassed with me, sweetheart. All I want is to give you pleasure."

I gather up the courage I have and channel the courage to say it. "I want you to touch my breasts."

"Good choice." His grin is sexy, and his eyes burn even hotter.

Those warm hands move down my arms, and then he lifts them over my head. Slowly the soft fabric of my top slides against my skin and is over my head. He tosses it to the side, and I shiver.

Miles looks at me, and there is so much desire in his eyes, I could melt. He moves his hands down my arms, placing them at my sides before he glides them from my stomach to my breasts.

My breath hitches as he just skims the outline of my bra.

His deep voice is rough and husky. "You have no idea how many times I've pictured this exact moment."

I look up at him as he undoes my clasp. Then he hooks his finger on my bra strap. Ever so slowly, he slides it down, and then it falls between us.

His eyes are on mine for a heartbeat, as though he's searching for permission, so I nod.

"My imagination wasn't even close to the perfection that you are."

"Touch me," I plead. I need to feel him, to know that this isn't a dream.

The last time a man touched me, it was to inflict pain, and I want that gone. I want him to replace everything in my past, by giving me this now.

He does. His hands cup my breasts, and he rubs his thumb across my nipple. "Do you like that?"

"Yes," I manage to whisper.

"Where else do you want me to touch you?"

Without a moment's hesitation, I tell him the truth. "Everywhere."

He squats down just a little, his hands hooking under my thighs, and then I'm being carried around to the side of the bed. Instinctively my legs wrap around his hips, and I hold on. I run my fingers through his thick, brown hair and then bring my lips to his.

He's like a drug, and I want to be intoxicated all night long.

He lays me down on the bed and tears his shirt off.

Now, I'm not saying that I didn't think he was going to be hot, because . . . he already was.

What I wasn't prepared for was this.

Thick muscles and a six-pack you could do laundry on. Over his chest and up his shoulder is a marine's emblem tattoo that is covering raised skin. I know what that scar is. My brother has a similar one.

He was shot.

As much as I want to ask, I won't. While I would gladly take his secrets, it's not fair to not offer him mine.

True intimacy is exposing yourself for another. To give your heart, soul, and secrets because you know you're able to be open with that person, but I can't give my secrets away. No matter how much Miles makes me feel safe, we aren't. I have to protect myself and my son.

He climbs onto the bed, hovering over me. His mouth finds mine, and I pour my emotions into it.

Everything I can't say but want him to feel.

When he breaks away, his tongue traces the contour of my neck, then down the center of my breasts before he finds one nipple, licking around it and then taking it in his mouth.

I moan when his teeth just gently bite down on my nipple. "Oh God."

I can feel his grin against my skin.

Then he moves lower, kissing all the way down as he goes.

He undoes the button of my jeans, then leans up, hooking his fingers and pulling them and my panties down. I lift my hips to help, and then I'm bare to him.

Completely naked and at his mercy.

"You're so beautiful, Penelope." I feel beautiful when he looks at me. "Now, you said you wanted me to touch you everywhere. Do you want that still, sweetheart?"

"Yes."

He grins at my immediate reply. His fingers move to my clit, and he puts just a small amount of pressure there. "You're so wet." He slides up and down my seam before pushing a finger inside. "So tight."

"It's been a long time," I confess. My heart pounds as I stretch, trying to open myself to him.

"Well, I better make sure you're ready." He continues to pump his finger in and out before adding another. There is a tight pressure, but it feels so good.

"Miles?" He looks up at me. "Take off your clothes, please."

"That's a request I'll happily comply with." He pulls out of my body and I feel the loss, the desire for more. To be full—with him.

He climbs off the bed and I sit up on my elbows—watching. I love that he doesn't look away from me. We watch each other as he moves his hand to his pants, unbuttoning and then sliding his jeans off.

I wait for the next item to go, but he stays put.

"You're forgetting something," I say with a smirk.

Miles is at the end of the bed a second later, and his fingers wrap around my ankles, pulling me to the edge. I gasp in surprise, and then his hands are framing my face. "I want you to do it. I need to know this is happening and you want this."

I'm pretty sure I've been clear about that, but I want to touch him too. "Okay."

With shaking hands, I inhale and then pull his boxer briefs down. His erection springs free, and he pulls my chin up and his green eyes are like glass. I can see through him, see the desire and the hope that lies just beneath the surface.

"If you don't like something or want to stop, just tell me," he says carefully.

"I don't want to stop."

Then he drops to his knees. "Lie back and open for me."

"You don't have to."

Miles grins. "Oh, I want to. I want it more than drawing my next breath. I want to taste you, and have you fall apart on my tongue. You'll come for me, and then I'm going to do it again. Lie back, sweetheart. Let me make you feel good."

It sounds like a freight train in my head as my pulse races faster, but I lie back as instructed. This wasn't something my ex ever did, even though he demanded I do it to him.

I'm not sure how to be with someone who is this giving.

Miles pushes my legs farther apart and hovers there. His warm breath is against my core, and I'm shaking with both anticipation and fear.

"I want to see your eyes, Penny. I want you to watch me worship you."

"I can't," I confess. It's too much. I can't watch him do it.

"You can. Push up on your elbows and keep your eyes on me."

His voice is like sandpaper against wood. It's rough and scratchy, but smooth at the end.

My stomach drops, but I do it. I lean up on my elbows and meet his gaze. "Good girl."

Why does that cause my entire body to tighten?

Without averting his gaze from mine, Miles leans down and makes a long swipe against my core.

"Oh God," I pant as the warmth from his tongue is felt throughout my entire body.

I watch him pleasure me. Licking, sucking, flicking his tongue, all while keeping our gazes locked. My climax is growing at lightning speed, and I'm running in the wind, everything spinning around me.

It's so much. Too much and yet not enough.

My head falls back, unable to watch him any longer as it mounts, ready to push me over the edge, but he stops.

I gasp and meet his gaze.

"Watch," he commands before I protest.

"Please don't stop," I beg.

His mouth is instantly back on me the moment my eyes meet his. His ministrations resume, his tongue swirling and adjusting the pressure. Then he starts to flick it and I'm moaning, gripping the sheets. "It's too much. I can't . . . I need to . . . please, please."

My words aren't even coherent, but I'm losing my sanity.

He doesn't stop, and I use all my control to keep watching because, dear lord, if he stops now, I might just die.

Then he moans against me and I fall apart.

I bite down hard on my lip, knowing I have to control myself, but being so out of it at the same time. My fingernails will probably puncture the sheets with how hard I'm gripping them, but Miles keeps going, relentlessly, as wave after wave of pleasure washes over me.

When my muscles finally relax, he stops and climbs up on the bed beside me, and the tip of his finger slides against the valley between my breasts. "You falling apart like that was the most exquisite thing I've ever seen."

"I'm pretty sure I'm a disheveled mess."

He shakes his head. "You're gorgeous, all flushed and perfect."

I roll onto my side and bring my hand to his chest. "We're not done yet."

"No, sweetheart, we're not. We're just getting started."

"I want to touch you." I push at his chest, rolling him onto his back, and he goes willingly. I run my hands down his abs, watching how the muscles ripple at my touch. "You keep telling me that I'm perfect, and then I look at you."

He really is a masterpiece. All muscle and power that lies underneath a heart of gold. How the hell this man is single, I'll never understand. Miles is the kind of man women dream of. He's smart, funny, caring, and he looks like this.

"I'm glad you like what you see."

I grin. "I do, very much." I slide my hand lower. "Show me how you like it."

I wrap my hand around his dick, and his hand covers mine. "Just like this."

We move our hands up and down slowly at first. Then he tightens my grip and goes faster.

His other hand snakes up, gripping the back of my neck and pulling me close to him so our foreheads are touching.

I keep going, and when his hand falls away, I stop.

He releases my neck so I can pull back and look at him. "Did I do something?"

"Yeah, you are too good at this. But I want to be inside of you when I come, and if we kept that up, it wasn't going to happen."

I reach over to the bedside drawer. Hazel was being funny by bringing me condoms, but I'm eternally grateful for that.

"You're sure?" He takes it from me.

"Absolutely sure."

And I realize that I really am. I'm not convincing myself of anything or coming up with excuses. I trust him. He's shown me over and over again that I can. He won't hurt me.

I don't even think he would be capable of it.

Miles slides the condom on, and then I straddle his hips. If I thought he wanted me before, this is a need.

"Penelope." He says my name on a whisper, a plea, a ray of hope, and I drink it in.

"I'm going to need to go slow," I warn him. I haven't been with a man since Kai was born.

"I won't move," he promises.

He positions himself at my entrance, and I slowly sink down. I can take him in only small amounts, and his hands are on my hips, holding me steady.

"God, you feel so good," he says through gritted teeth. "So fucking hot. So fucking mine."

I slide up a little and take him deeper this time. He's not small, and it takes me a few seconds each time to adjust to his size.

He makes a strange noise and I stop moving. "I'm sorry," I say, staring down at him.

"Dear God, you have nothing to be sorry for. If all we had was this, I'd die a happy man."

"I'm not hurting you?"

"No, the opposite. You feel so perfect wrapped around my cock."

I push deeper this time, taking much more than before, and even though it's a little painful, it's worth it. One more rock and then I sink all the way down. Our bodies are fully connected, and I don't move, allowing myself a moment.

He leans up so our faces are close.

"Miles" is all I can manage to say.

My heart and head are a mess. Everything about this feels so right and it hurts. Not physically, but in my soul. Something inside me has been broken for so long, and right now it doesn't feel broken.

I feel whole.

Complete.

His.

And then he rolls me onto my back, staring down at me, and begins to move, making love to me without saying another word.

twenty-one
Miles

We're lying here, Penelope in my arms, without speaking. Since she said my name, we haven't said another word, and I don't think either of us has been ready.

My hands roam up and down her back, and I kiss the top of her head. "Are you okay?"

Her head tilts and she looks up at me. "I'm . . . beyond okay."

Thank God. I worried that there would be regret after—not on my part, but hers.

I sift my fingers through her hair. "Are you sore?"

She mentioned it had been a long time, and I don't want her to be in pain. Penelope shifts, lying on her stomach, hand on my chest. "A little."

"Come on," I say, pulling her up with me. I take her hand, leading her into the en suite bathroom. "Sit there."

She sits on the edge of the tub, and I turn the water on. "What are you doing?" she asks with a little giggle.

"Taking care of you." Once it's warmed up enough, I put the plug in the drain. "Do you have bath oil or any of that stuff?"

She shakes her head. "I don't, but I have Epsom salt under the cabinet."

"Okay, well, that'll do." I open the door, grab the bag, and toss a handful in. "Here." I take her hand.

I help her over the ledge, and she slowly sinks down and then scoots forward. "Aren't you coming in with me?" Penelope asks.

I grin and climb in behind her. My arms wrap around her, pulling her to my chest.

I kick the faucet off with my foot, and then we lie here, the warm water soothing, but it's her that really gives me peace.

Tonight didn't go the way I planned, not a single thing, and yet it was the best damn night of my life. Dinner in the car was great, golfing with Kai was fun, and then . . . well, the rest was fucking perfect.

She was perfect.

Her long sigh fills the silence of the room, and then her head lolls to the side as she relaxes further into me. I cup the water, dragging it over the two of us so we don't get cold as she just rests.

"This feels good," Penelope says softly. "I don't want this night to end."

I grin, even though she can't see it. "It's not over yet, sweetheart. Just let me take care of you tonight. Here, sit up."

She does and I bring my hands up to her shoulders, gently rubbing them and then her neck, down her back, and up again.

"Your hands are magic."

"Just my hands?" I joke and she laughs.

"I think you have several magical appendages."

"Which is your favorite?"

Penelope shakes her head and then moans when I find a knot where her neck meets her shoulder. "Right now, your hands," she admits as I continue to work to get it to release.

"I'll be sure to work at getting another part to become your favorite."

There's this little massage-looking thing on the corner so I grab it. Strange it has points rather than circles, but . . . I don't know, girls are strange. I grip it against my palm and start to rub her back.

"What is that?" she asks as she leans forward.

"I don't know, it's yours."

I show her it over her shoulder and she bursts out laughing. "That's a scalp massager."

"A what?"

"It's for your scalp. Here, give it to me."

I hand it to her and she holds it the way I was, but makes small circles, moving it around her head.

I can do that.

"Let me."

Penelope gives it back and I start to do what she did. She lets out a low hum from her chest and I keep doing it. Seems girls like this. Okay then. Good to know.

I keep going and my other hand goes for the knot in her neck. Penelope is limp and compliant in my hands. I could keep her like this all day.

However, the water is cool and I'm pretty sure my ass is asleep so I put the massager down and help her out of the tub, wrapping her in a towel and rubbing her arms.

She lifts up on her toes and gives me a kiss, my heart swelling at her touch. When she drops back down, her blue eyes stare into mine, and the sincerity of her words takes my breath away. "Thank you for taking care of me."

I bring my hand to her face, rubbing her soft cheek with my thumb. "Always."

———

We're in bed with her head in the crook of my shoulder, and her fingers move to the tattoo over my right shoulder. She rubs the puckered skin, reminding me of a time I've tried to forget.

She doesn't ask, but I offer up the explanation, wanting to be close with her, to know my faults as well, share a true intimacy with her.

"It was during a deployment. Doug and I were part of a recon unit. Our job was simple, get in, get out, and don't get caught." My memories come back as though I'm watching it happen in real time.

"You don't have to tell me," she says quickly.

I want to give her parts of me so she might give me something of hers.

"I was lead of the team, and it was three of us who were going for a routine scout. I had a weird feeling, you know? Like something wasn't right in the air."

I look at her and she nods. "Quinn calls it his Spidey senses. They go off and he knows something bad is coming."

"A lot of us have it. Mine was flashing red lights, but I figured it was nerves or something because we were going to an area where something happened two days before. We had a source tell us the people we were looking for were at that location."

Doug didn't trust the source, but I did. It was my call, and I walked us into hell. I needed to believe it because we had a job to do and there were so many people's lives in our hands. That information was vital.

Penelope's crystal-blue eyes fill with unshed tears. "I have a feeling I know how this goes."

"We were being followed and none of us caught it. I'm trained to catch it. To know when the hunter is being hunted. Being a part of the recon team meant having good instincts."

She rubs her finger against the puckered skin. Then she leans in and presses her lips to it. "You survived and you're here."

"Barely."

It was the worst few days of my life. No one would tell me what happened to everyone else. Doug and Billy carried me out, but I didn't know if they were hit as well.

I was lying in that hospital bed, my skin crawling because I was so sure I was going to die there. Everyone dies in the hospital—I needed to leave, but they wouldn't let me.

I recall the way it felt, the fire burning through my shoulder as though someone was holding a match and wouldn't move it. The pain was unbearable, but it was nothing compared to the fear that my friends were killed.

"I remember the instant before," I confess. "I was scanning the area again because that feeling just wouldn't ebb, and I saw the muzzle. I acted on pure instinct. He was going to have a head shot on Doug. It was lined up perfectly. I threw him down, and I felt the bullet before the sound registered."

"You saved his life." The reverence in her voice is too much and undeserved.

"I walked him into it, Penelope. I made the choice and he

could've died. That doesn't make me a hero or noble. It means I was wrong and we were lucky."

She purses her lips. "You sound so much like my brother when he talks about certain missions. He had a lot of trauma, and most of the time he pretends it didn't happen. However, I can't imagine that Doug or Billy ever blamed you."

"They say they don't."

Her fingers go back to the hollow at the base of my throat. "And you don't believe them?"

"I don't know. I don't know that I deserve their absolution."

She scoots up so we're face-to-face on the pillow. "Absolution isn't yours to decide to grant. It's theirs, and if they've given it to you, accept it. It's as much a gift to the giver as the receiver. I think it's part of healing. If they carry that anger, that fear and rage, then they weigh themselves down. I used to think that forgiveness was a weakness. That if I forgave someone who hurt me, then I was stupid, but I think it's the opposite. It's the unwillingness to have hate fill you. I also think there is a difference between forgiveness or absolution and acceptance."

I kiss her forehead, breathing in her warm jasmine-and-rose scent and holding her so tight I'm not sure I want to ever let go.

I have never felt this much for anyone this fast. I've loved before, when I was in college, but as soon as I left for the military, we were done. It hurt, I was pissed, and then I got over it real fast.

This is completely different. I would've laughed at anyone who said you can fall in love with someone you know very little about other than surface level, that you've known for only a few months, but here I am, making a liar out of myself.

I stare down at her, hating the walls she's erected and knowing someone or something caused her to put them up.

I brush her cheek with my thumb. "Who hurt you, Penelope? Who made you so afraid to let me in?"

She looks away, and it's as though those blue eyes that were so open a minute ago have the shutters going down.

I lift her chin back up, waiting for her to open her eyes to me.

Slowly, her lashes flutter and her blue eyes are guarded. "There are things I can't give you, Miles. My past is one of them. And it's not because I don't want to tell you or that I don't trust you, but it's to protect Kai. I have to protect him, and allowing anyone . . . I just can't. It's better the less you know."

My primal urge is to fight. Whoever did this to her made her afraid and secretive. I'd like to kill them. To destroy them for ever hurting her. All those emotions rage inside me, but I know that violence and my unchecked masculine pride aren't what she needs.

I brush my finger against her cheek and keep my voice even. "Then I'll wait."

"Wait?" she asks.

I nod slowly and pull her closer, wanting to shelter her in my embrace. "I'll wait until you're ready to tell me, but just know that if you ever need me, despite whatever happens between us, I'll be here. I will never let anyone hurt you or Kai. Do you promise you'll call me if you're in trouble?"

"If it ever comes to that, I'll call," she promises.

I let that be enough for now and then shift onto my back, pulling her to my chest so I can hold her. "Sleep, Penelope, I'll make sure nothing hurts you."

———

The sun is just starting to rise, and Penny has slept soundly all night. On the other hand, I stared at the ceiling, thinking about everything that happened. Talking about that mission feels as though an old wound has been reopened.

Then I thought about what she said, and what could be haunting her. All my training kicked back in as I did a mental sweep of her house. Door locks, windows, entry points—I had to make sure there were ways out and a plan.

One niggling thing is her brother. He was a SEAL, and I would guarantee that he's behind her living here and her protection. I need to find a way to reach him and give him my word that I will do anything she needs to protect her.

I rub her bare back, sliding up and down the vertebrae, and she snuggles deeper. I could do this every day, wake up like this, her in my arms after I make her come over and over again.

However, we're not there, and I need to leave before Kai wakes up.

"Penny," I say her name softly. She wakes with a jolt, sitting straight up. The fear in her eyes has me lifting my hands. "It's just me."

Her chest is heaving and she works to calm herself. "Sorry. I just . . . waking up. I didn't . . ."

"It's okay, but it's almost morning and I have no idea what time Kai wakes up."

Those blue eyes go wide and she looks at the clock. "Oh my God! I have to be at work in thirty minutes. Shit. Kai's alarm will go off any second. You have to get dressed."

The two of us throw the covers back and are out of the bed. I find my shirt on her side of the bed, and when I turn to find my other clothes, I see her standing there, biting the tip of her thumb, staring.

I grin. "As much as I'd love to let you ogle me—and I definitely like you naked standing there—you need to get dressed before—"

"Mom!"

Her hand covers her mouth, and she runs to her door, turning the lock. "Give me a minute!"

He jiggles the handle and she stares at it, waiting to make sure it doesn't open, then turns to me. "Get dressed," she whispers aggressively.

"I'm trying," I say back as quietly as I can.

"Mom, why is the door locked?" Kai asks from the hallway. "Can I come in now?"

"No, Kai, I'll be out in a few minutes. Go get yourself some cereal before we have to leave for Prose & Perk."

I'm pulling my pants on and she's waving her hands at me like I need to hurry up. I'm doing the best I can without making noise. "Now what?" I ask.

She looks around the room like she didn't think about anything past getting me dressed. "I don't know. Can you hide and then we'll leave right away?"

I raise one brow. "My truck is in the driveway, blocking you in."

"Oh God! I hope he doesn't see."

I let out a soft chuckle and then sigh. "I'll go out the window once you're in the kitchen."

Thankfully, her bedroom faces the front of the house.

"You're not going to fit."

"I'll fit. I've climbed through much smaller places."

She walks to me, placing her hands on my chest. "Will you come back tonight?"

"If that's what you want."

Penelope nods and then lifts up on her toes, pressing her lips to mine. "I'll see you tonight."

She slips out of the room, careful to not open her door too much. I stand here for a second, until I hear her voice and Kai's walking away.

Then I slip out the window and count down the hours until I can see her again.

I'm exhausted.

I came home, showered, and drank two energy drinks. Then I went over the résumés to get another batch of interviews set up. We're down to the last set that can even be qualified.

I'm just . . . spent.

I sent off the names to Mrs. Hendrix so she can get everyone scheduled for this week and start to make contingencies if I don't have a teacher.

After writing down some ways I can shuffle staff around, I check my phone because it keeps vibrating on the table.

LACHLAN

So, how did the date go? (Ainsley made me send this.)

EVERETT

I forgot . . . it was the big night.

LACHLAN

We should've driven by his house this morning to see if his truck was there.

EVERETT

He didn't get that lucky.

Oh, but I did.

KILLIAN

Who did Miles go out with?

LACHLAN

Penny.

KILLIAN

Wow, didn't see that one coming. She's way too good looking for him.

EVERETT

Agreed. Miles looks like ass most days.

LACHLAN

He really does.

KILLIAN

Do you think he's purposely ignoring us?

LACHLAN

Or he's still sleeping . . .

I'm awake. I'm working. I know some of you aren't familiar with that concept.

LACHLAN

Yeah, being the fire chief is so fucking easy.

EVERETT

I own a very successful veterinary clinic as well as care for my mother, thank you very much.

KILLIAN

I won't dignify that with a response. I will, however, follow up to the first question that was asked. How did the date go?

It was great.

It was really fucking great.

LACHLAN

I'm glad to hear it, man. I know you really like her.

EVERETT

Penny is a great girl. Don't fuck it up or Hazel will kill you. She's incredibly protective of her.

LACHLAN

Which means she told you that she was off-limits.

EVERETT

Yup. After I screwed around with her cousin a few months ago, she's unwilling to let me around anyone she likes.

Gee, I wonder why. And the last thing I want to do is fuck it up, thank you very much.

KILLIAN

I wish you luck, my friend.

Thanks for the concern, everyone, but I've got this.

At least I hope I do.

twenty-two
Miles

"That was fucking incredible," I tell her after another round of mind-blowing sex.

She lets out a soft laugh, turning her head to face me and still panting. "Yes, yes, it was."

I came over around nine, and it's already one in the morning. I have interviews today, and I really should get some rest.

"I should probably go. I'm starving and need to sleep."

She rolls over, pulling the sheet up to her chest. "You can stay. I have food and a bed you can get some sleep in."

"I think we'll end up not sleeping."

Penelope smiles. "Probably."

I get up, looking over my shoulder to catch her staring at my naked ass. "You keep looking at me like that and I'm not going anywhere."

"What if I don't want you to leave?"

Fuck. This girl is going to be the death of me. I can't get enough of her. "Say the word and I'll climb back in bed and eat something else."

She pushes up on her knees, crawling toward me with her breasts swaying.

I nearly growl. "Fuck it, who needs sleep?"

I grab her hips, tossing her on the bed, and she giggles. I slowly crawl up her body, kissing my way as I go. My tongue circles her nipple, and then I suck it hard. I do the same to the other, listening to her moans and gasps.

Penelope's fingers tangle in my hair, holding me there so I continue a little longer, but that's not what I want to taste.

I take her hands and pin them above her head. "Keep them there," I command. "Do you trust me to make you feel good?"

Her blue eyes are wide, but she nods. "I trust you."

Those words fill me with a pride that has me ready to conquer the world. "I won't betray it."

"I know."

I'm not just talking about now. I would never hurt her. I'm going to test her trust, though.

"I want to tie your hands to the bed. I'm not sure you won't move otherwise. Will you let me?"

She nods.

I reach down and grab the belt off her robe she was wearing when I got here, and I walk over, wrapping it around her wrists and then to the wrought iron spindle on her frame. It's not tight—she could easily get out of it with one pull—but it at least gives the illusion.

"Are you wet for me, Penelope?" I ask.

"Yes."

"I bet you are. Such a good girl being sprawled like that for me. You are so beautiful like this. I got you."

"I know," she answers softly.

"Now, spread your legs for me. Let me see how wet you are."

Slowly she does as told. This week I've had her many ways, but seeing her like this, giving me the power, means everything to me.

All I want is for her to trust me, to share her pain so I can shoulder it for her. Something is weighing her down, keeping her from letting me in. I can feel I'm chipping away at it and, at the same time, completely falling for her.

"Miles," she moans my name. "Please."

I move between her legs, my face hovering over her cunt. "I'm going to make you come on my tongue, Penelope. I told you I was hungry."

She whimpers when I bring my tongue to her clit, flicking it gently. My hands are on each thigh, holding her apart. She can't move much, just her hips the smallest amounts. I lick and suck on her clit, then ease up, repeating the sequence over and over again. I push my tongue inside her, fucking her with it, wishing it was my cock taking her.

I lift her higher, devouring her, and she starts to tremble. I can feel her body tensing around me, and I move back to her clit, sucking it hard and then using my teeth.

Penelope detonates in my arms. Her head thrashes back and forth, and I keep going, riding out every minute of pleasure I can give her. She moans my name softly before biting down on her lip to keep quiet.

"Do you need to be untied?" I ask after her orgasm is done.

"More?"

"Yes, sweetheart, there's more. Answer me."

"No," she pants.

I grab her hips, flipping her over and pulling her onto her knees. Her upper half is suspended, and I push her knees closer for better leverage.

"I've got you," I tell her. "I'll hold you, just grab onto the bedpost."

She moves closer, and I spread her knees before driving into her. Her heat envelops me and she gasps, throwing her head back.

I reach up with one hand, grabbing her hair and just holding it. She looks at me from over her shoulder, her tongue darting along her lips.

"Just like that, Penny. Let me fuck you hard."

"Yes."

I slam into her over and over, my cock so hard as her pussy tightens. I release her hair and grip her hips tighter, needing more of her. Needing it all.

My hand moves to where we're joined, my fingers coated in her arousal, and I move to her ass. I don't know if this will be too far, but I want her. I want every part of her to be mine.

"Tell me if you want me to stop," I say as I move to her ass.

Just a little, I slide around the hole, warning her.

"Oh God," she moans.

I keep going, moving closer and closer to entering it. "Does it feel good?"

She doesn't answer at first, but the way she's rocking on my cock tells me it does. "Yes." Her answer is a whisper.

"Good. Tell me when it doesn't."

I breach the entrance just a little and she gasps, her head dropping. Her knuckles are white as she holds the metal frame. I go deeper, sliding my finger in and out in rhythm with my dick. Each thrust I do the same in her ass. Her pussy is so tight, milking me so hard that I'm not sure how much longer I can hold out.

The pleasure is like nothing I've ever felt before. My hand on her hip tightens. "I'm close, baby."

"I'm . . . I can't . . ." she pants between breaths.

I push my finger in again, and her head flies back, her arms go limp, and she comes apart, screaming into the pillow.

I can't hold back anymore. I come so hard, falling onto her back, jerking my hips until there's nothing left.

Wanting to make sure she's okay, I reach my hand up and untie the knot. I roll off to the side, careful not to crush her before pulling her to me.

"Are you okay?" I ask, pushing her hair off her face.

She laughs once. "I'm not sure what I am, but that was . . . unreal."

"It was," I agree.

Her eyes drift down and I know if I lie here, I'll fall asleep again, and then we'll have to worry about Kai. So I kiss her nose and extricate myself, needing to toss the condom away, and pull the covers over her.

Penelope nestles in and sighs. I grab my clothes that are thrown around the room—the two of us were in a hurry once I got here—and head into the bathroom.

I clean up, get dressed, and kiss her again, slipping out the front door before I don't have the strength to walk away.

———

"You know, passing notes to the girl you like isn't part of my job description," Mrs. Hendrix complains as she puts a coffee cup down.

"But you're so good at it."

Her one blond brow raises. "Uh-huh. So what's the deal with you and her anyway? I don't know much about her, just that she moved here recently."

"She did, and she has a little boy named Kai. He's six."

Mrs. Hendrix watches me as I read the note on the cup.

Date? Yes or No?

I grin and grab my phone to text her.

Yes.

PENELOPE

When?

You tell me, it was your idea. I have an interview now, let me know the details.

I look up and she's rolling her eyes. "I'm going to guess it's a yes?"

"It is."

"So you're going to buy more coffee that you won't drink?"

I nod. "I sure am."

I'd buy a million coffees that I'd never drink if it means I get to see Penelope and get to be with her.

"You look happy," she notes.

"That's because I am."

"Even with the fact that we start school in a week without faculty we need?"

Yeah, that part isn't so great, but I'm thinking my luck is going to change. I'm putting that out in the universe, because if there's not one in this bunch, I'm fucked. And not the good kind.

"It's going to sort itself out."

She shrugs. "If you say so. This first one is moving to Ember Falls. She's here for a few days, and I was able to get her in. At least we won't have to worry about you running into her if you don't hire her. I'll go get her."

I grab the résumé and look it over. I'm freaking exhausted, and reading it is almost difficult. I chug my coffee, waiting for the caffeine to kick in, and put my glasses on to review her résumé so I at least know her name.

"Mr. Anderson, this is Violet Leone."

I stand and extend my hand, but the two of us just look at each other for a minute. I know her. I swear I know her.

"Violet Leone? Have we . . . ?"

She smiles. "Miles, God, it's been a really long time."

So I do know her. How? Violet. Then it hits me.

"Oh my God, Violet Stewart?"

"Well, I was Stewart, but . . . anyway. It's so good to see you."

"It's been, what? Fifteen years?"

Violet Stewart used to come spend the summers here with her grandmother, who was friends with Gran, and we used to play as kids. When she turned sixteen, she just stopped coming. She was traveling or whatever with her parents, but it's been forever.

She smiles. "Sixteen, I think, but yeah, a long time."

"How are you? What are you doing here?"

"Good, I'm here for an interview with, well, you."

I motion for her to sit. "Please, sit, let's begin the interview. Tell me why you're interested in the position."

Everett is going to lose his fucking mind when he realizes she's back in town. The two of them were together, as kids do, and they promised each other the world. She broke his heart when she stopped coming.

"I've decided to come back to Ember Falls for a while, start over, maybe build a life like my grandma had. She was always so happy here. I have a master's degree in English literature, and I'm licensed to teach. I saw the opening here, and I got on a plane to leave California."

"Were you teaching there?"

Her eyes narrow a little, and she shakes her head. "No, not . . . really. I stopped teaching when I got married. Dylan didn't really want me to work, with his schedule."

"I see. Do you have any in-the-classroom experience?"

"Yes, I taught before I got married. I was or is or was married for just three years, so I have experience."

She stumbles a little over her words, and I feel like there's more to this than her just coming to Ember Falls.

"So you were married, but aren't now?"

I hear Mrs. Hendrix sigh heavily. "Mrs. Leone, what my boss isn't catching is that your husband is Dylan Leone, and you weren't working because your husband is a very famous actor."

"I was getting there," I bristle.

Maybe. I don't really keep up on gossip.

Violet smiles softly. "Yes, we're in the middle of a very public, very painful divorce. So I'd like to have this job. I'd be really good at it. I love kids and love English. I'll be able to guarantee one full school year. After that, I don't know if I'll . . . well, I don't know my plans."

"I see. So you'd be able to give me this school year, and we can assess the next? I'd need to know before the end of the year to be able to put out a hiring message."

She nods. "Yes, I can guarantee that. I'm going to be staying at my grandmother's, well, I guess it's my house regardless if I get the job or not."

There's not a doubt in my mind she's the right person. Honestly, she's the first candidate I didn't want to kick out. I look over to Mrs. Hendrix, and she nods.

I stand and extend my hand. "You're hired."

Violet lets out a long sigh. "Thank you. I'd like to go by my maiden name, if possible?"

"Of course, whatever you'd like."

"Thank you, Miles."

"Welcome to being a teacher at Ember Falls High School. You start next week."

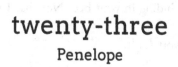

twenty-three
Penelope

"Why am I so nervous?" I ask Miles as I pace the kitchen. "I mean, he's going to be happy about this."

He stands and holds my shoulders. "Are *you* happy about this?"

"I'll be happy to stop having you sneak out of my bed each night. Not that I think having sleepovers right away is a good idea, but we don't have to hide it."

Miles moves his hands up and brushes my cheek with his thumb. "I want to be with you, Penelope. Not just sex, which is fantastic by the way, but I want to *be* with you. Dinners, movies, more golf, even though I suck. I want it all. However, I told you that I'll wait until you're ready. If you don't want to tell Kai, we don't have to."

My fingers wrap around his wrist. "I do want to tell him. He loves you, it's not that, it's just . . . it'll be so official."

"Yes, it will."

And that is really freaking scary.

For the last three weeks, we've spent each night together. We lie together, talk about our day, make love, and then he leaves before the morning. It's been . . . incredible.

He's tried in the last week to get me to go out publicly with him. To be more than just sneaking around. But before I can agree to anything more than what we've been doing, I want to talk to Kai.

"I'm ready to talk to Kai, and then we go slowly with this, okay? I'm still not sure this is a great idea."

His boyish grin makes my chest tighten. "It is definitely a good idea if I get to stop passing coffee cup notes and I can walk into the store and kiss you. It's a good idea if I don't have to pretend that each time I look at you, I don't want you more than the air I breathe. It's a good idea if I can take you and Kai to dinner, talk about everything we do when we're hiding in your bed. Not that I want that part to stop."

I laugh. "I bet you don't."

"Do you?"

"Not even a little."

"See, good ideas everywhere."

I let out a deep breath and nod. "You're right. I know it's time, especially because your free time is getting less and less."

School started two weeks ago, and it's been better than I could've hoped for regarding Kai. Meeting Ethan in the hockey clinic was the best thing that ever happened. Ethan really does know everyone, and Kai walked in on day one being welcomed into the group.

In his last school, he didn't have anyone. He ate alone, and I cried all the time.

Not this time. He's truly fitting in, and so am I.

However, with school starting, Miles has been really busy, and it's getting only worse as more and more after-school functions and issues keep arising.

Miles grins. "All of this will be good. Now that you're really only working during school hours, and Kai goes to my sister's on the days you're late, we will have the evenings, not just the nights."

I nod. Hazel adjusted my schedule so I can take Kai and Ethan to school each morning, and I work a little past when school is out. Eloise has been amazing and keeps Kai until I'm home the three days a week I work. Which is only really an hour.

"We'll talk to Kai, see how he feels, and then we can go from there. If he's reluctant or struggles with it . . ." I trail off, because he comes first, and I want to ease him into it.

"We'll see how he takes it. I promise we'll go as slow as he needs."

I roll my eyes because the reality is, we know he's going to be over the moon. He loves Miles and thinks he's the coolest guy ever. They went ice-skating yesterday with Ethan because Miles said he missed having pucks hit at his balls.

"Kai is going to be elated, and I'm going to have to rein his eagerness in to have you here all the time," I say with exasperation. "He thinks you're *sooooo* amazing. He's probably going to ask you to move in!"

Maybe that's what I'm really worried about. That Kai's attachment will be a heartbreak I've managed to keep him from until now. There hasn't been anyone who has been a good male role model, other than my brother, in his life.

Miles is the first.

"I'd rather you guys move in with me," he jokes. At least I hope he is.

Not wanting to risk saying something stupid, I turn and look out the window.

"Hey," Miles says as he wraps his arms around my shoulders, pulling me against his chest. "What are you truly worried about?"

I sigh, looking up at him. "I don't want anyone to be hurt, that's all."

He kisses my nose. "Then we make sure no one does. If this doesn't work out, we'll be civil and I'll never treat Kai differently."

"And that's why, even as nervous as I am, I'm ready to tell him. Plus, I really worry he's going to see your truck one morning and we're going to have to explain then. At least this is on our terms."

Sometimes he leaves when it's still dark. Other times we fall asleep and are woken by the alarm, and then he's sneaking out the window or hiding in my closet until we leave for the day. It's really becoming difficult since I want him to stay. I'm the one who moans and grumbles when he gets out of bed.

Miles squeezes me tight. "I'll follow your lead. If you want to tell him and it feels right, we will. If not, we wait."

Going public is a big step, but telling Kai and our friends feels like it's the right thing. Especially since it's becoming sort of obvious. We have his tournament in a few hours, so it'll be like ripping the Band-Aid off, that's for sure.

Eloise's car pulls up and Kai rushes out, waving to them as he heads toward the door.

Here we go.

"Mom!" Kai yells as he bursts inside.

"Hi, babe. How was school and hanging out at Ethan's?"

"It was great. I got to help the teacher, and then at lunch, we played freeze tag."

I smile. "That's great."

Miles comes around. "Hey, little man!"

"Coach Miles!" He rushes to him, and Miles gives him a hug.

"Glad you had fun today. Freeze tag was my favorite," Miles tells him.

"Is Coach staying for dinner?"

I straighten myself, preparing to try to remember the speech I planned. "We're going to have dinner and then go to Miles's tournament today, but first, we'd like to ask you a few questions."

"Okay," he says hesitantly.

Miles breaks the tension by lifting him up and carrying him sideways. Kai laughs and then Miles tosses him on the couch.

"All right, we have questions, or your mother does."

I exhale. "Would you be cool if Miles spent some more time with us?"

"Duh, Mom."

Right. I knew that one would be easy. "Okay, well, what if Miles and I were to be a . . . couple?"

"Like, what?"

I glance at Miles, who is grinning at me. "Like, we have dates and maybe Miles will have dinner a lot more and we'll go to his house so he can cook too. We'll be . . . dating."

I'm really freaking bad at this, but I've had zero practice, so this is the best I got.

"So you'll be boyfriend and girlfriend?"

"Yes," I say quickly.

He shrugs. "That's cool." Then he turns to Miles. "I got new Legos from Uncle Quinn. Do you want to help?"

"I'd love to." Miles gets up, winks at me, and when Kai is already in his room, he says, "Now you're all out of reasons."

I laugh. "Go build Legos and I'm going to get ready for our next hurdle."

Going to the tournament and admitting it to our friends.

———

"They're all looking at us," I say under my breath as we're walking into his Ultimate Frisbee tournament, holding hands.

Miles grins. "Because you're so beautiful."

Or it could be the fact that we're out, together, as a couple for the first time in Ember Falls. All our friends knew what was happening, so there was no reason to hide it once Kai was on board.

"I don't think that's why Everett has a shit-eating grin."

"Probably not, but I'll make sure to get retribution for you if you want," he offers.

I think about how much shit Everett gives me on a daily basis coming into the coffee shop and nod once. "I wouldn't mind it."

Miles kisses my temple. "Consider it done."

I glance down at Kai, who is smiling so big as he sees us share a sweet moment.

"Kai, Ethan and Briggs are waving at you."

"Can I go play?"

I nod. "Just stay where I can see you, please."

He's running and yells back to me: "Okay, Mom!"

Miles places his hand on the small of my back and then pinches my ass. "Hey!"

"What?"

I grin. "You know what."

"My hand slipped. Can't help it."

"Sure you can't," I chide.

We get close to the group and my anxiety spikes again. This isn't nearly as important as the conversation we had with Kai, but a part of me wanted to keep this to ourselves. There was no pressure or worries about what people thought. We just enjoyed each other and had weeks of it just being . . . us.

Ainsley is at the grill and turns to see us. "Hey, guys!"

"Ainsley, I'd like to introduce you to someone," Miles says, and her eyes narrow. "This is my girlfriend, Penelope. You can call her Penny. She likes that name. She doesn't like Pen, says it's stupid. I don't know, she's got weird quirks. Anyway, she's going to be around more, and I know you're the nicest out of this group."

Ainsley is smiling so big her cheeks look like they're going to crack. "So it's official?"

"It's official," I say, smacking Miles in the stomach.

She rushes forward, pulling me into a hug. "I'm so happy. He's a great guy."

"I know, I'm happy too."

And terrified, but I keep that part to myself.

twenty-four
Mile

"You hired Violet?" Everett says as he enters my office. "To be a teacher here?"

I'm going to kill Mrs. Hendrix for letting him in.

"Hello, Everett. Please, sit down, inform me of your complaint. It's not like I haven't had sixteen phone calls this week from parents and teachers. I've been dying to hear one from someone who has nothing to do with this school."

He huffs and then sits. "You didn't tell me."

"I didn't have to."

"She's Violet. You know . . . about us."

"I know, but she asked me not to say anything, and I really wasn't sure what to say. Her situation is unique, and I figured you'd find out. Besides, it was like . . . forever ago. You've clearly moved on and so has she."

We all know that's not entirely true. Maybe Violet has moved on, but I'm not so sure about my friend here.

He laughs once. "Do you know how I found out she's back?"

"I'm sure you'll tell me."

"Damn right I will. I was in Prose & Perk, just giving Hazel my normal daily dose of shit, and then the door chimes. I think, oh, Ainsley is here, she usually comes in now to write or do research. Only it wasn't Ainsley."

I cut in. "It was someone else?" I ask dramatically.

He flips me off. "It was Violet. All grown up and absolutely fucking breathtaking."

No matter what Everett says, she's the girl that no other woman measures up to.

"I honestly didn't think to tell you."

"You should've."

I shrug. "Maybe, but she asked me not to, and I was respecting her wishes."

He runs his hand through his hair. "She's married. Or was. I knew that, I mean, we all knew since it was so fucking public."

"I didn't know."

"Seriously, you are supposed to be up on all the things because you're around the kids all the time, and you didn't put that together?"

"I don't follow celebrity gossip," I explain. I usually hear the major things, and I honestly never cared enough to look it up.

"You know about music."

"Well, I dare you to work in a high school and not know about the world's most famous pop star. So did you guys talk?" I ask.

Everett sighs heavily and it's clear this is really bothering him. "A little. She said hi. I said hi. Hazel went absolutely nuts and hugged her like she was her long-lost sister."

"She kind of is."

"Yeah, yeah, but then I stood there, pissed and hurt and shit that I shouldn't feel. It's been like fifteen years since we spoke. I don't know why I care."

I know why he does, but it's not my place to enlighten him. He loves her. He will always love her. She was his first everything, and the two of them made promises to each other and she broke them. Well, as much as young lovers do.

He wanted a future with her, and she went off and left him. Then his parents got in their accident, his father passed and his mother has struggled with the effects of the accident, leaving Everett as her primary caretaker.

Since then, he hasn't let himself even consider dating when his primary focus is his family.

He glances up at me. "Did you look online to see what has her living back here?"

I shake my head.

"I'd like to beat her asshole soon-to-be ex-husband with his own arms."

I chuckle. "I'm going to assume it's bad."

Everett stands and shakes his head. "Dude, they made the internet for a reason."

"Dude, I don't look up my employees' personal lives. She promised she'd give me one full school year. She's incredibly qualified, and we've known her since we were kids. Giving her the job was a no-brainer, and giving her her privacy was also one. If she wants to tell me, she will."

Thinking that would mollify him was my first mistake. "You should've told me she was back. She fucking lives next door. I can't avoid her."

"Well, I'm sorry you think that. It's been, as you said, many years. I didn't realize it would set you off." I stand. "Now, I need to do principal things, and that doesn't include standing here, listening to you." I grab my favorite mug, take a sip, and place it down. "I'll walk you out."

"I forgive you—well, I will after I kick your ass at practice," Everett says.

"You can try."

Everett leaves, and Mrs. Hendrix is at her desk, smiling at me with mischief in her eyes.

"You're fired."

"Please, you'd fall apart without me."

I wish it wasn't true. "Probation then."

She grins. "I've been on probation since the day I started."

"I'm learning the error of my ways."

Her hand motion is dismissive, and then she juts her chin toward the two students sitting in the chairs.

Great.

"Hawk? Blaire?" I call their names and both look over. "Let's go inside and see what trouble we're in, shall we?"

Today is really going to hell in a handbasket.

———

"I'm really nervous," Penelope admits in the car.

"It's going to be great. I promise. Gran will love you."

She already does. Eloise has told her just how much she adores Penelope. Gran called me two days ago, informing me that I would be going to her house today—with Penelope and Kai. Then I had a two-hour-long lecture about how old she is and the fact that I don't even consider her tender emotions, making me no longer her favorite.

I'm going to remedy that.

"I just really want her to like me."

I take her hand in mine. "She will. She's grumpy only to me and Eloise. It's our penance for making her suffer."

Penelope squeezes and nods. "Okay. I'll relax."

She won't, but at least she is saying it.

"Is Ethan going to be there?" Kai asks.

"He is. Eloise, Doug, Ethan, and Cora are all coming to dinner."

Because I basically threatened I'd break Doug's other leg if he didn't get his family there.

Gran is amazing. I love her with my whole heart, but she's old and crotchety. We need buffers.

"Cool!" Kai says and then stares back out the window.

We make the turn onto Gran's driveway and go past the large rock that I climbed all the time. "I would stand on that rock and pretend I was a pirate, looking out across the ocean. Other times it was an explorer who found the town."

Her eyes soften. "That's so cute."

"Cute or . . . adventurous and imaginative?"

"Cute."

I tried. I park and get out of the truck to open her and Kai's door. He's jumping down before the door is fully open, and then Penny gets out.

She looks at the house that I grew up in. It's the same in some ways as the day she bought it. It's two stories with white siding and blue shutters. She's painted those a few times, but the blue was the last color she changed it to before my mother died. The back is wooded, and there's a small clearing on the right where Eloise and I would play.

The porch is small but has two rocking chairs in which I spent many nights beside her as she knit.

"This house is adorable," Penelope says.

"It's home."

"She's close to the falls, right?"

I nod. "Yes, the falls are about a five-minute walk that way." I point past the trees.

Last week I finally broke down and told her the legend of the falls. I dragged it out as long as I could because it was fun, and I also wanted us to be public, so it was just a way to push her into it a little bit.

Not that I think it's even a small reason as to why she finally agreed to date.

We get to the front porch, and I lace my fingers with hers and open the door. "Gran? We're here."

Ethan comes darting out of the living room before we can even step foot through the threshold. "Kai! You're here! Come on, I have to show you this!"

Kai looks up at Penny, and she shakes her head. "But, Mom."

"You two can wait a second and say hello."

"Oh, you're here!" Gran exclaims and comes out of the kitchen, wiping her hands on the dish towel. "Hello, Penelope. Welcome to my home. And this must be Kai."

Penelope steps toward her, releasing my hand. "Thank you for having us. Eloise and Miles have told me so much about you."

She eyes me speculatively. "All good things, I hope?"

I grin and kiss her cheek. "There are only good things."

She scoffs and slaps my chest. "You keep your lies to yourself, Miles Anderson."

Ethan is practically bouncing out of his skin. "Granny, can I please take Kai to see the tree house? Please!"

Gran smiles. "Of course, you boys go play. It was nice to meet you, Kai."

"Nice to meet you too!" Kai says as Ethan drags him by the arm.

I chuckle. "Those two are really best friends."

I get a death stare from my grandmother. "I'm angry with you." She answers to what I'm sure is the puzzling look on my face. I just walked in. This is a new record, even for me.

"Me?" I ask in horror. "For what?"

"You brought this beautiful girl to meet Marge before me? How dare you?" Gran looks affronted, but I know better. Or at least I know how to butter her up.

"Don't be mad," I say, giving her my best pouty face. "I love you most. That's why I wanted you to meet her in a special way."

She shakes her head. "I believe nothing you say." Then she turns to Penny. "You come in the kitchen with me, dear. Miles . . . go away."

I laugh once. "Unreal. I've been dismissed."

Penelope grins and heads into the kitchen with Gran, and I'm sure my sister is there too.

Doug is sitting on the couch, the game on and my niece, Cora, passed out on his chest. I clap his shoulders as I walk behind him. "What's up, douchecanoe?"

He places his hand on her back. "Well, well, if it isn't the prodigal son coming for dinner. You know, all I've heard is how you didn't bring her here and she had to practically beg for you to agree to this."

I roll my eyes and sit on the opposite couch. "She'll get over it."

"She always does for you."

I laugh. It's only funny because it's true.

"How are you feeling? The leg better?"

Doug is fully out of a boot and walking. He's slow, but healing really well. "Doctor says I have maybe another two weeks of physical therapy, and then it'll just be doing what I can without pain. Already it's a million times better. The fact that I'm mobile has made things so much easier."

"I'm sure Eloise appreciates it."

He nods and mindlessly pats Cora's back. "She does. However, she warned if I set foot on the ice again, I won't have to worry about breaking a leg, because she's going to kill me."

"Sounds like Eloise," I say, leaning back. "So do you want to plan a game in a month?"

Doug grins. "Make it two."

I laugh softly, careful not to wake the baby. Although both of Eloise's kids seem to be able to sleep through a war. I have pictures of Ethan passed out on top of a speaker that was playing music. They never believed in being quiet when they were babies, and while I thought it was a little bizarre, it seems to have worked.

The two of us catch up, talking about how much he hates his job and is looking into becoming a fireman. "My military time would count and give me a loophole as I approach the age limit."

"I know you're miserable."

"It's an hour commute each way. Then I get home and Eloise is pulling her hair out with the two kids, and I'm exhausted and up at four in the morning. This would be closer to home, and I know everyone on the squad."

"Anything I can do to help, you know I will. I'm sure you've talked to Lachlan, but I'm happy to back you up if you're really interested," I offer.

"I'd appreciate it," Doug says, and then my sister and Penny walk in.

"Well, Penelope has been thoroughly indoctrinated, and Gran is half in love with her," Eloise says with her arm linked in Penny's.

"I don't know about all that," Penelope says, walking over to sit with me on the couch.

I smile, looking at her warm blue eyes. "I knew she'd like you. How could she not?"

Eloise makes a gagging noise. "Anyway, now you have to keep her because we all adore her."

"That's my plan," I say, just needing to find a way to make her want to be kept.

twenty-five
Penelope

Tonight has been much better than I could've anticipated. Miles's family have welcomed us with open arms, and I promised Gran I would come by this week to pick up something she wants to make for Kai.

Being here tonight was both wonderful and a little heartbreaking.

I don't have this.

I never did. My parents didn't live anywhere near our grandparents, so we never saw them, and they didn't speak to me. Miles's family loves him so much. They're close and warm, and it was beautiful to be a part of.

During dinner we laughed and they told old stories. Then we had the best chocolate cake I've ever had in my life. Gran was a baker and used to own the bakery in town. She definitely still has all the skills.

Now Miles and I are out walking down toward the falls, my hand laced in his, and I rest my cheek against his arm.

"I feel like we've been walking more than five minutes," I say as we wander along the tree line.

"I may be taking you the long way."

I smile. "I don't mind. I like having quiet time with you."

It's the best. We don't need to fill the silence, we just are together.

I never knew there could be so much peace with another person, but with Miles, it's effortless.

"Good. Do you remember what I told you about the falls?" he asks.

"Yes, that Gran owns half, which doesn't make any sense."

Seriously, how do you split a waterfall?

Miles chuckles. "The land splits right down the middle of the river. So the right half is Lachlan's and the left is Gran's. Of course, they're not putting ropes in the middle, but it was divided to protect the falls from ever being one person's."

"I think that's kind of cool. The ancestors of this town really thought about it."

"They did. They wanted everyone in the town to have a chance to heal themselves." He kisses my temple and veers us to the right. "When the land was divided, it went to two families who hated each other."

I glance up at him, surprised anyone would do that. "Really?"

"I always thought this was such a cool part of the story, and it always gets left out. This land has been in my family's name since the beginning. Gran's great-great-great-grandfather was the hated one."

"What?" I ask, jaw falling slack. "Why did you leave this part out?"

He chuckles. "Honestly, most of the time I just forget. Anyway, the Andersons and the MacLeroys hated each other. It was ugly. I think they stole cows and one slept with the wife of the other. I don't know, it was very messy and caused huge issues. So the town came together because they'd often suffer during their fights."

I'm honestly fascinated by all of this. "You make it sound so serious."

"Well, it was. I mean, old man MacLeroy could've taken my great-great-great-grandma, and then . . . I wouldn't be here."

I laugh softly. "That would be tragic."

"See, I knew you'd understand."

I shake my head. "Go on."

"Okay, so, the rival farmers hated each other, and there was drama so the mayor, or whatever he would've been of the town, stepped in. He decided that the only way to make the families stop feuding was to re-divide the land ownership. He made some bullshit decree, and they moved the river to be the buffer, but their beloved falls, well, they still needed those."

"Right, we need to magically heal the sick," I say in agreement.

"Exactly. The only way to do that was to divide the river itself in half. The Andersons and the MacLeroys were very powerful. They had a lot of cows."

I snort. "The testament of wealth, no doubt."

"Anyway, they split the land, and the demand the town made was either the people of Ember Falls were permitted unfettered access to the magical falls or the land would be seized from them both. If there were any more issues, they'd redefine the property lines again, and the falls would be off-limits. Since my family were definitely the most reasonable, we agreed immediately. After that, the MacLeroys left town, and we've stayed."

We reach the falls, and I stare at the beauty of it all. "I'm glad you stayed."

He turns me to look at him. "I'm glad you came."

I lift up on my toes, kissing him softly with the sounds of the rushing water behind us, and thank every star in the sky that I found my way here too.

———

My sister-in-law was right: Orgasmville is a lovely little town.

"Am I sneaking out your window again?" Miles asks as he curls his body around mine.

I turn, rolling to face him while he has his elbow propped up, watching me. "I was thinking . . ."

"About me, I hope."

I smile. "Yes, it's about you."

"Can I guess it?"

"If you must."

His grin causes my stomach to flutter. "I was thinking that you might be thinking that we should start sleeping together every night, and I don't have to leave before Kai wakes."

He's not that far off.

"You're close."

"I knew it."

I lean closer and kiss his lips. Miles makes me feel like a teenager experiencing her first crush. From the rush of nerves to the butterflies in my belly when I see him. Each time I think it'll lessen, but it hasn't.

"Do you want to know what I was actually thinking?" I ask.

"Of course I do. I want to know everything."

I know he does. He's been so patient, and I've appreciated it more than he can know.

"Okay, so I had two thoughts. First is that I think we should maybe go visit my brother. I know you have football games every weekend and you're busy, but I think you'd like Ashton and I'd love to visit."

"I'm never too busy to spend time with you, Penny. I'll always make the time. We can go any weekend you want."

The butterflies take flight again. "Ugh." I groan and flop on my back.

"That upsets you?"

I turn my gaze to meet his as he looks amused. "Yes, because you're so perfect. You're not supposed to be perfect. I keep waiting for this fatal flaw to emerge so I can convince myself that . . ."

That I'm not falling in love with you.

"That what?" he asks, his fingertip brushing across my lips. "Tell me what you're trying to convince yourself and I promise I'll find you a flaw."

I take his fingers in mine, intertwining them and staring at our hands. I may not be able to give him all he wants about my life, but this isn't the past.

This is the now and . . . if I have to walk away tomorrow, I would want him to know what he truly means to me.

Miles's warm green eyes glimmer in the soft light of the bedside lamp.

"That I think I'm falling in love with you."

He shifts his body closer and slowly leans down to kiss me. Each kiss feels different. It's as though he tells me something more and more every time. In this one, I feel his love. The tenderness pours from him and I drink it in.

He deepens the kiss, pulling his hand from mine and bringing it to my face, moving me to be closer to him. My hand goes around his back, leaving no gap between us.

He gentles the kiss and then pulls back. "I think I've already fallen in love with you."

Instead of feeling absolute joy, my heart is swarmed with pain and anger.

He can't love me.

He can't love a person he doesn't even know.

God, I didn't think it would feel like this. I had no idea that love could hurt because it might not last.

I let the tears come. They wouldn't stop even if I wanted them to.

I let all the sadness that I've been feeling for years come to the top, because I know Miles won't let me drown. Every emotion of fear, shame, despair, and hate bubbles up, making every part of my body ache.

I've struggled so much, I've been so fucking alone.

I've tried to keep it together, only crying in the shower, where no one could see or hear. To make the best of the situation because Kai deserved a better life than what I could give him.

All I've wanted was better for him and me.

Now I have it. I have it with Miles and he said he loves me. Why? Why can't I dream for more?

Because I made bad choices, that's why.

Miles pulls me against his strong chest, holding me together as I fall apart.

"Penny, sweetheart, please don't cry."

I wish I had any control, but he shattered me with his confession.

He doesn't let go and murmurs words of encouragement as my body is racked with sobs.

I cry for the life I lost.

I cry for the fear I've been living in.

I cry for the man I don't deserve who loves me.

I cry for the loss I know I'll have to suffer.

Losing Miles will be a pain like I've never known. I won't heal from it because it'll be so deep in my soul.

Finally, the sobs start to subside and I gain control. He lessens his hold and stares down at me.

"I'm sorry," I say, sniffling. "I know that's definitely not the reaction you were looking for."

The concern in his eyes almost breaks me again. "I'm more worried about you."

I owe him an explanation. Yet, it's more than owing it to him. It's that I *want* to tell him. I want to give him a part of me and hope that he'll understand.

"I've spent the last six years avoiding allowing anyone in," I tell him, staring at the vein in his neck.

He tenses. "Do you feel comfortable telling me why?"

"Only part of it."

Miles nudges my head up to look at him. "You can trust me, Penelope."

"I know, but I can't tell you everything. I wasn't exaggerating when I said it's best you don't know. It would've been honestly better if you never came around me. You wore me down," I admit as a tear trickles over my cheek. "You broke down every defense I had, and now I don't know how to get it back."

"I'll be your defense."

How absolutely perfect is this man. He has no idea what he'd be defending me from, yet he gives it so willingly.

"You can't defend me from the past, Miles."

"Did you do something? Are you running because of it?"

"Who said I'm running?" I ask, fearful of how close to the surface he is.

"I'm not saying this to scare you, but I'm trained to read and find secrets, Penelope. I know you're running from something. I'm pretty sure your brother doesn't work for a start-up, and he's helping to keep you hidden. I haven't asked about it because I don't want to push you. I've waited for you to open up because no one just randomly moves to Ember Falls. So what is it that has you hiding?"

I let someone's money and influence destroy my life because I thought he loved me. Edward's words were pretty, but his actions were those of a monster. I remember thinking how wrong he was, how cruel he could be, and explaining it away because he'd buy me something pretty and say how sorry he was after.

If I accepted his faults, surely it meant he'd accept mine.

But his weren't just fissures, they were fucking fractures.

Miles waits patiently, and I work to find my courage. My eyes meet his beautiful emerald ones, and I say all that I can. "I fell in love, or what I thought was love, with a very wealthy and powerful man. We'll call him John. John is Kai's father. John was the kind of man who wanted more—always. He wanted more money, more control, more of anything he could. I'm sure I wasn't the only woman he dated at the time, either, but I don't know for sure. He was brutal and savage and absolutely fucking awful."

"Did he hurt you?" His voice is full of restrained anger.

I close my eyes, remembering the pain of the back of his hand, and nod. "Yes, but it was always . . . calculating. Mostly he used other ways than brute force to scare me when I tried to leave. He broke into my apartment when I didn't sleep at his place and slashed my couches after I tried to leave him the first time. He would threaten me, more than anything, and I never knew if it was going to happen."

It was the fear that was the worst. That may sound impossible to someone else, but I could handle a backhand; the stalking and mind games were worse to me.

Miles draws slow circles on my back, telling me it's safe for me to go on.

"I found out I was pregnant. In that moment, when I saw that test with a plus sign, I knew I had to leave. There was never a doubt in my mind that he would either kill me or use the baby as a way to manipulate me."

There had never been a more clear moment in my life. I refused to bring a child into this world with Edward VanderGroef. Even if it meant spending the rest of my life on the run.

"Does he know about Kai?"

I shake my head. "No."

"But he's searching for you?"

"No."

His eyes narrow, and I can see the confusion on his face. "Penny, I'm not sure I understand."

"I know, and I'm sorry, but if I tell you more, if I give you this secret, your life will be in danger. I can't do that to you. I can't risk that you'll be dragged into this. The reason I didn't *want* to love you, damn it, is because I might have to leave. No, I *will*. They'll find me. They always do."

"Who will find you? If John, as you call him, doesn't know about Kai, why would he be hunting you?"

I look down, my heart aching from this conversation. Once again, the tears come, because the agony of this situation is eating me alive.

I love him.

God, I hate him for making me love him, but how could I not?

My hand balls into a fist and I rest it on his chest, wanting to push him away, but then needing him close.

"I can't tell you more."

He moves his hands to cup my face. "I will not let anyone hurt you. Telling me, giving me that risk, that's mine to take."

I shake my head. "It's mine to give and I won't."

The men that killed Edward know me. They saw me that night. They know what I saw, what I took from his office, thinking it would protect me, but it didn't. It made me their top target.

Even if I gave it back to them, they'd kill me. I know too much—names, places, certain players that are involved, all of it in that stupid book Edward kept in his top drawer. There is a missing link, though, the person who is at the top of it. Edward was smart enough to leave that out. That person will never stop.

"What will you tell me?"

"That I wish this could be different. That while I'm here, I'm yours, but I need you to promise when I have to go, that you won't follow. You won't look for me. You will let me and Kai go and know that leaving you is going to be the hardest thing I ever do."

"So one day you're just going to pack up your things and leave? You won't even give me a chance to protect you?"

I nod. "Yes. One day you'll come here because I won't be at work or Kai won't be at school, and it'll be like I never existed."

I won't lie to him about that. He deserves whatever truth I can share.

Miles sits up in the bed, shifting his legs over the side, and rakes his hands through his hair. "You have no intention of giving me a chance?" he asks, looking out the window.

My jaw trembles and I wrap my arms around my middle. "I'm giving you the truth. If I don't go, when I'm told I need to go, Kai or I could be taken, killed, beaten, or have to watch them torture the people I love. I've seen what they do."

He turns quickly. "So, what? I love you now? I come here one day to an empty house, and I just go on with my life as though I never loved you?" He shifts, taking my face in his hands. "Like I don't know what it felt like to hold you? To kiss you? To have you in my arms? Do you really think I can do that, Penelope?"

My heart breaks all over again. "I don't know."

"Well, I do. I can't do it. I will search for you, Penelope. If you leave, I'll be right behind you, because I'm not going to give you up without a fight. If someone is hunting you, then it's time I hunt them." He kisses me softly, and the pressure in my rib cage increases.

Miles pulls back and I gasp. He releases me and gets out of the bed, pulling his clothes on. "Where are you going?" I ask with fear that this is it. I would've prepared myself better if this was the end. I scramble out of the bed, pulling the sheet with me. "Miles? Are you leaving me?"

He has his pants on and grabs his shirt from the end of the bed. Once it's on, he steps closer. "I'm going to do what I need to do in order to protect you, because I'm not losing you."

And then he walks out and I rush to grab my burner phone out of the top drawer.

"Penelope?" Quinn answers on the second ring.

"I need you."

twenty-six
Miles

Doug is standing outside his house, arms crossed. "What's going on?"

I don't know what to tell him, but if there's anyone in this world who can help, it's him. "It's Penelope."

"Okay . . ."

"There's something that I can't fully say."

He nods once. "I'm going to assume it's bad."

"It is. I'm worried for her safety."

Doug watches me carefully. "What do you need from me?"

"I'm not even sure, but she needs to be protected until I can figure out who wants to hurt her."

"Consider it done."

There are people in this world that you know you can call at midnight on a Tuesday who will answer and be ready to fight, just because you asked. Doug is that person.

Just the same as I am for him.

"Thank you."

He shakes his head. "You'd do the same. What's your plan?"

I run my fingers through my hair and pace. "I don't have one yet. I don't even have the full fucking information. I guess that's step one. I need to know who and what exactly has her scared."

"So she's on the run from something?" he asks. "I only say that because it all seemed weird to me. Someone just randomly picks

Ember Falls? She had no ties here, just a desire to be a barista in a small coffee shop? I was suspicious, but I'm also built this way."

"You mean we were formed to be this way," I say, sighing heavily.

"True. It's done us well, though."

It has. Right now, more than ever. "Yes, but I wish I had all the tools I needed, and it's been so long since we were in, there's this feeling like I can't do anything. I can't provide her with the safety she's so desperately seeking."

Doug sits on the step at the edge of the porch. "Maybe she doesn't need that. Maybe she has that already; she just needs you to be there for her."

"She basically told me, in no uncertain terms, that she's going to have to leave at some point and she won't even come to me."

He falls silent for a minute, and then I sit next to him, a heaviness in my chest that won't weaken.

"You love her."

"Yes."

He grins. "Knew it would happen someday. You with all your bullshit about not wanting kids or a family. Then you fell in love with a girl who would give you both."

"I love him too, you know? Kai is a great kid and he's a part of her," I confess.

"Which probably makes it easy for her to love you back."

If she loved me, she'd give me a fucking chance to protect her. She'd tell me everything so I wasn't fighting in the dark with a blindfold on, swinging aimlessly. I could narrow in, focus, and be the man she needs.

"Not enough." The two words fall out, settling dread through me.

Doug inhales deeply and lets it out through his nose. "You've always had this issue, Miles."

"What?"

"You think, just because you're you and you're smart and have always been able to accomplish the things you set your mind to, that things will just happen. If they don't happen the way you want them, then there's some reason. Sometimes the things we don't know are because we're not meant to at that time. Look, I have never questioned your leadership, but when that mission went bad, you blamed yourself over and over because you acted on that intel."

I fall silent, waiting for the anger that I deserve. When it doesn't come, I say the only words I can. "I believed them."

"And we did too. If I really doubted it, I mean to my bones, I would've fought you. I didn't because you were always good at being patient. It was me who would jump off, and you'd rein me in. That didn't happen that day, and when I looked back, I blamed myself more than anything."

I turn to look at him, my eyes wide as I take that last statement in. "Blamed yourself, for what?"

"For not saying anything. That day, you were like a caged animal. You thought if we'd provided the information, then nothing bad would happen. We all went into that mission without proper planning. You're like that right now."

No. No, I'm just . . . worried.

I just don't want to lose her. I don't want anything to happen to her. "All I want is to protect her and Kai. To make sure that nothing ever makes her scared again."

"So why aren't you with her right now? Why are you outside my house in the middle of the night, ready to fight some invisible threat?"

"You'd be the same if it were Eloise."

"Probably, but I'd be sitting outside your house, and you'd be telling me to go to her, comfort her, be the man she can come to if she needs you so she never wants to leave. I'll reach out to some guys I know and do what I can. Go back to Penelope, Miles. Give her every reason to run to you instead of away."

Doug stands, clasps my shoulder, and heads inside.

I sit here for a few seconds, wondering when my friend became so wise, but knowing every word he said is true.

After another second, I'm in my truck and driving back to Penelope.

The light is on in her bedroom, and I see her moving around. I head over, knocking twice on her window. I see her jump and then look out. Her shoulders slouch slightly when she sees it's me.

Penelope slides the window up and waits. "Why are you here?"

"Will you let me in?"

She chews on her lower lip.

"Please, Penny, let me come in."

She releases a heavy breath and nods. I head over to the door, and the lock clicks open before I see her standing there in sweatpants, her hair in some weird haphazard mess on the top of her head, eyes red rimmed and puffy.

"I made you cry," I say, stepping toward her.

She retreats and I swear, my heart breaks from that one step. "No, you made me realize what I knew all along."

"And that is?"

"That I can't do this. That loving you was going to break my heart."

"It's not. You were right."

Her eyes widen. "What?"

"I have to decide if I can handle what you can offer me."

Penelope places her hand over her chest. "And?"

I move closer, and this time she doesn't retreat. "I will take any and everything you can give me. Even a small part of what we have is worth any possible heartbreak. I love you, Penelope. I love you and Kai, and I won't give up this time in fear of what may come. I'll stand beside you and in front of any danger that comes your way. I'll fight your past because I want your future."

She swipes at a tear before it can fall. "And if I have to leave tomorrow?"

"I pray you won't, but then I want tonight."

I take another step, and she lifts her head to look at me. "You came back."

"I never planned to leave you," I confess. "All we have is here and now, Penelope. I don't want to worry about anything else."

Every part of me wants to beg her to stay with me. To be with me as much as she can. If I can show her that I'll be her safe place, maybe she'll make other choices.

Her hands lift to rest on my chest. "I'll be right back."

"What?"

"I need to make a phone call."

My brow lifts. "Okay? It's almost two in the morning."

She nods. "I know, but I decided that staying is worth it. You're worth it. Even if I might have to leave, I want all the days I can have now."

Penelope lifts up and kisses me, and I vow I'm going to do whatever I have to in order to keep her with me for as long as I can.

twenty-seven
Penelope

L ast night was probably the longest of my life. I'm exhausted and eternally grateful that I have the day off today.

I got Kai off to school without issues, and now I plan to take a very long nap.

Until my phone—the burner—rings.

I quickly rush to it and answer. "Yes?"

"You're sure you don't want me to come get you?" Quinn asks again.

"I'm sure," I say apologetically.

"Will you explain what happened now?"

My poor brother must hate me at this point. He was an hour into the drive, about halfway to me because he was driving like a lunatic, worried as I was sobbing, and then I told him to go back home when Miles came back.

He kept asking what the hell happened, and I gave half answers because I wasn't really sure how to explain it all. However, he deserves an answer.

I relay most of the details of the evening, about how I told Miles some of the truth, his reaction, the fact that I love him and he told me he loved me. Quinn listens in silence as I prattle on and on, hearing how absolutely batshit I sound.

In that moment, though, it felt like the right decision.

To leave town before anyone got deeper or Miles's life became at risk.

It's bad enough carrying the guilt that my son suffers for it, I didn't want to add another person on the list.

Quinn is quiet after I finish explaining how he came back and my feelings around what I want now.

"Hello?" I ask after another minute passes.

"I'm here. Just wondering if I should come get you anyway, because you're clearly a mess."

"You're the one who told me to date him," I remind him.

"Yes. You're right. I was the dumbass who forgot that women are incapable of not flying off the handle."

I grumble. "I'm not certifiable."

"Penny, you called me at one in the morning and told me that you needed me to come move you. I had activated everything. We were already looking for a new town, names, plans to mobilize, while I frantically was on my way to you because I thought— somehow—they found you. Not that you were scared because you've fallen in love. You just cried and said you had to leave. Over and over."

I huff, bristling at the fact that I was . . . irrational. "I *am* scared," I admit.

"I bet. It's fucking terrifying falling in love. It's the single best and worst thing that ever happened to me. I couldn't imagine my life without Ashton, and yet she drives me bonkers. At the same time, I know that I would quite literally die without her. I've felt the pain of losing her once, and I know that I could never do it again."

Quinn and Ashton went through literal hell to get to where they are. I'd never seen my brother so broken, and when she left him, he fell apart.

"Then you understand why I'm so afraid of this?"

He lets out a long breath through his nose. "I understand. I just also think that you have to give Miles the chance to make his own choices. If he loves you, he's not going to give up. I think you should trust him with your secrets. If there's anyone in that town who is capable of doing what you need them to do, it's him. Just think about it."

"You're telling me to risk his life too?"

Quinn chuckles. "If he loves you, his only concern is you, and he doesn't care about risks, because protecting you is worth it."

The three of us are curled up on the couch, just finishing a movie that Kai picked out. We have family date nights at least once a week. Tonight was the only one we could make work. Tomorrow is the first hometown football game, which I was instructed I had to attend. Not by Miles, but by everyone.

The entire town shuts down.

Like, closed.

Every business, the parks, everything.

Friday nights in Ember Falls are for football, and the entire town attends to support the Bulldogs. So, tomorrow, we are going. Not just to support the football team, but because Miles will be there and we get special seating as his guests.

Kai is beyond excited, since Ethan and Briggs talk about it nonstop. They've been going to games since they can remember, and it's "the best time ever."

Kai looks over at Miles. "That movie was stupid."

Miles laughs. "It really was, but you picked it."

"Mom only gave me two choices."

I roll my eyes. "I liked it."

"Because you're a *girl* and it had kissing," Kai informs me. Apparently, my status as a female has definitely knocked me down a peg in the cool category.

Whereas Miles is the coolest person in the world.

Miles does his best to hide his smile. "I think guys like kissing too."

Kai's eyes flash to him, and the absolute horrification on his face is comical. "No, they don't."

I lean back, wondering how he plans to get out of this one. "Well, maybe not in movies."

That seems to mollify my son. Kai lets out a long sigh. "Next time we get to watch something with fights."

Oh boy. "Or we watch an animated film," I offer as an alternative.

Kai shakes his head. "No way, Mom. We need war."

I burst out laughing and Miles chuckles. "Okay, soldier. Go get ready for bed. You have school tomorrow."

He stands, salutes—badly, I might add—and rushes off.

"Come here, love," Miles says with his arm open. I scoot over, closer to him, and rest in the crook of his arm.

When he's here on family date nights, we keep the PDA to a minimum, increasing it each time to get Kai comfortable with it. Tonight, he kissed me when he came in the door, which was the first time we've done that.

Kai didn't even seem to care.

"That movie really was terrible," I say, smiling up at him.

"Seriously, so far, you've picked two movies, and each one was worse than the last."

I chuckle and nuzzle in more. "Whatever. Yours are all fighting and destruction."

"I pick movies Kai will like. I'm just cementing my spot with him."

"Any more cement and you'll become a statue," I mutter.

I don't think Kai could like Miles more than he already does. He includes him all the time, puts an incredible amount of consideration into everything he does regarding him, and shows up. Every time he makes a promise, he delivers, and he's honest when he doesn't think he can do it.

Kai asked him a few days ago if he could take him to the rink, and Miles explained he couldn't that day, but that he'd be able to on Saturday. Sure enough, Saturday morning, Miles was at the house to pick Kai up and spend the day with him when I had to work.

Miles hugs me close. "All part of my plan, sweetheart."

Since my breakdown a week ago, we've been fairly smooth sailing. We haven't brought it up again, but there's this tension that sometimes builds, having given him the reality of our situation.

I talked to Ashton yesterday, and she assured me that there have been absolutely no indications that anyone is close to figuring out where I am. She also encouraged me to open up and give this burden to be shared.

She said her therapist also agrees.

There's that.

I've been thinking about all of what I've been through and how it's led me here. I feel safe and I know that Miles would do anything for us. He loves me. I love him with my whole heart and maybe all my worry was for nothing.

My brother is doing everything to protect us from afar and Miles is doing it here.

"Stay tonight," I say, looking up at him.

"I was hoping you'd say that."

I smile back at him, hoping tonight goes well.

———

"Yes," I moan as he thrusts harder.

"You feel so fucking good," Miles says, gripping my thigh as he holds it in place.

"You always feel good," I tell him.

Miles adjusts his hips, somehow finding a way to drive even deeper. I feel him everywhere. Like he is a part of me, and my heart is pounding.

"Look at me." His voice is harsh through his teeth.

My eyes meet his. There is so much emotion that it takes my breath away. I see his love, his devotion, his desire and promises all in there. I open myself up, letting down every ounce of self-preservation, hoping he sees the same in my gaze.

I plan to give him everything, no more restraints, and pray it's the right choice.

Miles slows his thrusts and glides inside me. It's no longer sex. It's so much more than that.

Another orgasm is building. Each thrust I get closer and closer. He feels so good, so right, and his cock hits the perfect spot each time he slides in and out.

"I love you," I say to him as he fills me again.

His hands take mine and he lifts them above my head, entwining our fingers. "I love you, Penelope. More than I ever knew was possible."

"I need you," I confess.

"You have me."

"I want you." I continue saying what's in my heart.

"I'm yours."

"I can't lose you."

Miles stills, buried so deep inside me. "Then don't leave me. That's the only way you'll ever lose me."

A tear slides down my cheek, and then another one. It's not sobbing. It's just so much emotion. So much love that it has to spill out or I'll die from it.

"I won't," I promise.

Miles's mouth is on mine again, his cock filling me, and he pulls his hips back one more time; then we fall apart together.

He lies there, still throbbing inside me. "I'm not ready to leave you yet."

I feel the same way. "I like you inside of me."

"I like being there."

I grin. "How about we clean up and climb back into bed, where you can hold me and we talk?"

"That sounds ominous," he says, pushing my hair back.

"It's not. I mean, it kind of is, but not in the way you think."

He nods and we head into my bathroom. Miles has a toiletry bag he keeps under my sink for nights just like this. We shift around each other effortlessly, which makes me smile, and he does the same in the mirror.

Miles kisses my forehead and heads back into the bedroom while I finish up.

I grab his shirt, pulling it on and buttoning the bottom four buttons. I love to sleep in his shirt. It smells like him, the deep notes of amber from his cologne clinging to the fabric, his deodorant, and . . . just . . . Miles.

I inhale it as I walk over to the bed, where he's propped up on the pillows, glasses on as he checks his phone. He puts it down as I get near, my knees hitting the mattress as I stand there.

"Do you want to lie with me?" he asks.

I shake my head. "I'd like to sit."

"Okay."

I climb up, crossing my legs and facing him. "I told you a small amount about my past, but I left out what I thought would be dangerous for you to know."

"Penelope," Miles says, stopping me, his hand reaching out to rest on my knee. "I'm not afraid of your past."

"You should be," I say on a whisper. "You don't even know what you're involved in."

"Did you kill someone?"

"No."

"Did you maim someone?"

I shake my head. "I wish."

"Okay, so are you running from the cops?"

"No."

Miles shifts closer. "Then tell me so I can better protect you."

"If I tell you this, you have to let me say it. Don't ask questions until I've somehow managed to explain it in full, okay?" He nods. I inhale deeply and force the story out. "John is really named Edward VanderGroef. We met in Chicago when I worked in the same high-rise. Edward owned a lot of different companies. He was beyond wealthy. I was working for a commercial interior design company, fresh out of college with big hopes and dreams.

"When we started dating, things were beyond my comprehension. He bought me gifts and clothes and jewels and everything. He had money that people like me only imagined. We were together for a year before things started to change. Gone was the sweet man who showered me with love and affection. He became cold and distant at times. I just figured it was something with his business."

Miles stays quiet, but his hand moves up to find mine.

"The first night he hurt me, we were at a party. He was drunk and I made an offhand joke to one of his friends. He squeezed my upper arm so hard I bruised. The next morning, he sent me flowers and a bracelet. He swore he didn't mean to do it, that he was drunk and didn't know his own strength. I withdrew from him, but he was relentless in pursuing me.

"Eventually I forgave him. It continued in this pattern until he backhanded me so hard I swear I blacked out. That next day, I got all my stuff from his house and told him it was over. Only that wasn't acceptable for Edward. That night, he threatened that if I tried to leave him, I'd see how hard that would be, because he had ties to everyone in Chicago."

I take a breath, making sure he's still with me. Miles keeps quiet, and I tangle my fingers with his.

"He got me fired and then broke into my apartment to slash my couch. A week later, I found out I was pregnant and I knew. I knew I couldn't have a child with this man. He would never stop, and I couldn't do it. I called my brother, who, as you guessed, doesn't do what he says. He works for a security company that does things I'm not even sure about, but personal protection is one of them. He wanted me to tell Edward that I was going out of town for a friend's wedding. To invite him, knowing he couldn't and wouldn't come. Edward didn't do anything that wasn't going to benefit him."

I stop there, feeling the fear starting to mount. This is where the story becomes dangerous for him.

Miles nods, encouraging me to go on, but I need to give him one more chance of an out. "If I tell you this next part, it's where I put you at risk. Do you understand?"

"Penelope, the only risk I care about is what would happen to you and Kai. I know I'm not a marine anymore, but I do have train- ing. I know how to protect myself and others. You're not risking my life, because there is nothing I won't do for you. Nothing I won't give if it means you and Kai are safe. I know the risk, and I'm sitting here, unmoving."

The story becomes so real, I see it all like a movie.

"You can do this, Penelope. You are going to leave and protect your unborn child, who will never know the horror that is their father," I told myself as I stood outside Edward's office door.

It was late, dark, and I felt like I was going to be sick—again. This was a common part of my days since I found out I was pregnant, but that time, it wasn't morning sickness.

I called my brother from the lobby.

"Did you do it?" Quinn asked.

"Not yet, I'm not sure I can. Maybe I can just leave without telling him," I suggested, hoping Quinn changed his mind.

He didn't.

"No, we need some time, and if he thinks you're only gone for the weekend, it allows us to get the pieces into place. You've got this, Penny."

I exhaled. My heart pounded so hard against my chest, I thought it would break a rib. "I'll call you when it's done."

"I'll be at the meeting spot. Come right here."

I disconnected the phone and took the elevator up to the fifty-third floor. There was only a lamp on in the front room, and Edward's office was bright. There were the sounds of three men talking. I didn't recognize any of their voices.

"You'll bury the body on your property," the one man said, and I stopped exactly where I stood.

Edward huffed. "Absolutely not, Michael. I'm done hiding your fuckups. I'm not excavating a new location."

The same man spoke again. "You forget who I am and what I can do if you refuse."

"You forget what information I hold as well. I don't think your voters will put you in for another term if they know you're laundering money and responsible for the last incumbent's death." Edward's voice was harsh.

I moved closer to the door, peeking in. There stood the senator I'd met at a party a few months ago, someone in all black, who definitely looked like a bodyguard, and Edward's business partner, Anthony.

"Don't try me, Edward."

Edward spun around in his office chair. "Or what? You'll kill me too? I don't think so. I'm the one who holds the cards, and if you so much as try to fuck with me, all your secrets will come out. I'm not stupid, Michael. I keep all the information safe as insurance."

He looked so smug, so sure that he was completely safe. I'd seen that smug superiority so many times. After he'd hit me or taunt me about what my life would be if I tried to leave. I was done being scared, though. I was ready to live on the run if it meant my child would be safe.

Anthony scoffed. "You're such a pompous prick."

"And you're a fucking pussy," Edward spat back.

Then, I saw the most infinitesimal movement from the senator. He stepped forward, and his bodyguard also moved. "You should really think twice about threatening someone." The senator's voice was as cold as ice.

Before I could move or blink, the bodyguard moved to the back of Edward's chair with something in his hand. He wrapped it around his neck, pulling it tight. I watched in horror as Edward clutched at the wire wrapped around his neck. It lasted what felt like an hour, but it was really only a few seconds.

They turned and looked at Anthony. "Find the book and kill anyone who's seen it."

"Penny," Miles says quickly. "My God."

"I hid. I knew I had to or I would be dead too. I tucked myself under the front desk of his assistant, staying as small as I could. They left the room, after tearing his office apart. Edward told me that if anything happened to him, I needed to go to one place. He told me it was going to keep me safe. Even in his games, he knew that I was at risk. He explained there was a book in his office and they'd want it. Once I was sure they left, I went to the couch they'd flipped over, pulled the staples back, and took the book that was secured in the wood frame."

"So they know you have it?" he asks.

Again, in my haste, I was stupid. There are so many things I should've done differently. If I had called Quinn before I left the office or when I was in there. If I had called the cops, I had the proof, but the book was . . . off. It had half answers and things left out. There were first names but not last ones or vice versa. Nothing in that book could actually prove anything, and that book that he thought would protect me became a liability because I knew *some-thing*. Enough that people would want to gain that information.

"They were watching the building and saw me come out with it. I called my brother as I was running out of the building, and he told me where to go. I got in my car and headed to him. Anthony and the senator must've assumed I was just going somewhere and they just needed to wait for the right time, but I was protected by Quinn and his friends by then."

"What was in the book?" Miles asks, playing with my fingers.

I take the strength he offers and say the rest: "Dates, locations of bodies, money that they were laundering. But the book is flawed. The list of names are half there. The thing is, even if I gave them the book, they'd kill me. They've hunted me, finding me each time Quinn moves us. I hoped they'd give up after six years, but I don't think they ever will. Until we crack what's in that book, I'll never be safe."

Miles reaches forward, pulling me into his arms. I let him hold me, because I'm absolutely drained.

Miles pulls back after a while, taking my face in his hands. "Their days of coming after you are over, Penelope. I protect what I love, and I will make sure you and Kai are safe."

twenty-eight
Penelope

Protecting what he loves means spending the next two weeks trying to constantly surprise me by grabbing me, tossing me around the house, and teaching me ways to get out of his hold.

"Good, Penny, keep your arms in next time."

I glare at him. "I know all of this is your way of controlling the situation, but you're killing me."

"No, I'm trying to keep that from happening," Miles says after flipping me over.

This week, we're doing choking maneuvers. I swear, he's enjoying this a little too much. However, since doing this with him, I feel a little . . . calmer.

"If someone grabs you, where does this arm go?" He lifts my right arm.

"I hook it under and twist," I say.

"Exactly, love. You duck at the same time you twist."

I can really see why he was such a great teacher. He's smart, calm, and explains things in a really clear way. Last week, we talked about what to do if someone grabbed me, all the ways to break a hold, if someone grabbed me by my hair, but Miles was adamant I learn how to get out of a choking situation.

Today, he's shown me if they grab me standing up, or against a wall.

"You do realize that even if I get out of this, it doesn't mean they won't grab me again," I remind him. "There was more than one person."

He nods. "I don't think the others like to get their hands dirty. Killing someone isn't as easy as it sounds. I would guarantee the reason they had their henchman is because they don't have the stomach for it. You just worry about one person, and their weakness. Then you run, and you do whatever you can to get away." His hand cups my cheek and then moves to my neck, his eyes staying there for a moment. "You get away and find help. What is the other thing you do?"

I roll my eyes. "I call for help and make a lot of noise."

Miles grins and leans down. "Good, now I'm going to choke you, and I want you to break free."

I exhale and grab his wrist, twisting the way he showed me. "Ha!"

He chuckles. "Just like that. Okay, now we're going to go through what I think will be the most likely way they'd try to choke you."

Great, more choking. "You know, if this was my kink, we'd be doing something totally different. We could be naked and sweaty, instead . . . we're sweating for another reason."

Miles's eyes go wide. "Don't worry, you're going to be naked and sweaty very soon. Now stop trying to distract me."

I tried. "All right, show me how not to die."

Miles grabs me quickly, putting me on the floor and mounting me, his hands going to my neck. Fear fills me instantly. I know he would never hurt me, but I don't think I can get out of this. His eyes are focused on me. "If someone has you this way, it's the most dominant and probably likely to hold. I have complete control. All of my weight will push onto your neck, making it a much easier way to choke you. You have six seconds before you'll pass out, and if they continue, you'll be dead."

"Miles, I can't," I say, panting, my anxiety the highest it's been. They killed Edward by choking him to death.

"You can. Look at me, Penelope. Get your elbows in as tight as you can get them against your side." I follow his instructions. "Now take your right arm and cross it over your chest, hooking my wrist." I do that and he shakes his head. "Put your thumb next to your fingers, not wrapped around."

"Why?"

"Remember how you can break a hold because the thumbs can't hold body weight? Same applies here."

Okay, that makes sense. I adjust my grip.

"Like this?"

"Perfect. Keep your elbows tight to the body and move your left arm to hold my tricep. This makes it so I can't pull my arm out to break your hold. Right now, you have control of this arm completely." Miles tries to move his arm side to side and out, but he can't. "Hook your leg over mine. Other foot in the center." I move that one. "Now keep your arm locked against your side and use your hips to push."

There's no way I'm getting him over. He's got at least fifty pounds of solid muscle on me.

However, I try it. I push up with my hips, keeping my grip as tight as I can, and he rolls. I break the hold and I'm running the way he's shown me.

"I did it!" I say when I'm at the door. "I rolled you! Did you let me?"

"Did it feel like I let you?"

I shake my head. "No."

"Because you used my hold against me. This isn't a fight. This is break and escape."

He walks to me, hands up, indicating he's not about to push me against the wall to choke me. "Come here," he says softly.

I eye him suspiciously, because he did this to me before. "Truce?"

He grins. "Truce. I need to kiss you, Penelope. You have red marks on your neck, and I can't look at it."

My heart melts when I see the regret filling his beautiful eyes. "You're teaching me."

"Still, I don't like it."

I go to him and he dips his lips, kissing the angry skin. "You'd never hurt me on purpose," I say, running my fingers through his hair as he places feather-light kisses on my mouth.

"No, I wouldn't."

I dip my head back to look in his eyes. "Again. I want to see if I can do it again."

He nods once and then grabs my legs, putting me back on the floor, and we keep going until I can do it when he's at full strength.

———

It's a Sunday afternoon and we're at the Ultimate Frisbee Championship. Who knew there was such a thing?

Miles, Everett, Lachlan, and Killian have been here since seven in the morning, setting up, getting loose or whatever, and preparing for what will surely be an ass kicking.

Their first match is at noon, and I'm in the car with Ainsley, Kai, and Rose.

"This goes all day?" I ask.

"All. Day," Ainsley says with a huff. "Although, this is the first time they're competing in a championship in this league, so it actually may go really quickly since they suck so much."

"Daddy said they're going to win," Rose pipes up.

"I hope so!" Ainsley says and then gives me a look saying there's not a chance they do.

We ride the thirty minutes, laughing and talking about Ainsley's job. She's heading to Washington, DC, to cover a story she thinks is going to blow up. She spends about one week a month up there as she works for a newspaper in New York.

"I really think there's something off about this senator," she says as she makes a left into the parking lot.

"Is that what you're investigating?" I ask.

She nods. "There's just a hunch I've had, and my boss has shot the story down like ten times, which is weird, because we'd want to be on the breaking side of it. I have a source who is adamant I need to dig in. All the places I've looked so far have come up empty, though. I guess I get why my editor isn't all in. I need something concrete before I can spend weeks on it."

I know nothing about journalism, so I'll take her word on it. "Can you tell me who?"

"I wish I could, but I really can't. Not that I think you're not trustworthy, I do. I just have to protect the story always."

I can't help wondering whether it's a certain senator I know. I wonder whether Ainsley knows and could . . . I don't know, help.

No. I'm not dragging her into it.

"Don't apologize, your discretion is actually admirable," I say softly.

"If I'm wrong, which I could be, that could destroy his or her life, you know? I don't ever want to be that person. Accusations can do just as much damage as facts sometimes. We see that constantly in politics."

"In life too," I say.

"True. People often overlook things based on their own opinions. It's just the way it seems lately. It's why I'm very cautious with any story I put out. I protect my source as well as making sure all the information is verified."

I respect that completely. "I think that's what makes you a good journalist."

Ainsley smiles brightly. "You think?"

"I do."

"Well, who knew that me writing about the love of my life and Ultimate Frisbee would've been the break in my career I needed."

"The last part especially," I say with a laugh.

She sighs deeply, glancing at Rose in the back. "It was the break in my life too. It brought me to Ember Falls and to Lachlan."

We pull into the parking lot, and there are hundreds of cars. Frisbees are flying around, people sitting at the backs of their cars with grills, tents, and chairs everywhere. I had no idea this was such a big thing.

"Yeah, they do Frisbee big in these leagues," Ainsley says when she sees my face.

"This is . . ."

"Yup. Just wait, the guys have a great setup, and hopefully they brought a physical therapist this time, because one of them is bound to pull something."

I laugh. We park and then I turn to Ainsley, wanting to ask her something, but I'm not sure I should.

"Penny?" she asks as I stare at her. "Are you okay?"

Here goes nothing. Ainsley has been a friend, and she probably understands the fear I have about all of this.

"Were you scared?" I ask her. "When it came to Lachlan?"

Ainsley's eyes flash to mine, and there's a mix of understanding and sisterhood in her gaze. "Very. Love is terrifying. At least I think so. Moving to Ember Falls after fighting so damn hard to be a reporter in New York was also a big risk. I think that without taking any chances, you never know what rewards might be awaiting you. Look at you and Miles. If you hadn't come here, you'd never have met him."

"That would've been a really sad thing," I say with all the honesty in the world. "He's a great man."

"He'd do anything for you, Penny."

"I know he would."

She reaches her hand out, gripping my wrist and squeezing. "I'm glad you came to Ember Falls."

I cover her hand. "Me too."

"Now, let's go watch them lose and pretend we care."

twenty-nine
Miles

I wrap my arm around Penelope's shoulder, pulling her against my sweaty chest.

"Eww, stop," she complains with a laugh.

I kiss her temple and lower my voice. "You like when I'm sweaty."

She ducks her head and I imagine her pink cheeks. "Not like this."

"Oh, only when you can be sweaty too?" I tease.

Her eyes meet mine. "You're ridiculous."

"You're adorable."

"You need a shower."

I grin. "You should come home with me and make sure I don't miss a spot."

Her blue eyes flash with heat, and she plays with the silver medal around my neck. "Maybe I will. You are a podium winner, after all."

We played really well today. Much better than we have all year. I was actually quite remarkable, if I do say so myself. It was almost like the team of last year, where we were in sync and all the plays just clicked.

"That I am. We almost had the gold too," I remind her.

"You did very well."

I kiss her softly, and then Kai rushes to us. "Can we go to Mr.

Lachlan's house today? Rose said that she can swim in the falls, and I want to swim in the falls, too."

Penelope shakes her head. "Not this time, buddy. You have school tomorrow, and I'm pretty sure you still have homework to do."

He grumbles a little but then sighs heavily. "Fine."

I chuckle and watch as he runs off. "I have homework to do too," I tell Penny.

"Oh?"

"I need to study some anatomy."

She laughs. "You do, huh?"

"I do and I need a live model," I tell her.

"Wow, I hope you can find one on such short notice."

"I was thinking a redhead with blue eyes might be open to it."

Penelope's smile is slow. "I wonder where you plan to find one of those?"

I pull her back to my chest, her hands splayed there, and I grin down at her. "I think I already found her. What do you say? Will you let me strip you down and see if I remember what goes where?"

God, I really hope she says yes. The last few nights I've had to work late and haven't been able to go to her house. I've missed her. So fucking much.

"What part of the body are you studying?"

"The lower half."

She lifts up on her toes. "I think I could help with that."

I pull her up so we're eye to eye. "I can't wait. Come on, I'll drive us home."

We make the thirty-minute trip back to Ember Falls. Kai asks a lot of questions about why we did certain things and the rules of Ultimate Frisbee. Afterward, we come up with a schedule for the week. Friday is our next home game, and Penelope and Kai will be there with me again.

"Did you like the game the last time?" I ask him.

"It was super cool!" Kai exclaims.

"This time, do you want to come on the field with the mascot? You can even hold the leash," I offer up to him. Everett will really appreciate this. Brutus is an absolute menace, and watching Everett try to control him is priceless.

"I can?" Kai asks.

Penelope, seeming to know what I'm up to, cuts in. "No, you cannot hold the leash. You can stand with Mr. Everett—if he says it's okay."

Well, there goes my fun.

Kai is still smiling. "Okay, I'll ask him!"

I grin at Penny. "Killjoy."

"Troublemaker."

I shrug. "You love it."

We pull up to my house, and I feel a bit of nerves hit me. Penelope and I have been together for almost three months. We've been at her house, or on nights when Kai is with my sister, or when last week he went to stay with Quinn, we're at my house.

Lately, I just want every night with her. A lot of it is that I'm constantly on alert, and when I'm not near her, I feel unsettled. I worry and find myself making every excuse to spend each night together. She's safer when she's close to me, where I can protect her and Kai.

This week I had a new security system installed in my house. I want one more barrier to entry. One more way that if someone tries to get to her, they have an obstacle, and it gives her time, which is what she needs to hide or run.

On top of that, I asked Eloise for some help to do something else for her and Kai.

Once we park, we get out and I let them in, putting in the code.

"You have an alarm system?"

"Yes, I had this put in for when you're here."

She smiles at me. "You're sweet."

"I'm prepared."

I'm also sweet, but this isn't about that. It's about something else, and I have to ask her, but I have no fucking clue how it's going to go over.

"Kai, can you go into the game room for me? I got you something."

His eyes widen. "You did?"

"I did, but I also need to talk to your mom. You're welcome to open and try it out, and we'll come in as soon as we're done, okay?"

"Okay!" He rushes out of the room, and I hear him scream when he sees the arcade game I bought. Every kid should get to play arcades.

"What did you do?" she asks.

"Don't worry about it. Listen, I want to talk."

Her body tenses just a little. "Okay, is there something wrong?"

"No, just the opposite. I want you to move in with me."

Penelope steps back. "What?"

"Move in with me. Stay here. We're together all the time anyway, and you'll be safe here. I have the alarm system, put in a new door that's reinforced and can't be breached. Doug is installing cameras next week, and I did something else."

Here it goes.

"What did you do?"

I take her hand and walk her to what used to be a guest room. I slowly push open the door and show her the transformation.

Gone is the neutral guest room with a queen bed and two night-stands, and there is a bunk bed with a full on the bottom. There's a Lego table off to the right and a dresser with a television mounted on the wall. The room has lighting around the top that changes to every freaking color combination possible. My sister was adamant that I didn't do a bedding with characters on it, and so I went with a blue-and-gray color scheme.

Penelope inhales, her hand on her chest. "This is . . ."

"For Kai. If you don't want to move in with me, that's fine, but at least he has a place of his own. He and Ethan can use this room for sleepovers or—"

Before I can say another word, Penelope has her arms wrapped around my neck and her mouth on mine. I wrap my arms around her, pulling her to me, and return her kiss.

Instead of letting this kiss get carried away, I pull back and lift her up so her legs are around my middle. "Are you happy?"

"I can't believe you did this," she says breathlessly.

"Why can't you?"

"We're so new."

"I love you. I want you both with me."

She stares at me as though she can't really believe what she sees. "I love you too."

"Will you at least think about moving in? You'd save money on rent, and I make a pretty good bodyguard."

Penelope's hand moves to my face, and she brushes the stubble there. "I'll think about it."

"Good."

I hope the answer is yes.

———

"Where's Penny?" Hazel asks as she finds me at the football game.

"She should be here any minute," I reply, although she's about fifteen minutes late.

This week I had a huge issue at the school with two students who got in a fight, and when I suspended them both, both of their parents wanted to have meetings with me. That meant that Tuesday night, when I was supposed to have dinner and watch a movie with Penny and Kai, I was here until nine, because no matter what I said, the family wasn't hearing me. One day missed with Penny and Kai. Then on Wednesday it was the other family. I didn't think it could be worse than the first, but I was proved incorrect.

Thursday is the day before game day, and I always have to stay late because home games in Ember Falls often get out of hand. I met with the sheriff and county police to establish whatever safety protocols they want. Tonight's game is against our biggest rival, and last year the benches and the stands cleared.

It was absolute mayhem.

"How did the threats go?" Hazel asks with a smirk.

"You mean the entire school assembly, where I had to basically inform everyone that if they participated in any kind of altercation, they'd be expelled? It went over like a ton of bricks."

I've been the cool principal since I started. I don't hold that title anymore.

I'm now the asshole. As an Ember Falls alum, I should know

better. We're playing against Spring Hills. They're the worst. They're dumb. I'm supposed to support the anarchy.

"You are a traitor," Hazel informs me.

I glare at her. "I'm trying to stop a riot."

She laughs. "Oh, please, you were the one who led the fight when we were seniors."

"I did not."

One brow lifts. "No? I think you're mistaken, friend."

Okay, so I might have done that. They were worse back then. It was also a different time. We didn't worry about them bringing weapons.

"Whatever."

She nudges me. "So I heard you asked Penelope to move in?"

I try not to think about it all the time, because she still hasn't given me an answer. We planned to discuss it again. I was hoping we could tonight, but between our schedules, we just haven't had the time.

"I did."

"And?" Hazel asks.

"I don't know."

Her eyes go soft. "It's a big step. She's got a kid to think about too."

"I'm aware. I would never do anything I wasn't sure about."

I'm sure about her. About us. About the fact that she is the only person I can see myself with.

"As someone who has known you almost my entire life, I know this, but it's still new. I can imagine that I wouldn't be rushing to move in with a guy after just a few months. Give her some time."

"Did she say something?" I ask, knowing Hazel and her penchant for pulling information out of people.

She shakes her head. "No, we didn't talk. I mean, we kind of did. She told me you made a room for Kai and asked her to move in." Hazel places her hand on my arm. "If you want my opinion, and this isn't based on anything that Penny said, just from what I know about her from working for me, it was probably a little scary. She's skittish in some way. I assume there's a good reason for it, but I don't know.

She sent me a text yesterday morning, saying Kai wasn't feeling well and she'd be out of work for a bit."

"He's sick?" I ask.

I figured she would've at least said something.

"I guess. I told her it was no big deal, and that I would cover the store. She's off the next two days after that for her normal schedule."

Why wouldn't she tell me? I know I've been busy, but even just a text message would have been fine.

I grab my phone, wondering if maybe I missed it, but the last text was last night, when she said she was really tired and asked if I could just see her at the game today instead of coming by.

"Maybe she's sick too," I say, relaying part of the text to Hazel. "Maybe that's why she didn't want me to come there last night."

"Could be if she was feeling sick or Kai was."

I shoot off a text.

> Hey, are you okay?

I wait, but nothing.

"Mr. Anderson? It's time for the coin toss."

I turn to Hazel with a sigh. "I'll be back in twenty. Keep an eye out for her and sit over in that section there. I saved us a row."

"Sure thing."

I head out onto the field to help keep the peace. The principal of Spring Hills and I agreed to come out together and do the coin toss to avoid the kids talking any kind of shit while standing there. While I may have grown up hating Spring Hills, bunch of assholes, Damon is a great guy, and we have no issues.

We get to the center and shake hands.

"Miles."

"Damon, good to see you."

He smiles. "You as well. I've given the best warnings I can."

I chuckle. "Me too. Let's hope this one goes better than last year."

"Seriously."

The referee nods to both of us, and Damon calls heads.

Dude, tails never fails is a saying for a reason.

It lands on tails, and I was told by the head coach that under no circumstances were we to defer.

I let the ref know of our choice, and Damon and I shake hands again. "Good luck."

"You too, Miles."

The teams all line up, and the national anthem is played. We continue to stand in the middle with the referees, again to show that we can be civilized, and then it's time to kick off.

I check my phone to find still no response from Penelope and go up to my seats.

"Did you hear from her?" I ask.

"No, nothing," Hazel says.

"I'm going to call," I say, having this unsettled feeling in my stomach. I get around the side of the snack stand, where I can get a little privacy, but it just rings and goes to voicemail.

Maybe they're napping or . . . I don't know.

Still, I can't help but worry a little.

I send a text off to Doug.

> Me: Hey, can you swing by Penelope's house and just check and make sure she's okay? I'm at the game and I can't leave, but she's not answering her phone.
>
> DOUG
>
> We're pulling in now, but I'll drop Eloise and the kids off then go by if you want.
>
> Thanks.
>
> DOUG
>
> You're so going to owe me.
>
> Put it on my tab.

Eloise, Ethan, and Cora make their way to where we're all sitting.

"No fights yet?" my sister asks.

"It's only been two minutes."

She shakes her head. "Slackers."

I keep my phone in my hand, in case Penelope or Doug calls.

I wait.

And wait longer.

Finally it rings and it's Doug. "Hey," I answer on the first ring. "Did you check on her?"

"Miles . . . she's gone."

thirty
Miles

I'm in my car, not even caring about the game. As soon as Doug said the words, I was running.

She's gone.

No. She's not gone. She wouldn't leave like this. Not after everything we talked about. Not after all the fucking promises made.

She said she'd come to me. She said she wouldn't leave.

I slam my hand on the steering wheel, pissed that my worst fucking nightmare is coming true.

My phone rings and I pray it's her, telling me where she is and to come to her. It's not. It's Mrs. Hendrix.

"I had to go," I say quickly.

"I understand that, but we have a small issue."

Of course there is. This entire day is coming unraveled. Why not have my job be part of it? However, everything else in the world could crumble, and this is where I would need to be. I need to get to her place, sort out what the hell my brother-in-law thinks is happening, and fix it. "There is an emergency, Lois. I have to deal with it."

"Okay, *Miles*, I'm just telling you that the sheriff is upset. I explained there was a situation, but he's saying if you're not back in an hour, he's going to demand we forfeit based on the agreement that both school principals were in attendance as a show of strength. I don't want to try to explain what will happen if that happens."

"I'll be back within the hour. I just . . . I need to do this."

"All right. I'll stall and give you that hour."

My foot is heavy on the accelerator, and what should take me fifteen to twenty minutes to get there, takes ten. When I pull into the driveway, Doug is outside with the front door open.

I'm out of the truck, rushing to where he is, ready to search and find her.

"Miles!" he calls, but I shove him aside and enter.

The minute I do, my heart stops.

There is no way to deny what he said is true. Every item that was in this house is gone.

It's empty.

No couch. No dishes. No tables or chairs.

It's like she was never even here.

"I'm sorry, man," Doug says from behind me. "I know you said this was possible, but I didn't think she'd leave like this."

I can't speak. My head is spinning, and all the fucking conversations play like a loop in my mind. The way she laid with me, telling me she loved me. How she looked at me after we'd made love. The self-defense lessons and how she seemed like she was trying because she wanted to stay and fight.

I shake my head. "No. There's no way she just left like this."

He comes around, looking at the empty house. "I'm not sure what else this could mean. It's all gone."

I walk through the rest of the house, looking in Kai's room, then the bathroom, hers, out to the backyard, where the fucking tree in a pot sits.

I call her phone again, but it goes to voicemail.

"Penelope," I say, my voice cracking, the pain of her name slicing through my heart. "I don't know where you are or why you left. I don't know if it's because you got scared and we were moving too fast or you're in trouble. Just know that I'm not giving up. You may have broken your promise, but I'm not breaking mine."

I clench my jaw tight, wanting to scream and fight the fucking world, and at the same time, not being able to deny the truth.

Penny left.

She's gone. Kai is gone.

Everything is fucking gone.

And my heart feels like it's been ripped from my fucking chest.

————

I go back to the school, watch the rest of the game, don't give one shit about the score, and after the crowds file out without a goddamn war, I'm ready for my own.

Doug is watching me carefully, probably worried that I'm going to fly off the handle, but instead of anger and frustration, which I definitely felt when I got to the game, now I'm just strategizing.

How do I find someone who doesn't want to be found?

Someone who has an entire group of people who do nothing but hide her?

Hell, I don't even know what her real name is.

Fuck.

All I know is that her brother is in Virginia Beach and works for a security company.

I need to make calls and find out how to reach Quinn. I need to gather what intel I can find and go from there.

"I see your mind working," Doug says.

"I'm going to find her."

He opens his mouth to say something and then closes it. I wait, knowing Doug can't keep quiet for too long, and then he sighs. "I'll do whatever you need."

"I need to find her brother."

Doug nods. "Okay, and how do you want to do that? All you know is his name and that he's in Virginia Beach."

"I know."

"Okay, so what's the plan?"

I turn and glare at him. "I don't know."

Doug puts his hand on my shoulder. "Listen, I know you're upset, but let's reach out to some guys from our unit. A lot of them went out to work with private companies. You never know, maybe they know someone or something. Let's start at the beginning."

I barely get the next words out, my heart in my throat. "What if she doesn't want me to find her?"

"Then you cross that bridge when you get there." He squeezes once. "Come on, let's get to work."

On my way out of the parking lot, I find Lachlan, Everett, and Killian standing by my car.

"What's going on?" Everett asks.

"Penelope left."

"Left town?" Lachlan asks.

"Yes."

Everett comes forward. "Bro, I'm sorry. I really thought . . ."

"I'm going to find her," I tell him resolutely.

"Okay."

"Something scared her off, and I'm not going to just let her go. I love her and I'm going to find her."

Lachlan gives me a sad smile. "I know you will, Miles. We're all here for you no matter what."

Then I remember Lachlan has strong military ties in Virginia Beach. His father was a captain, and Ainsley's father was an admiral. Both of them probably know people down there who were SEALs and can help.

"I need your help, well, your dad or Ainsley's father."

"What?" Lachlan asks. "How can we help?"

"Her brother, he was a SEAL and lives in Virginia Beach."

Lachlan lifts a hand. "Dude, there are millions of people down there and . . ."

"He works for a security company. His name is Quinn. He has a best friend, Liam, I think." I rack my brain, trying to come up with something more. "His wife's name is Ashton. Please, just ask him. He works for a company there. They are all SEALs. Please."

"Okay, I'll call," Lachlan says. "I can't promise anything."

"I know. We're making calls too. I need to talk to her. Even if it's just to say goodbye."

If she wants to leave me, I want to hear it.

It's now almost midnight and I can't sleep. I throw on my hoodie and walk up to Penelope's house.

It's dark, quiet, and empty—just like I feel.

I miss her.

I don't know when she left, and all I want is to hear her voice and for her to let me make it right.

I walk inside, looking around, somehow hoping the furniture magically reappeared. It didn't.

How the fuck did she leave me so easily?

All she had to do was tell me that moving in was too fast and she wasn't ready. I would've slowed down, but she gave no indication that it spooked her.

I walk out to the backyard again, going to the tree I gave her, wanting her to plant roots in Ember Falls and watch something grow together.

Seems her putting it in a pot said it all.

She didn't want that, she couldn't give me more than just a small space to grow, and she outgrew the container we were in.

I kick the rocks in the back, watching them scatter around, hating how they mirror my thoughts.

Each memory that replays causes another tear at my soul. I let myself love her, telling myself that even if this happened, I would be grateful for the time we had.

She warned me. She told me that one day this eventuality would come and she'd have to choose Kai's safety over her own wants and needs. Even knowing that, I can't give her up.

I need to find her. I promised I would never stop searching, and I won't.

Exhaling deeply, I look back at that tree in a pot, symbolic in so many ways.

Then my phone rings and I see Lachlan's name.

"Hello?"

"I think I found her brother."

"I'm on my way."

Time to get some answers and find Penelope.

thirty-one
Miles

Lachlan insisted on riding with me to Virginia Beach. His father has connections within a SEAL team, and he reached out, gathering some information and calling us back to say that he thought he knew who Quinn was.

According to him, there is a Quinn Walker that might be Quinn Miller who works for a security company run by all former SEALs, with offices in California and Virginia. He is married and has a son, and Lachlan thought it could be him based on the other name I gave him—Liam.

Lachlan clears his throat as I stare out the window, counting trees. "You know we'll find her, right?"

I nod. "I just don't know in what state. If someone took her . . ."

"Don't go there. We'll find Quinn, somehow, someway. If the guy my father found isn't her brother, then maybe he knows of him. I thought Penelope's last name was Walker?"

"That's what she told me," I say, and my voice sounds dead, even to me.

"Maybe there's an explanation?"

"There is."

She would've had to change her name several times to keep on the run. Penelope's brother wouldn't take any chances.

We go over a bridge-tunnel and come out on the other side of the water, where there are large ships and more military members in a square mile than anywhere in the world.

"We'll be at the security company location in about ten minutes. Do you have a plan?"

"Yes, find Quinn and find out where the fuck Penelope went, and then I bring her home to me."

"That's definitely one way," Lachlan says and keeps driving.

We weave through the streets and pull up to what looks like an old factory. The brick building is inconspicuous and appears to be vacant.

"You're sure it's this one?" I ask with disbelief.

"Yeah, this is what my dad said."

"I'm going to check it out." I'm out of the car before he can say anything else.

As I approach the front door, two men exit the building. "Can I help you?" a tall man with dark-brown hair asks.

"I'm Miles Anderson. I'm here to see Quinn Miller."

"I don't know anyone by that name," he replies.

"Tell him it's about his sister and nephew. Penelope and Kai."

The man pauses and then says something through a radio. A minute passes, maybe two, and I've assessed a lot more about the building than from my original glance.

There are two posts on the top where snipers would be perched. I'm pretty sure there's at least one there now, but I can't tell for sure. All over the doors and windows are cameras. They're small, hidden very well, and anyone would miss them, but I see the lens moving now.

This isn't an abandoned building.

This is a fortress.

After another minute goes by without a word being spoken between anyone, Quinn exits the building. He looks slightly concerned, but also a little irritated.

"What do you mean it's about Penelope? What about my sister?"

"Where do you have her?" I ask.

His eyes widen just a smidge. "What?"

I shake my head, not wanting to play games. "She left me, and I know you have her hidden. I just need to talk to her. Tell me where she is."

Quinn looks to the other guy, who shakes his head. "Miles, I'm going to say this very clearly, and I'm not fucking around. I didn't move Penelope from Ember Falls. So if she's gone, she either moved herself, which she would never do without telling me, or someone has her."

"Everything is gone," I say quickly. "Everything. Not a single item was left in that house."

He shakes his head and looks to the other guy. "Go!"

Quinn starts to walk away, but I grab his arm. "I'm going wherever you are. I love her, and I'm not going to sit around doing nothing. You can either let me help, which as a recon guy, you know I can, or I'll do it my fucking self."

"Let's go then, but you didn't see anything when you were here, understood?"

I follow him inside, pulling out my phone to text Lachlan that I'm staying and that I'll meet up with him later.

When we enter the building, it's almost unbelievable. There are monitors in a row against the back wall and people walking around. It reminds me of the inside of our tents on a mission. Start-up company, my ass.

Quinn stops at a desk. "Penelope and Kai were taken. Find anything you can. Traffic cams, receipts, anything, ping the burner as well."

"She has a burner?" I ask.

"She does. Hopefully she has it on her."

There is so much about her that I don't know.

I sigh, pointing out the obvious. "If someone took her, they'd have searched her."

Quinn nods. "I'm aware, but I'm going to hope we find something."

"Will you let me do something? I want to dig into her ex. Maybe there are some common-tie names. She mentioned his partner was there that night," I remind him.

"That's one of the guys we keep tabs on. He's in Chicago still."

"You don't think that someone with his reach and money could send someone to get her?"

He rolls his neck. "He does, but I have to go with what information we have, so I can't just jump that she's in Chicago. Now, if you want to help, this is Liam and Ben, and we have a lot of work to do, so we'd appreciate any help you can give."

The four of us work together, going through hours of video data. There's so little, it feels overwhelming and frustrating. Each minute that passes, my fear for what's happening to her grows.

I've been trained to not let my emotions overwhelm me, but this is different. This is Penelope and Kai.

After another hour, we finally get our first break. "There!" I yell, looking at a video from the small airport west of Ember Falls.

I reach out to the sheriff, and he is able to get them to turn the tapes over when I explain part of the situation. He gets them to us in fifteen minutes and wishes us luck.

"That's not . . ." Liam starts to say, and I cut him off.

"That's her. I know her. I'd know her anywhere."

And I do. I know it in my gut. Not just because I want it to be her. To have a lead, somewhere to start looking, but because it *is* her.

We continue through the coverage. The first fifteen minutes was too grainy to see anything, but I know her body. I know her shape and how she moves. I know it's her.

Liam turns to Ben. "Let's get the flight logs."

Ben goes to his computer and pulls up the information. "At that time there were two planes. One went to Oklahoma, and the other went to a small town in Illinois."

She's in Chicago. She has to be.

I turn to her brother. "Where is the book?"

His eyes widen just the smallest amount, but I catch it. "I don't know what you're talking about."

"Penelope told me she gave it to you. She said it was her last-ditch effort to save her and Kai, if ever it came to that. I need that book, and I'm going to get the woman and child I love."

Quinn stands still for half a minute. "The book is worthless."

"What?"

He runs his fingers through his hair. "It's filled with nothing but riddles. There's nothing that ties anyone concretely. The book is, however, powerful in the hands of someone who has the key. We've had every analyst we know try to work through it while we've kept Penelope and Kai away from the people who want it."

"So what? They want the book back. We'll exchange her for it, and ..."

"And what? You're going to run with her? You realize that if we give the book back, it changes nothing. She still had access to this information. They will never stop hunting her until the book has value to someone outside of the group of people in it."

"Let me look at it," I say.

He huffs out a laugh. "And what?"

"Let me try. Either way, we have to go to Chicago. So let me study it, see what I can find my way. I will do anything to protect your sister and nephew from anyone who wants to hurt them. I'm going to find out who has her, and I'm going to get them out, with or without you. At least with the book, I have a fighting chance."

Quinn looks to Liam, who shrugs. "I'll give you the book, and we'll play this out the best way to keep them safe. You can go in to negotiate their release, but my team and I will be standing perimeter. I'll breach if I have one moment of doubt that anyone's life is in danger."

As much as I'd love to go in there half-cocked, I know this is the best way to protect my family.

"I hate to be the bearer of bad news and all, but Chicago is a big fucking city. We have no idea where they are and who even has her," Liam chimes in.

"I'll find her," I say, not doubting I can. "I just need to get to that airport and read that fucking book."

———

"If that principal job doesn't work out for you, I'm sure I can get you a job here," Quinn says as we're in the building across from where we believe Penelope is being held.

I was able to get enough information and track her here. It took us two days to narrow it down to three possible locations to run surveillance on for any sign of Penelope.

All three buildings are owned by one of the names in that book. I spent the entire flight reading, making notes, mulling over possibilities, and coming up with a strategy that would allow us to get answers as quickly as possible.

While we have been watching each one for a sign of them, I reached out to Ainsley for help. She's a journalist for a newspaper, and there was a name in the book that she'd mentioned once in regard to a story she's working on in Washington, DC, about a senator.

It wasn't the same one, but the name I gave her was heavily involved. She asked me to give her a day so she could do some digging. She called this morning with information that makes this book far more dangerous.

It wasn't long before we could figure out the bigger names—high-ranking judges, police who were being paid off, and the senator who was definitely making money off all of it.

He has the most to lose, and I will make sure, once Penelope and Kai are safe, he does.

I speak to Quinn, staring up at the skyscraper. "I'm still not sure this building is right."

While we didn't see the senator or anyone, I entered the other two buildings we were watching, posing as a member of the janitorial staff. I did a scan of the floors, hoping I'd just stumble upon them, but there was absolutely no sign of them. The other one that Ben was sitting on, I can't explain it, but I just felt they weren't there.

When we arrived here, where Quinn has been doing surveillance, I felt it. My instincts were ringing, telling me they're here.

"It's your call," Liam says.

"I can go in, scope it out, be sure," I suggest.

Quinn shakes his head. "It's too risky. You've been in two buildings, and if someone recognizes you, then this will be over before it starts. No, we have to play this right, and my gut says they're here."

I've made the wrong choice before, and it almost cost someone their life. I don't want anyone else to get hurt because of this, but at the same time, each minute we spend out here, second-guessing things, is another minute Penelope and Kai are in danger.

Please let them be here.

For five days they've been gone. Five days of enduring God only knows what. Feeling like it's now or never, I make the call. "I think we should go in. We have a plan, we've gone over contingencies. The only thing I think might be better is if we release what's in the book in smaller doses. That way, it could give us a chance if he doesn't kill me."

Liam looks to Quinn. "He's right. If Penelope and Kai are alive and Miles goes in, there's nothing saying that they won't just shoot him immediately. If that happens, we can enter and inform them that something will be breaking soon unless they give us your sister and nephew."

"Fuck," Quinn grumbles and looks to me. "You realize you're putting your life at risk right now."

"I don't care about me," I say.

Quinn stares at me. "She does."

"Then she has to trust us. We'll figure it out, but my only goal is to get them safe."

"Then let's roll."

I'm coming for you, Penelope.

thirty-two
Penelope

"Just be calm, Kai. Stay quiet." I brush my hands over his face, imploring him to do as I say. The last five days have been the worst of my life, and that's saying something.

Kai and I were in the house, I left the door unlocked because I've become complacent, and we were discussing moving in with Miles.

I needed to know that Kai was really okay with it, not just in theory.

He was happy, smiling, wrapping his arms around me in absolute joy.

That's when everything changed.

Two men entered my home and grabbed us.

There was no time to do anything, and I knew all I could do was cooperate so they didn't kill us right then.

Now that they have us, there's no way I'm getting out of here alive. No one knows we're gone. There's no way anyone could find us, even if they were looking for us.

I'm devastated at the reality I'm facing—the end.

It'll leave Kai without any parents, but my brother will be there for him, and in my heart, I know Miles will too.

I fight back the tears. I need to be strong. Kai needs me to hold it together, even though I'm falling apart.

I love my son.

I love him so much, and I'm never going to see him grow up.

I won't watch him graduate from school or start college. I won't see him when he has his first crush or comfort him during his first heartbreak. So many things I won't witness on this earth.

Kai clutches at me, his fear palpable. "I'm scared, Mommy."

"I know, baby. Remember what we learned?" I ask him.

He nods.

I stare into his beautiful blue eyes. "What do we do when this happens?"

My brother may not have given me self-defense lessons, but he did teach us what to do once we're captured. How to speak, where to look, what to observe, and how to buy time.

That is my only goal. To buy us as much time as possible. I don't know if Miles or my brother will realize we're missing, but I pray that they do.

"We stay strong and I let you talk," Kai says softly.

"That's right, and if they take you away from me?"

The words feel like knives cutting through me, but it has to be said. I have to do what I can to protect my son.

He shakes his head, as though this can't happen. "I don't want to be away."

"I know, but if it happens, do you remember what Uncle Quinn said?"

"I be quiet and look at my feet and be brave."

I brush my thumb across his cheek, then clutch him to my chest. My jaw trembles as the fear of the situation overwhelms me. "That's right. You be brave and know that someone will be looking for you. So you don't worry about Mommy. You have to be strong and do whatever you can until help comes."

Help has to come. If not for me, for Kai.

All I can do now is pray that Miles realizes I never would've disappeared on him and searches for us.

Not that there's a strong trail to follow. When the men entered my home, they forced me to send the text message to Hazel, saying I couldn't come into work.

We were then bound and put in a car as I watched them clear our house.

All knowing that they were going to make it look like we left and that it would be days before someone realized we'd been taken.

I hold my son, whispering fervent silent prayers that someone will save us both, but at the very least—him.

As I hold him tight, a sickness fills my stomach at the fact that none of the safeguards that had been put in place could be activated. I couldn't run or get to my phone. There was . . . no time to do anything.

That night we were on a plane and have spent the last five days in this room overlooking Chicago.

"Food." I hear a grunt, and then the door unlocks. It opens slightly, and two bags of food are dropped in before we're alone again.

The room we're being held in is luxurious in a way. We're in a high-rise office building, and this room has a bathroom attached and two sleeping bags in the corner, which we've used, huddled up together.

Food is brought three times a day, and we wake up with clothes to change into. As far as kidnappings go, they're not treating us horrifically. I'm not sure if that's a good or a bad thing.

There are no buildings that are our height, and there's a film on the windows so you can't see us—trust me, I've tried.

This location was chosen for a reason.

Since they've been after me for six years, I can be assured they've planned in great detail.

What will be my downfall is that the book is not in my possession. No matter how much they've searched through the things in my house, they won't find it.

I'm praying that a bargaining chip is what saves Kai.

Kai and I eat the food. They brought me a burger, and he has chicken nuggets.

No one has spoken to me yet. It's been a lot of grunts and hiding faces. It's the opposite of what Quinn warned me about when we discussed a capture. He said if they really planned to kill me, they wouldn't hide faces. They'd look me dead in the eye because there would be nothing for them to fear.

We haven't had that. It makes me both nervous and hopeful.

The door lock clicks again and opens and I reach for Kai, pulling him against me.

Then the senator and two other men walk in. The senator's brown eyes meet mine without trying to hide anything.

"Hello, Penelope, we've been looking for you for a long time."

thirty-three
Penelope

"I don't have the book," I repeat.

"We know you have it," Anthony says with frustration. "Edward would've had a contingency, and he told me where the book was, but it wasn't there. You were the only one he would've said anything to."

Playing dumb is what I'm going for as long as I can. All day they've asked the same things, and I've given the same answers.

"I don't have this book you keep talking about. I don't even know what kind of a book? I mean, maybe I have it and I don't know? Maybe I took it when I left Edward—by accident."

Anthony's jaw clenches. "Penelope, don't play games. I really would hate to bring your son in here and see if we can make you talk."

My stomach drops. I hoped I could keep this up for at least another day, but if . . . if they hurt him. If they threaten to hurt him . . . I can't do it. I . . . I can't.

I do my best to school my emotions and shake my head. "Why? He doesn't know anything, and I don't either. Why are you doing this? Why?"

A hard slap across my face causes my head to whip to the side. Fuck, that hurt. Immediately my hand flies to the spot the body-guard hit.

"You know why!"

I rub the tender skin, biting back the tears. My time is running out. I'm not going to be able to stall much more, and I'm terrified.

They'll use Kai.

I know they will.

"You keep saying you want this book, but you won't tell me anything about it."

The senator, who has been quiet through the entire process, pushes off the desk and walks toward me and turns to his bodyguard. "Let's show some restraint and not hit a woman, shall we?"

Good cop.

Bad cop.

Got it.

I tense as he grows near. "I'm not going to hit you."

I try to appear relaxed, but I'm anything but that. I'm terrified, and I know that I'm nearing the end of being able to stall until my brother or Miles realizes what's happened. I've tried my best, but I don't know how else to delay this.

For six years I've run, and this is when I finally have nowhere else to go.

"This is ridiculous!" Anthony bellows. "The bitch knows. She knew everything from the start. We should kill her and the kid and get it over with. She's a liability. Let's get rid of the loose ends and be done."

The senator sighs and shakes his head. "I don't enjoy killing women and children."

He scoffs. "No, you just like to use them to gain the power you want."

The senator's eyes get hard and his jaw tightens. "And you don't?"

"I'm not a wolf in sheep's clothing. I'm well aware of the monster I am," Anthony spits back. "Now let's get this shit over with or I'll do whatever I have to, because I have business to attend to. If you don't have the balls to handle her, then I will, and I'll handle you as well."

Anthony starts to move toward me, but the senator lifts a hand and signals with two fingers, and before I can turn and shield my eyes, the bodyguard pulls a gun out with a silencer and shoots Anthony.

I gasp and feel like I'm going to be sick. Oh God, he just killed Anthony. Right there. Shot him like it was nothing.

Oh God.

I start to tremble, and the senator looks to me. "I'm sorry you had to witness that, but I don't appreciate threats, and he was a liability."

I nod, fear causing all my limbs to shake. I try not to look at the dead man on the floor. I focus on the senator's face as tears leak down my cheeks.

"I don't have your book," I say, my voice barely a whisper.

It's true. I don't have it.

He sighs heavily. "We went over every inch of Edward's office. We went through his home, your apartment, and anywhere else he spent time. Then I found a note in a file that was hidden. It just had your name and the word . . . book. I haven't gotten to the place I am by being stupid. I've amassed wealth and power by being smart and calculating. Why would Edward leave something like that? Why would he point the finger at you and name the one thing he knew we'd want?"

"Because he was a sick asshole. He would hit me and he knew I was leaving him."

"Or . . . he told you where the book was if anything happened to him."

That's exactly what he did. While I may not have wealth and power, I'm also not stupid. I gave the book to my brother because I knew at some point I'd need it as a bargaining chip.

I try once again to be stupid about the book, knowing the sand in the hourglass is running out.

"He wouldn't. He didn't trust me or even like me. I was a toy to him, and he wouldn't give me information. If anything, he kept me in the dark about everything he did."

It's true. I didn't learn about Edward's illegal dealings until much further in our relationship. There were no signs that the money he made came from illegal gambling, drugs, and backdoor deals that he was paid off to keep quiet. To be honest, I didn't care to ask. He lulled me into a false sense of trust.

I didn't get the rug pulled out until it was much too late.

The senator shakes his head, walking around. "If you truly know nothing, why did you run?"

"Because he was dead."

"And that upset you?"

I scoff. "Not in the least."

"So you didn't call the cops? You just chose to pack your belongings and spend your life on the run? That doesn't make much sense, Penelope. Here's what I think. You're a smart girl and knew what he was up to. You also knew about the book, because Edward needed insurance and a way to barter for his life. Just as you do now. So you have or had the book, and when you realized he was dead, you set into motion your plan of spending your life in hiding. It worked, much better than I could've ever thought."

Every word of what he says is true, and I keep my features schooled, but inside I'm freaking out.

I shake my head.

"You have it or at least know where it is, so let's stop the charades," he says, coming to crouch in front of me. "I've been patient and let this go on long enough. However, I have a plane to catch, so we're going to speed this up." He jerks his head, and a minute later the door opens as they bring Kai in.

"Mommy!"

I gasp, trying to stand, but I'm grabbed and shoved down. "Please don't hurt my son," I beg, tears falling rapidly as I stare at my little boy. My innocent child who did nothing wrong. His decisions didn't bring him to this—mine did. "Please," I say again.

Kai's eyes are on me, and the fear shines so bright and I feel so much pain in my chest that I can't breathe.

God, I hate this. I hate that he will have felt a moment of fear because of me.

"Tell us where the book is, Penelope, and no one will get hurt."

The lie wraps around me, shattering me to my core. The moment they have that book is the moment I will draw my last breath.

Time is up.

The last piece of sand has fallen and I have to save Kai.

I look into the senator's eyes, knowing that there is no more I can do, but give him what he wants. "Kai goes back to the other room," I say firmly. "He isn't here or hurt. Do you understand?"

He nods once.

"I want to talk to him," I say pleadingly.

I have to say goodbye.

The senator waves his hand. "Bring the boy to his mother."

Kai is released and runs to me, his arms wrapping around my neck as I cry into his. This is goodbye for us. How do I do this? How can I say goodbye to him? My heart is not only broken, it's shattered. I've failed as a mother.

I've failed in every way.

With strength I didn't know I had, I release him, pulling his face to look only at mine. "Everything is going to be okay, baby."

I lie to him, needing him to see me this way. That I was strong and unafraid. He needs to know that I did this for him. To save him because he's worth my own life. He's worth more.

"Mommy." His voice breaks, but I force a smile.

I rub my thumb along his cheek and then brush his hair back. "I love you more than anything in this world, you know that, right?" He nods. "You are smart, and kind, and everything good. I am *so* proud of you." It's as though someone is punching a hole through my chest, but I soldier on. I need him to know how much I love him.

"I love you too," he says, his eyes swimming with tears.

"Don't be scared. Just know that no matter what you're going to be okay, and I am *always* going to be with you." I sniff and kiss his nose. "You are never alone, my sweet boy. If you close your eyes, I'll be right there, in your heart, guiding you wherever you need to go." I hiccup on the last word. He has to survive this. He has to be okay, because I'll lay down my life now, if it means he has a choice. I suck in a breath, rubbing his beautiful face, memorizing every curve. "Now you have to go back in the other room and stay there, okay?"

He shakes his head so fast. "No, no, I want to stay with you!"

"I know, but I need to talk to some people, and it's an adult conversation," I try to explain. "Can you be brave for Mommy?"

I stare into Kai's warm eyes, the ones that mirror my own, and pray the rest of my plan will work—for his sake.

Kai's jaw trembles, and tears fall down his face, so I clutch him to my chest once more, sending all the love I have for him in this embrace, needing him to feel it, to know deep in his heart that no matter what, his mother loved him.

Everything I did was to keep him safe, and I'll do it now too.

I force air in my lungs, gathering the little strength I have left, and pull him back. "Go with them. You'll be safe and it'll work out."

Kai cries as the other man pulls him from me. He's kicking and screaming, and I watch him, trying to calm him with my eyes, but I can't. He wails and I cry harder as soon as he's away from me. I bury my face in my hands, despair and sadness coming like waves, drowning me in a sea of grief.

Minutes go by, and my tears don't stop until Kai's quiet. Even after he finally settles and I can't hear him, I cry because I can do nothing else.

I think about all I've lost. My son. My family. My home and the man I love.

I'll never see Miles again. I won't get to tell him how much I love him and we wanted to live with him.

I replay our first date. The way he packed the food up and left so we could get Kai. The first time we made love and his tenderness. The moments when he made me feel safe, loved, and important. He would've been the one. I know it in every fiber of my being.

I wanted to make Ember Falls my home, because Miles is my sanctuary.

The life we could've built fades into the background.

I thought I knew heartbreak before, but it was nothing compared to this. To lose both of my loves in one moment.

A hand touches my shoulder and I gasp, looking up into the senator's eyes. "It's time to talk."

Before I can say a word, a door flies open and the bodyguard lifts his gun. When I turn to see who it is, my stomach drops.

"Miles," I breathe, and pain tears through me for a whole new reason, because in his hand is the fucking book.

thirty-four
Miles

She's alive.

Seeing her face, that she's breathing, is a relief like I've never known. I prayed we weren't too late. That I could set things into motion, and it seems I'm just in time.

I shake the book in my hand, bringing the attention to me. "Hello, Senator," I say evenly.

"You're the boyfriend?"

"Yes, and also the owner of the book you're so desperate to find."

I assess the room, taking in the dead body on the ground across the way and Penelope's red-rimmed eyes. There's a mark on her face, and I instantly see red. Someone fucking hit her.

He'll pay for that.

Her lips are parted, and confusion fills her beautiful eyes. "Miles? What are you . . . ?"

I take a step and the dickhead with a gun shifts. "I wouldn't shoot me since I'm not an idiot, and you should know there are contingencies in place if that happens."

The senator lifts his hand and the bodyguard steps back. "You have contingencies?"

"Yes, I'll warn you now that if I'm not walking out this door with Penelope and Kai in ten minutes then everything in this book, all the names, dates, locations of bodies, and all the other fun things that are in here will be blasted out in an email to fifteen different news agencies. There will be no rock you'll be able to hide under. No corner of the world where this won't touch you. So I'd put that gun down, and let's discuss the options," I say, stepping farther into the room.

They have no idea that Ainsley's newspaper already has the contents of this book, and there will be nowhere they can escape this, but I bluff until I have Penelope out of this room.

It's clear that this doesn't sit well with him as he shifts and waves his hand, indicating his man should lower the gun. Once that's out of the way, I walk over to Penelope and pull her up against me.

"Are you okay?" I ask softly.

She nods quickly. "Kai," she breathes.

"He's fine," I whisper. "Trust me."

I heard him screaming, assuming they were together, but when I opened the door, there was only one man, who had Kai in his grasp, and I didn't hesitate. I was able to take care of him quickly and grabbed Kai, sending him to Quinn, who was waiting two doors down.

Once I knew he was safe, I came to get Penny.

I return my attention to the matter at hand. "This book was an interesting read. I can see why you were so eager to get it back."

The senator's jaw tics, and I push Penelope slightly behind me.

I continue on: "Here's how this is going to go. You're going to let Penelope walk out of here right now, and then we can negotiate."

Penelope gasps. "No!"

Her hands are at my back, and I have to fight to keep my eyes forward and not comfort her. The only thing I give a shit about is getting her out of here to reunite with Kai and her brother.

He laughs. "I don't think so."

"That's fine, your clock is ticking either way, so it doesn't matter to me. I wonder what the news will report first. Maybe the way you've funded a crime ring? That might be too mundane, though. It could be the fact you're funneling money through a charity for children but it's only lining your pockets . . . that would be a good one to start with. Taxpayers just love those kinds of stories."

While we were planning, I strategized every option, and the only thing we knew was that we had to prepare for the worst. That all of us might not make it out or I would die trying to save Kai and Penelope.

No matter what, this will be over today.

Taunting him is the only thing I can see that will allow Penelope to walk out the door.

The senator looks at Penelope, me, and then his bodyguard, whose jaw is clenched tight. He definitely doesn't want Penelope to leave, but his options are really limited.

"What assurance do I have that if I let her go, you won't release the information?"

"You don't. You just have to believe that I would never let harm come to my family." We may not be married. We may not be together, but I love her and Kai. They are my family, and I will protect them until my dying breath.

Her fingers tighten in my shirt, and then I feel her forehead against my back.

He rubs his tongue against his teeth, and I wait in silence. "If she goes and she speaks a word, I'll kill the kid."

Little does he know that's not an option. "Understood."

"Go," he says to Penelope.

Penelope doesn't move, so I step back, forcing her to go closer to the door I came in. "Penelope," I say firmly, keeping my eyes on the two in front of me. "Go now, I'll be there soon."

She shakes and her breathing is labored. "I don't want to leave you," she whispers.

"Know that I love you and plan to marry you, but now you need to walk out the door." It's the first time I said it, but if I die, I want her to know how I feel. "Now, go."

"Come back to me," she whispers, and then I feel the warmth of her body leave me.

Her loss is a physical ache that I feel in my bones. I just had her back, and I had to let her go, but I have no regrets. If I die here, it'll be for the woman and little boy I love. For the people who made me the happiest I've ever been, and that's a sacrifice I'd make every day.

I glance at the clock. I have six minutes remaining, so I don't delay. "Here's option number one . . . I'm going to leave this book with you and all the disgusting shit you've done and walk out, with nothing ever being said. We'll forget you, everything we've read, and you'll forget *all* of us. The second option is . . . you hurt anyone that I love and every single fucking detail is leaked. If you follow us, every detail is leaked. If you ever come near us, every detail is published. I have every safeguard in place for this, and I swear to God, if I feel even one ounce of these things happening, I won't hesitate to ruin your life to protect the people I love."

"You think I'm an idiot? The fact that you have copies of it is enough of a reason to kill you."

I shrug. "Maybe, but it's been six years where she could've destroyed your life, and not a peep. Six years that all she did was want to live a life away from this hell. If you let her and Kai go, stop chasing them, then the information stays hidden, but that's a choice you have to make."

He has no idea that the contents of this book are basically in another language. I was just fortunate enough to find someone who was able to put the pieces together. Even now, Ainsley is working on compiling all the information to release her story in two days.

I don't like that he'll have two days where he could come after us. None of this sits well with me, but I have to believe I can keep them safe that long. He may have the power now, but the tides will change, and when it does, he'll pay for his sins with Penelope and Kai well away from it.

"Well, you've surely thought of everything," he says.

"The choice is yours, Senator." I glance down at my watch. "You have less than five minutes."

thirty-five
Penelope

I hold Kai in my arms, tears streaming down my face as I rock back and forth. We're in a room, and Liam, Ben, and Quinn are standing around us protectively.

None of us speak as we wait for either time to expire or Miles to come through the door.

I kiss the top of Kai's head and keep chanting to whatever higher being there is to please let Miles come back to me.

I need him.

I love him, and want to spend the rest of my life with him—no, that's not how it ends.

He loves me and that was not a proposal, I want him to say it to my face. Not as a way to get me to leave him in the hands of men who won't hesitate to kill.

Ben steps closer to Liam, keeping his voice low. "One minute."

Liam nods, and I track him moving around the room to Quinn. "We should move her and Kai. Get them out of the building."

Quinn shakes his head once. "Not yet."

"We are running out of time, Quinn. We need to get out of this building."

I get to my feet. "We're not leaving him," I whisper. "He saved me, and we are not walking out of here without him, do you understand, Liam Dempsey?"

My brother and Liam both sigh at the same time. "Penny . . ."

"No." Even though the word is barely audible, it rings out like a gunshot. There is no option here. "No, you go get him then. We're not leaving here without Miles."

Quinn turns to Ben. "You stay here with them and be ready to hit send to Ainsley, telling her to push the information immediately. Liam and I will go get Miles."

Ben adjusts, moving us deeper into the room. "You both stay in that corner."

I rest my hand on his arm. "Thank you."

"Stay down and listen to whatever we say, okay?"

"Okay," I reluctantly agree.

The three of them look at each other. "If we move, we can't undo this."

"It's been a minute," Ben says.

No, no, no.

No.

I refuse to accept this. That after all we've been through, I've lost Miles. I can't.

He's too good. He's everything to me and he found me, just like he promised. Even though he didn't know if I went willingly or not, he came for me and then saved me.

Tears fall unbidden down my cheeks in rivers. I have had my heart break more in the last five days than I ever knew was possible. I've felt despair deeper than I knew anyone could feel. I've also felt loved more than I deserve.

Miles walked into a room that he knew he might not walk out of —for me, for us. He allowed himself to be sacrificed just because he loves me.

It would be so cruel for the fates to give me this outcome after everything, but I see all three men check their watches, and the realization that time is up is clear in their eyes.

It's been ten minutes, and Miles hasn't come back.

He's most likely gone, and it's too late to save him.

I sink to the ground and cover my mouth as a sob tears through me, full of anger, sorrow, and anguish. Even though I muffle the sound, it rips through the room.

"We give him one more minute," Quinn says after his eyes meet mine. "We don't press send until we have Penelope and Kai secured out of the building."

Liam looks to me with a sadness I've never seen there. He knows the outcome of this story. There is no happily ever after. The princess gets saved by the handsome prince only to be left planning his funeral.

I'm not living a romance—it's a tragedy instead.

They check their watches and Quinn gestures his hand forward. Ben moves to me and I get to my feet, pulling Kai with me and starting to fight. "No. No, please, Ben. Please don't . . . I can't leave him. I can't go."

"Penelope, we have to move. Your brother and Liam will do what they have to."

I can't give up on him. He didn't do that on me. Not when I was scared or pulling away or threatening to leave him.

"Mommy, where is Miles?" Kai asks, and I keep him against my body so he can't see me fall apart.

I hold it in, looking up to the sky as the agony of his loss is felt through my body. I hear Quinn and Liam open the door, but before they can take a step out, Miles is standing there with a smile.

His voice is thick as he stares into my eyes. "It's over."

Relief rushes through me, and he's moving to me before I can unlock my muscles. Then he's in front of me, his warm hands cup my cheeks, and his lips are on mine. It's not a long kiss, but it's the best one of my life.

He pulls back. "Are you okay?"

I nod. "You're okay?"

He smiles and looks down at Kai. "And you, buddy?" Kai wraps his arms around Miles's torso as an answer, and he pats his back. "Good. Now let's go home."

We are on a private plane back to Ember Falls. Ben, Liam, Quinn, and Miles have spent the last thirty minutes debriefing, or whatever they call it, with me sitting on Miles's leg. He hasn't let go of me since we were reunited.

Kai is sound asleep on the couch toward the back.

"I don't think we have to worry," Miles says, rubbing his thumb in circles on my hip. "He looked through the book before he made his choice, and he thinks we don't understand anything that's in it, since it was no help. Plus, he doesn't know that Ainsley was already working on a story that he would've been tied up in, and with the new evidence she's collected, I think he'll be arrested within a day or two."

Quinn nods. "I agree, he's arrogant enough to think that him having the book is enough."

"All of this sounds great, but they know where I am," I say.

Miles pulls me tighter. "It doesn't matter. We have the upper hand now, and the story Ainsley's paper is going to run doesn't mention you or the book. No one will hurt you or Kai. This is going to be over very soon."

I nestle into him more, feeling like even if I could burrow inside him, it wouldn't be close enough.

"Liam and Ben are going to stay in Ember Falls for a few days. Once the information breaks, it'll be over," my brother says with confidence before turning to Miles. "I was worried this would go much differently. I wasn't sure . . ."

Miles's body tenses. "I wasn't either for a minute. I think he thought we were bluffing at one point, and then I informed him time was up and he better kill me now or be ready to wish he was dead."

"I'm glad he picked the right option," my brother says as he extends his hand. "You have my respect and gratitude. Even if my sister drives me crazy, I couldn't imagine my life without her. Thank you for not being willing to let her go."

Miles shakes his hand. "There is nothing I wouldn't do for her and Kai."

Quinn nods once. "I know. You two should talk. We'll head over there and give you some time together."

The three guys get up, and Liam and Ben both shake Miles's hand as well. We're alone and he moves me so my legs drape over him. I'm tucked in the corner, and the back of the chair is providing us some privacy.

My fingers brush against his stubbled cheek. "Hi."

He grins. "Hi."

"You love me?" I ask, even though I've felt his love in everything he does.

"Very much."

"I love you too. With all that I am."

The words come out much easier than I thought possible, but it's the truth. He is everything I've ever wanted, and I've spent our entire relationship fighting this, but I don't want to anymore.

He is the man I love, and he needs to know it.

Miles wraps his hand around my wrist, pulling it to his mouth and kissing the inside. "I love you with my entire heart, Penelope. When I thought you left me, I wanted to . . . well, I was a bit dramatic. All I knew was that I had to find you, bring you back to me, find a way to make you see that we were right for each other."

With my other hand, I brush his hair back. "I didn't leave you."

"I didn't know. I . . . I didn't know and then I didn't want to believe it."

"I know, but I need you to know now. I would never have left you like that. Ever." He must've felt so betrayed when he found my house empty. "How did you figure it out?"

Miles lets out a huff with a grin. "I found your brother and went to him, demanding he tell me where he moved you."

"Oh God. You both must've been out of your minds."

"No, sweetheart, we knew something was wrong and immediately sprang into action, looking at how someone would've gotten you out of Ember Falls."

"It felt like it happened so fast. I was at the table with Kai, and next thing we were in the back of a van. I didn't have time to do anything."

The anxiety I felt bubbles back up. I wanted to believe they were coming for me, but I was prepared for the other outcome. I will never forget how it felt to think it was the last time I would see Kai. To recall Miles and the fact that I couldn't tell him I loved him.

Miles brings our foreheads together. "I should've been there with you."

I let out a small huff of a laugh. "No, this is not your fault." I lean back to look him in the eyes. "You found me. You came for me, even though you thought I left you."

"I told you I'd always search for you. I would've never stopped, Penelope. Never." His eyes move to my cheek, and he brushes it. "Which one of them hit you?"

I blink in confusion. "What?"

"You had a red mark, right here." Tenderly the pad of his finger slides against my right cheekbone. "I saw it when I entered the room."

When I was backhanded. "It doesn't matter."

"I think it does."

I shake my head. "None of that matters anymore. I'm here, in your arms, and safe."

"Yes, you are."

It's the only place I want to be. I lean in, bringing my lips to his, still a little dazed that he's here. His hand moves up my spine, gripping my neck and keeping pressure there before releasing it and pulling back.

The two of us look in each other's eyes, saying so much. I want him to know how much I love him. How much he means to me.

"I love you," I say the words again.

"Now, I meant what I said. Marry me."

My eyes go wide. I thought maybe he forgot he said that. I didn't really want to bring it up, but apparently, he wasn't lying. "You . . . what?"

"Marry me, Penelope Walker. I love you. I want to spend the rest of my life with you. We've both experienced the pain of being apart, and I never want to feel that way again. I love you and want you to be my wife."

I suck in a breath, my mind going in a million directions. It's too soon. We never even moved in with each other. Marriage? That's . . . nuts.

But is it?

I love him. He loves me. He literally walked in front of a bullet for me. Miles has shown me over and over that I come first. That he'll always be there, whenever I need him. Whether it's a storm or a hostage situation, I'll never be on my own.

My hands cup his cheeks, staring into his eyes, looking for any glimmer of hesitation, but it's not there. All I see is love.

"I'll marry you," I tell him. "Also, it's Penelope Miller."

I kiss him again, until I hear my brother gagging, and then I smile and bury my head in his neck.

———

I'm sitting on Miles's bed—well, our bed, I guess now—drying my hair with a towel after taking the longest and best shower of my life, in his robe I found hanging.

Miles called Eloise when we were driving back from Virginia Beach, asking if she would go to the store to bring me some necessities and some clothes she had that she thought would fit. Since Ethan and Kai are the same size, she grabbed some of his stuff as well. She had everything in bags when we arrived home, because I have nothing.

Absolutely nothing.

They cleared out my house and destroyed all my belongings, leaving me and Kai without a thing.

It's a funny feeling, being completely without. A lot of the things I owned I didn't have an attachment to anyway. The furniture was used and there when we moved in, but Ember Falls, and that house in particular, became a home.

It was where Kai and I would laugh as we danced around the table where he did homework, and it was the first place I felt safe in. It's where I first made love to Miles and where we spent most of our nights. That house held a lot of memories, and a part of me feels as though it's been stripped from me.

I squeeze the excess water from my tresses, trying not to let my mind get hung up on things that don't really matter. I have my life. I have my son and I have Miles. The rest is just stuff.

"I'll trade you a penny for your thoughts," Miles says as he's leaning against the door, the light behind him making him almost look angelic. He enters the room, closing the door behind him. "Although, I already have the only Penny I want."

"You do?" I ask with a grin, instantly feeling better just from the sight of him.

"Yes, you are the only Penny I want or need."

He comes to the edge of the bed and scoops me up in his arms. I wrap my arms around his neck. "Well, you have me."

"I do."

I do. Those two words strung together mean something monumental. I want nothing more than to be with him for the rest of my life, but I worry that his proposal was a spur-of-the-moment, we-almost-died kind of thing, and now that the dust has settled, maybe he wants to take it back?

I would completely understand, and it wouldn't change anything, but I want him to be sure.

He sits down, keeping me in his lap, and I decide to give him the out if he needs it. "Miles?"

"Yes, love?"

"Are you sure about . . . what you asked me on the plane?"

I feel him tense a little, and then his eyes meet mine. "Of course I'm sure. Are you having second thoughts?"

"No, nothing like that. I just . . . it's a lot and it's fast and we almost died and . . . you know. Sometimes people make really bad decisions in the heat of the moment."

I would know, I've done it enough.

He reaches over, grabbing something out of the bedside table.

"What did you get?"

He places a velvet pouch on the bed and then with one hand opens it.

I gasp when I see the ring resting in his palm.

"Penelope, I knew I wanted to marry you after our third coincidental date. I knew there was no other woman in this world who could make me as happy as you did after our first real date. I would've married you the night we made love, but I knew that might scare you a bit. This was my gran's ring that she wore until my pops died. It's been in my family for a long time, and I went to her after our first official date and told her I met the woman I wanted to marry."

Tears spring to my eyes as I look at the ring, not sure what to say. "Miles . . . you don't . . ."

"I planned to do this right, take you and Kai somewhere, ask him for his permission to marry you. Clearly that went a little sideways."

"Clearly." I brush the tears away, not wanting to miss anything from blurry vision.

He takes my hand. "I've never been more sure of anything, and while I didn't get to ask you in a way that you'd know I was sure, I hope this proves it. I love you, Penelope Miller. I love you and want to spend the rest of my life with you. Will you marry me?"

I smile, the weight of the world lifting. My tears fall and I nod. "I already said yes, but I'll say it a hundred times. Yes, I want to marry you."

"You're sure?" he asks with a grin.

"I'm sure." Miles slides the gold ring with a pear-shaped diamond on my finger. "It's beautiful," I say.

In the last few days I've felt the lowest of lows, and Miles just gave me a high I didn't know was possible. I hoped that he wasn't just asking me because of fear, but this shows it. How did I ever get so lucky?

"Not as beautiful as the woman whose finger it's resting on."

The diamond shimmers in the light, and I bring my hands to his face, kissing him softly. I pull back, knowing this next part is tricky. "I do want to ask if you're okay if we wait a bit, let Kai settle in before we spring it on him."

"I understand. He's been through a lot, and I think we need to make sure he's okay before we tell anyone. I'll keep the ring, and when you're ready, I'd like to ask you with him."

The fact that he worries about my son above his own wants is why I love him so much. "I love you."

"I love you, Penelope."

He kisses me softly, and I imagine what this life could be.

When will we marry? Will it be a small wedding or does he want something big?

A part of me wants everyone to see us happy and in love. Also for Kai to get to watch us choose each other.

I want him to witness a relationship and how special and beautiful it can be.

Obviously, we'll live here since he owns his home and our house is . . . gone in a way. I'll also want to make some bigger changes in my life regarding work. And then who knows about a family and if he'll want more kids. It's definitely something I wonder about.

I brush my thumb against his lips. "Do you want kids someday?"

I know I always wanted another, but I don't know if he does. Miles is quiet for a bit, and then his voice is soft. "I didn't. For a long time I was completely fine with being an uncle. When you came into my life, it became different. I not only fell in love with you, I fell in love with Kai as well. I want to be his father in every way that matters. You know my mother died four days after giving birth to me and Eloise, right?"

I nod and my chest aches at what he must've felt. "I know."

"So I don't know if I want more kids. I want to want them. I know, logically, that millions of women have perfectly normal births and don't die from it, but I . . . I can't lose you, Penelope. If Kai is the only child we have and raise, I'd be okay with that. I promise I will love him like he's my own. However, if we're blessed with a baby, then of course I'd be happy. Terrified," Miles says quickly, "but happy. Do *you* want another baby?"

My immediate reaction is to say yes, because I always have wanted a bigger family. I sort of gave up on that dream because life took me in another direction. Now it's going in another turn, and the future feels so wide and unknown.

"I'm open to it, but"—I sigh, placing my hand on his chest—"I just want you for now."

thirty-six
Miles

Her saying that I'm enough makes me want to give her more. I don't want enough. I want better than enough for her. Looking in her eyes makes my chest grow tight. I love her with everything I am.

That may seem cheesy or cliché, but it's how I feel about her. There is nothing I wouldn't do to make her happy.

I lean in, our lips so close, and I breathe in her jasmine and floral scent. For days I wondered if I'd ever have her in my arms again or inhale that perfume that is all her.

Now she's here and I swear, I can't let her go.

"I missed this," I tell her.

"What?"

She climbs up in my lap. "You. This. Us."

Her blue eyes are soft and open, more so than I've seen in the past. "I missed you too. I thought about you, about us, about how I wanted to see you again, to tell you I loved you. I should've told you when I first felt it."

There was no way she would've, and I understand why she couldn't. She lived in a constant state of fear, but that's over now. Or will be in a few days.

"I knew I'd wear you down."

She laughs softly, rubbing our noses together. "I knew you would too."

"I want to make love to you," I say softly, spinning the ring on her finger. "I want to lay you down in this bed that we'll share and show you just how much I love you."

Penelope turns in my lap, moving her hands to clasp behind my head. "Show me."

We both shift at the same time, our mouths coming together in a clash. My tongue slides into her mouth, moving against hers, and then she moans as I cup her ass.

I want this to be slow, but right now we're both almost frantic.

I roll us onto the bed, gentling the kiss and gaining back control. "Slow, sweetheart," I murmur before taking her mouth again.

God, I love the way she tastes. Sunshine, sweetness, and all mine.

Penelope's hands pull at the bottom of my shirt, yanking it up over our heads. Then she's removing my shorts and boxers, her eyes roaming over my body. "You're so perfect."

"No, my love, you are."

She pulls my head back down to hers, and I give her what she wants. We kiss long and vary between rough and soft. I taste her moans and drink in the sweet sounds of pleasure she makes at just this.

Moving to my side a little, I push her robe open and cup her breast. "There are other added benefits to you living here," I say, pinching her nipple.

Penelope groans and arches her back. "Yes, I can see that."

"Do you want me to name them, Penelope?"

When she doesn't answer, I move my mouth to her breast, running my tongue along the peak.

"Miles," she sighs heavily.

"Mmm, I'm not sure that was an answer."

She whimpers when I do it again, this time flicking it. "Yes."

I know she's not talking about the question, but I'll give it to her anyway. "Well, there's the fact you'll be naked far more often."

Her fingers move to my hair. "That is a benefit."

"I agree." I kiss the valley between her breasts and then bring my mouth to the other one. "You'll also be in our bed each night, so I can wake you up in some inventive ways."

Penelope's eyelids close. "I can't wait to see them."

I can't either.

"I think I'll show you one of them now," I say, needing it more for myself than anything else. I kiss my way down her body, over her flat belly, and then I nip at her thigh. She gasps and allows me to part her legs. "I'm going to make you come this way. Do you want that, sweetheart?"

"Very much so."

"Then your wish is my command."

I lick up her seam, and she pants while I hold her legs open. I play with her, bringing her to the brink and then backing off when I feel her body start to tremble. My tongue pushes a little harder at her clit, and her knees tighten around my head. She tastes so good, I could do this for hours, listening to the sounds she makes.

"Oh God, please don't stop," she begs.

I have no intentions of it. She starts to breathe rougher and I flick faster. My eyes lift to see her, and she's so fucking glorious. Her back arches, and then her hands cover her breasts, playing with them as I keep up the pace.

She's close.

I push a finger deep inside her, curling and searching for that place that will make her lose it.

Then she shatters. She sucks in deep breaths of air, and then she bites down on her hand. I continue licking her, drawing out whatever pleasure I can as I pump my cock. Watching her like this, I can't help it.

When I can feel she's done, I move back up her body. "Penelope, open your eyes," I command. I want this moment with her, when I push inside her body, to have that connection.

Slowly her lashes flutter. She slides her hand up my back. "Not yet, baby."

I stare down at her, and she uses her other hand to push at my chest. I go willingly, lying on my back. "You see, there are benefits for us both."

Well, I'm not going to argue with that. "And they are?"

She grins, using one finger to move slowly down my chest, just like I did to her. "First, you'll be naked, and I plan to take advantage of that."

"I think I need a demonstration."

Her hand wraps around my cock and she pumps slowly. "Are you a hands-on learner?"

The saucy tone in her voice is so fucking hot, but her wearing that ring while wrapping her hand around my cock is beyond words. "I am. Especially with your hands on me. Your diamond shining, telling the world you're mine."

"I'm all yours, and I was hoping you wanted to learn by doing." She continues to move her hand up and down, and I wrap my own around hers, increasing the speed and pressure.

"Fuck, Penelope," I groan.

Her breasts brush my chest as her lips slide along my ear. "I was actually hoping you also like learning orally."

Fuck me.

"Sweetheart, there is nothing I'd like more than your mouth around my cock right now."

"Nothing?" she asks, her tongue licking before her voice is there again. She takes my hand, moving it down to her pussy. "Not even this?"

"I'll take anything you'll give me."

"I'll give you everything."

Then she moves down, and without any preamble, she takes me deep in her mouth. "Fuck," I groan as the heat of her mouth surrounds me.

She bobs her head, using her tongue along the underside of my dick over and over. My fingers lace in her hair, and I use every bit of restraint I have not to push, but Penelope moans when I tighten my grip.

I make the mistake of looking down at her, watching her take me deep. The heat in her eyes is enough to send me over.

"Penny," I say her name and her eyes find mine again. "Looking at you like this is too much. I need to be inside of you."

Her mouth comes off me, and I move so she's under me. I take this moment to stare into her beautiful denim eyes.

"Miles?"

"I love you."

She smiles softly. "I love you."

I adjust my hips and her heat calls me. I push just the tip inside and keep my eyes on her. "I love you," I say again.

"I love you," she repeats.

We do this until I'm fully seated in her tight, hot cunt. I lace our fingers together, putting them above her head. I pump my hips and she squeezes.

I push deeper, needing more, and she wraps her legs around me. "Miles," she breathes my name. "God, I love you. I love you so much I can't breathe without you. I need you. I love you."

My head falls into the crook of her neck as her words slay me. "Come with me, Penny. I'm close."

We both grip each other's hands tighter, her ring digging into my finger, and I move my hips, rubbing her clit as I slide against her. "So close," she pants.

"Tell me when," I say through gritted teeth, trying to hold back my orgasm. She feels incredible, and I can't keep it at bay for much longer.

I move my hips like that again, and her cunt grips my cock so hard I clench my jaw harder.

"Now, baby, now."

She lets go and I follow right after. I fuse my mouth to hers, drinking in her cries all the way down to my soul.

When it ends, I slide out, and after we clean up, we climb back into bed. I pull her to my chest and kiss the top of her head while her arm is draped across me. We lie here in silence, my heart still pounding as the weight of the last few days settles.

She's here and safe.

She doesn't have to run anymore.

We can build a life together, and I never have to worry about her disappearing again.

———

~One Month Later~

Kai and I are at school while Penelope went for a job interview. There is a girl that Eloise used to work for who started an online interior design business. They are looking for young, smart people, and

Eloise put in a good word for Penelope. She happened to be about an hour away and wanted to meet Penelope.

"Do you think Mom will get the job?" he asks, glancing up at me.

"I hope so. She was really excited about the interview."

He nods. "I think she'll get it."

"You do, huh?"

Kai lets out a long sigh and I grin. "She's smart and doesn't want to smell like coffee anymore."

That is true. "No matter what happens, I'm sure she'll find something she wants to do."

Even though Hazel will probably lose her shit when Penelope quits.

We've settled into becoming a trio pretty effortlessly. I hang out with Kai if Penny has to work on the weekends and after school. He's taught me a lot about the world of video games and influencers, things I thought I knew but actually was pretty ignorant about.

Every Thursday I pick up Ethan, and we head to the rink where the boys practice and laugh at me for anything they can. It's fun, and I love spending time with Kai just as much as I love being with Penelope.

He's a great kid with a big heart, and I'm a better man with him being in my life.

The only thing I've yet to have to tackle is any kind of parenting, which Penelope and I argued about last night. I agree that I need to fill that role, especially because we are becoming a family and she wants me to be not only his friend, but his dad as well.

Of course I want that, too, but . . . I'm not going to make up an argument just to have a disciplinary moment.

When it happens, I'll handle it—maybe.

For now, I'm happy to let Kai set the pace.

The most settling part of the last month is that Ainsley's article did everything we hoped. She was able to bring down a large crime ring, and the people who were hunting Penelope are now behind bars. There is so much information that we were assured Penelope doesn't need to testify. They have documents and many other eyewitnesses who will ensure a victorious trial.

I'm eternally happy for that.

Kai and I make it back to my office. All the extracurricular activities are over and we can finally leave.

"Are you ready to head home?"

He nods. "Let's go."

We gather our things and walk to the car. On the ride home, he tells me about his teacher and her new dog.

"I think we should get a dog," he informs me.

"I think we can talk about it, but dogs are a lot of work."

"I can handle it."

There's not a doubt that he can. "Maybe we can talk to your mom about it in a few days? Let's let her get through the interview stuff, okay?"

"Okay," Kai agrees easily.

I park in the driveway, leaving room for Penelope to park to the right, and Kai doesn't immediately unbuckle like he always does. He sits there, seeming to contemplate something.

"You all right?" I ask.

"Are you going to marry my mom?"

Umm, definitely not what I thought was coming.

I'd planned in a few weeks to take Kai out for ice cream, maybe the candy store, or somewhere he could buy whatever he wanted. Once I had the bribery portion of the day in order, we would talk about this.

This is no buttered-up version, but at the same time, Kai is way too smart for his own good, and I want to build a relationship—a father-son one—based on trust and communication.

"How about we go inside and talk about this with a snack?" I ask.

"Can we have a brownie?"

I laugh once. "Sure, little man."

Kai unbuckles and we head inside. Penelope made brownies, cupcakes, and a cake last night because, apparently, she's a nervous baker. I'm not going to complain one bit, because all three of them are amazing.

Once I cut him a square, I put the plate down in front of him and sit across the table. Kai takes a bite and then puts it down. "So are you going to marry Mom?"

I fold my hands and lay them on the table, just like I plan to do with my heart. "Man to man?"

This impresses him and he nods.

I fight back the urge to smile. "Okay," I begin. "Would you like me to marry your mom?"

"Yes."

No hesitation. Not even a blink. "I would like to as well. I'd like to talk about what this means for us, though. You're a big part of this too."

Kai straightens in his seat. "I am?"

"Yes. Not only do I want to be your mom's husband, but I'd really like to be your dad. This means that me asking her also means I ask you if you'd like to be a family. See, I love your mom very much, but I also love you. In a way, we'd be more than married, we'd be a family as well. I think that's a decision that you have to be involved in too."

I lay it all out, my heart pounding because all of it's true, and also it's fucking terrifying to leave some of this up to a six-year-old.

"You would be my dad?"

"If you want, or we can just be a family, and whenever you want me to be more, I'll be that."

I'm pretty sure all of this is going over his head since I'm winging it, but Kai leaps out of his seat and wraps his arms around me. "I want you to be my dad."

I hug him tight, so fucking grateful this kid is in my life. "It will be my honor," I say, holding back emotions that are thick in my throat. "My absolute honor."

thirty-seven
Penelope

I'm so excited. That was the best interview I've ever had.

"No, Eloise, she's amazing," I tell her as I'm driving back. As soon as I got in the car, I had to call her.

"I know, Nicole is great. So tell me about the job!"

I launch into the description of how her company works differently from other online design businesses. She has been doing this forever and really knows her niche. I'll be working with higher end budgets and also some that need thrifting. Everything we do is custom and really creative.

"I'm just so excited."

"And you don't have to move? I know Nicole is in Tampa, so I didn't know . . ."

"Nope! Since it's all online, it means I can do it from Ember Falls."

Eloise squeals. "That's amazing. Hell, I may go back to work for her."

"You should!"

"Not yet, but I'm so happy for you!"

It's been such a whirlwind of life changes. I'm living with my boyfriend-slash-fiancé that I can't tell anyone I'm engaged to. Kai is thriving in school, and I'm going to go back to working in a field I genuinely love.

All of it feels too good to be true.

"Thank you again," I say to her as relief and joy wash over me.

"No thanks needed, Penny. All of this is great, and it means that you'll stay in Ember Falls, which is the best news ever. I think my brother would lose his mind if he thought you were leaving."

"I would never take the job if I had to do that."

Leaving Miles isn't an option. I love that man with my soul, and having almost lost him once makes me never want to experience that again.

I'd do any job if it means I stay here. Although I know he'd move if I really wanted to go somewhere else, but I'd never ask him to do that. Ember Falls is just as much my home as it is his, and I can't see myself growing old anywhere else.

She chuckles softly. "My brother is a lucky man."

"I think we both win."

"You know, I always worried about Miles," Eloise says with concern in her voice. "He loves so deeply, but always held a part of himself back. I know that losing our parents wasn't easy. Although we never knew our mom, we knew her through Gran. He struggled so much with thinking that having a family and being vulnerable was a risk that he didn't think was worth it, even though he knew how happy I am with Doug."

I stay silent for a second. "Do you think he's happy now?"

"Beyond happy, Penny. He's . . . I don't even know what to say he is because I've never seen the man like this. You really changed him. You and Kai. So, what I guess I'm trying to say in a very long-winded way is . . . thank you. Thank you for making Miles see that love and family isn't a risk, but a reward that never ends."

I'm not sure what in the world she's thanking me for. I didn't give him anything, but the sincerity in each word settles over me. "He's given me the same, and I'm just thankful we found each other."

"Me too."

Cora wails in the background and Eloise sighs heavily. "It never ends. Give me a call tomorrow. Maybe we can grab lunch?"

"I'd love that."

"Great. Talk soon!"

She hangs up and I send a text to Miles that I'm on my way, but he doesn't reply.

Strange.

He might be at the rink, though. It's Thursday, and they always do that. He did say before I left that he had to work and couldn't do their usual plan.

I finish the rest of the drive, bopping in the car, singing to some of my favorite songs, not caring that I look ridiculous as I pass people on the highway. Nothing can top this mood.

I pull into the driveway, and Miles's truck is there, but I never got a text back. Oh, well, I can tell him face-to-face.

"I got the job!" I yell as I walk in the house. Only I'm met with silence. "Hello? Boys?"

What the heck?

I walk into the kitchen, no sign of them. "Miles? Kai?"

My heart starts to race and anxiety fills me.

"Miles! Kai!" I scream again. They're probably playing a video game with those headphones on.

Then I hear a tapping on the window outside. "Mom!"

I jump, my hand flying to my chest, and I let out a breath.

Kai runs off, and I take it that I should go out there since no one is coming in.

After I get my heart under control, I head to the back door and slide it open.

As soon as I do, my chest is tight for a whole other reason.

There is the potted tree and a hole that's surrounded by candles. Beside it stand both Miles and Kai, dressed in slacks and matching shirts.

"What's all this?" I ask, stepping deeper into the yard.

Miles walks forward. "I asked you to plant this tree and let the roots grow, but you weren't ready then, were you?"

I shake my head. "Not really."

"Are you ready now?"

I smile and look over at Kai, who is grinning. "I am."

"Then I think we should plant the tree and let it grow together." Miles winks and then drops to his knee.

Oh God. He's proposing. Now.

Even though he's done this already and I've said yes, I've been hoping this would come soon. Between his finger and thumb is the ring that comes out only when he needs to be reminded that I'm with him—always.

He explained that he was going to approach it with Kai soon, and I agreed that it was time. I just didn't know it would be today.

Miles takes my hand in his. "Penelope Miller, my life was just fine before I met you. I had a great job, home, friends, and was a world-renowned Ultimate Frisbee player." I laugh and then suck in a breath as my tears come. "I thought I had it all. I thought I knew what true contentment felt like, and then you came into my life. That's when I realized that I had nothing. All of those things were menial without someone to share it with. From the first day I met you, trying to lace up hockey skates and refusing to believe we were dating, the storm, our first date, to when I came to find you, I knew that you were the only person in this world I would want beside me." He kisses the top of my hand, and then I sink to my knees with him. "You are my here, my now, my forever. Marry me?"

I look over at Kai, who is grinning so wide, and he has a sign in his hand that reads *Say yes*.

I laugh through my tears and nod quickly. "Yes, I'll marry you."

He slides the ring that his grandfather gave his grandmother onto my finger, where it will stay until the end of time.

epilogue
Miles

"Relax," Doug says, brushing at my shoulders. "She'll be here." I grumble under my breath and glance down at my phone again. Instead of a long engagement, Penelope and I agreed to a small, intimate, and fast wedding.

No need to wait months, we waited long enough to find each other, and I didn't want more than a month to pass.

Today is the day—well, if the bride shows up.

Lachlan enters the room, closing the door quickly. "She's not here yet, but I talked to Ainsley and she said it's fine, everything will be okay."

"Where is she?" I ask.

"You know, she didn't mention it. My fiancée wasn't very forthcoming with her information."

I roll my eyes. "If she went to the falls . . ."

Along with telling Penelope the story of the falls and how they came to be, Hazel also informed her that it's tradition to go there on your wedding day and jump in with your bridal party.

Is that a thing?

No.

Am I going to kill Hazel?

Yup.

No matter how much I told Penelope that Hazel was fucking with her, she kept saying that other people also informed her, my sister being one, that this is a thing, and she didn't want to break with tradition.

Everyone in my life sucks.

The door opens again, and this time it's Everett. "You doing okay? I mean, I know getting stood up at your wedding isn't easy, but I secured a back door where there's no one that'll see you."

I flip him off. "Dickhead."

He chuckles. "I'm sure it'll be fine."

Well, I know one way to piss him off. "Hey, can you do me a favor, since you're a groomsman and everything?"

"Yeah, what's up? Do you need a getaway car?"

"Can you find Violet and make sure she's not sitting alone? I worry since Hazel is with the girls."

He glares at me. "Sure."

I grin. "Thanks."

I grab my phone, calling Penelope again, but it goes to voicemail. "Hello, my love, I'm here . . . at the church, you know, where you're supposed to be because we are getting married today. Not sure what you're doing, but you know . . . if you could get here, that would be great."

I hang up and Doug chuckles. "She'll be here. She loves you. Trust me, it'll be fine."

Trusting him isn't the issue. It's that she's not freaking here.

Quinn enters the room next, because at this point it's just a revolving door. "I called her again and Ashton, no clue what they're doing, but if my wife has any say in this, it's trouble."

My phone rings in my hand a second later and I answer. "Hello?"

"Miles, this is Sheriff Smith."

"Yes?"

"There was an accident, and everyone is okay, but we brought the girls here to be checked out just as a precaution."

"Oh my God, is she okay?" I ask, grabbing my jacket.

"Yes, she's fine. No one was injured."

I hang up and I'm running to get to the hospital. It'll take me fifteen minutes to get there. I'm rushing out the door when the guys call after me, coming with me.

"Miles!" Quinn yells.

I turn to face him, relaying what I know. I look to Doug. "Keep Kai busy. I'll be back as soon as I can."

"What do you want me to do with the guests?" he asks.

"Sing and dance, I don't know, but I need to go," I explain, and then I'm running out the door.

Quinn is in the car with me, and then his phone rings. "Ashton?" I can only hear his side of the call. "You're fine? Everyone else?" A pause. "We're on our way. Yes, dear, I know that you said you were fine and I don't need to come, that you planned to order a fucking car to get you, but we're coming." Another pause, and I can hear her yelling at him. "Well, they already have bad luck, so what's a little more?"

He hangs up and releases a heavy sigh. "They're fine. They figured we'd never know and they would've just ordered a car to come get them, but I said we were on our way. Penny is just waiting to be released."

We pull into the hospital, and I'm out of the car as soon as it's in park. Both Quinn and I push through the doors, and then I'm at the front desk. "Penelope Miller."

She types on her computer and rattles off the area she's in.

I slide the curtain over and she's sitting on the bed, in her wedding dress, with the girls around her.

"Hi," she says, biting her lower lip.

"Hello," I say, keeping my voice even.

"Can you give us a minute?" Penny says to the girls. Each of them heads out, leaving us alone.

I take a step in, my throat growing tight. "You're okay?"

She nods. "Yes, they took x-rays because my wrist was hurting, but the doctor said it's fine, just sore."

I move to her, touching her hands, arms, and then her face. "You're fine?"

"Completely."

I rest my lips on her forehead. "I lost a decade off my life. First I thought you were going to stand me up, then I heard you were in an accident, and I just . . . I couldn't think."

Penelope leans back to look at me, a sheepish look on her face. "You're in a hospital."

I blink and look around. "I am. I didn't even . . ."

"Hesitate," she finishes my sentence.

"Not even a moment. I had to see you, touch you, know you were okay," I explain.

She smiles and takes my hands in hers. "There was nothing that was going to keep me from marrying you today."

"Except the fact you guys hit a bus."

"It was a tap, and even that wasn't going to stop me," she says quickly.

Life with Penelope will never be boring, that's for sure. Even with the mini heart attacks on a daily basis and the fact that she's going to cause me to go gray much too early, I wouldn't change any of it.

I sit in the chair beside her, still holding her hand. After a minute the doctor enters.

"Ms. Miller, you are cleared to go. All the tests came back great. I'm going to sign the paperwork, and I'd like you to just follow up with your doctor."

"Thank you," Penny says with a heavy sigh.

"I hope you both have a beautiful wedding."

He leaves and I stare at my soon-to-be wife. She swings her legs over the side of the bed and I grab my jacket, laying it over my arm. "Hopefully we still have guests at the wedding when you're done."

Her eyes widen. "Why?"

"Doug is entertaining them. It's going to be a shit show, and they'll probably leave just from his bad jokes and singing."

She laughs softly. "It's fine if they all leave. I only need a very small group of people there."

"Me too. I just need you and Kai."

Her eyes turn soft and then she rests her hand on my cheek. "I think there's one more we will need with us."

"Who?" I ask, confused because . . . I thought we were having a moment saying the three of us are what matters, but clearly I'm wrong.

Her hand moves to her stomach. "It's a good thing you got over your fear of hospitals, because I really didn't want to have a home birth."

My hand covers hers, and my brain starts to catch up to what she's saying. "You're pregnant?"

"I am."

"You're sure?"

She laughs once. "I am. That's why they brought me to just check on things. As soon as Ashton opened her big mouth, they demanded I come here."

I stand, no longer able to contain the excitement that's running through my veins. "We're going to have a baby?"

My mind goes blank for a second, and then I start to see our new life. A baby. A little boy or girl who will have their mother's eyes and be so loved. A child that will have a big brother to love them and protect them.

A smile forms on my face, and there's not an ounce of fear. I always thought I'd be different, upset even, but I'm not. Not even a single bit.

"We are. Are you happy?" she asks with hesitation.

I kiss her softly and then move to kiss her belly. "You have made me the happiest man in the world. Now I'm going to carry you out of here and marry you before some other catastrophe happens."

I lift her up and she giggles. "You're supposed to carry me over the threshold at home, not out of the hospital."

"I'll take no chances with you injuring yourself. You worry about the baby, I'll worry about everything else."

"I love you, Miles," she says, smiling at me.

"I love you more than you will ever know. Are you ready to spend the rest of your life with me?"

"Absolutely, and you?"

"Forever has never looked better."

Dear Reader,

I hope you enjoyed Here and Now! I wasn't ready to leave Miles and Penelope behind! I wanted to give just a little more of a glimpse into their lives, so ... I wrote a super fun scene.

Since giving you a link would be really difficult, I have an easy QR code you can scan, sign up, and you'll get and email giving you access! Or you can always type in the URL!

https://geni.us/HAN_Signup

If you'd like to just keep up with my sales and new releases, you can follow me on BookBub!
BookBub: https://www.bookbub.com/authors/corinne-michaels

Join my Facebook group!
https://www.facebook.com/groups/corinnemichaelsbooks

books by corinne michaels

Want a downloadable reading order?
https://geni.us/CM_ReadingGuide

The Salvation Series
The Belonging Duet
The Consolation Duet
Defenseless
Evermore: A 1001 Dark Night Novella
The Indefinite Duet

The Hennington Brothers
Say You'll Stay
Say You Want Me
Say I'm Yours
Say You Won't Let Go: A Return to Me/Masters and Mercenaries Novella

Second Time Around Series
We Own Tonight
One Last Time
Not Until You
If I Only Knew

The Arrowood Brothers
Come Back for Me
Fight for Me
The One for Me
Stay for Me
Destined for Me: An Arrowood/Hennington Brothers Crossover Novella

acknowledgments

My husband and children. I love you all so much. Your love and support is why I get to even have an acknowledgment section.

My assistant, Christy Peckham, you always have my back and I can't imagine working with anyone else. I love your face.

Melanie Harlow, you have no idea how much I cherish our friendship. You are truly one of my best friends in the world and I don't know what I would do without you.

My daily writing loves: Lauren Blakely, Laura Pavlov, and Natasha Madison. This little group of misfits is my favorite thing in the world. You have no idea how much I love you guys.

My agent, Kimberly Brower, thank you for having my back and always being on my side.

The team at Sourcebooks, my editor Christa, Thank you for believing in this story and my work, I am beyond grateful.

My publicist, Nina Grinstead, you're stuck with me forever at this point. You are more than a publicist, you're a friend, a cheer-leader, a shoulder to lean on, and so much more.

The entire team, Maddy, Meagan, Tori, and Kayla who support me, rally behind me, and keep me actually functioning.

James, my editor for taking such great care with my story. My cover designer who deals with my craziness, Sommer Stein. My proofreaders: Julia, and Michele.

To my author friends who are truly the best support system I could ever wish for. Thank you for showing what women uplifting women looks like. Catherine, Elsie, Lena, Amy, Willow, Laura, Kandi, Rebecca, Samantha, Amber, Kennedy and so many more.

Every influencer who picked this book up, made a post, video, phoned a friend ... whatever it was. Thank you for making the book world a better place.

about the author

Corinne Michaels is a *New York Times, USA Today, and Wall Street Journal* bestselling author of romance novels. Her stories are chock full of emotion, humor, and unrelenting love, and she enjoys putting her characters through intense heartbreak before finding a way to heal them through their struggles.

Corinne is a former Navy wife and happily married to the man of her dreams. She began her writing career after spending months away from her husband while he was deployed—reading and writing were her escape from the loneliness. Corinne now lives in Virginia with her husband and is the emotional, witty, sarcastic, and fun-loving mom of two beautiful children.